melt

lisa walker

melt

lisa walker

[Lacuna]
2018

Published in 2018 by Lacuna in Armidale, New South Wales, Australia
www.lacunapublishing.com

Lacuna is an imprint of Golden Orb Creative
PO Box 428, Armidale, NSW 2350, Australia
www.goldenorbcreative.com

Cover design by Golden Orb Creative
Cover image "Two Gentoo penguins" © Dmytro Pylypenko | Dreamstime

Text design and production by Golden Orb Creative
Typeset in 11.5pt Adobe Caslon Pro

A National Library of Australia Cataloguing-in-Publication entry has been created for this title:

ISBN 9781922198327 (pbk)
ISBN 9781922198334 (ebook)

Contents

To John. Thanks for all the well-built igloos.

Chapter One

I encounter an existential elephant

Project:	Monday morning routine
Objective:	Arrive at work on time, healthy, rested and ready for action
6.15:	Wake up (exact wake time determined by 'wake easy' app to ensure optimal brain function)
6.15–6.25:	Visualise day ahead (visualisation leads to peak performance)
Critical event:	Waking up on time

The alarm wakes me at 6.17. The air is cool. Inside my apartment it is always twenty-three degrees Celsius – the optimum temperature for sleeping. Adrian slept over but left at five am to go running. He's been running a lot lately. At first it was once a week, then twice, then three times, then daily. He's training for the City to Surf.

My dream lingers. I banish it. Unproductive energy. I only have eight minutes for structured goal visualisation. Dream analysis isn't on the schedule – I work with the conscious, not the subconscious; the concrete, not the airy-fairy. Airy-fairy has been evicted from my life.

Generally speaking, I don't dream much these days, but when I do it is always the same. Awake, my eyes scan my room. The pristine white walls reassure me – everything is as it should be. The apartment was a dreary yellow when I moved in but that couldn't last. *White.* It had to be white. I had no idea white came in so many varieties.

The hardware shop man raised his eyebrows when I showed him the colour chip. 'Enough for a one-bedroom apartment please,' I said.

'Are you sure you wouldn't prefer *White on White*, *Natural White* or *Whisper White*?' he said.

I shook my head. Despite their names, these colours were varieties of cream. If there'd been anything whiter than *Antarctica* I would have bought it. My apartment is like a hermetically sealed compartment – white as snow, surgically clean. No cobwebs hang across my lights, no cockroaches loiter in dark corners. An antiseptic fragrance greets me as I open the door each evening. *Bliss.*

Cleaning products are my one indulgence. Over the last year I've discovered I love to clean. Under the sink I have Vim and Ace, Gain and Gumption. I have products for glass and products for wood, three types of dishwashing detergent and four types of laundry detergent. I use different products depending on my mood and the task at hand. Softly is for quiet moods and Tornado for energetic ones. I think of myself as a domestic artist.

I subscribe to electronic newsletters that keep me up to date on the latest cleaning breakthroughs and look forward to Saturday morning – cleaning time. The tricky area between the bathroom tiles is my favourite. I use cotton swabs for that, discarding each one as it becomes soiled. This makes me feel like a surgeon – *forceps, nurse!* I don't understand why some people have an aversion to toilet-bowl cleaning – the modern products make it a joy. Once I've cleaned the bathroom I am elated, practically euphoric.

Sometimes I have sexual fantasies of being scrubbed head to toe with a toothbrush or gently polished by Mr Sheen while he sings his little song. *Oh Mr Sheen, oh Mr Sheen …*

I haven't shared these fantasies with Adrian. Adrian and I have a lot in common, but he might find my cleaning fantasies strange. And, given the state I was in when we first met, I've had to work hard to convince Adrian I'm the opposite of strange. I think I have succeeded.

Maybe one day I will tell him. Imagine the things one could do with a feather duster and a roll of extra-strong Chux. But I should be visualising, not daydreaming. Adrian says daydreaming is my worst habit. It's lucky he is not fully acquainted with all my habits.

Adrian and I have been together for one year – one gloriously, gloriously productive year. If it wasn't for Adrian, I don't know where I'd be.

I'd like to hear Marley's thoughts about Adrian. I've started emailing him again lately. Pulling my laptop onto the bed, I open last week's email.

To: Marley Lennon Wright
From: Summer Dawn Rain Wright
Subject: I encounter an existential elephant

I expect you've been wondering why I sent you that text, Marley. I'll get to that. First, let me tell you about Adrian.

Adrian and I met on a plane from Kathmandu, of all places. I shudder to think of the impression I made at the time.

I'd been lucky to make the flight at all. I'd woken late, rushed out into the street and squandered the last of my rupees in a bribe to my taxi driver. We'd narrowly avoided a garlanded cow, almost driven a man on a bicycle off the road and run a gauntlet of beeping cars. Check-in had closed, but I talked my way through.

You know me, Marley, this was the way I always travelled – close to the edge.

Stuffing my backpack into the overhead locker, I squeezed my way past a pair of knees to the window, collapsed onto the seat and fastened my seatbelt. A quick glance at the man next to me assured me we had nothing in common. He was thirty-ish – button-up shirt, dark grey trousers and business shoes. He was unusually clean, as if buffed up in a car wash. Staying clean in Kathmandu was no mean feat. A small briefcase rested under the seat in front of him and he held a notebook computer in his hands, waiting for the all clear to turn it on.

He reminded me of Adam Carrington, the oldest child of Blake and Alexis. You remember how Adam was kidnapped at birth and the woman who stole him confessed on her death bed that he was a Carrington? Then, when he went to find his birth family he ended up falling in love with his sister?

Aargh, Marley – my greatest fear!

'Good morning,' the man said to me.

I nodded in response. *Australian.* So we did have that in common, but if I kept my mouth shut he'd never know.

He held out his hand. 'Adrian. Adrian Robertson.'

I toyed with the idea of feigning poor English skills before replying. 'Summer. Summer Wright.'

If he noticed my feeble parody, he showed no sign. While the plane taxied down the runway he told me he'd been on a seven-day Business

Leaders of the Future trek. He'd been pushed to his physical limits during the day and drilled by a leadership consultant at night.

It was like we'd been in different countries.

I'd been up all night partying with a group of Swedes, Irish and Israelis. A cocktail of the usual stimulants was leaching out of my system. For the moment I was buzzing, but I knew that soon an existential crisis would hit me like a rampaging elephant. This elephant had been lurking in the wings for weeks now, stamping its feet. I'd kept it at bay with determined activity, but it was butting at the flimsy support of my wildlife hide.

That's a metaphor, Marley. There were elephants in Kathmandu, but not in my part of town and definitely not on the Air Nepal flight to Sydney.

Over the last two years I'd worked in a range of occupations. I'd been a chalet girl in Chamonix, a bartender in Biarritz, a dish-washer in Dublin, a waitress in Wales and a secretary in Sussex. I'd followed my whims all over the globe, not knowing what I was looking for. Not knowing how to find it. Not like you, Marley – you knew what you were doing from the moment you were born.

One week previously I'd woken up in the Annapurna Guesthouse next to Owl, a handsome Canadian I'd met in Lukla en route to Everest Base Camp. I'd examined him closely while he slept, cataloguing his many assets. He had a tattoo of an owl on his chest, a black spike through his ear, the softest skin I'd ever felt, curly hair like a poodle, teeth so white they glowed in the dark and, most notably, he was some kind of genius in bed. Despite all this, I rolled away from him, stared at the cracks in the ceiling and a desperate certainty smote me. I couldn't do this anymore. I needed to start.

Start what? whispered a voice inside my head. It sounded like you, Marley. *Anything*, I replied to you. *I need to start my life.* Before I changed my mind, I pulled my phone towards me and sent you that text – *coming home.*

On the plane, I closed my eyes and, for the first time since I booked my plane ticket, acknowledged the existential elephant's existence. *What? What? What do you want?* I asked it.

The elephant raised its trunk and trumpeted a question that made me quake.

❄ *lisa walker*

After a two-year binge of travel, parties, crappy jobs and even more crappy relationships

what do you do hoo hoo
with the rest of your life life life?

My eyes flew open as the plane taxied down the runway. I was almost surprised not to find the elephant on the seat next to me, it had been so loud. I swear, that trumpeting would have blown my wildlife hide right into the ground.

The elephant had your voice, Marley.

I found myself staring at my grubby feet propped on the embroidered shoulder bag in front of me. And then at the polished leather shoes of my companion. I stifled a giggle – we were the odd couple. Stick-on stars decorated my toenails and a tattered red string, given to me by the guy I met in Lukla, hung around my ankle. *A romantic keepsake*, I told the elephant. *You can't knock that.*

'I'll come and visit you in Sydney,' Owl had said as we stumbled out of the Rum Doodle Bar. His teeth shone in the lights from the window and he stroked my arm in a way that almost made me forget that there is more to life than good sex.

I pulled myself together. 'Better not to try and hang on to something that is wonderful but fleeting.' A sad sound track started in my head. A romantic ending – *Last Tango in Kathmandu*. 'Let's keep it like this – a perfect memory. You and I' – I wiped away a tear – 'are two free spirits who have connected in a very, very, meaningful way.'

He ran his hand down my back as we made our way back to the guest-house, reminding me of how meaningfully we had connected.

'Very, very meaningful,' I repeated, as his hand slid around my waist and his thumb stroked my stomach. I stopped as we reached our guest-house and put my hand to his cheek. 'Maybe we'll meet again in another lifetime and take up where we left off in this one. But for now, I must take the path less travelled, while you' – I pondered – 'will also take the path less travelled, but a different one.' I pressed my hand to his. 'You are a beautiful, beautiful person and I wish you joy on your path, but I don't expect it to ever intersect with mine again.'

He did a reasonable job of looking disappointed. Maybe he was.

'After tonight, I mean,' I added, as I took out the key to our room and pulled him in after me, almost tripping over his guitar in the process.

Sorry, Marley – too much information.

As the plane took off, I gazed out the window. The Himalayas were glorious as always and the world looked as it always does from on high – exciting and full of possibility. But after two years roaming the globe, this was the sum total of what I knew about life: I was broke, tired and going home.

I close the email.

Shutting my eyes, I imagine the day ahead of me, step by step – I will succeed and impress at every opportunity, I will succeed …

lisa walker

Chapter Two

I ascend the Cone of Certainty

Project:	Monday morning routine (continued)
6.25–6.55:	Morning yoga (remember to stay in moment, breathe, relax)
6.55–7.15:	Breakfast (home-made muesli with low-fat yoghurt, goji berries and chia seeds)
7.15–7.45:	Wash and dress (outfit laid out the night before to facilitate this step)
7.45:	Walk to Chatswood train station
7.58:	Catch train to Town Hall (travel pass pre-purchased to prevent delay). On train: Check and respond to email, Twitter, Facebook, LinkedIn and Instagram (remember: one third respond, one third communicate, one third encourage)
8.27:	Walk from Town Hall station to office
8.39:	Arrive at work, change shoes, brush hair
8.45:	Work commences
Total time:	2 hours 30 minutes
Critical events:	Leaving home on time Train arriving on time

Visualisation over, it is time to proceed at a relaxed and orderly pace through my morning routine.

I glance at the clock. Unaccountably, it is 6.50. I am behind schedule; ground must be made up. While I'm much more disciplined than I used to be, I am not as disciplined as Adrian. Adrian's morning routine always runs to plan. Soon mine will too. I will absorb his effectiveness through osmosis. I will become a better version of myself. I just need to try harder. I leap out of bed, mentally revising my morning routine.

Yoga. I rush through a few half-arsed sun salutes. *Check.* Adrian does Bikram yoga – the one where you exercise in a room heated to forty degrees. I tried it once but had to crawl out and lie on the cold floor outside after fifteen minutes. To be honest, it wasn't only the heat; I was psyched out by the bikini girls in the front row next to the wall-length mirror. The contrast between them and me, in my baggy sweat-soaked T-shirt, was stark.

Adrian told me not to come again unless I was going to try harder. I intend to, but every time I think about it I get flashbacks of my face reflected in the mirror – I looked like a sinner in the fires of hell. Adrian tells me it's all in my mind and I'm sure he's right. In the near future I will do Bikram regularly in a red bikini which displays my flat and lightly muscled stomach. I have added this to my morning visualisation. Adrian says creating a vision of success is half the battle.

Breakfast. Unfortunately my home-made muesli currently consists of ten unopened packets of ingredients in a shopping bag. I'm not sure how that happened as muesli-making was definitely scheduled for Sunday afternoon. Then I remember – there was that special episode of *Dynasty* on the box. It's lucky Adrian didn't stay for breakfast. I stuff down some cornflakes and instant coffee while re-scheduling muesli-making for my evening project plan. *Check.*

Some sad lettuce leaves, a hard lump of cheese and an unidentifiable bowl of leftovers greet me as I place the milk back in the fridge. Strangely, my cleaning fetish only extends as far as the surfaces on display. I can't find the same enthusiasm for the insides of cupboards or for removing dust balls under my bed. I don't know why that is, but never mind. Once Adrian and I get married and move to our new house, I'm sure this defect will be overcome. I will dust and polish our lovely home in my red bikini and grow a herb garden which is the envy of the neighbourhood. I'm so looking forward to it.

Dress. I glance at my cupboard where today's outfit hangs on the door handle. After work I'm meeting Adrian for dinner at six-thirty pm. The grey pantsuit will carry me from work to dinner at Le Max. I have a slinky black top to replace the un-slinky work top. I do need to make some effort. It's the first anniversary of the day we got together and I think tonight he's going to propose. Pantsuit on, I run a comb through my short hair – so much more practical than those flowing locks. *Check.*

Departure. 7.45. *Check.* Yay – I'm back on course.

As I step out the door, something remarkable happens. White flakes drift past my eyes. It's like I'm in Chamonix again. It's snowing!

I stretch out my hands and flakes land softly on my palms. I register their warmth. Of course they're not snowflakes. This is Sydney. It's ash from a fire in the mountains, carried here by the hot westerly wind. I watch the flakes fall and a stillness comes over me. Closing my eyes, I breathe in the faint scent of smoke. Then a man in a suit brushes past, jabbing my hip with his briefcase. The stillness is gone. I have a train to catch.

On the train, my mind returns to Adrian. Adrian has taught me so much about time management. Before I met him, I used to fritter away hours and hours smoking dope and watching clouds. But there is no point in regret. Adrian tells me to think of each day as the first day of the rest of my life.

I've learnt from Adrian that everything important in life requires a plan. I'm not sure how I got through the first twenty-six years of my life without one, but I've made up for lost time. I suppose it's only natural that I'm not yet on Adrian's level, I'm coming from a low base. Whenever I have doubts, the red bikini spurs me on.

'Prior planning and preparation prevents piss-poor performance,' Adrian says.

He can be funny sometimes.

It seems weird to admit this, but I'm not sure what Adrian does for a living. He explained it to me, but I couldn't grasp it. And now it is way, way too late to ask him again.

As far as I can work out he is a free-ranging man of influence – a gun for hire. He told me once he uses his outstanding project management skills to advance his clients' goals. Last month he was responsible for getting the Mayor of Sydney re-elected, but he has moved on. He mentioned something about federal politics. Whatever it is he does, he is good at it.

On my laptop I open the Project Adrian Plan (never to be referred to as PAP). Six months ago I entered a line item: *Engagement*. I left it a little open. Any time between December and February would have been fine. But I'm ready to increase the certainty on that now. I delete *Dec–Feb* and put in a new target date: *Tonight*. It is time to ascend the

Cone of Certainty. Imagine, I could have gone my whole life without hearing of The Cone if it wasn't for Adrian. Oh, to reach the perfection of the point. Oh, to reach it with Adrian. *Tonight.* Tonight I will ascend. Using my drawing tool, I make a little picture ...

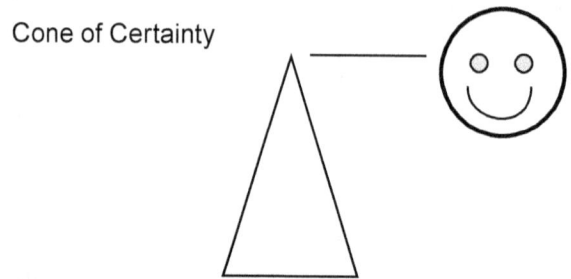

Cone of Certainty

Then, as I often do on the train, I start a new email.

To: Marley Lennon Wright
From: Summer Dawn Rain Wright
Subject: My first encounter with taskeddling

It was funny how I hadn't liked Adrian at first, Marley. I had woken, two hours into the flight, bleary and fractious, and pulled myself upright.

My hair was a tangled, snaky mess. Next to me Adrian had his computer turned on. With nothing better to do, my eyes were drawn to it.

A colourful bar chart filled the screen. Each bar had writing next to it, but I couldn't read it from where I sat.

He looked up. I was struck by how indecently healthy he was. The whites of his eyes seemed freshly bleached, his cheeks had a slight blush of pink, his brown hair was lustrous, thick and neatly cut. He was like a horse spruced up for a show. A handsome and well-toned horse. 'Where would we be without Gantt, huh?' he said.

I sighed. I wasn't feeling good. The drugs and alcohol had drained out of my system and I wasn't too sure if he was speaking English. I felt a pang of loss for Owl. He would have known better than to talk to me this morning. He would have known exactly what I needed. And he wouldn't have looked so dauntingly energetic while he was about it either. 'Gant?' I murmured in a discouraging way.

'Henry Gantt, the father of project planning.' Adrian's eyes lit up. 'Gantt revolutionised project management.' He could have been spruiking a new deodorant – *stay fresher longer, no white marks* … 'A project without a project plan is like' – he paused – 'travelling to a strange land without a map, a guidebook or an itinerary.'

'Oh.' That confirmed it – I was seated next to an alien. I'd never met anyone who planned things before, especially travel.

My friends all listened to their inner voices and went with the flow. They thought the universe would provide and all we ever have is now. The people I knew didn't have itineraries. We shunned guidebooks in search of real experiences, often ending up in out of the way places without any evident attractions. 'So much better', we said to each other. 'No tourists'. Except for us, obviously.

Adrian was still talking about the contributions Gantt had made to scientific management through 'taskeddling' (it was some weeks before I realised he was saying 'task scheduling'). Adrian, it was clear, worshipped Gantt, whoever he was. If Gantt did a world tour, I bet Adrian would camp out to get tickets.

'Project management,' Adrian said, 'is the art of ascending the cone of certainty.'

He seemed to think I was captivated. As a matter of fact I was, but not in the way he thought. It was an insight into a strange culture, like watching a reality TV show. And it was distracting me from my existential crisis.

'When you start a project, there is so much you don't know.' He held his hands out wide. 'And then, as you work your way in' – he brought his fingers to a point – 'you have it – perfect certainty.'

Perfect certainty. As he said that, the sun poked through the clouds outside the plane. A ray of light came through the little window and illuminated him.

Adrian's fingers were still steepled together. Almost like he was praying.

'What do you call that point?' I gestured at his fingers.

His teeth flashed in the sun. 'The Point of Complete Certainty.'

I felt it then, Marley – a shiver of possibility. Could this man have something I needed?

Adrian says if you take care of the little things, the big ones will take care of themselves. Turns out I'd been tackling things the wrong way around my whole life.

Clicking on the email, I press 'send'.

I stretch as I look out the train window, remembering the first time I heard of The Point of Complete Certainty. What bliss, to know exactly where you were going, exactly what you were doing. I never would have conceived of such a possibility without Adrian.

Adrian and I are incredibly compatible. We have discussed our life goals – two children, a house on the North Shore, private schooling. Preferably we will have a girl and a boy. There are ways of choosing gender I believe, something to do with yoghurt.

Oops. I glance at my watch. My daydreaming has put me a little behind schedule with my social media, but that's alright. Social media is not a critical event. I can reduce it to fifteen minutes. Opening Facebook, Twitter, LinkedIn and Instagram, I carefully work through my contacts. One third *encourage*, one third *respond*, one third *communicate*. Building a social media platform is critical to success in the entertainment industry. Not that I could be said to be in the entertainment industry as such. Not yet. But I have ambitions.

Dramatic music fills my head as it always does when I ruminate about my career aspirations. The correct musical accompaniment is important to set the scene. The music stops abruptly as I remember I haven't told Adrian about my secret goal.

Adrian used his extensive influence to get me an entry-level position at a TV station. He thinks I will use my new-found management talents in production. 'Project management skills will get you a long way in television,' Adrian says. One day I will have to tell him I have no intention of moving into management. And I will tell him soon – just not yet. I'm waiting for the right time.

At the moment I am only a humble production assistant at Channel Five, but now I have a foot in the door, I am one step closer to realising my secret, secret, secret and long-delayed goal.

Chapter Three

My secret goal

My secret goal has its own soundtrack.

> *Drum-roll please.*
> *Are you ready, chorus?*
> *Chorus (to the tune of 'Paperback Writer'): Oo oo. She wants to be a*
> *famous scriptwriter. Scriptwriter.*

Yes, that's right. I am a closet scriptwriter.

> *Chorus: Oo oo, scriptwriter.*

But it is not the Academy Awards that beckon, it is soap opera.

> *Oo oo – soap opera?*
> *You got a problem with that, chorus?*

I don't suppose many people remember *Dynasty*. While I missed its heyday – it last screened in 1991, the year I turned one – my dear Aunt Patsy gave me a box set for my twelfth birthday. She thought I could use some glamour in my life. While mud was plentiful, glamour was in short supply on our commune in the hills.

'Happy birthday, Summer.' She placed a gold-wrapped present with a shiny bow on our rough wood table. 'Enjoy.' Her scarlet lips drew up into a naughty smile. 'You'll have to watch them at my place.' She glanced at my mother. 'We've moved out of the stone age there.'

Aunt Patsy lived in a neat brick house in Lismore. It was close to my high school and I got into the habit of visiting her after school. It was a novelty to sit on a leather couch in a house with walls that weren't made of mud-bricks.

From the moment I slipped the first video into Aunt Patsy's player, *Dynasty* filled a gap I hadn't known was there. I inhaled the sheer glory of the settings, the dresses, the beautiful women, the dashingly handsome men, the intrigue, the bizarre but excruciatingly addictive plot lines …

The first wife, Alexis, returns!
The illegitimate half-sister departs!
The husband leaves his wife for another man!
The hotel is set on fire by the amnesiac wife!
The wife has a torrid affair with a business rival!

There's never been a soap opera to touch it. I'd pull on my mud-stained boots in the morning imagining they were stiletto heels and arrange my daggy sunhat as if it was a milliner's creation.

'What are you walking like that for, Summer Dawn?' Marley would yell as I flounced down our weed-infested path to the school bus. Only Marley called me Summer Dawn. It was a joke, but it stuck.

'Call me Sophia, darling,' I would murmur, languorously.

'Wait for me, you vixen,' he'd call after me.

Marley. I gaze out the train window. For the last few days the sun has been reddish – a light haze of smoke blankets the sky. The firefighters will be out in force.

Only Marley knew about my secret career goal.

'Go for it, Summer Dawn,' he said. 'It's what you were born for.'

If I was born to be a scriptwriter, my twin brother Marley was born to be a firefighter. His number is there on my phone. I touch my finger to it. They say we're in for a hot, dry summer – a treacherous summer. 'Stay safe out there,' I murmur. 'Don't forget to look up.' Falling trees are more dangerous than flames, Marley always said.

Marley never got what I saw in *Dynasty* but he was happy to take part in my role plays. Under duress, he would be Blake to my Alexis but he preferred being the gunman at the royal wedding. The Moldavian Massacre was one of the great moments of *Dynasty*. Dead bodies were strewn like confetti in this season finale. Viewers had to wait six months to find out if their favourite characters had escaped unharmed. What a cliff-hanger! What suspense! I can only hope to emulate this amazing scene one day.

I don't suppose Marley would understand what I see in project management. Or Adrian. He wouldn't like my apartment or my new life. He wouldn't understand why I need certainty. Why I plan everything now. Why I live in the city. Why I refuse to come home. I guess there are a lot of things Marley wouldn't understand about the way I am now. But there's nothing I can do about that.

Before I went overseas, Marley gave me his tattered old copy of Jules Verne's *An Antarctic Mystery*, the one Mum had given him on his tenth birthday. 'Leave it behind somewhere when you finish it,' he said. He'd got a new version of the complete works of Jules Verne so he didn't need it anymore.

An Antarctic Mystery was Marley's favourite book. When we were kids we used to sit on a log out the front of our house and he'd read from it. I can still hear him:

> Great flocks of royal and other penguins people these islets.
>
> These stupid birds, in their yellow and white feathers, with their heads thrown back and their wings like the sleeves of a monastic habit, look, at a distance, like monks in single file …

When it was Marley's turn to control our games, we would get in a tree and pretend we were on a ship, making our way through a sea of towering icebergs. Sometimes he'd make me be a penguin, while he was an Antarctic explorer. Marley didn't know that while he was visualising icebergs, in my mind I was in front of a roaring fire in the Carrington family mansion.

I glance at Marley's number again then put my phone away as the train pulls into Town Hall station.

Despite what people may think, project management and soap opera are not poles apart. While soap opera is designed to give the appearance of surprise and unpredictability, in fact nothing is more tightly controlled. That is how I know soap opera is my destiny.

Adrian doesn't have much time for soap opera. I know this because he sprung me watching *Dynasty* once when he came back from a run unexpectedly.

'What are you doing, Summer?' He sounded horribly disappointed. 'I thought you were going to do yoga while I was away, not fritter away your time on rubbish.'

I flicked the remote, changing stations. 'I was watching *Philosophy Now*, it had an excellent interview with Peter Singer, but there was an ad break, and I didn't want to waste my time so I …' I hit the *off* button before it became clear there was nothing on the box but trash.

Adrian thinks soap operas and the people who write them are an unnecessary evil. But we're so compatible in other ways I'm sure he'll come around if I introduce him to it in the right way. Once I'm an ace project manager and Bikram yogi in a red bikini, the fact I want to write soap opera won't matter as much.

I know soap operas are not high art – that doesn't matter to me at all. There is something about the love triangles, the family feuds, the bitter business rivals and the dark secrets, that reaches out and grabs me. I love how whenever the action flags, you throw in a brain tumour, a long-lost son, or an evil blackmailer. I even love the way the characters talk to each other in a way no real person ever would – how whole conversations take place where they tell each other stuff they already both know. In soap opera, villains always get their come-uppance. In soap opera, things always make sense in a way they never do in real life.

The train stops and I get out. On the way to the office I see a guy I know slightly from his appearance on a Channel Five sports show. I wave. 'Hi, George, that was such bad luck you didn't make the foot-ball team. You've been training for ages and I know you wanted to make your father proud of you because he's always thought you were a sissy, not like your older brother Michael who plays for Australia.' My head is so full of scripts I sometimes sound like an extra in *Neighbours*. It's an occupational hazard.

George is a silent type. He smiles vaguely. 'Hot day.'

I stop at the corner and buy a copy of *The Big Issue* as always. 'Hey, Bill, this issue looks great. I loved the story in the last one about the woman who met up with her brother after thirty years. The story about the Titanic was excellent too.'

'Hot day,' says Bill as he pockets my change. He is obviously a silent type too.

Bill and George are right. It is a hot day. The sun beats on my head as I walk the last block to the office. *State is a tinderbox*, screams the headline on a newspaper stand. But they always say that, don't they?

My fingers itch and I reach into my bag. I try to restrain myself to once a week but today, although it has only been three days, I touch Marley's number on my phone. It rings, and I hear him: *Hello, Marley here, please leave a message.* 'Hey, Marley, it's Summer here, I miss you.' I press 'end' and suck in a gulp of hot air as I drop the phone back in my bag. That is it. That is definitely it for another week. I have got to stop calling Marley. I have got to stop.

The glass doors swish open and a delicious cool envelops me as I step inside the foyer of Channel Five. Twenty-three degrees. Perfect. A huge bunch of red roses decorates the reception desk. As Jacinta the receptionist is a hipster, these must be an ironic statement of love from her boyfriend, a lank-haired indie muso. They only just got back from a holiday in Iceland where they had a ball writing doleful poetry in bars. For short breaks, they usually do the same thing in Melbourne. Melbourne, according to Jacinta, is much hipper than Sydney, but nowhere near as hip as Reykjavik. Hipness appears to be inversely proportional to sunshine. Hobart, Jacinta says, is about to become the hippest city in Australia.

'Hi, Jacinta,' I say. 'Wow, is that bunch of flowers from your boy-friend? I'm so glad you've finally got a nice guy. You've been going from ratbag to ratbag for ages and you deserve much better, especially now you've dyed your hair that gorgeous colour and ditched those heavy glasses.'

Jacinta tucks her fire-engine red hair behind her ears. She is used to it. All the scriptwriters speak like that. 'Hi, Summer. Maxine's in a state. Harry from *Up and at 'Em* got a better offer at Four.'

'Damn. They can put him in a coma, can't they?'

Jacinta shakes her head, her teardrop-shape retro glasses shining in the down-lights. 'Jo's already in a coma.'

Jo is Harry's screen wife, who in real life is currently getting married in Hawaii, hence the coma. 'It could be contagious?'

'She was in a car crash.' Jacinta puts her head on one side.

'True.' I consider this. 'Hospital bug?'

'Maybe. But there's still the long-lost uncle plot.'

I wave my hand breezily. 'Let him stay lost.'

'You should be a scriptwriter, Summer.' Jacinta flicks through her notes with her long, black fingernails. 'Production meeting for *In the Wild* is in meeting room two.'

In meeting room two, Maxine, my boss and Channel Five's creative director, is looking anxious. Consequently, the rest of the team are even more anxious. This is nothing new. People are always anxious in production meetings for *In the Wild with Cougar*.

Maxine has perfectly coiffed flaxen hair and large blue eyes. While she looks like a fifties-style Stepford Wife she is in fact one of the most feared people in television. I have seen large men weep after meetings with Maxine. Even in an industry rife with neurotics, divas and power-hungry stress-heads, Maxine has a reputation.

When I first joined Channel Five Jacinta took me aside. 'There's something you need to know about Maxine.'

I waited expectantly.

'Never say *can't*, only *can*. If someone says *can't*, it sends her berserk.' She drew her finger across her throat. 'I'm not joking. There was a meeting once, it was before my time, but I've been told about it.' Jacinta's eyes darted around the room and she whispered, 'She sacked everyone in the room. On the spot.' I must have looked doubtful because she added, 'You can ask anyone. Just mention *Charlie's Adventure*. You'll see.'

I thought Jacinta was exaggerating until I saw a set designer tell Maxine he couldn't find a live elephant for a dream sequence in *Up and At 'Em*. It was horrifying, like that scene in *Alien* where a fanged monster bursts out of John Hurt's chest and tears its victim to shreds. So far, I have managed to avoid being on the receiving end of that attack.

In the Wild with Cougar is one of our highest-rating shows. This makes it high stakes in the ratings war against Channel Four, our closest competitor. We put it up against their popular *Kitchen Talent* show at seven-thirty on Thursday night. So far, *In the Wild* is thrashing *Kitchen Talent* but far from making our team cock-a-hoop it has the opposite effect. The problem with *In the Wild* is that it all rests on the dynamic, beautiful, charismatic, highly intelligent and unpredictable Cougar Gale.

This is problematic for two reasons. One being that a star performer can so easily be lured away. Two being that Cougar Gale is poison to work with and only becomes worse as each TV poll shows her to be one of the biggest stars in Australian television. Cougar has cross-demographic appeal. Both men and women love her tough-girl sexiness while kids are drawn to her can-do attitude to wilderness survival. Cougar is that rare star who families, singles and, it is rumoured, even the Prime Minister, love to watch. Hence, as I walk into the production meeting, right on time, the anxiety in the room hovers as palpably as the smoke haze outside.

I take my seat at the table and open my laptop. 'Is Cougar coming?'

Maxine takes a sip of her coffee, leaving bright red lipstick marks on the paper rim. She gestures with her chin. A glass of freshly squeezed mixed vegetable juice sits in front of an empty, expensive, ergonomically-designed chair with a knee rest but no back support. Cougar believes the human race started declining when we discovered chairs.

'Fill us in on the details for the next series while we wait, Summer.' Maxine's voice is controlled, but I sense the monster stirring within.

Can, not *can't*. I call up my spreadsheet. The next series will be filmed in Antarctica. It's ground-breaking and all very hush-hush. Anyone who breathes a word about it outside the walls of Channel Five will be found the next morning with their throat ripped open. It has been rumoured Maxine lists *hit-men* as a deduction on her tax return.

We're calling our new show *Cougar on Ice* and it's going to blow Channel Four out of the water when it goes to air in the peak ratings period. It will be the first Australian commercial TV series to ever be filmed totally in Antarctica. There have been one-offs before, but this is different – seven episodes with major product placement. The advertising people have been working their butts off pulling in new clients and the publicity team are glassy-eyed with excitement. It's been made clear to me that I am honoured to work on logistics and I'd better not stuff it up.

'Right.' I clear my throat. 'We have four seats confirmed on a flight departing from Hobart on the nineteenth of December. Cougar will be travelling with cameraman Rory Fleming, producer Mary Hogan and stylist Alicia Waring. Her Antarctic liaison is Lucas Nilsson.'

Lucas Nilsson. Thank goodness I'm not the one who's going to be stuck in Antarctica with Lucas Nilsson. Good luck to Cougar, is all I can say. Dealing with Lucas, who is based at the Australian Antarctic Division in Hobart, has been beyond frustrating. If there was ever a man with no concept of project management, it is him. I make a mental note to check that he's got my latest spreadsheet and continue. 'The trip to Antarctica takes four and a half hours—' A rumbling noise interrupts me.

Cougar skateboards into the room. Instantly everyone is on full alert. Cougar radiates star power. An aura moves with her, lighting up her long, tanned limbs, her bouncy black hair. She flicks her skateboard with her toe and carries it to the table, drains her vegetable juice in one gulp. Wiping her mouth with the back of her hand, she perches on her chair.

She glances at the clock on the wall. 'Okay, guys, let's move it. I've got a date at the rock-climbing gym in half an hour.' She manages to sound as if we've kept her waiting for hours.

Chapter Four

I evaluate for improved performance

Project:	Becoming Mrs Adrian Robertson
Objective:	Depart restaurant with ring on finger
17.45:	Finish work, go to bathroom and change to night-time 'look'
18.15:	Leave office
18.30:	Arrive at Le Max
18.30–18.45:	Glass of wine and light conversation with Adrian
18.45:	Adrian proposes. I accept graciously. The entire restaurant, which has been briefed, claps and cheers.
Critical event:	Adrian proposing

I am at Le Max at exactly six-thirty pm. My hair is fluffed up and I have added lipstick, the slinky top and a spray of the Le Nuit perfume which Adrian gave me for my birthday. I inspect my reflection in the restaurant door as I open it. I look neat, clean and efficient with a touch of sex appeal. Perfect. No-one would ever know I was a hippie chick from Nimbin.

I am not trying to be a *Dynasty*-style vixen or a *The Bold and the Beautiful* seductress. No, I aim to be the type of woman a man wants on his team – an asset to the corporation, a suitable candidate for a merger and expansion.

'Romantic love is a modern concept,' Adrian told me the other night. 'For most of history, marriage was about improving your lot in life, finding a partner to forge ahead with.'

He didn't say as much, but it was clear to me he thought I was the partner with whom such productive forging could be achieved.

The waiter shows me to our pre-booked table. We always take one near the window. Adrian and I are valued customers. Renaldo has a special smile tonight. He has probably been briefed by Adrian.

'Bring me a glass of chilled cabernet sauvignon please.' Adrian has been teaching me about wine. I was strictly a beer and mixed spirits girl before I met him.

Renaldo's brow creases.

Damn. Cabernet sauvignon must be the red one. Lucky Adrian isn't here. 'On second thoughts, make that a sauvignon blanc.'

His face clears and he departs.

While I wait for Adrian, I pull out my laptop and start a new email.

To: Marley Lennon Wright
From: Summer Dawn Rain Wright
Subject: The Project Adrian Plan

I had never intended to see Adrian again after I got off the plane, Marley.

Sure, I'd felt something when he talked about the Cone of Certainty, but it was like watching an animal in the zoo. It was entertaining, but you don't want to get intimate with an armadillo. I had nowhere near accepted that I needed what he had.

But when I touched down in Sydney everything changed.

I switched on my phone as I got into the airport terminal. It beeped immediately. I had a text message from Mum – *Call me.*

I rolled my eyes. Mum would want to know when I was coming home. I had no intention of moving back to Nimbin, but I planned to visit once I'd sorted out some accommodation in Sydney.

I wanted to see you, Marley, if nothing else.

I pressed 'call' as I waited at the baggage carousel.

'Summer?' Her voice was high-pitched. 'You need to come home. Marley's in hospital. A tree fall.'

I swayed on my feet, my fingers tingling.

In the press of people jostling for their luggage, a hand gripped my arm. It was Adrian.

His touch was comforting. More than that, it held me up. 'Is he, going to be alright?' I croaked into the phone.

'We don't know. You'd better come home.'

It was Adrian who sat me down, retrieved my bag, bought me a cup of sweet tea, booked me on the next available flight to Ballina and sat with me while I waited, not talking, for my flight to depart. His capable aura dispelled my panic – I would have been a gibbering wreck without him.

He pressed his card into my hand as I stood to board the flight. 'Get in touch? When you're back in Sydney?'

I stuffed it in my pocket, not expecting to ever see him again. My mind was on you.

But six weeks later in Nimbin, when the rain was turning our garden to a quagmire and I still didn't know what I was doing with my life, I found his card. As I turned it in my hands, I remembered the Cone of Certainty – how the light shone through the window as he said it. And, being the hippie chick I was, it seemed like destiny. I gave him a call.

Adrian was so sweet those first few weeks. He used his contacts to help me find a flat. We went to the movies, out to dinner, and took long walks around the harbour. He was courtly, always the gentleman. He walked on the traffic side of the footpath, took my arm to help me over puddles. I'd never been treated like that before. In Nimbin you knew a guy liked you if he passed you the joint first.

And he was so competent. If he said he'd be there at ten, he'd be there at ten precisely, like a Japanese train. He said he'd find me a flat and a job and, voila, he did. I'd never met anyone like him. It was clear if I stayed in Adrian's wake, doors would open.

On the third week we were dating, he introduced me to his favourite hobby – running. We ran somewhere in the bush near his apartment. Adrian ran around me in circles as I huffed and puffed. He might have noticed I wasn't all that into it as the running wasn't repeated.

Instead, he took me to art-house movies. I hadn't encountered these before – we only had the multiplex in Lismore – but I soon got the idea. Good movies have one or more of the following features: they are shot in black and white; feature grimy, desolate housing estates; have no dialogue; or have long shots of empty corridors. In addition, they are often made by directors with multi-barrelled surnames.

After the movie, we would discuss the meaning of the seven-minute segment where two characters walked silently through the desert. And if I happened to think the movie might have been improved by a dash of witty dialogue or a smidgen of romance, I kept this opinion to myself.

Despite all these lovely excursions, Adrian never touched me. No-one could call him a quick worker – by week four he'd progressed to a kiss on the cheek. I do wonder if anything would have happened at all if I hadn't taken matters into my own hands.

Over the weeks Adrian courted me, he taught me a lot about project management. His way of doing things might have been alien to me, but it was effective. It got results. It minimised uncertainty. And to me that now seemed like a very good thing indeed.

I needed a fresh start. Mum kept asking me to come home, but there was no way I was going back to Nimbin. If I stayed there it wouldn't be long before I'd be back with the old gang, back in the old habits. I'd gone overseas to get away from all that. Although sometimes it felt like I'd taken it with me.

I'd tried blowing with the wind and, frankly, it sucked. Predictability, I'd decided, was the zeitgeist. And where was I going to find it if not with Adrian? After four weeks I was determined to move our relationship on to, ahem, the next level. To be honest, I was baffled: it had never taken more than four days in any of my previous relationships.

Even with Jack the dope dealer, Marley! (And you know how slow he was.)

Adrian was a mystery. And there is something sexy about a mystery. He was always so cool, so in control. And – this hadn't been immediately obvious to me – he was very attractive. Charismatic. Adrian exuded the magnetism of someone who knows what he wants. Women responded to him – waitresses lingered, shop assistants blushed. I must have been the only woman in the world who hadn't wanted to lay herself at his feet at first sighting.

I decided to put my new-found knowledge of project management to work. The Project Seduce Adrian (PSA) scheme revolved around the incredible attractiveness of my assets. I don't mean the usual; Adrian had been seemingly oblivious to those. No, after browsing a few issues of *Project Manager Online* magazine, I knew what he couldn't resist. I downloaded an advance copy of the latest project management software on my home computer and outlined my master plan. It had two critical events:

- persuading Adrian to come back to my apartment for software viewing
- distracting him from software to softer wear.

The first of these was a piece of cake; Adrian was excited about the software, but as it turned out, moving him on from that was tricky.

I'd installed him in front of the computer with a glass of wine and leaned over his shoulder to demonstrate the finer features of the program.

'Summer, we've been together for a year,' says Adrian.

I nod.

'It's been … good.'

I smooth my hair behind my ear with my right hand, leaving my left on the table.

'As you are aware, there comes a time when you need to evaluate and decide what course of action to take next.'

'Yes, I know, Adrian. Evaluation is the key to improved performance.'

'Summer, this is a little hard for me to say …' Poor Adrian looks bashful.

I decide to make things easier for him. 'Yes.'

'What?'

'Yes! I'll marry you.'

Chapter Five

Extreme Project Management

Project:	Brain-wipe
Objective:	Blot evening from memory
0.00–1.00:	Aargh!
1.00–2.00:	Aargh!
2.00–3.00:	Aargh!

I fumble with the light switch. My heart is thudding from the usual dream, but the hum of my air-conditioner reassures me. Twenty-three degrees. I check my phone. It's three am. I've barely slept. *Yes! I'll marry you.* Why did I say that?

I pull the laptop towards me and open a new email.

To: Marley Lennon Wright
From: Summer Dawn Rain Wright
Subject: Use of the 'f' word

Adrian shook his head after I said I'd marry him. His cheeks were pink. 'No, what I'm trying to say is … I think we need to take a break and consider our options.'

'Take a break? Consider our options?'

Adrian waved his hand in a *keep your voice down* way. 'You don't seem fully committed to project planning … to the vision of Gantt.'

I glanced around the restaurant. Perhaps they hadn't been briefed but they were paying attention now. Let them look, I didn't care. 'How am I not committed to the vision of Gantt?'

Adrian didn't reply.

'But Adrian, why? We've been together for one year. We have wonderful sex. (That wasn't quite true, Marley, but I'd always let him think so.) We're totally compatible. We both love the same things (if you discount running, Bikram yoga, art movies and wine-tasting). We have the same goals. Why?'

'I'm sorry, Summer.' Adrian fingered the bruise on his hand.

'Is this because I didn't make muesli?'

'What? You told me you'd made muesli.'

'I lied.' I thought of the dust balls. 'Did you look under my bed?'

'No, why?'

'Never mind. Why then? Why?'

'You're not achievement-focused, Summer. I should have realised when I met you. I thought I could change you, but I was wrong.'

'No, you were right. I've come so far already. I'm a different person.'

Adrian sighed. 'I didn't want to have to say this, Summer, but … I've been seeing someone else.'

'What? Who?' I felt sick. Some other woman had lured Adrian away with her amazing project management skills. I hadn't been trying hard enough.

Adrian fingered his hand. 'It doesn't matter who, but she's … incredibly focused.'

'Who? Tell me.'

A dreamy expression spread over Adrian's face. 'Cougar Gale.'

'Cougar Gale?' I glanced at the bruise. The rock-climbing – of course.

'Cougar made me realise – life is not a dress rehearsal.' He said this like it was the most insightful thing he'd ever heard.

I snorted. 'Oh for fuck's sake. We used to have a poster saying "life is not a dress rehearsal" pinned up in our outside toilet on the commune. It's hardly profound.'

Adrian's eyes widened. 'You don't normally swear, Summer.'

'That goes to show how much you know about me, Adrian. The first word I ever said was "fuck".'

That wasn't true but, as you know, Marley, I did grow up around a lot of people who used the f-word as an all-purpose adjective.

Adrian blinked. 'It's not nice, for a woman to—'

'Fuck, fuck, fuck. Ha. You want me to use the c-word? I can. I've done it before.'

Adrian cringed. He shook his head.

I salvaged what was left of my dignity and got to my feet. 'I hope your spreadsheets get a virus.' I walked away leaving him to pay the bill.

'Don't be like that, Summer,' he called after me. 'There's no need to let this come between us. I still respect your abilities as a project manager.'

I didn't dignify that with a reply.

Fuck Adrian. Tears prick my eyes. How could he do that? And to say I'm not committed to the vision of Gantt ... I love project planning. It's been a revelation. My phone lies on the bedroom table taunting me with its file of Adrian projects. I'd already started a wedding project plan. It would have been the best organised wedding ever. And he threw it all away. For what – rock-climbing with Cougar Gale? Wait until his rope breaks, he'll be wishing life was a dress rehearsal then.

I grind my teeth. *Adrian and Cougar* – it's so unexpected. How do they even know each other?

In reality, I have no idea what kind of person Cougar is. I've been in meetings with her and bought her juices and organic tofu rolls, but I don't know her. On television she comes across as a friendly, girl-next-door type. If you happen to live next door to a multi-talented adrenaline junkie. But who is she really?

Sitting up in bed, I pull my laptop towards me and type *Cougar Gale* into Google. Her standard publicity photo comes up. She is paddling her kayak over an apparently bottomless waterfall. Our toilet wall *life is not a dress rehearsal* poster had a photo of someone doing exactly that.

Cougar is wearing her usual quick-dry singlet and leaning backwards in the kayak. Her thick, black hair is flying out behind her. She looks ecstatic. Does she look like that when she has sex with Adrian? Perhaps not. Sex with Adrian is more like finding a great parking spot than plunging over a waterfall – satisfying, but not exactly transcendent.

I read the blurb beneath the photo. *Cougar Gale has solo kayaked from Australia to New Zealand. She has climbed the six highest mountains in the world. She has a PhD in glaciology from Cambridge.*

'And she looks amazing in quick dry shorts and singlets,' I add.

If I had a publicity blurb, what would it would say?

Summer Wright doesn't like exercise much, particularly if it involves contact with nature. She has a Bachelor of Arts from a university no-one has ever heard of and is a self-taught project manager who aspires to be a soap opera scriptwriter.

'And I look comfortable in track pants and T-shirt,' I say to my imaginary biographer.

Cougar: flowing hair, rippling muscles.

Me: functional brown bed shirt. Functional body. Functional hair. In one year I've refashioned myself from spunky hippie chick to nerdy project manager – I thought it was what Adrian wanted.

Cougar. Adrian. Adrian. Cougar. Even with the addition of the hair wax, leather jacket and rock-climbing, Adrian doesn't seem like Cougar's type. Unless she is attracted by the Cone of Certainty?

I turn on the radio and lie down again. Sometimes when I'm restless, background noise helps me sleep. 'The state is a tinderbox … worst year for bushfires on record …' I lean over and turn it off, but it's too late. Marley's voice is in my head. I turn on the light again and pick up my laptop.

To: Marley Lennon Wright
From: Summer Dawn Rain Wright
Subject: Remember?

'Our garden has a greater diversity of snakes than most national parks, Summer Dawn,' you used to say.

Like that was a good thing. Remember that snake book you showed me? There were night tigers, small-lipped snakes, green tree-snakes, brown tree-snakes and carpet pythons. These ones I didn't mind much. *Not dangerous.*

I wasn't so happy the day I found a brown snake on the verandah, or had to leap over a rough-scaled snake that emerged from under the fridge, or almost sat on a death adder which had curled up for a snooze on the couch.

'We're having a bumper snake season,' you said, like a farmer expecting a good crop.

They had come for the bats apparently.

Our house was like a tree. In the top level, the roof, lived the bats. They were tiny, smaller than my hand, and chocolate brown. During the day they squeaked and scuffled in the roof. It was hard to imagine they slept soundly with all the snakes slithering around. At dusk they took off in a cloud. Often one or two got lost and ended up inside the house.

You'd pick them up off the curtains or corners where they landed and escort them gently outside. They bit and clawed you, but their mouths were too small to do damage.

Not many of my high-school friends visited me at home. Their parents didn't like them going to the commune. The valiant souls who made it out were scared off by the wildlife. The snakes and bats were bad enough, but it was the ticks and leeches that sent them running.

The funny part is you and I roamed for hours without a problem. Bring in an outsider, however, and they couldn't step outdoors for more than fifteen minutes without being mobbed by blood-sucking predators.

'They sense weakness,' you said, as we waved goodbye to my friend Madeleine, who'd arrived unblemished but departed with blood trickling down her ankles from leech bites and at least five separate lumps where we'd removed ticks.

I felt the truth in that. You and I were strong. But I didn't want to be different from my friends, Marley.

Marley's *An Antarctic Mystery* is over on the bookshelf. Throughout all those years of travelling I never opened it. Looking at its creased spine, I picture him reading out loud, a mug of tea in his hand:

> Not a single iceberg is to be seen on this fantastic sea. Innumerable flocks of birds skim its surface, among them is a pelican which is shot. On a floating piece of ice is a bear of the Arctic species and of gigantic size.

I smile, remembering Marley's face. It used to be like looking in a mirror when we were kids – before the hormones kicked in. But my life is the opposite of Marley's. I'm heading for the top of the Cone of Certainty – the pointy end where there are no surprises.

There are no trippy 'go with the flow' friends at the point of the Cone. You don't wake up to find your drug-dealing boyfriend has taken off with your life savings and was last seen strumming his guitar on a yacht bound for Hawaii. Or that he's crashed your uninsured car after an all-night party. No, it's stable up there at the point. You start each day with a sense of purpose and the satisfaction of knowing what lies ahead. You have life insurance and car insurance. You are the master of your destiny.

Adrian nudged me off the top of the Cone last night but he's not going to derail me. With or without him, my life is running according to a plan.

I think of what he said – *You're not achievement-focused, Summer.* He had a point. While my task management has improved, I'm a long way off perfection. The unmade muesli, the daydreaming … I didn't think he'd noticed. But it seems he had. Not to mention my lack of interest in running, Bikram yoga, art-house movies and wine-tasting. Who can blame him for deciding Cougar is a worthier acolyte to induct into the ways of Gantt?

I blink away tears at the thought of Adrian telling Cougar about the Cone. This seems like the worst betrayal – the Cone is our special thing.

I take a deep breath. I will try harder. Surely if I improve, Adrian will return. Cougar is a test. I'd been pretty half-arsed about it all. No wonder he was disappointed.

My eyes wander back to the bookshelf. Adrian has left some books here for me – 'Essential reading,' he said, but I'm yet to open them. Was he waiting for me to discuss them with him? I walk over and inspect them. *Seven Habits of Highly Effective People, Elegant Account-ing, Manage for Success, Extreme Project Management* … This one sounds like it might be what I need.

Picking it up, I flick through the pages. It's enlightening. I thought I had a handle on this project management thing, but there's a lot I wasn't aware of – the history, for one thing. Apparently the 1950s were the beginning of the modern project management era (MPM). Before that (BMPM – the Dark Age!), projects were managed on an ad hoc basis. I'm not sure what this means, but it sounds loose, very non-Cone of Certainty. Imagine – all those centuries of ad hoc project management before Gantt came along … People bumbling around doing whatever they pleased.

I turn the page. Where would project management be without such tools as Gantt's famous Work Breakdown Structure (WBS)? Not to mention the Gantt chart – a revolutionary tool of project management, developed in 1910 and used during the First World War to control shipping movements.

How did the pyramids ever get built without these tools? I bet there was a lot of waiting around for blocks to be delivered and extra slaves sourced. What about the Great Wall of China, Stonehenge, the Easter Island statues … The mind boggles to imagine how they pulled those off without spreadsheets and pie charts.

Extreme Project Management is for people who find normal project management isn't enough – those who have tried the soft stuff and are up for something harder. People like me. 'Hard core project managers don't give up when the going gets tough, they get extreme', says a line on the first page.

For some reason this reminds me that I still haven't heard back from Lucas Nilsson in Hobart about my latest spreadsheet. I flick him off a quick email.

> Please respond at your soonest convenience to my latest breakdown. It is imperative that the production schedule is followed to the letter. If you foresee any difficulties the Work Breakdown Structure must be revised before Cougar departs for Antarctica.

I press 'send'. That should get him moving. By now it is four am – only a couple of hours until I need to get up. I get into bed with the book and turn the pages.

Chapter Six

Igloo builders are in short supply

I wake only when sunlight falls on my face. It is 7.15. I've slept through my alarm. The book is open on my chest, but extreme project management will have to wait. My morning routine, that's what I need to think about. Today's project plan requires a quick edit. I pick up my laptop and work through the line items, pressing the *delete* button.

Project:	Tuesday morning routine
Objective:	Arrive at work on time, healthy, rested and ready for action
~~6.15:~~	~~Wake up (exact wake time determined by 'wake easy' app to ensure optimal brain function)~~
~~6.15–6.25:~~	~~Visualise day ahead (visualisation leads to peak performance)~~
~~6.25–6.55:~~	~~Morning yoga (remember to stay in moment, breathe, relax)~~
~~6.55–7.15:~~	~~Breakfast (home-made muesli with low-fat yoghurt, goji berries and chia seeds)~~
7.15–7.45:	Wash and dress ~~(outfit laid out the night before to facilitate this step)~~
7.45:	Walk to Chatswood train station
7.58:	Catch train to Town Hall ~~(travel pass pre-purchased to prevent delay) On train: Check and respond to email, Twitter, Facebook, LinkedIn and Instagram (remember: one third respond, one third communicate, one third encourage)~~
8.27:	Walk from Town Hall station to office
8.39:	Arrive work, ~~change shoes, brush hair~~
8.45:	Work commences
Total time:	~~2 hours 30 minutes~~ 1 hour 30 minutes

There – *look at me, Adrian* – extreme project managers are adaptable! I still haven't made the muesli but I will move on to getting dressed and leaving for work. I have a production meeting at nine and a lot to do to get Cougar's Antarctic trip on course.

As I slide *Extreme Project Management* back onto the shelf my eyes fall on Marley's book. I should read it properly one day.

᪉

'Hi, Summer,' says Jacinta as I come in. She is wearing a polka-dot dress, like something my grandmother might have owned, but on her – and teamed with black Blundstone boots – it is hip. Her forehead creases as I come closer. 'Are you okay?'

'Fine thanks. Adrian and I have separated by mutual consent, so he can pursue his need for rock-climbing with Cougar Gale. This was a surprise as I'd already worked out which universities our children were going to, but I'm fine.' I smile brightly. 'Which room are we meeting in for *In the Wild*?'

'Oh.' Jacinta seems lost for words. 'Room three. Can I get you a chai or something? A juice? Some wheatgrass? Are you sure you're okay?'

'Yes, I'm fine. If Cougar wants to rock-climb with a man who thinks the female body is a difficult engineering problem, who am I to stop her?'

Jacinta frowns. I'm over-sharing.

Maxine approaches the glass doors and I decide to move on. 'Ha, ha,' I add.

For some reason this does nothing to remove the frown from Jacinta's face.

I'm the first to arrive at the meeting, which is good. I might have skipped most of my morning routine, but I'm on top of things. The Cone of Certainty is operating at an acceptable level.

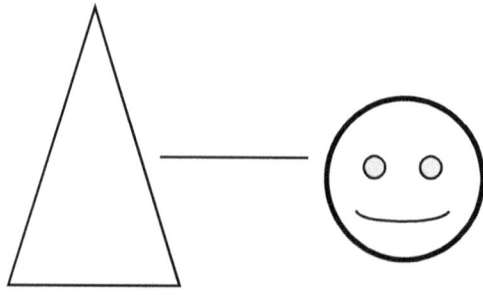

I open my project plan and check through the details for Cougar's Antarctic expedition. It's only two days until she leaves and there are still a few loose ends.

Antarctic liaison: Australian Antarctic Division will supply scientific talent – Lucas Nilsson.

I snort and check my emails. He has replied: *Looks fine, Lucas.*

Looks fine? Has he even read it? There are five hundred and twenty actions in my spreadsheet. They can't all look fine. A second email from him pops up: *But you have to remember. This is Antarctica. It's unpredictable.*

Unpredictable? That is completely unacceptable. He needs to be told that's not how television works. I grind my teeth, make a note to follow up by phone, and continue scrolling through my project plan.

Series storyboard: Script to be finalised by creative team headed by Dianne …

The rest of the production team straggle in.

Another email pops up: *PS. Emailing at four am? Sleep is more important than spreadsheets.*

Not to me it's not, I reply.

Maxine's arrival is heralded by the clack of her heels.

You will see, pops up in my inbox.

I delete Lucas's email and sit up straight. I'll deal with him later. Full focus is now required.

Taking her seat, Maxine looks towards Cougar's chair. Her nostrils flare as she glances at her watch. 'Give us a run-down on the financials will you, Damien? While we wait.' She places her phone on the table with a bang. Maxine and Damien the financial controller are at the same level in the station hierarchy, but this is Maxine's turf and she is asserting her command.

'The good news,' Damien says, 'is we have extensive advertising bought up already for this series.' Damien is relaxed, confident and full of himself. He presses a button on his laptop and a bar chart fills the screen on the wall. 'You can see last season's advertising.' He picks up a small laser pointer and indicates the smaller bar. 'And this season's.' He points at the larger bar. 'I think it's safe to say *Cougar on Ice* is going to exceed our projections.'

At the mention of Cougar, I grit my teeth, controlling my emotions. I imagine them as three lionesses called Anger, Hurt and Betrayal. At the moment they are well behaved, but that doesn't make them any less dangerous. *Down, girls.*

'What type of advertisers?' says Maxine.

'Two car companies, two airlines, white goods ...'

Maxine fiddles with her phone.

'We also have some interest in product placement,' says Damien.

Maxine looks up at this. 'What products?'

'Tim Tams, Jimmy Choo, iPad, Baileys—'

Maxine's phone rings. She snatches it up. 'What? But? How long? That's impossible. Where? Let me talk to her. Very well. As soon as possible.' Beneath the blusher and foundation her face has paled. All eyes are on her as she puts the phone down. This is clearly bad news. 'Cougar Gale has' – she breathes deeply – 'broken her ankle. While skateboarding down the ramp at Bondi. With a surfboard. She is in hospital while her leg is put in plaster.'

Damien gasps. 'Is she ... alright?'

Maxine's baby-blue eyes would freeze the heart of a braver man than he.

He sinks into his chair. His laser light – previously so jaunty, so cock-a-hoop – moves down the screen and vanishes quietly off the bottom.

Maxine glares at him. 'Her PA says she is resting comfortably.' She slams her hand down. 'This. Is. A. Total. Disaster.'

I remember Jacinta's story about the *Charlie's Adventure* meeting. *No-one got out of there alive.*

The production team fidgets and I sense they are all thinking the same thing. *Cougar on Ice* is the new *Charlie's Adventure*. Mascara-coated eyes slide away from Maxine's gaze. One man ferrets around on the floor for an invisible pen. Damien is three shades paler than he was a few moments before – almost *Whisper White*. The potential for loss of advertising has hit him hard.

Maxine bangs her pen on the table. 'Don't just sit there. Suggestions?' Her eyes are china-doll laser beams, her scarlet lips drawn back from her incisors. Beneath her black silk top I swear there's a bulge where a fanged monster is about to burst out.

'She could still go. On crutches,' pipes up Damien.

I clear my throat. My heart is thudding wildly, but I can't just sit here – this is my area. 'They have very strict medical requirements for travel to Antarctica,' I say in my most efficient production assistant manner. 'She had to have a lengthy doctor's examination to be accepted. She won't be allowed on Australian Antarctic Division transport with a broken ankle.'

'We could p-postpone the series,' says Dianne the scriptwriter. 'Until she is out of p-plaster.'

Maxine raises one perfectly shaped eyebrow. 'Summer?'

I am mesmerised by her eyebrow. It is too smooth, too perfect to be real. Perhaps it is tattooed. 'Well,' I say to the eyebrow, 'we can try for another flight in January or February, but, um, if we pull out … They could offer the media spot to Channel Four. There's a waiting list, you see.'

Maxine bangs her fist on the table again. Her blonde coif sways like a building in an earthquake.

Everyone jumps.

'There is no way on earth Channel Four is getting that flight,' she snarls. 'No way on earth.'

Everyone shakes their heads. Muted murmurs of sycophantic agreement spread around the table.

'We'll substitute another presenter.' Maxine clicks her fingers at me. 'Who's available?'

I shake my head. 'I'm afraid we can't do that at this stage.'

The table gasps as one. A sea of horrified round eyes fix on me as if I'm holding a gun to my temple. Damien presses his hands to his cheeks.

What have I said? *Can't.*

Maxine's two eyebrows draw together. They are amazingly versatile.

I should be terrified, but I am hypnotised. 'The application was for Cougar,' I say to her eyebrows. 'The place is in her name. If she doesn't take it herself, we have to begin the application process for someone else. We can't take that time.'

There is another audible gasp in the room. I've said it again. Under the table someone kicks me.

I press on. 'And I'm pretty sure Channel Four is on that waiting list.'

'No.' Maxine's eyebrows are almost in her hairline. 'That is not happening. There is no frigging way. Even if I have to dress up as Cougar myself ...' She pauses. 'Hm, with all that snow gear on' – she gestures around her head to indicate a puffy hood – 'who's to know? Yes, that's an option – a Cougar impersonator. Who have we got?'

This is the most ridiculous suggestion ever. Cougar's face is one of the best known in Australia. How can you impersonate her? Surely Maxine can't be serious?

But everyone else at the table is nodding eagerly. Obsequious murmurs fill the air – *great idea, terrific, absolutely*.

'It has to be someone who can build igloos.' Dianne's cheeks are flushed. She speaks quickly. 'I'm finalising a fun Christmas Day script where everyone gathers in the igloo which Cougar has secretly built overnight and they all open their presents and eat mince pies and it's like, you know, they're all so far from home and yet she's brought them all together, it will be beautiful ...' She stops as her breath runs out.

'Summer can build igloos.' Damien points his laser at me.

The whole table turns to me as the red dot hits my chest.

I shake my head. 'No I can't.'

There's another audible gasp.

'You told me,' says Damien. 'When you were in Chamonix ...'

I stare at him. It's all coming back to me. Over someone's birthday drinks a while back I'd told Damien the igloo story. I'd had a few wines at the time and I may have exaggerated slightly.

The True Igloo Story

When I was working in Chamonix, there was a man staying in the lodge who built an igloo for his kids. I happened to be wandering past and admired the igloo. He was patting snow on the outside and I helped him smooth it out.

The Igloo Story as told to Damien

When I was working in Chamonix there was a guy staying in the lodge who asked me to build an igloo for his kids. Going way beyond the call of duty, I built it all by myself and slept in it for two nights with his kids. Because that's the kind of person I am.

Damien had seemed awed and I saw I'd changed in his eyes – become more adventurous and capable. I wasn't just a television production assistant anymore – I was an igloo-builder.

'Once. I've only done it once,' I say.

'Well, that's more than anyone else here has done.' Maxine is unnaturally calm, but the corner of her eye is twitching. She speaks sweetly. 'Is that correct, or do we have another igloo-builder here? Leanne? Steve? Dianne?'

Shaking heads confirm that Channel Five's production team does not harbour any closet igloo-builders.

Maxine turns back to me. She puts her head on one side. 'It could work. There's a resemblance now I think about it.' Her eyes assess me. 'At a pinch. If you're not looking closely.'

'But I ca—' I stop myself. 'I don't know anything about—'

Maxine snaps her fingers at Steve, the publicity guy. 'Photoshop her.'

'Huh?' I say.

But Steve pulls out his phone, snaps a photo of me, does something techo on the computer and within two minutes a photograph is projected on the screen. The image is the standard publicity shot of Cougar going over the waterfall. But instead of Cougar's face, it is mine. I have my mouth half-open, caught in the middle of saying *huh*? I have Cougar's hair and body. It's a strange feeling, like getting an extreme makeover. And the weird part is, I do look a bit like Cougar.

Maxine looks from the image back to me and her mouth turns up at the corner. 'You've got the same nose.'

She's right. I've always hated my long nose. On Cougar though, it is striking and glamorous.

Maxine clicks her pen in and out then waves her finger at Steve. 'Put her in a snowsuit.'

A couple of minutes later, there I am on the screen again, still with my mouth half-open, but now I'm wearing a puffy, red snowsuit, with the hood pulled up. Steve has split the screen, so the other side has Cougar wearing the same snowsuit.

Everyone's eyes flicker from one side of the screen to the other and I know I'm coming out of it badly. But … our lips are similar too. On Cougar, of course, they are luscious, not just thick.

'Interesting,' says Maxine. 'The snowsuit hides a multitude of sins.' She lays her hands on the table. 'Okay, that's our solution. Summer, you are Cougar.'

Everyone at the table smiles with the relief of having dodged a bullet. Everyone except me.

I gaze at Maxine. Don't I get any say in this? *Antarctica?* I don't want to go to Antarctica. My heart beats faster at the thought. Anything could happen in Antarctica. People die in blizzards and are devoured by starving huskies. 'But Cougar has a PhD in glaciology. I don't know anything about glaciers. Or about presenting.'

'You've got two days to learn.' Maxine sounds as if this is more than generous. 'Okay, let's move on. Fill us in on the coma scene for *Up and at 'Em*, Dianne …'

Everyone relaxes from the rigid position they've assumed over the last few minutes – disaster has been averted. Dianne, her cheeks still flushed, gives a rapid run-down on the multiple-coma issue.

I open and shut my mouth like a dying goldfish, but as far as the production team is concerned I am yesterday's news.

Chapter Seven

My life becomes a string of spaghetti

Project:	Wednesday routine
Objective:	Become Cougar Gale
6.00:	Wake up
6.00–7.00:	Running
7.00–10.00:	Eat home-made muesli and watch old episodes of 'In the Wild'
10.00–11.00:	Weight training
11.00–12.00:	Dye hair black and apply fake tan
12.00–14.00:	Buy outdoor clothing
14.00–24:00:	Study glaciology
Total time:	18 hours

On Wednesday morning I wake at six am. The meeting yesterday seems like a bad dream. It was as if the whole group was hypnotised by fear of Maxine. I've heard of that sort of thing happening before, but I've never experienced it. Group think, I believe it's called when people make bad decisions in order to conform to social norms.

Am I really about to impersonate Cougar Gale? I turn my head and bang my nose against something hard. *Extreme Project Management* is open on my pillow. I'd fallen asleep reading it last night. I now know extreme project management (XPM) is used to manage complex and uncertain projects. In contrast to traditional project management (TPM) it is open, elastic and non-deterministic. The book has a couple of helpful diagrams.

TPM is like a waterfall

_____

    _____

        _____

XPM is like a string of spaghetti

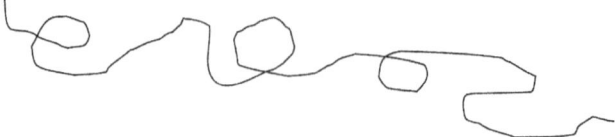

While my life bears more resemblance to a string of spaghetti than an orderly cascading waterfall, I suspect it is worse than that. My life is more tangled, like this:

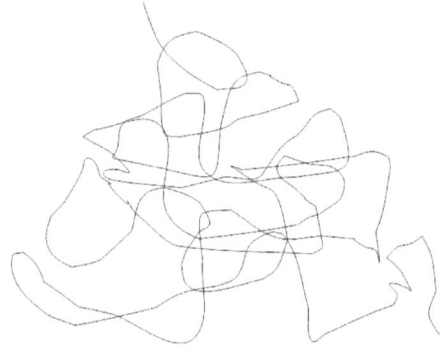

Opening my laptop, I check today's objective – *Become Cougar Gale.* *Ha.*

I can't believe a table full of seemingly rational adults has agreed that no-one will notice if I turn up on TV in Cougar's place. But I suppose it does happen in long-running soap operas when one of the actors leaves. The viewer knows that Charlene's a little different today but after half an hour you forget there was ever another Charlene.

Pulling on a T-shirt and shorts, I stagger out the door. It's ridiculous to expect I'm going to transform my body into Cougar's in one day; however, I must make some effort. I will pound the streets of Chatswood for an hour.

I pound the streets of Chatswood for ten minutes before relapsing into a brisk walk, which soon becomes a stroll. It's too hot for running. The sun, even filtered through a thin layer of smoke, is bitingly hot. It's lucky I thought to stuff a twenty-dollar note inside the groovy armband that holds my phone. This armband was a present from

Adrian. 'You can listen to music and take calls while you run,' he said. 'And once you upgrade to a voice recognition phone, you'll be able to send texts too.' This sounded feasible, but if I was to send a text now it would be nothing but gasps and pants and I'd get booked for harassment.

By six-thirty, I'm ensconced in a coffee shop with a double-shot latte and a muffin on order. I would have been there earlier, but the cafe only opens at six-thirty.

My ten-minute run has illustrated how unsuited I am for this job. It's ridiculous. I can't go to Antarctica. I can't impersonate Cougar. I'll make a fool of myself if I'm not eaten by huskies first. Something weird happened in that meeting room yesterday but I'm sure they'll have come to their senses by now.

At nine o'clock I will go and see Maxine. I'll be firm and assertive while avoiding *can't*. Surely she will see reason. We can reschedule *Cougar on Ice*.

On the TV in the corner a talking head presents *The Morning Show*. A graphic pops up on the screen showing little bushfire symbols across the state. I would leave, but I have food coming. Instead, I try to ignore the interview with a man in orange overalls. A few words penetrate – *long, hot summer … high fire danger … total fire ban … working to control …*

'Here's your coffee.'

I turn back to the table, just in time to see him. It's only a glimpse, but it is him. Marley is pulling out a hose, running towards a burning tree. *File footage*, says a note at the bottom of the screen.

'Are you okay?' The waitress places a glass of water in front of me.

'Yes, thanks.' I drum my fingers on the table and breathe slowly to steady myself. The image on the screen changes to a parched paddock; *no prospect of rain*, says the announcer.

Things got a bit sad between Marley and me before I left to go overseas. We'd never been apart for so long – I think we were both trying to avoid thinking about it.

I tap on my phone and start an email.

To: Marley Lennon Wright
From: Summer Dawn Rain Wright
Subject: Remember? (part two)

I was reading on the couch when you sat beside me, bouncing up and down the way you always did.

I looked up from my book. 'Hiya.'

'Hey.'

You were so tall and broad-shouldered, Marley. You were the kind of guy I'd want to see coming to help if I was stuck in a house with a bushfire advancing. And, if you weren't my brother, I'd say you were kind of cute.

'What're you reading?' you said.

I held up my book. It was a guide to scriptwriting.

'Still into that stuff, huh?'

'Yeah, you still into that firefighting stuff?'

We always paid each other out, didn't we?

'I'm going to miss you, Summer Dawn.'

'I'll miss you too, you old silly.' I punched you on the shoulder. 'We'll email, right?'

'Yes.'

'You could come,' I murmured.

'Yeah. But I've got *stuff* to do here.'

I knew that – you'd only just got a professional firefighting job after being a volunteer for almost ten years. You were hardly going to leave.

'Hey, you're going to have a great time. Make sure you send lots of emails,' you said.

I send the email and take a sip of water. I have a queasy feeling, like I'm sliding down the Cone of Certainty at high speed. Damn Cougar Gale and her broken ankle. Damn Adrian and his sudden thirst for rock-climbing. They've pushed me off my rightful position on top of the Cone. I desperately need to tell Maxine I'm not going to Antarctica. I'm not looking forward to it, but it has to be done and I'll feel much better afterwards.

I draw a little picture on my phone with the pointer:

Before meeting with Maxine

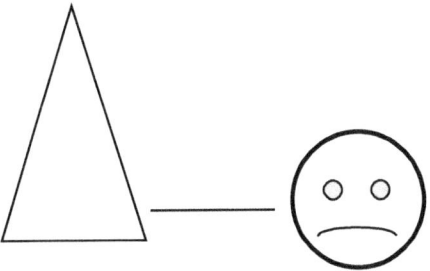

After meeting with Maxine

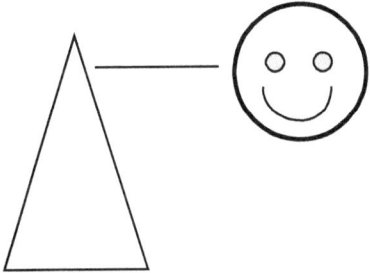

Extreme Project Management had something to say about rapid change – what was it? *When chaos and uncertainty reign, a good project manager does not call in sick.* Something like that … I may need to revise my life plan to take Adrian's temporary absence into account, but the extreme project manager isn't fazed by change, they just re-schedule. Once I've mastered XPM, Adrian will return. He won't be able to resist my sexy project planning.

Adrian is probably rock-climbing right now. Or possibly visiting Cougar in hospital. Somehow I can't summon the expected emotions. Anger, Hurt and Betrayal must be snoozing in the sun. They're not the angry lionesses they should be. Here I am, betrayed on the eve of my engagement and yet … Instead of three lionesses, I seem to be saddled with three old tabby cats called Irritation, Annoyance and Pique. No doubt I'm in shock.

As I nibble on my chocolate muffin I recall that my project plan stipulated home-made muesli for breakfast. Too late. My phone rings and I check the number. *Mum*. I can't resist thinking of her like that – it's my little rebellion. I'm never allowed to call her 'Mum', only Euphoria. Euphoria's not the name she was born with, but on the commune changing your name is de rigueur. Our neighbours are Serenity and Rock.

While my full name is Summer Dawn Rain Wright, Summer is more than enough for me. Marley got off easily; he was named after Bob Marley, hero of hippies the world over. His middle name is Lennon, for obvious reasons.

Mum almost never rings me on my mobile – she's worried about radiation – so this must be urgent.

'Hi, Euphoria,' I say.

'Summer, I'm worried about you.' Mum speaks quickly; she wants to get off the phone as soon as possible. I picture her standing in the mud-walled lounge room, holding the phone away from her ear to lessen radiation. While it is me, if anyone, who is being irradiated, Mum believes it works both ways. 'I had a dream about you. You were buried in snow. You're not going anywhere snowy, are you?'

'Um.' The Antarctic trip flashes through my mind, but of course I'm not going. And if I was, it would be top secret. 'No. I had my apartment painted white. That's probably it.'

'Oh, get out of here. Not you, Summer, it's those bats, they're running rampant. There's always one flapping around. Yes, that's probably it. I'd paint it blue if I were you – much more calming. Well, don't go anywhere snowy, will you? Not until after the summer solstice.'

'Why?' I was born on the summer solstice, hence my name.

'Really, Summer, you should know – after your birthday is a much safer time for you.'

'Okay, Mum, that's fine, I'm not going anywhere.'

Mum's frozen silence reminds me I've called her 'Mum'.

'Euphoria, I mean.'

'You should come home for the New Year's Eve ritual. That was always one of your favourites. Marley preferred Halloween and ...' Euphoria stops. 'Those bats, I've never seen so many of them.'

'Mm,' I murmur in a non-committal way. I have no intention of going home to make corn dollies and harvest altars or to beat drums with Mum and her friends. It might have been fun once, but I've moved on.

'I'd better go before we get too much radiation. Don't talk on your mobile phone again today, will you?'

'I won't.'

Mum hangs up.

I finish my muffin thoughtfully. Summer solstice used to take the place of Christmas on the commune. It was a huge celebration with friends and family. I never missed not celebrating Christmas and we got our presents early so there was no cause for complaint. Although I've put that hippie pagan stuff behind me, I used to love celebrating the power of the Sun Lord – the moment he reached his zenith.

As I pay my bill and step out of the air-conditioned cafe into the heat of the morning, it feels like the Sun Lord is doing way too much celebrating for his own good.

Chapter Eight
I discover my inner Alexis

Project: Meet with Maxine

Objective: Get out of going to Antarctica

Critical events: Say 'can' not 'can't'

Cool air surrounds me as I step inside my apartment block. I press the lift button, mentally rehearsing what I'm going to say to Maxine. If I get there early I can catch her before she rushes off to any meetings.

The lift doors open on my floor and I freeze. An unexpected and unwelcome visitor lurks outside my door.

Cougar Gale is wearing short shorts and a black singlet which shows off her biceps. If it wasn't for the crutches and the plaster-encased foot, she'd look ready to run a marathon. The folly of impersonating her strikes me anew. It's like a spaniel trying to pass for a wolf. It's lucky I've ditched that idea. I'm about to press the 'doors close' button and retreat, when she spots me. Reluctantly, I step from the lift.

Cougar has never acknowledged my existence before. In meetings she acts like I'm a piece of furniture. She is the star and I am but a humble assistant. But now … we have a lot in common.

As I approach her I wonder, again, what she is doing with Adrian. He doesn't seem her type. I've seen Cougar in the social pages linked to ruggedly handsome and successful men – the Australian surf champion, a B-grade Hollywood actor and the son of a media magnate. Cougar is as beautiful in an off-the-shoulder evening gown as she is in her quick-dry clothes. They never last long, these men. She is clearly a man-eater.

Adrian is handsome and athletic – all that Bikram yoga and running. He is organised and good at his job, whatever it is. He projects an air of focus and dependability. Although, as it turns out, he is not so dependable after all. He has the charisma that comes with being sure of himself. But … he is not in Cougar's league.

Cougar raises her eyebrows as I approach. I am instantly aware of my sweaty tattered T-shirt and shorts. She's right in front of my door so I can't ignore her, though that's what I'd like to do. Whatever she wants, I'm sure I don't want to hear it.

'We need to talk,' she says.

I'd rather kick her crutches out from under her, but common courtesy is hard to overcome. I open the door and stand back to let her go first.

Cougar swings on her crutches ahead of me into the flat. She gazes around. 'Into white, are you?'

'Yes. It's … calming. Do you want to sit down?'

Cougar perches on a stool at the breakfast bench.

I lower myself onto the couch and immediately feel at a disadvantage. I should have remained standing to look her in the eye, but it's too late now.

'I'm not happy,' says Cougar.

This should have been my line. I'm the wronged partner confronting her fiancée's seductress, after all. I have to admit she doesn't seem happy. Her exquisitely plucked eyebrows are drawn together. Cougar appears to be nursing a grudge against me.

This is unfair and a little confusing. It leaves me lost for words. Where is a scriptwriter when you need one? A few obvious lines flash through my brain. *How dare you show your face here? Get out and never darken my doorstep again, you man-stealing tart.* But these seem misplaced in the face of her indignation.

I jump as Cougar bangs a crutch on the ground. 'I'm not happy about you impersonating me in Antarctica.'

Oh that. 'I'm not happy about it either. Maxine didn't want to lose the spot to Channel—'

'I know all that.' Cougar puts her hand up. Her eyes move down my body then come up to meet mine. It is clear I have been appraised and found wanting. 'It's most ridiculous thing I've ever heard and it's not going to work.'

Right up until she says this, I would have agreed wholeheartedly, but now my hackles rise. Alexis from *Dynasty* wouldn't stand for this from a woman who'd stolen her man. The words leap out before I can stop them. 'Well, I don't care what you think. I'm going to do it.' I'm just putting on a show. I have no intention of going to Antarctica.

Cougar looks faintly amused. 'They'll find you out in the first day and send you home. I'm one of the best known faces in Australia. You'll never carry it off.'

'Ha, that's what you think.' I'm not going to roll over and let her walk all over me. 'Everyone is replaceable.'

'The media will get onto it and you're going to look preposterous. It's almost certainly illegal. I've had the clearance, not you.' Her eyes linger on my face. She touches her mouth with a forefinger. 'You've got chocolate ...'

Damn. I wipe my mouth with the back of my hand.

'I doubt you'd have passed the medical. And you'll be travelling overseas with a false identity. You'll end up in jail.'

I hadn't thought of that. 'You can go to the media yourself. That'll put an end to it.'

'Don't you think I would if I could? My contract has a clause for this sort of thing. It's completely sewn up – commercial-in-confidence. You're the one who needs to stop it. You're never going to be able to carry it off.'

Cougar sounds so sure and she's probably right. But I waggle my head in a careless way. 'We'll see.'

'It's a joke. You' – her lip curls – 'impersonating me.' She focuses on my mouth again.

I resist the urge to wipe it. She's trying to psyche me out.

'Sorry about Adrian by the way.' She doesn't sound sorry at all. 'He's quite the high-performer in bed, isn't he?'

I'm gobsmacked.

'And in other places.'

Anger stirs at last. She emits a low, dangerous growl. I can't believe this woman. She's doing a better job of sounding like Alexis than I am and she isn't even trying. Is that what Adrian likes? Has he been longing for a prima donna? Anger shows her teeth, she snarls and roars and I have an epiphany. If that's what Adrian wants ...

I will go to Antarctica! I'll be a better Cougar than she ever was. I'll show him who's a focused high-achiever. I'll show him who's the face of Australia. And damn it, I'm the soap opera scriptwriter here, not her. I'm taking control of this scene, starting now. Standing up, I look her in the eye. 'I want you out of here. Now.'

Cougar's mouth twitches. 'No need to come over all melodramatic.'

I walk over and open the door. When I turn back she's still perched on the stool. 'What?' You want it in writing?' I hesitate, take a deep breath and say my next line. 'You man-stealing tart.' My cheeks flush red at my daring.

Cougar seems more puzzled than angry. 'What did you say?'

'I said' – I draw myself up to my full height – 'you man-stealing tart.'

Cougar laughs. 'You've been watching too much daytime TV, Autumn.'

'Summer.'

Cougar lowers herself onto the floor. 'You're going to regret doing this. You're out of your depth, Winter.'

'Summer.'

'It's going to end badly. For you.'

I'm waiting for her to add *Spring*, but she doesn't. I shrug. I don't want to go to Antarctica and I don't want to impersonate Cougar but I'm committed now. I stand back to let her through the door.

Cougar pauses at the doorway and sniffs the air. 'I don't mind a bit of Mister Sheen.'

I stare at her, unsure how to take this. She gives the impression she's waiting for a reply. As if *Mister Sheen* is a secret password. 'Me neither.'

She winks at me.

My eye twitches but I am *not* winking back.

Cougar swings down the corridor towards the lift like a woman on a mission. She turns as the lift doors shut and the last thing I see is a flash of teeth like the Cheshire Cat, then she is gone.

Shutting my door, I lean against it. *Antarctica. Damn.* How did that happen? If only the word *igloo* had never passed my lips.

I remember Mum's warning – *encased in snow*. I make a mental note to Google igloo-building. Structural integrity may be important if I don't want to end up buried in snow.

Chapter Nine

I encounter a hairy scientist

Project:	Thursday routine
Objectives:	Travel to Hobart
	Be Cougar Gale

'Glaciology is the study of ice,' I say to my reflection. 'I am a glacio-logist, which is to say I study ice.'

I am practising for Antarctic conversations. If I'm going to be Cougar Gale I have some work to do. I remember that episode of *Days of Our Lives* where a character had a chip inserted into her brain which made her become someone else. That would be good.

My phone dings and I check it. It's time for my scheduled call with Lucas Nilsson to finalise logistics. Even though I'm now Cougar, I'm also still the production assistant.

I dial his number and he picks up.

'Lucas Nilsson.'

He sounds distracted. I try to imagine what he looks like. He's a scientist so I expect he's old and hairy and perhaps wearing a moth-holed woollen sweater over shorts which expose his knobbly knees.

'It's Summer Wright. From Channel Five. I need to check through the spreadsheet with you.'

'Mm.' The phone bumps and there's the sound of rustling paper. 'Where is it? Oh here.' There's a bang. 'Damn.' There's more rustling and more banging. 'I spilt coffee on it.'

'You have the electronic version.'

'Yes.' There's the sound of keyboard tapping. 'Yes. Here it is. Five hundred and thirty-five actions.'

'And two thousand sub-actions. Have you familiarised yourself with it all?' I feel a knot in my chest. I'm going to Antarctica and my liaison officer is not on the ball. In fact, he seems downright non-chalant. I pick up a pen and gnaw it. 'It's very imp—'

'Mm. Just looking through it now. Oh dear, just deleted it. Never mind. I'm sure it will be fine.'

'No, that's not good enou—'

'Summer, I'm sorry, but the probability of us sticking to that schedule is very low. There are many factors to consider. Antarctica is not Sydney. I have to go now. I have a paper to write. Goodbye.' He hangs up.

I can't believe he hung up on me. I try dialling again, but he's switched his phone off. I gnaw at my fingernails then snatch up Adrian's book for some inspiration on how to deal with such situations.

Adrian's book tells me extreme project management requires improvisation, the ability to relax controls and keep the process loose. I must remember my life is no longer a waterfall, it is more like a scrum. I must stay on my toes – be prepared, but not over-prepared, alert but not alarmed. Okay. That is the way to tackle Lucas Nilsson. I breathe deeply. Alert, not alarmed.

The Extreme Project Manager doesn't get bogged down in extraneous facts. Okay. Don't worry about facts. I concentrate on breathing deeply.

There is no point in trying to remember details about boring ice holes, measuring ice flows and whatever else it is that glaciologists do. Not only are ice holes boring, they are tedious and dull. I can do this, I tell myself. I can.

I smile at my reflection and articulate clearly; 'Ice is of great interest to me. Do you like ice?' I sound like Eliza Doolittle: *the rain in Spain falls mainly on the plain.* I imagine there will be a lot of people in Antarctica who like ice. Why else would you go there?

Penguins, I suppose. 'I like penguins too,' I say to my reflection. 'Ice and penguins are two of my favourite things.' Now I sound like Maria from *The Sound of Music.* I shouldn't be channelling musical stars, I should be channelling Cougar. How do I do that? I narrow my eyes and purse my lips like a supermodel with indigestion. A bolt of inspiration strikes. I put one hand on my hip and raise an eyebrow. 'You can take your ice and your trampy penguin and get out of my igloo.' Yes, Alexis the bitch queen is a perfect match for Cougar.

I did attempt to study glaciology yesterday afternoon, but got bogged down in facts: reams of information about sea ice and sea level rise, ice shelves and icebergs. Who would have thought there was so much to learn about ice? I've decided it's best to keep it to two key messages – ice and penguins – for the time being. Later on, I can expand my repertoire to snow and seals.

I tilt my head to one side. I have the glaciology part of the equation mastered, but how about the appearance? After a visit to the chemist, my brown hair is now black and my pale skin brown. There is definitely a resemblance to Cougar Gale. It's like one of those separated at birth things. I'm the twin who was brought up in the trailer park and spent her leisure hours watching television, while Cougar went to a private school and had elite training in gymnastics from an early age. I'm glad Adrian can't see us side by side as I wouldn't come out of it well.

Clothing-wise, however, I'm right on top of it. I'm wearing stylish quick-dry shorts and a tank top. Underneath I have a quick-dry bra and knickers. I glance at my bed where a huge mound of clothing sits waiting to be packed. My visit to the outdoor shops yesterday afternoon was a revelation. I'll have to share it with Marley. I open my laptop and write:

To: Marley Lennon Wright
From: Summer Dawn Rain Wright
Subject: You should have told me this!

I had never ventured into an outdoor shop before. I'd imagined them as hard core affairs, frequented and staffed by earnest hairy types in Birkenstocks or walking boots. I expected they would not give the time of day to someone who'd never tramped through thigh-deep mud like the guy in the poster on the shop window.

So I pushed open the door to Outdoor World timidly, like a stranger entering a wild west saloon bar, half expecting the shop to fall silent as the hairy types eyed me with suspicion. Nothing was further from the truth. I wonder why I waited so long. Outdoor shops are an Aladdin's

Cave of goodies, staffed by sensitive, muscular, handsome, men who are also good at sales. Why did no-one ever tell me this?

I'm not sure what happened there in Outdoor World. My memory is hazy, as if I'd had a big night out. I've never had much interest in shopping – our hippie upbringing I suppose. That anti-consumer ethic is hard to overcome. But buying outdoor gear isn't the same – you can consume, while being anti-consumer. You're buying the simple life. It's a win–win situation. Wielding a Channel Five credit card also helped.

Not only did I leave the store with a down jacket, mittens, down booties, thermal underwear, quick-dry casual wear, a puffy sleeping bag, walking boots, sunglasses, a nifty outdoorsy toiletries bag, karabiners, crampons, a rope and much, much more, I also left with the phone number of my helpful sales assistant, Dave.

I'm not sure what I'm going to do with the karabiners, crampons and rope, but Dave seemed to think they were essential equipment for a glaciologist embarking on a journey to Antarctica.

'You'll be wanting to climb some glaciers, I imagine,' he said, fondling the rope in a suggestive manner with his manly, muscular hands.

I nodded decisively. 'Yes. Absolutely. The more the better.' I was pretty sure my relationship with Dave went beyond his desire to earn sales commission. There was a meaningful connection going on. Something about the way he held my feet when he fitted my crampons reminded me of Owl from Lukla. His broad shoulders stretched out his 'Save the Dugong' T-shirt. His hands knew exactly what they were doing.

Yes, I flirted. A little. It's been a long time since I've done that, Marley. I needed to restore my confidence. It was nice to feel acknowledged as a woman. Let's face it; Adrian wasn't exactly a powerhouse of lust. I never felt like he was overwhelmed by desire. *A conscientious performer* is what I would have written on his report card. But Adrian has other strengths that are much more important and I do miss him terribly.

After we'd concluded our business Dave handed me a card with his mobile phone number scribbled on it. 'In case you need any after sales service. I teach rock-climbing if you're interested. It's good to know how to tie knots.' I was definitely picking up on some double entendre. It seems like everyone's talking about bondage these days.

'You don't play guitar, do you, Dave?' I asked as I was about to go.

'Yes. How'd you guess?' he said.

'A woman's intuition.' I dropped his card in the bin down the road. As you know I have good reason to avoid guitar-playing men, Marley.

You are the exception to the rule.

My cameraman, Rory, knocks on my door at eleven am. He blinks when he sees me. 'Wow. You look different.' Rory is about six foot three with flaming red hair and chubby pink cheeks. I expect his ancestors excelled at caber tossing and bagpipes. Rory himself plays the drums in the Inner West Marching Band.

Rory and I don't know each other well, but we have a water-cooler relationship revolving around him showing me pictures of his cute two-year-old twins, Rory Junior and Beth. Like most cameramen, Rory affects an air of worldly cynicism, as if he has just emerged from the trenches of Afghanistan. His evenings are spent changing nappies and playing peek-a-boo though, not carousing in bars or dodging bullets. I suspect the thing he is most looking forward to on this expedition is a good night's sleep.

'So, Summer, I never knew you were an igloo-building expert,' says Rory. 'You've been hiding your light under a bushel.'

'Who told you that?'

'It's all around the station. Changed my whole impression of you.'

'Why, what sort of an impression did you have before you knew I could build igloos?'

'You just seemed normal. But now I know you build igloos, I realise you always did have this mystery woman air about you.'

'Yes, well ...' I spread my arms out. 'There you go, igloo-builder extraordinaire – that's me.' There is no accounting for the aura that comes from being an igloo-builder.

'That's a cool skill to have. I wish I could build igloos. Not that you get many opportunities, I suppose ...'

'No, I don't.'

'We're meeting Alicia and Mary at the airport, by the way.'

I grimace.

'I know,' says Rory.

Alicia and Mary, the stylist and producer, are Maxine's protégées. They will be reporting back on my every move.

'So, you're all ready?' Rory takes in my outfit. 'Been shopping?'

The karabiners on my backpack jingle as I twirl, displaying my outdoor regalia. 'Good, huh?'

'Well, you look the part. Think you can pull it off?'

I put a hand on my hip and channel Alexis. 'I can't wait for the day I see you walk out into the snow with those two trashy seals you came in with.'

'Pardon?'

I twirl my hand in a *get with it* gesture and repeat my line, but he still looks baffled. 'I'm Cougar. Get it? I'm like Alexis from *Dynasty*.'

'You watch that show? How come I've never discovered this about you before? I love *Dynasty*. Alexis, huh?' His brow furrows. 'Good call, but you don't sound bitchy enough. Try this.' Rory points his finger at my chest, narrows his eyes and puts on a female American accent. 'I want you. Your seal. And the other seal. Out. Now. I need to lie down before I'm on camera.' He puts the back of his hand to his forehead and sighs dramatically. 'Why do I have to work with such a bunch of incompetents?'

I laugh. He is as close to Alexis as a red-haired giant could be. 'Oh – you're amazing. I thought I was a major *Dynasty* fan, but you have way outperformed me. I can't believe it. You're going to have to help me with this.'

Rory raises one eyebrow. 'Try rephrasing that.'

'You' – I assume a commanding tone – 'You with the camera.' I click my fingers. 'Feed me my lines.'

'Right on.' Rory raises his fist in a power salute. 'You're going to be a natural at this, Summer. Ready to go, bitch queen?'

'Yep. I'll close up.' I go around the flat, closing the windows. I'm almost out the door when I see it – Marley's book. I touch the spine – there will never be a better time. I stuff *An Antarctic Mystery* in my backpack next to my new bible, *Extreme Project Management*. Slamming the door behind me, I follow Rory down the stairs.

Hobart is much cooler than Sydney. I pull on my polar fleece jacket as we step off the plane. We have the rest of the day to get organised. Our plane to Antarctica leaves tomorrow morning.

'Australian Antarctic Division,' Mary the producer tells the cab driver. 'We've got to get kitted out,' she says to the rest of us. 'Puffy jackets.' Her phone rings and she answers it. 'Chickens,' she says. 'Twelve.'

Alicia the stylist pulls out her notebook and shows me some sketches she's done of Cougar wearing a snowsuit. 'I did have in mind a few styling options for Cougar. Hood up, hood down, balaclava on or off, goggles on or off. But, considering ...' She flicks to the next illustration. 'It's best to stick with this look.' She holds up the notebook and shows me the sketch.

It looks like an old photograph of an Antarctic explorer weathering blizzard conditions. She or he – there's no way of knowing – is encased in down from head to toe. A balaclava and goggles cover every inch of face; only the tip of a nose is exposed. The Abominable Snowman could be hidden in there and you wouldn't know.

'That's my look?' I must admit, I was hoping to cut more of a dash on my television debut.

Alicia nods. 'We've got a few different balaclavas and goggles, so we can mix and match. The snowsuit only comes in red though, so that limits our options.' She unzips a small sports bag revealing a collection of woolly balaclavas. 'We'll stick with the primary colours. Black for serious stories, yellow for lighter ones.'

It seems this will be a fairly undemanding assignment for Alicia. 'Makeup shouldn't be too much of an issue,' I say.

'I don't know about that.' Alicia inspects my nose. 'I've got a few products to cut down on shine and redness, so don't worry about it too much.'

How did I get to the age of twenty-seven without realising I'm the human version of Rudolph the Red-nosed Reindeer? 'Thanks.'

Alicia pats my knee. 'I've dealt with worse.'

At the Antarctic Division storeroom we are given boots, balaclavas, mittens and a huge puffy red suit each. Mine seems excessively large, but I suppose they have to be roomy to go over the top of all the other warm clothes. This accomplished, we check into our hotel.

Alicia and Mary mutter something about a conference call with Maxine and disappear.

I decide this is a good opportunity to try out my new look away from their critical eyes. 'Give me ten minutes,' I say to Rory, 'then knock on the door. I'm going to get dressed in my snow gear. I want you to tell me if I look like Cougar. Bring your camera.'

It's cool in Hobart, but not that cool. By the time I don the puffy suit, balaclava, goggles and mittens I'm perspiring profusely. I hate to think what my nose is like. Luckily Rory knocks at the door before I keel over from heat exhaustion.

He wolf whistles when he sees me and comes in leaving the door ajar. A cooling breeze blows into the room so I don't shut it. 'Hot stuff.' Rory fans his face.

'Yeah, ha, ha. Okay, so do you think you could film me doing a piece to camera and we can see how I can improve?'

'No, no.' Rory puts up his hand. 'Way too polite. Cougar, remember?' He snarls and claws at the air. 'Ready when you are, ma'am.' He shoulders his camera.

'Right. Okay.' I breathe deeply trying to channel Cougar – *snarl*. My shoulders go back and I thrust out my breasts. I expect this is a wasted effort, encased as I am within about a metre of down. 'I need a close-up. Stand there. Get my best angle.' I look square at the camera and speak with Cougar's rounded vowels. 'Here we are in Hobart, the gateway to Antarctica. Already the temperature is well below zero, which is why I am wearing the special Antarctic clothing issued solely to Antarctic expeditioners by the Australian Antarctic Division. On my hands are special Antarctic mittens, designed for temperatures down to minus fifty degrees Celsius.' I hold up my hands. I'm ad-libbing, I have no idea what temperatures we're likely to get. 'On my feet—'

A cough interrupts us.

Rory and I turn towards the door.

A tall shape is silhouetted against the light. As I'm wearing my dark goggles I can't make out much else.

'Hello.' The voice is lightly accented. 'Are you Cougar Gale?'

I look towards Rory, trying to signal, *am I supposed to know him?* Rory stares at me blankly. Of course, my balaclava and goggles make non-verbal communication impossible. The man must be a fan. My inner Cougar takes over. 'Can't you see we're filming here? I can't sign autographs, you'll need to speak to my producer. Move out of the light.' I gesture with my mitten and the shape moves away. It's only then that it occurs to me that he sounded familiar. 'How was that?' I say to Rory.

Rory laughs and puts his camera on the bed. 'Perfect. I think that was Lucas Nilsson, our scientific liaison officer, so you're off to a great start.'

'Lucas Nilsson?' I rip off my hood, balaclava and goggles. 'You could have said something. Oh God.' I unzip my suit and pull it off. I'm drenched in sweat. 'I felt like I was about to die in there. It was almost as bad as Bikram yoga.'

Rory shakes his head. 'That is exactly what Cougar would have said: no autographs.' He guffaws. 'That's priceless.' He looks at me with new respect. 'I had no idea you were such a bitch.'

'I do my best.'

I hear raised voices outside – Alicia and Mary. They don't sound happy. Mary bursts into my room without knocking. Alicia's not far behind.

'Un-fucking-believable.' Mary's phone rings and she puts it to her ear. 'No, dolphins. I told him dolphins three times; I don't know why he keeps going on about porpoises. You're not going to believe this, Maxine. They've bumped two places off the flight.' She pauses. 'No, just for one day. They're flying again the day after. This guy called Lucas Nilsson. Antarctic liaison? Said there was an urgent demand for seats. Some VIP. Aren't we VIPs?' She listens again. 'Yes. Summer and Rory. Will do.' She pauses. 'Cows would be okay.' Ending the call, she turns to us. 'I'm afraid you're not going to like this, Summer.'

I think I already have the gist of the situation, but Mary confirms my reading. Rory and I will be travelling to Antarctica without our entourage. 'It's just for one day,' Mary says. 'The plane's making a special trip back the next day to pick up this VIP from Antarctica and they'll take Alicia and me down then.'

I let my mouth droop as if I'm devastated. 'Rory and I will do our best.'

As soon as Alicia and Mary are out of the room, Rory and I exchange a high five. 'Yes!' I say. 'It's you and me Roars.'

'Roars?'

'I think it's time for nicknames, don't you?'

'Rightio, Lexie.'

'Lexie?' Of course – Alexis. 'Don't worry, I've got it. Let's take a look at the footage.'

Rory plugs the camera into the television and we sit on the bed. I cringe as I see myself. The puffy red suit encases an equally red nose. Alicia is right, some serious touching up is needed – it's like a cherry tomato. The camera pans to the shape at the door. As the light adjusts I can see him. I remember my image of him as hairy, knobble-kneed and old. The only part of my description that fits is 'hairy'.

Lucas Nilsson is tall with thick sandy hair that sticks up from his head as if he's just come out of a wind tunnel and a matching sandy-coloured beard. He's wearing faded blue jeans and a threadbare T-shirt. He is maybe thirty-ish. It's hard to tell with that beard. It covers most of his face.

'Speak to my producer,' I hear myself say.

His face tightens before he walks away dangling a bicycle helmet in his hand. That might explain the wind tunnel effect.

Looks like I've made myself an enemy already, but that's the price one pays for being Cougar.

That night in my hotel room, as I delve around in my backpack trying to find my toothbrush, I feel the edge of Marley's book and pull it out. *An Antarctic Mystery* – it seems appropriate. Sitting on the bed, I thumb through it, seeing the familiar pen and ink illustrations scattered through the text. Men clinging to a boat in high seas with icebergs all around, men peering at icebergs through a telescope, a boat perched on the side of an enormous iceberg, a man running away from another man on an iceberg …

I read the first paragraph:

> No doubt the following narrative will be received with entire incredulity, but I think it well that the public should be put in possession of the facts narrated in 'An Antarctic Mystery'. The public is free to believe them or not, at its good pleasure ...

I climb into bed with the book and by the time I put it down one hour later my head is full of creaking ice, barking seals and the prospect of adventure.

Chapter Ten

I learn to behave badly

Project:	Friday routine
Objective:	Travel to Antarctica
7.40:	Leave hotel
8:00:	Arrive airport
8.30:	Plane to Antarctica departs
8.30–13.00:	Study glaciology and discuss filming arrangements with Rory
13.00:	Arrive Antarctica
15.00–22.00:	Filming, discussions about ice, dinner etc

'Come along, Rory.' I stride across the crossing into Hobart International Airport, carrying a daypack. Behind me Rory struggles with his camera gear and several bags. Being Cougar has its advantages – I doubt she carries her own luggage. The sun is out and I've reluctantly abandoned the puffy red suit, balaclava and goggles. In their place I'm wearing large sunglasses, a nifty quick-dry sunhat, quick-dry shorts and a polar fleece jacket. It's still cool here in Hobart compared to Sydney. At some stage before we land I'll don the appropriate clothing, ready to hit the ice.

Mary and Alicia have not accompanied us to the airport. They've taken the opportunity to sleep in after a late night fielding last minute dramas about *Wildlife Wonder* – Channel Five's funky new kids' show.

Alicia's stand-in stylist was apparently not up to the mark. 'She has no idea,' Alicia said over pre-dinner drinks in the bar. 'Obviously donkeys wear hats with flowers. I shouldn't have to tell her that.' She took a long swig of her G and T. 'Unbelievable.'

Mary did brief us thoroughly on the need to stay on script. 'The most important thing is to keep the advertisers happy,' she said. 'So whatever you do, don't forget the product placement. It's essential. If you have to choose between story and product placement, you choose product placement. Got it?'

'Product placement. Essential. Got it,' I replied.

Lucas Nilsson is standing outside the airport. His hair still looks like it's been dried in a wind tunnel and he's dressed in the same style as yesterday.

I peer at him over the top of my sunglasses. Closer inspection reveals he's wearing exactly the same clothes as yesterday. It must be his favourite outfit. 'So sorry about yesterday.' My tone implies I'm not sorry at all. 'Thought you were one of my fans. I'm sure you know how it is. They follow me everywhere.'

'No.'

It takes me a moment to work out which part of my speech he's responding to. 'Oh yes. Everywhere.' I turn and wave gaily at a woman on the other side of the road. 'My stalker,' I murmur. 'Thank goodness she won't be able to follow me to Antarctica.'

Lucas lifts a hand to the woman. 'That is Cherie, our cook. She will be on the flight with us.'

The woman walks across the pedestrian crossing towards the airport.

'Ha ha,' I say. 'Looks a lot like my stalker.'

'You will get to know each other well,' says Lucas. 'You're sharing a room at Casey Station.'

I notice his accent again – Scandinavian? 'Oh.' I eye the woman. She is muscular, with a round suntanned face and short blonde hair. I like the look of her.

But behind Lucas's back Rory shakes his head.

Of course – Cougar would never share a room. 'Oh no, no, no. I must have a private room. I never share. I'm sure my producer would have told you that. It was on the spreadsheet.' It hadn't been, but I'm pretty sure he never looked at the spreadsheet.

'Everyone shares. It's not a resort,' says Lucas.

I shake my head and steel myself for some prima donna action. 'Absolutely not. Just because you've got my producer bumped off the flight, doesn't mean it's open slather.' There's a perverse pleasure in behaving badly. That must be why people do it. What did Krystle say about Alexis, the bitch queen from *Dynasty*? You love her or you hate her and she's equally satisfied either way? 'Rory.' I point at him. 'Call Mary and get this sorted out.'

Rory winks at me behind Lucas's back. He pulls out his phone.

Cherie, the cook, is beside us now.

'Cherie, this is Cougar Gale,' says Lucas.

She puts out her hand. 'Hi, Cougar. It's so great to meet you. I love your show, you're the best thing on television.' She sounds a little overwhelmed.

I shake hands. Cougar is sometimes gracious to her fans.

Cherie studies me. 'You look different on TV.'

'Everyone looks thinner on TV.'

'Oh. I always thought it was the other way around – fatter, I mean.'

'No. Thinner. Television is slimming.' The trick of being convincing is to not hesitate.

'That's interesting.' She puts her head on one side. 'I suppose they make you up, when you go on.'

'Yes, of course. She, I mean *I*, am not really anything like that. As you can see.' I stretch my arms out. 'This is the real Cougar. Usually I travel with a makeup artist, but she got bumped off the flight. When she comes over tomorrow I'll be more like the Cougar you know.'

Her brow crinkles. 'I hope you don't think … I didn't mean to be offensive. You look different, that's all.'

'No, no.' I laugh. 'I'm used to it. No-one looks like they do on TV or in magazines. Have you ever seen Elle McPherson in the flesh?'

She shakes her head.

'You'd walk straight past her. She's actually short and plump.' I'm tempted to add she has freckles and buck teeth, but that might be stretching things too far. 'They do so much with airbrushing these days,' I murmur.

'Fascinating,' says Cherie. 'I mean, it's obvious it's you now I know. You have such a distinctive nose.' She touches her own.

I'd never realised my nose was so unique before. Unique to me and Cougar, that is.

'We might be able to do some ice-climbing together? When we get to Antarctica. You're into that, aren't you?' she says.

Am I? She seems to think so, and she knows more about Cougar than I do. I take in Cherie's muscular body. 'I go hard. Are you up for that?'

She beams. 'Yeah. I'll be training on the rock-climbing wall at the station if you want to join me. You get soft pretty quickly in Antarctica if you don't make an effort – all that time indoors. And the food's good, if I say so myself. A lot of people come back a couple of sizes bigger than they go down.'

And here I was thinking we'd be fighting each other for the last morsel of pemmican – whatever that is. I'd never imagined avoiding weight gain would be a problem in Antarctica. 'Sure. I train every day. Rock-climbing, weights …' – I rack my brain – 'that sort of thing.'

'So, we're sharing a room?' says Cherie.

A phone rings at that moment. Lucas extracts it from the pocket of his faded jeans. 'Lucas Nilsson.' He listens, expelling a sharp breath of air from his nostrils. 'Okay. Fine.' He slides the phone back into his pocket. He runs his hands through his hair and it takes a moment for him to speak. 'You have a room to yourself.'

I nod, as if it is no less than I expected.

Cherie looks at him questioningly.

His mouth twitches. 'You will be with Maria, the krill woman, Cherie.'

I almost laugh – not Catwoman, not Superwoman, but … *Krill Woman!* I've heard of krill, but I don't have a clear picture of what they are – some kind of small sea creature. I had Sea Monkeys when I was a child. They were disappointing – not monkey-like at all and I imagine krill to be like that – tiny with lots of incessantly waving legs. I can't wait to meet Maria the Krill Woman. Perhaps she is small with restless legs.

A police car cruises past the airport entrance. A glance passes between the cop and Lucas. Lucas raises his hand. Hobart's a small town – they probably know each other from cricket or badminton.

Rory and I head into the airport. Before the glass door slides shut behind us I hear Lucas mutter to Cherie, 'Prima donna'. I wince internally, but straighten my shoulders. I'm not here to make friends with tall, hairy Scandinavian scientists; I am Cougar Gale.

'Going well, Cougar.' Rory touches my shoulder and winks. 'Growl,' he snarls.

Rory's a good mate. He knows I'm doing my best. Outside the glass windows I can see what must be our plane. It's average-sized and shiny silver with no logos.

'The Airbus A319.' Rory has the world-weary manner of one who's been extracted from multiple war zones by a variety of aircraft. 'Slightly smaller than the 320, but still with long-range flexibility.'

Aircraft fetishes are a boy thing. All planes are alike to me, unless they do something special with the paint job. 'I loved the way they painted those Air New Zealand planes with Lord of the Rings scenes a while back.'

Rory seems unsure how to respond. 'Should do a piece to camera.' He unzips his camera bag. 'Before we take off.'

I sigh. 'Better get my gear on.' Alicia has given me strict dress code instructions. I'm to be wearing the suit with the hood up, balaclava and goggles for all close-ups. She's also supplied me with some greenish cream to put on the end of my nose – to neutralise the glow, she said. As if I were a glow-worm.

Five minutes later, I'm sweating it out in front of the window in my puffy red suit. 'Is my nose red?' I say to Rory.

'No redder than your suit.'

'Thanks a lot.' I rummage around in my bag and extract the green cream. 'Dab this on it for me, will you?'

Rory is horrified. 'I don't do makeup. I'm a cameraman. Union rules.'

'Oh come on, pretend it's camo paint and it's vital to ensure we don't get spotted by enemy bombers.'

'I suppose if you put it like that.' Rory takes the tube from me and squeezes a little of the green cream onto his finger. 'Hey, it really is camo paint. Why do you want a green nose?'

'To stop me glowing. The ways of the makeup artist are mysterious. Put it on and see what happens.'

Rory rubs his finger around on the end of my nose.

'Have I stopped glowing?'

'Hm.' He stands back. 'I suppose you are less red. And if I cross my eyes …' He assumes a cock-eyed look. 'It's kind of impressionistic.'

'Like Picasso, you mean?'

Rory nods. 'Is that what you're after?'

A trickle of sweat makes its way from my armpits down my sides and into the top of my pants. 'God, I don't know. Maybe everyone wears green makeup on TV. Let's get it over with so I can take this suit off. Where's the script?'

'Oh yeah, I've got it in here.' Rory riffles around in his backpack and pulls out a folded wad of paper. He hands it to me. 'Practise a couple of lines, then I'll shoot.'

I clear my throat. 'Not many people know llamas and alpacas are different species.' I'm trying so hard to sound like a presenter, I don't notice what I've said until I see Rory's face.

'Not sure of the relevance,' he says.

'You're right.' I flip to the next page. 'Donkeys are widely used in many countries ...' I feel queasy. 'Rory, did Mary give you this script?'

He nods. 'She pointed at the table and told me to take it.'

'Rory, this is the script to *Wildlife Wonder*. You picked up the wrong script.' I can hear the shrillness in my voice.

'I'm a cameraman. I shouldn't be asked to pick up scripts.'

A small river of sweat makes its way down my neck and across my chest. I have no script. I am doomed.

Chapter Eleven

I express an interest in Inuits

Sweat is streaming down my face as Rory and I stare at each other. *No script.* My first test and I've failed it. What would the extreme project manager do? What would Cougar do?

I rack my brain and summon thoughts of Antarctica – barking seals, icebergs. *An Antarctic Mystery* comes to mind. I imagine I'm on board a sailing boat, warmly dressed in my wool suit and upholding my Victorian manners, despite the extreme situation in which I find myself. Yes, that's it … I lick a trickle of sweat from my lip.

'Oh for Christ's sake, let's do it,' I say. 'I'll make it up as I go along. How hard can it be?'

Looking miffed, Rory raises his camera to his shoulder. 'Okay, rolling.'

I take a deep breath. 'Needless to say, we are bound for the desolation of Antarctica. Notwithstanding the potential for peril, we are launching into an adventure that seems likely to surpass all my former experiences. Soon, our plane will set forth. I desire to lay stress on the fact that once, this voyage would have taken … a long, long time, but now, it will only take … a few hours.' I haven't got my head around the finer points of my itinerary.

Rory frowns. He presses the 'stop' button.

'What?' I say.

'Mm, it's just, you sound … weird.'

'Weird?'

'Notwithstanding the potential for peril?'

'Oh.' I replay what I've said. Have I ever used 'notwithstanding' in a sentence before in my life?

'Sorry, I've got Jules Verne on the brain. I'll stop now.'

Rory presses 'go' and gives me a thumbs up.

'As we bid farewell to Australia, I'm sure all of us here are wondering what the future will hold in the icy southern continent. So many have come to grief in its frozen wasteland – Scott of the Antarctic' – I try to remember the names of his team but fail – 'many huskies, ponies and several other brave souls. Let's hope we make this perilous voyage successfully.' I remember Mary's directive – product placement is essential. 'Luckily, I have packed Tim Tams – a chocolate treat is what you need when you're stuck in a blizzard.' I pull a packet out of my snowsuit and open it. 'Goodbye, Australia.' Tim Tam in hand, I wave at the camera. 'I'll be with you every day for this special feature of *Cougar on Ice*.' I bite into the Tim Tam and chew with wild abandon. 'Mm, delicious.'

Rory gives me another thumbs up and, stuffing the last of the biscuit in my mouth, I rip off my hood and balaclava. 'God, I hope it's going to get colder than this.' Crumbs spray out of my mouth as I talk.

'I'd say that's guaranteed.' Lucas is leaning against the window nearby. He looks pleasantly cool in his jeans and T-shirt. 'I think Oates was the name you were after?'

'Oats?' Chewing, I turn to him. He's so tall, I have to bend my neck. '"I may be gone some time"?'

It comes back to me. Oates is the one who was injured and wandered off into the snow to die so the others might have a chance to live. Tragic. Especially since they all died anyway. 'Yes. Of course. I know who Oates was.'

Lucas's eyes seem to be focused on the tip of my nose.

I notice a spray of Tim Tam crumbs on his cheek, above the beard. 'Sorry.' I point to the crumbs and he wipes them off leaving a smear of chocolate behind. I decide not to tell him. 'I don't even like Tim Tams all that much, but I have to eat them for the show.' I offer him one.

He takes it. 'I suppose someone has to.' He bites into the Tim Tam.

'Going to make a call' – Rory pulls out his phone – 'before we're out of range.' He wanders a short distance away.

Should I be ringing someone? Mum? But I'm sworn to secrecy. No-one must know I'm here.

'You spent a year living with the Inuits, didn't you?' says Lucas. 'I saw that show you did. That must have been interesting living in the Canadian Arctic.'

Don't tell me he's a Cougar fan too. 'Oh, yes, Inuits.' It was the first I'd heard of it, but it wouldn't surprise me. Seems like everyone around here knows more about Cougar than I do. I unzip the front of my snowsuit to let in some air and buy time. 'Mm, it was fascinating. Built a lot of igloos. You know how it is. They're always at it. Igloos, igloos, igloos.' I wave my hand around.

'Oh. I thought they lived mainly in houses these days.'

Damn. Things must have changed since I last took an interest in Inuits. I suppose it's been a few years. What was that film we watched in primary school – *Nanook of the North*? 'Not the Inuits I lived with. They were back to nature types. Traditional,' I say.

'How intriguing. Did they go hunting?' There's something strange about his vision – his eyes are still focused on the tip of my nose.

'Oh yes. They loved hunting.' I wish Rory would come back and rescue me, but he's having a long phone conversation with either Rory Junior or Beth. 'Daddy is going somewhere cold,' I hear him say.

'What sort of food did they hunt mainly?' Lucas gazes at me intently.

Why is this guy so interested in Inuits? Can't we talk about something else? All I know about Inuits is that they live in the snow. Perhaps they hunt seals. Do they have seals in the Arctic? Probably, but I can't be sure. 'Polar bears.'

'Mm. That must have been interesting.'

I'm relieved he's buying it, but alarmed that he now seems even more interested. 'Yes, it was. Very … dramatic. Yes.'

'Did they use dog sleds?'

I hesitate. Is this a trick question? I nod. I have a fifty per cent chance of being right. It's time for me to ditch him before I get myself further into hot water. I've already overstepped the limits of my Inuit knowledge.

'How did you feel about that?' He sounds like he's interviewing me for a current affairs show.

I blink. There's something about him that prevents me from pulling a Cougar Gale and flouncing off. For a hairy and poorly dressed scientist, he seems used to having his questions answered. 'How do I feel about polar bears being hunted?' This is a technique Adrian taught me prior to my interview for the job at Channel Five. When in doubt, repeat the question.

'Yes. Considering they are at risk from climate change.'

This question isn't getting any easier. Now I feel like I'm on a TV quiz show with a million dollars and a fast car at stake. My heart beats faster and sweat trickles down from my armpits. Climate change? I could do with some of that myself. Peeling off the top of my suit, I expose my sweat-soaked quick-dry singlet. 'Hot, isn't it?' I flap my hand around my face. I have nothing to say on the topic of polar bears and climate change. Polar bears, yes. Climate change, maybe; at a pinch. But polar bears and climate change together? There must be a connection or he wouldn't have mentioned it. 'That's a good question.' Another Adrian technique.

'It's tough, isn't it?' Lucas gazes off towards the plane, apparently contemplating polar bears and climate change.

A surge of confidence runs through me. I might be able to bluff my way through this. I nod sagely, to suggest my complete mastery of the topic. 'It's like, polar bears … climate change … hunting. What can you say, right?'

Lucas's brow wrinkles. 'It's a dilemma.'

I have no idea what we're talking about. I shrug in what I hope is a *je ne sais quoi* kind of way.

'I don't know either,' he says.

I smile as if we're in agreement.

'People get emotional about polar bears,' he says. 'I get emotional about polar bears myself. I am sure you do too.' He runs a hand along the rim of the window and taps out a little drum beat with his fingers.

I nod. 'Yes. I mean, I think about them a lot. They're so …'

'Iconic.'

'Exactly.' It's time to extricate myself from this conversation.

'I wonder though, whether they are over-emphasised in the debate.'

'I couldn't agree more.'

There's a hubbub behind us. Hooray – a distraction. Three news crews scurry into the building.

I straighten my shoulders. Has someone leaked my – that is, Cougar's – departure to the media? But no, they turn and focus their lenses on a black car that's pulling up outside. The car stops and a long pair of legs encased in puffy red material emerge followed by the rest of the body, also encased in a puffy red snowsuit. The man stands and I recognise him.

I turn to Lucas. 'Isn't that …?'

He nods.

It's the Federal Minister for Science, Nathan Hornby. He is known for his brash, populist style and his changeable policy decisions. But I suppose that's what you get when you're part of a government that's ruling by a hair's breadth.

Another pair of legs emerges from the car. They're encased in moleskin pants that seem familiar. The man stands and his thick, brown hair ruffles in the breeze. *Oh my God, it's Adrian.* My stomach flips. He did tell me he was working for a federal politician now. Why didn't he tell me he was coming to Hobart? I suppose we haven't been talking.

Hornby comes through the glass doors and turns to face the media pack. Three microphones are pushed towards him.

Holding up my snowsuit I shuffle closer, to listen in. Adrian catches sight of me. He doesn't look surprised. Cougar has clearly filled him in on the situation.

He might have warned me our paths were going to cross. My angry lionesses feel like three dejected sloths called Disappointment, Rejection and Longing. I've missed Adrian.

Adrian doesn't acknowledge me – he is wearing his alert professional expression.

'What is the purpose of your trip to Antarctica, Mr Hornby?' says a blonde girl who doesn't look old enough to be driving a car, let alone interviewing politicians.

Hornby must be the VIP who bumped Mary and Alicia off the flight. But they took two seats, which means Adrian …

'I'm on a fact-finding mission. As you know, the government is currently debating a number of measures connected with climate change. The polar regions are said to be the canary in the bird cage.'

Bungled metaphors are part of Hornby's signature style.

'Australia is a significant partner to the Antarctic treaty which aims to protect the continent. I thought I should see for myself what is happening there.'

'Is this part of the lead-up to the international climate change conference in Sydney next week?' says the blonde.

'Yes. I am reluctant to commit the Australian people to an environmental policy which will be a burden on the economy without being fully across the facts.'

'What is your opinion on global warming? Should we be worried?' This was from a young man with his curly hair tied back in a ponytail.

'Personally, I think the climate-change science is far from settled. Why, if carbon dioxide is such a villain, hasn't there been a steady increase in temperature since the eighteenth century? And of course, as we all know, ninety-seven per cent of all carbon dioxide occurs naturally.'

'But don't all the climate scientists agree carbon dioxide emissions are leading to global warming?' This is the blonde again. She's nowhere near as silly as she looks.

'I am hugely unconvinced. It is contentious to say the least. In my humble opinion, climate science is crap.'

The reporters murmur in an appreciative way. They've got their sound bite. This is exactly the type of statement for which Hornby is famous.

'How long will you be in Antarctica for, Mr Hornby?'

'I'll be back tomorrow, unfortunately. I'd love to stay longer, but we have this new carbon policy to resolve and time is of the essence. That's all thanks, I've got a plane to catch.' Hornby raises his hand and turns away, heading in our direction. Seeing us, he smiles in the hail-fellow-well-met manner of politicians everywhere. His eyes skim over me and he must have been briefed because he sticks out his hand. 'Cougar Gale?'

My eyes dart to Adrian. 'Yes.'

'It's a pleasure to meet you.' Hornby squeezes my hand in a firm grip. There's chocolate on his palm as he takes it away. Hopefully the Tim Tams will be less messy once we're in Antarctica.

I don't think the media pack have caught our exchange, which is lucky. Cougar Gale and Nathan Hornby together would be quite a story and I have no standing orders on what to do in the event of a media scrum in Hobart Airport. Maxine would be most unhappy to have my cover blown before I leave the country. It might be best to take evasive action. 'Bit cold in here,' I murmur and pull up my hood. I'm not sure where I put my balaclava, but pulling it on would make me look deranged anyway.

The reporters wander away.

Hornby's gaze turns to Lucas and he puts his hand out. 'How do you do?'

Lucas hesitates for a fraction of a second before extending his hand. 'Lucas Nilsson.'

'And what do you do, Lucas?' Nathan sounds politely interested.

'I am a climate scientist.'

The politician barely flinches.

'Time to catch the plane, Minister.' With a quick glance my way, Adrian ushers his boss away.

The young blonde reporter turns back, steps toward Lucas and holds out her microphone. 'What do you think of the Minister's comment that climate science is crap, Doctor Nilsson?'

Lucas opens his mouth and shuts it again. He pulls at his beard. 'I'm afraid I am unable to comment.'

Chapter Twelve

I am honoured to receive a Channel Five pen

Following my Inuit discussion with Lucas, I update my project schedule.

8.30:	Plane to Antarctica departs
8.30–15.00	Study glaciology and Inuit hunting methods and discuss filming arrangements with Rory

There are only twenty passengers on our flight to Antarctica. The other passengers have a serious air about them and most have beards. In fact, if you discount the five women, they all have beards. Both men and women are dressed in unisex-type clothing – a mixture of quick-dry pants and T-shirts or button-up shirts. I decide they must be scientists.

I buckle my seatbelt and wait for the safety briefing. Although I've flown a lot, I've never got over the feeling that strapping yourself into a metal compartment and blasting into the air is a most unnatural thing to do. I once read that people who listen to safety briefings have a higher chance of survival in aircraft crashes. I don't know if that's true, but I figure it's worth a shot so I always listen carefully.

The captain – close-cropped grey hair, military bearing – strides down the aisle. He stops and surveys us with a practised eye, as if separating the sheep from the goats in readiness for a dangerous mission.

I sit up straighter and assume a vigilant air. If there is separating to be done, I want to be a goat.

'There are no passengers, only crew on this flight', the captain tells us.

I nod.

'You should all have your survival gear close at hand. Survival suits will be donned before arrival at Wilkins Runway.'

I almost salute at this point. Already I feel like an intrepid adventurer. This is no cushy commercial flight, this is the real deal.

'You may have noticed you have all been seated down the back of the plane. This is to allow the nose of the plane to get up, which it might have trouble doing otherwise due to the weight of fuel,' says the captain. 'For safety reasons we carry enough fuel to do a turnaround without landing should the weather deteriorate rapidly in Antarctica. I don't expect that to happen today. The runway is currently being prepared and I'm not anticipating any problems,' he adds.

The way he says this makes me anxious. Why do we need to know about the runway? Isn't that a given? I clear my throat and raise my hand, remember I am Cougar, drop it again and pretend I was stretching. 'What's involved in the runway preparation?' I hope this sounds like a journalistic inquiry, rather than a plea for reassurance.

'The runway is on an ice shelf,' says the captain. 'Prior to landing, the ground crew scour the surface to provide increased friction. They test it by driving vehicles on the ice and braking sharply to ensure there is sufficient traction.'

An ice shelf? We're going to land on an ice shelf? And right now some lunatics are doing burnouts on it to see if we can stop? I survey the cabin. No-one else looks perturbed.

The captain, apparently deciding I share his interest in runways, regales me with further details. I stare at him, catching only the odd phrase here and there – *the runway moves a few centimetres every day …* – the runway moves! – *check the runway for crevasses …* – the runway has crevasses! 'So it's all quite safe,' he concludes.

In my experience, the more someone feels the need to reassure me, the less safe it actually is. Like that speedboat trip on the Mekong that ended in a nearly fatal encounter with a Chinese tanker and a small waterfall … *Very safe, Miss*, I'd been assured. I close my eyes and say a silent Om to calm myself as the captain retreats to the front.

'All right, Cougar?' murmurs Rory.

I nod.

'The Airbus 319 is one of the safest planes in the world,' says Rory. 'It's the Airbus 330 you need to worry about.'

Until then, it hadn't occurred to me to worry about the mechanics of the plane.

Hornby and Adrian are seated opposite Rory and me. The Minister leafs through official-looking documents with an urgent air. Is he uncomfortable being on board with a planeload of scientists, having said that climate science is crap? Apparently not. He projects the confidence of one who is sure he's the most important person in the vicinity.

Adrian meets my eyes. He shakes his head slightly and pulls some documents out of his briefcase.

I don't know what that's supposed to mean. *Lie low*, I assume. My dejected sloths sigh and curl up for a sleep.

Lucas comes down the aisle as the plane doors shut and slides into the seat in front of me. Clearly he's not concerned about missing the safety briefing. Through the gap in the seats I see him open a book. *The Worst Journey in the World*. He must sense my eyes on him as he glances back. I turn away in case he feels inclined to continue our polar bear discussion.

He rustles a plastic bag and pops something into his mouth. It looks like dried pineapple or pawpaw. I have quite a weakness for dried fruit but restrain myself from asking for some.

We taxi down the runway, accelerate and for a moment it seems the nose of the plane is not going to rise, but soon it lifts and we are airborne. Tasmania disappears, then we are over the sea and in the clouds. That's it – I'm on my way to Antarctica.

Antarctica – the frozen continent … If this was a movie they would play sinister music to provide a sense of foreboding. Fifteen scientists, a minister, his minder, a cameraman, my liaison officer and me. Twenty set out, but how many will make it back alive?

My reflection in the window gives me a strange sense of dislocation. I'm not the Summer I know. I flick back my newly dark hair in a Cougarish manner. But what's that on my nose? I touch it and my fingers come back stained with a smudge of green. 'Rory.'

He turns.

'I can't believe you didn't tell me I had a big, fat green nose. Why'd you put so much of that stuff on?'

'I told you I wasn't a makeup girl. You said to put it on until your nose wasn't red. It took a lot—'

'Great. I'm going to be on television looking like a freak.'

'Not my fault,' Rory mutters. 'I'm a cameraman. I was bending union rules as it was.'

'Alicia's going to flip out.'

'Well maybe *Alicia*' – Rory accentuates every syllable – 'should have made it to the airport instead of wearing herself out styling llamas. Not my job description.'

My first ever television appearance and I've got a green nose. *Terrific.* Using the window as a mirror, I wipe off the makeup.

Rory plugs in his iPod in a sulky way and stakes his claim on our shared armrest in the manner of one severely wronged.

I lean against the headrest. It's been such a whirl of activity over the last two days, I haven't had time to think about anything except getting ready. I haven't had time to be nervous.

Now it hits me – for the next week, I am Cougar Gale. Nathan Hornby and Adrian will be going back to Hobart tomorrow, but I'll be at Casey Station until the plane returns on Boxing Day. Can I pull it off? Here I am impersonating a TV star with amazing outdoor skills and a PhD in glaciology. I know nothing about either of those things. How did I let Maxine press-gang me into this?

On Wednesday afternoon I had my first ever private meeting with Maxine … She'd pulled up her scarlet lips in a facsimile of a smile and gestured at the chair on the other side of her vast shiny desk as I came in.

I sank into the chair, ending up about a foot lower than her. No doubt she planned it that way. A faint aroma of terror clung to my chair. How many people had been eviscerated by Maxine in this very spot? I wiped my sweaty palms on my skirt.

'There's a lot riding on this, Summer.' Maxine focused her eyes on me.

I felt like a mouse gazing into a snake's eyes. I nodded to convey my complete understanding of the situation.

'It's the ratings period and Channel Four are pushing us every inch of the way. We need this to work. Do a good job and you have a rosy future ahead of you at Channel Five.' It was clear the reverse also applied – if I failed, I had no future at all. Maxine opened her desk drawer and pulled out a box. 'A little gift for you. For being a team player.'

It was a Parker pen embossed with the Channel Five logo – the traditional Christmas gift for the executive team. I'd never been given one before. 'Thank you, Maxine,' I said. 'I feel honoured.' The sad part was, I did. The future of Channel Five was in my hands. I felt like an undercover spy being equipped before a crucial mission.

'No-one must find out you are not Cougar.' Maxine's eye twitched. 'I've gone out on a limb here for you. Even the directors don't know what you're doing.'

For me? I blinked. She hadn't told the directors? What was she going to say if they found out? Would I be cut adrift? I felt like I was in a Wilbur Smith novel.

Maxine smiled as I stood up to leave. 'Good luck, Summer. We're counting on you.'

'I won't let you down, Maxine,' I said but she'd already picked up her phone.

Now, as I click the end of my pen in and out, I feel weird and scared – like a Cold War double agent about to cross over into East Germany. I'm leaving Summer behind and becoming Cougar. *I am a glaciologist. I am a TV science superstar.* I wonder what the real Cougar Gale is doing. The broken ankle will restrict her rock-climbing. And at least Adrian is here, where I can keep an eye on him.

I glance across the aisle, but he is immersed in his documents as if I'm not here. As if we'd never talked about the house on the North Shore, the two kids … As if he'd never introduced me to the Point of Complete Certainty. And I'd thought I was so close to the Point, but I've slid right to the bottom again.

I sigh. We'd felt so right – so stable, so solid. I didn't tremble when I thought of him or grow sick with longing, but that was good – you can't live like that, it wears you out. Being with Adrian made me feel like an adult.

I'd spent my teens and most of my twenties falling in and out of love countless times and become way too familiar with both euphoria and despair. Finding Adrian was like getting off a rollercoaster and onto a steady train. Or so I'd thought. We had shared goals, we were a team. And the sex was fine. There's more to a relationship than uncontrollable lust. He was a damn fine project manager and you can't have everything.

I feel like that girl on the plane from Kathmandu again – the one I'd left behind. *Impersonating a TV star in Antarctica.* It's hard to imagine I could get any further from the Point of Complete Certainty.

But I must stay positive. Adrian and Cougar won't last. And, it now occurs to me, what luck he is here in Antarctica. What better way to show him I'm the woman for him? I'll be more Cougar than Cougar ever was. I will be erudite, beautiful, talented … My pulse beats an anxious tattoo at the thought. My three sloths whimper. I ignore them. Yes, once Adrian sees what I can do he'll come running back.

Adrian rustles his papers and makes a note with his pen. I subdue an urge to snatch the ballpoint off him and stab him in the thigh. Instead, I breathe deeply. *I am Cougar Gale.*

First things first – I'll start on the tasks I have allocated for this plane trip. I check my list. *Study glaciology and Inuit hunting methods and discuss filming arrangements* … That sounds strenuous. Maybe I'll have a little look at *An Antarctic Mystery* to get in the mood first. The adventurers are setting off for Antarctica. *The Halbrane was a schooner of three hundred tons, and a fast sailer*, I read.

I yawn. It's been a tiring couple of days …

Chapter Thirteen

The lone wildebeest

'Cougar, we're descending.' Rory wakes me.

I open my eyes, blink, and look out the window. I can't believe what I'm seeing. Below me, the sea is dotted with white lumps which can only be icebergs. But ahead, as far as I can see, there is nothing but whiteness. Is it glare on the ocean? It goes on and on. Slowly, I pick out some relief. It isn't glare, it's snow – *Antarctica*. I hadn't expected it to be like this. What I'd expected, I couldn't say, but not this vastness, this unending snow …

Rory's face is near mine at the window.

'I had no idea it was so big,' I say.

'Twice as big as Australia.'

'I had no idea,' I repeat. 'No idea.'

Rory gives me a quizzical look. 'Are you okay, Cougar?'

I'm not sure if I am. My heart thuds in my chest. It's so bright out there, so white and so immense it makes me feel small and a bit frightened. It's like looking into the night sky and realising your utter insignificance. I imagine a space explorer might feel like this. It doesn't seem like a place meant for humans.

'Puts things in perspective, doesn't it?' Lucas peers through the gap in the seats. 'I've been here three times, but it still takes me unawares.'

My mouth is hanging open, so I shut it.

Rory nudges me in the ribs. He's reminding me I am Cougar, not some gobsmacked idiot. Cougar has seen this sort of thing before.

I force a yawn. 'It's quite pretty.'

Lucas blinks, then turns back to the front.

The captain's voice comes over the intercom. 'Survival gear on, folks.'

There are rustles as people pull on their snowsuits. Rory and I do the same. Seatbelts click as we settle in for landing.

❄ *lisa walker*

The plane drops lower and that vast whiteness becomes more defined. There are mountains – huge mountains. I hadn't expected that. For some reason I'd thought it would be flat. The sea edge is rimmed with turquoise cliffs of ice. They are brilliant, luminous. I hadn't dreamed they'd be that colour. My mouth is open again. I shut it. We drop lower and I see black dots on the white. 'Penguins,' I squeal.

Rory jabs me hard.

'Ow. Penguins,' I repeat in a more subdued manner. 'As you'd expect.' But nothing is as I expected. I've seen pictures of Antarctica before – movies of penguins waddling on the ice, seals emerging from blow holes. I've seen all that, but the reality is different. The reality is so much more. I'm not sure why, but then it hits me. No people. All that vast, vast land and no people – hardly any, anyway. This is nature in the raw. Marley would have loved it here.

The sun shines off the snow in a dazzle of diamonds as we touch down in Antarctica. I lean across Rory, my nose to the window, drinking it in. Stuff keeping it cool – it's Antarctica! I'm as overcome as a kid at Disneyland.

The plane lands, bounces lightly then taxis down a blue ice runway. Outside are some tents, shipping containers and a large red truck thing with a rubber tread around its wheels. Four figures dressed in red suits stand on the edge of the runway. Red appears to be a popular colour in Antarctica.

We come to a standstill and soon the door is opened. A rush of cold air fills the plane.

'Doesn't feel much like global warming to me,' murmurs Nathan Hornby.

Adrian smiles at his boss politely.

Lucas, having disregarded the Captain's earlier instruction, gets to his feet and pulls on his snow suit. What if we'd crashed? He would have perished instantly. Lucas clearly is not the kind of guy who understands the Cone of Certainty. Unlike Adrian, who is already encased in down and ready for action. Being in Adrian's orbit is like partaking in a well-organised tour – everything runs to plan. My sloths whimper. *Don't worry, girls, we'll get him back*, I tell them.

I eye Adrian across the aisle and twitch my head. He gets the message and hangs back as everyone else leaves the plane.

'Why didn't you tell me you were coming to Antarctica?' I mutter.

'It was a last minute thing. Hornby decided he needed to do some fact checking. I thought I'd better come along. He needs someone to keep him on message. You should get him on your show. He's good talent.'

'Hmph. Maybe I will.'

'Anyway, it's a quick trip. We're heading back tomorrow.' Adrian pulls up his hood. 'Better get out there.'

I shuffle up the aisle after him. These snowsuits take some getting used to.

Outside it is still and cold, though not as cold as I'd imagined. I was visualising howling winds, blasting snow, men crawling for shelter gnawing on the remains of a husky. But this isn't much colder than Chamonix on a mid-winter's day. Still, I pull up my hood. Goggles are essential – the light is blinding.

Adrian takes a photo of the Minister posing next to the plane. The politician looks rugged in his snowsuit, a serious expression on his face, which must be his fact-finding look. He's not a bad-looking man, in a latter day Jack Nicholson sort of way. I wonder what sort of facts he expects to find out in one day in Antarctica.

Adrian lies on the snow to shoot upwards. I envisage the picture – a looming man with an expanse of snow behind him – and the caption: *Warming? What warming?*

Seeing the Minister in action reminds me I should get a shot in front of the plane as well.

Rory is already onto it, he has his camera over his shoulder. He points. 'Stand there, Cougar, where there's no-one in the background.'

'Have we got a script for this part?'

'Um' – Rory pulls more paper from his bag – 'Not unless you want to talk about dolphins.' He shrugs. 'It's just welcome to Antarctica, isn't it? No biggie.'

I open and shut my mouth. What little I know about Antarctica I've already used up in my airport speech. I can't do it. Then I remember Adrian's book. *Extreme Project Managers fire first and take aim later.* This suggestion seemed bizarre and potentially dangerous when I read it – what were the authors thinking? But … perhaps that is the approach I need. 'Okay.' I pull up my balaclava. 'Is my nose red?'

Rory gives me an exasperated look. 'I'm just the cam—'

'Joking.'

'Okay, rolling.'

Taking a tip from the Minister, I assume a rugged, serious expression. This is Antarctica, after all, the last frontier. Despite having flown here in a nice, warm plane, instead of battling our way through stormy seas, we are still heroes in the tradition of the great polar explorers. We all had to pull together to get ourselves off the ground. No refreshments were served. It was tough.

I have no idea what I'm going to say but my mouth opens – *shoot first, aim later.* 'Welcome to *Cougar on Ice.* To recap, many people have come to grief in the frozen wasteland of Antarctica – Scott of the Antarctic, Captain Oates and numerous others. We have touched down on the ice sheet.' I pause for effect. 'That's right, we landed on ice. It was touch and go there for a few moments but our captain brought it off. We, the crew, were ready in our snowsuits with survival gear at hand in case anything went wrong. While it might look sunny and warm here, it is in fact bitterly, bitterly, bitterly cold. Unprotected, you would soon die from exposure.' I shiver in an exaggerated manner. 'And other misfortunes would follow upon that one.'

Rory raises his eyes from the camera at my relapse into Victorian English. He pulls down his goggles to block the glare and opens his mouth.

I forestall him. 'Flying over the continent gives you an appreciation of its amazing, amazing vastness. Antarctica is twice as big as Australia. And while there are bases, no-one lives here permanently.'

I can't read Rory's face through his goggles, but I sense I'm being dull. If only he'd picked up the right script. Human drama, that's what we need. I should be able to do that – I've been living and breathing scripts since the age of twelve. A love triangle or a baby switching would be good, but failing that … I eye the scientists in their red suits as they head towards the snowmobile. Nathan Hornby follows behind like a lone wildebeest separated from the herd.

melt ❄ **87**

'Here in Antarctica, we are a long way from help. We must fend for ourselves, make our own rules. In these rugged conditions one person can impact on the whole group. It's like Big Brother, but if you're evicted there's nowhere to go. Twenty people boarded my flight to Antarctica and already tensions are being felt. Those of you who've watched the news will know the Minister for Science believes climate science is crap.' I gesture towards the scientists and Rory follows, panning over the red suits.

'There are a lot of scientists here in Antarctica. A lot of scientists and only one Minister.' I point at the lone wildebeest. 'And his minder.' I scan the ice but Adrian is nowhere to be seen. 'I'm not suggesting anything, but I think there is one person in Antarctica who should be locking his door tonight. Antarctica might be a big place, but there is nowhere to run.'

The snowmobile roars – time to sign off. In this part of the show there's usually some light relief. A cute animal would be good, but failing that … I lean down and scoop some snow together. 'Yeeha.' I'm not aiming the snowball at Rory, but if I was I'd miss him for sure.

Rory's mouth drops. The snowball is the size of a basketball. He picks up his camera and runs. The snowball misses the camera and splatters as it hits his shoulder, spraying snow all over his face. He trains the camera back on me as he wipes it off. He seems a little pissed off.

'Whoops.' I smile gaily. 'Nothing like a snowball fight.'

Rory shakes his head and points downwards.

I pick up the bottle I've strategically placed at my feet. 'Oh, look what I found! My Bailey's Irish Cream should be nicely cooled. I can't wait to curl up next to the fire and have a drink. Stay tuned for more *Cougar on Ice* after the break. Notwithstanding.'

'How was that?' I say to Rory. 'Did I sound like Cougar?'

Rory puts the lens cap on his camera. His shoulders are shaking.

'Are you okay? Sorry about the snowball. I didn't mean to hit you.'

A snorting noise comes out from beneath his hood. He looks up. 'Sorry, but that was nothing like Cougar, it was more like Monty Python.'

'Oh.' I stare at him. 'So I guess we can't use it?'

Rory snickers. 'I'll send it to Maxine when we get to the station. What's to lose? If they wanted something different they should have given us the right script.' He zips up his camera bag. 'Notwithstanding.' He snorts again.

Adrian appears from behind the plane. Did he hear what I said about the lone wildebeest? Like everyone else, he's wearing goggles and it's hard to read his expression. When he sees my eyes on him he turns and walks towards the snowmobile.

Chapter Fourteen

The krill issue

Project:	Day one in Antarctica
Objectives:	Give the impression I know my shit
	Impress the hell out of Adrian
16.30–18.00:	Study glaciology
18.00:	Dinner

My room at Casey Station has a small single bed and a little desk. I'm in a building called the Red Shed which is like a shipping container but is surprisingly civilised on the inside, like a ski lodge. I'm relieved not to be sharing even though I've had to be a diva to achieve it. It would have been hard keeping up appearances as Cougar constantly. At least this way I can relax occasionally.

The station is on a rise, not far from the sea. I would have liked to go for a walk and investigate, but Lucas made it clear I was only to venture into the field when escorted by him.

He showed me the board by the door, where everyone at the station must move their tag from 'in' to 'out' if they go outside. 'It is essential we know where everyone is at all times,' he said. He was quite the bossy boots – especially for someone with no understanding of the Cone of Certainty or spreadsheets.

It was a three-hour drive from the airstrip to the station and the whole way here I had my nose to the window. While the terrain we crossed was flat, mountain peaks and rocky outcrops loomed out of the whiteness in the distance. It was hard to get any sense of scale. The mountains could have been hills or of Himalayan proportions – there was no way of knowing. It was late by the time we got here although the sun was still high in the sky.

Now, I gaze out the window of my room. The sky has a particular quality here. It's so clear it sparkles. When I got out of the snowmobile it seemed like there was fairy dust in the air – it shimmered all around me. I wanted to stop and stare, to soak it in, but I didn't want to look like an idiot. I will ask Lucas about this shimmering, if I can find a way to do that which doesn't make me sound ignorant. No doubt glaciologists are well up on such things.

I've been trying to study, but all I can do is press my nose to the glass. Outside are a few more buildings. Although there is snow not far away, here we are on bare rock. In the distance – it takes me a while to figure this out – is the sea. It's not like the sea back home. Snow-covered ice stretches from the shore, breaking up into pancakes further out. And beyond that is water. I'm desperate to get out there, but I suppose I must follow orders.

I feel like I have travelled not to the end of the planet, but to another world. Somewhere magical.

I drag my eyes back to my laptop. It's lucky my room has an internet connection. I hadn't thought to check beforehand. With what little concentration I've mustered, I have so far learnt that polar bears are only found in the Arctic, not the Antarctic. I felt like I'd been hit with a snowball when I read that. I had no idea. I could so easily have come undone in conversation with Lucas. I remember his eyes crinkling. Had he been trying to catch me out? No, why would he? I'm being paranoid.

The alarming polar bear revelation spurred me on to further wildlife research. I've discovered there are four types of seals and seven types of penguins in the Antarctic and memorised their names for future use.

All of this I have gleaned from a website called *Polar Fun for Kids*, which is pitched at just the right level. After one and a half hours of study I have the Antarctic knowledge of a five-year-old.

I check the dinner objectives I've typed into my project plan. Adrian would not be happy. The objectives are loose. They are not measurable, or possibly even achievable. Adrian is big on stretch objectives. They have to be hard enough to work for, but not so hard you give up. Sounding like I know my shit could be a stretch too far but I'll give it a crack. The same goes for impressing Adrian.

Extreme Project Management is poking out of my travel bag. When I open it at random it tells me that *The Extreme Project Manager is a relationship manager not a task manager.*

This is heartening – *tasks, shmasks*. The Extreme Project Manager focuses on the vibe and lets the tasks take care of themselves. I can manage that.

Alicia would no doubt have had an outfit planned for my dinner debut. I pull my small pile of clothes out of my bag and lay them on the bed but nothing jumps out at me. It's warm inside the Red Shed and the mood is casual, so I decide on my quick-dry pants that zip off at the knees and a 'Save the Dugong' T-shirt – they were on special at Outdoor World. This outfit makes me look like an outdoorsy, rugged and environmentally-concerned TV celebrity.

Dinner is awkward as, naturally, being Cougar, I have special requirements. Everyone else tucks into steaks, but I've instructed Cherie to prepare me a lentil salad and fresh vegetable juice. Cherie gives me my food with a face that is not as friendly as it used to be. This makes me feel bad. I don't know how Cougar does this. Her skin must be like the Antarctic ice cap. *Four kilometres of cold, hard frost before you get to the frozen rock layers beneath*, I say to an imaginary audience. I am becoming quite the expert.

I am seated at a table with the scientists. Lucas is back in his favourite jeans and T-shirt and his book rests on the table next to him. He must be a keen reader. He introduces me to Maria, the krill woman. She is not small with waving legs as I had imagined. Maria is from Holland. She has smooth brown skin and shiny blonde hair cut in a straight fringe across her forehead. She is tall and shapely and seems devastatingly intelligent – scarily so. I resolve to avoid her if possible.

Maria and Lucas are having a rapid-fire conversation about ice-core samples. I know from *Polar Fun for Kids* that scientists drill deep holes into the ice to learn about past climates – the site was a little short on detail. My knowledge of ice-core samples isn't enough to get in at the ground floor on this conversation.

'One hundred and fifty per cent?' says Maria.

Lucas nods, his beard going up and down. 'In the last hundred and fifty years.'

What is it with scientists and beards? I try to imagine what he would be like without hair all over his face, but fail.

'I knew it was bad, but I didn't think carbon dioxide had gone up that much,' says Maria.

Carbon dioxide. Now at least I know what we're talking about – climate change. I think of Nathan Hornby and his *climate science is crap* comment. The Minister is at a table up the other end of the room with Mike, the station leader – fact-finding, no doubt. Adrian is perched on a chair at the same table. Of all the dining rooms in all the world, Adrian has to turn up here. At least I'll be able to relax once he goes home tomorrow. It's bad enough being Cougar, but having Adrian watch my performance is doing my head in. No doubt he will compare the two versions of Cougar in his head and find me lacking.

I open and shut my mouth a few times as Lucas and Maria continue their conversation. Rory glances my way and flickers his eyebrows. I know what he means. Cougar would not sit here mutely. Cougar would be the centre of attention. Cougar is like Alexis from *Dynasty*, she always makes her presence felt. I rack my brain to recall what I know about climate change, but suspect there is no way to dumb down this conversation enough for me to make a contribution. I now wish Mary was here. Annoying as she is, she would be able to brief me on the best tactic to take control of the situation.

As we finish dessert – luckily sticky date pudding is on the menu for Cougar – there is a break in the conversation. Rory gives me a meaningful nod. I clear my throat. 'Ahem.' Maria and Lucas turn to me. I straighten my spine. 'I'd like to brief you on my program. Then we can be sure we're all on the same page.'

Lucas's blue eyes crinkle. 'Are you planning to include climate change in your show?'

I am jolted out of my happy sense of taking control. I have no idea what he is talking about. This show is about Antarctica. It's about ice and penguins, snow and seals. That's what you always have in shows about Antarctica. No-one is interested in climate change – and certainly not at seven thirty pm on a weeknight when the alternative is watching *Kitchen Talent* on Channel Four. Climate change is boring. The ABC might get away with it, but our audience has a trigger-happy grip on the remote control and they're not afraid to use it. I'm about to tell him this, but he continues.

'All we get is documentaries about ice and cute little penguins.' Lucas snorts. 'It drives me crazy. When are we going to see some real science? You are a glaciologist?'

I nod – *whatever that is.*

'Good. Then you know all about it.' He smiles. His teeth are very white.

I cough. I'm keen to divert the conversation away from my broad knowledge of glaciology.

Lucas taps his fork on his glass and the hum in the room lowers.

I wasn't expecting the whole room to listen in. Even the Minister's table is turned my way. *Even Adrian.*

'Cougar is going to brief us on her program,' Lucas announces. 'I expect this will be of interest to everyone.'

There is much scraping as everyone swivels their chairs to face our table.

Rory raises his eyebrows at me.

I get to my feet. For some reason the music from *Dynasty* runs through my head. I think of how when the show starts they run a rapid recap of recent developments. *It's not your baby! Give it to me straight, doctor! He's not dead!*

Lucas's eyes are focused on me. Maria's head is cocked to the side. Adrian looks alert and ready to rate my performance. The Minister folds his arms as if awaiting a controversial policy announcement from the opposition. And I think it is this that sends me off in an unexpected direction – *shoot first and take aim later.*

I take a deep breath. 'Hurricanes are increasing! Bushfires are raging! Polar bears are at risk of extinction!' *Polar Fun for Kids* filled me in on the polar bear situation. It seems the thin sea ice in the Arctic is leading to polar bears having difficulties in catching seals.

Rory is wide-eyed. It's hard to know whether he's impressed or alarmed. Lucas and Maria seem puzzled but interested. Maria opens her mouth, but I hold up my hand. I am Cougar. I have the floor. I have no idea what I'm going to do with it, but I haven't finished yet. What would Alexis do?

If this was a soap opera, someone could return from the dead. A long-lost relative might knock on the door, there could be a murder, an unexpected pregnancy or an arrest for shoplifting. I could blow something up, give someone cancer, or crash a car. But none of that is going to happen now – they are waiting for me to talk about climate change. With the possible exception of Rory, there is no-one here who knows less about this subject than me. My mouth is drier than Antarctica, which despite all that snow and ice is apparently the driest continent on earth. I lick my lips, my mind sorting and discarding random facts I've absorbed from my favourite website.

Up the other end of the room, Nathan Hornby clears his throat, but this isn't parliament and I'm not going to let him rain on my parade. I decide to stick with what I know.

'I am a glaciologist. Glaciology is the study of ice.' I cough again. 'But I suppose you know that. Antarctica has a lot of snow and ice.' That seems safe enough. 'And, em, if the planet warms up, it is likely to melt.'

Lucas's sticky date pudding has gone down the wrong way but I press on – drama, that's what I need. Antarctica doesn't have oil barons, lying lawyers, evil despots or aging sex kittens, but … 'Antarctica has penguins in seven varieties, although technically speaking three of them, the king penguin, the macaroni penguin and the rockhopper penguin, are only found on the sub-Antarctic islands.' I use my most authoritative tone. This is a trick I learnt from Adrian: *People don't care what you say. They care how you say it. Project confidence and they will assume you know what you are talking about.*

Maria opens her mouth again, but I silence her with a frown and continue in my best Cougar style. 'The true Antarctic penguins are the Adelie, the chinstrap, the emperor and the gentoo. Antarctica also has four varieties of seals: the crabeater seal, the Weddell seal, the elephant seal and the leopard seal.'

Lucas looks like he's waiting for the punch line.

Like a true television pro I go in for a big segue from cute wildlife to climate change. 'If it gets too warm, the Adelie penguins will have to move south.' I'm proud of this, it sounds plausible.

Lucas nods.

I feel encouraged – a surge of confidence races through me. 'The emperor penguins won't like that. What's going to happen then? It's going to be war out there. Those emperor penguins, they don't like to be disturbed. You've all seen *Happy Feet* – they don't like Adelie penguins much. And what about the leopard seals? If the ice gets too thin, they'll leap out through it and eat penguins whenever they want.'

The Minister mutters something.

Adrian pulls out a phone and types something into it. Perhaps he is briefing the Prime Minister on my insightful analysis of climate change. Or sending sexy texts to Cougar.

'It's going to be war out there,' I repeat. I've lost my train of thought. *War* – this reminds me of the Moldavian Massacre episode of *Dynasty* … 'The leopard seals will be, like, total terrorists and the penguins will be refugees, driven to stealing food from the tourists when they're not fighting amongst themselves.' I think that's what happened in Moldavia …

Rory leans back in his chair and behind Lucas's and Maria's backs he makes a slashing gesture across his throat.

I decide to wrap it up. 'So, anyway, that's the angle I'm planning to take for *Cougar on Ice*. My producer will be here tomorrow, she can provide more detail for those who want it.' I sit, my heart thudding in my chest. I feel like I've had an out of body experience. If this was *Big Brother* I have no doubt I would be voted off the show.

There's silence for a moment, then murmurs spread across the room.

Lucas spoons up the last of his pudding. 'That sounds like an interesting approach.' He chews with a thoughtful expression. 'At least it is not just cute penguins.'

I smile as if the thought I was about to be ejected into the snow for impersonating a scientist was a million miles from my mind.

But I am not home and free yet. The krill woman's eyes are narrowed as she takes a sip of her water. 'What about krill?'

My smile snap-freezes in her icy glare. I have no idea how to answer that question. She may as well have said, what about krypton, for all the sense it makes. I am tempted to scream, 'The cabin is on fire! This is all your fault!' Anything to create a distraction. What would Alexis do? I lift my nose. 'My producer is totally on top of the krill issue,' I say with all the hauteur I can muster. 'You can talk to her about it.'

It's time to beat a retreat. 'Rory,' I snap, getting to my feet, 'we need to run through our shooting schedule for tomorrow.' I stride from the room with Rory following. Once we're out of earshot I lean against a wall to recover. My legs are weak from the strain. 'How do you think that went?'

'I was getting worried for a moment, but I think you pulled it off, Summer.' He puts up his hand. 'High five.' Rory's massive hand meets mine with a smack. He laughs, sticking his nose in the air. 'My producer is totally on top of the krill issue,' he mimics.

Now the fright is wearing off, euphoria sweeps through me – I can't believe I did that. 'What *is* the krill issue, Rory?'

'The krill issue is' – Rory ponders – 'serious. Very serious.'

'Indeed.' I put on my presenter voice. 'The krill issue is at the heart of everything. We will never understand anything about Antarctica until we get to the bottom of the krill issue.'

'The krill issue is profound, more profound than you can imagine,' says Rory in a deep baritone. 'It is, in fact, the essence of profundity.'

I nod. 'We are in accord on the krill issue, Rory. Krill is … the answer.'

'Amen.'

We giggle like schoolgirls.

Rory and I part at the end of the corridor. On the way to my room I pass a noticeboard. Some sheets are pinned up there with news stories from the outside world. I flick through them. *Fire blocks highway on north coast*, one of the headlines reads. *Firefighters are backburning to control a fire in forest* … I don't need to read any more.

Back in my room, I press my nose to the window again. A gust of wind hits the building making it shudder. Outside the sky is still light. Snow drifts across the ground in flurries. It's not anywhere near as pleasant as it was a couple of hours ago.

It's hard to imagine people frolicking on the sand in Sydney. It is harder to imagine they're fighting bushfires back home. As I close my eyes, I think I hear someone playing guitar, but that may be because I am thinking about Marley.

I open my eyes feeling uneasy, like I'm late for something important. It's light outside. Have I slept in? I reach for my phone. It tells me it's three am. Three am? Outside the sun is low on the horizon. It doesn't look like three am. But if it was light when I first tried to go to sleep at eleven and it is light now, maybe it never got dark at all.

It soon becomes clear I'm not going back to sleep. In fact, I'm not sure if I have slept at all. I sit up and stare out the window again. It is three am and I am wide awake – what to do? Maybe I should make a start on my igloo? After all, it's only four days until Christmas and it might take some time. Mary will be here later today wanting a progress report. It would be good to have something to show her.

While I could co-opt Rory to assist in this endeavour, a foolish pride prevents me. Rory thinks I am an igloo-building guru. It's my one claim to fame. And besides, Cougar is supposed to be building the igloo in secret. Although it will need to be captured on camera …

My phone is still in my hand. This gives me an idea. I can do this indie-style. It will be authentic, cutting edge – a hand-held phone camera, amateurish composition – *The Blair Witch Project* on ice. But where to build my igloo? I look out the window.

I'd expected to be surrounded by snow in Antarctica but in fact the station rests on rock. This makes igloo-building a challenge. But it can't be far to the snow – I will have to go out and investigate.

First, I do a quick Google. *Fun with Igloos* tells me that *an igloo is a great place to spend the night and will take three to six hours to build.* That's okay; I can do a couple of hours then finish it off tomorrow. *You will need a spade and a saw.* Hm … I gaze out the window. Several sheds are scattered nearby. They seem like the kinds of places that would house spades and saws.

The website assures me that, if I follow its instructions correctly, the igloo will not collapse. This sounds like a butt-covering exercise – if it does collapse, clearly I didn't follow instructions. I remember Euphoria's vision of me encased in snow. But, I reassure myself, most of Euphoria's visions never come to pass. While I was travelling, she had visions of me falling off the Leaning Tower of Pisa, getting bitten by a scorpion in a pyramid, being abducted by an Indian guru and trampled by an elephant. An elephant did, in fact, stand on my toe in Thailand, but it was only a minor injury.

I scan through the instructions, trying to commit them to memory ... *don't make it too big, large blocks on the bottom, entrance with vertical blocks, L-shaped entrance, ventilation hole, smooth out the ceiling* ... It goes on and on. I had no idea so much effort had gone into that igloo in Chamonix. Never mind, I'm sure if Inuits can do it, I can. How hard can it be? All I need is to find a nice, quiet, snowy location where I won't be disturbed.

Putting on my snowsuit, I sneak down the corridor, hoping no-one will spot me going out of bounds. Though that's hardly likely at this time of night – I glance out the window – *day* – whatever.

I have a pang of guilt at the tagboard. I can't move my tag to say 'out', because I'm not allowed to be out by myself. This is a stealth exercise. I'm going out into Antarctica alone ...

Outside, it is freezing. I pull my balaclava up over my nose so not a single part of me is exposed. The first shed I come to is deserted, as you'd expect, so I open the door a crack and peer inside. Tools lie against the walls and hang from hooks. Soon I am out the door with a spade and saw under my arm and heading for a nearby rocky outcrop. Dragging my equipment, I climb over the rocks to the snow.

The location is what I need – flat, snow-covered and private. Although the station is over the rise, I feel isolated and intrepid, like an early settler about to erect his first shelter – *here, I will build my igloo.*

This is going to be fun! I can already picture the jolly time we'll have inside the igloo on Christmas Day. There will be presents and candles and maybe some hot mulled wine. And when Adrian sees me on TV, he'll be so impressed at what I've achieved he'll realise I'm the girl for him. I can't wait. Now, I just need to remember what to do. First, I need to stomp the snow so it becomes firm, then I use my saw to cut some blocks and I pile them on top of each other in a circular dome shape. Easy.

One and a half hours later, I sink to the snow, panting, and survey my creation – a ring of crumbling snow blocks about two metres in diameter. You couldn't call it a shelter, although if you lay in the middle it might cut the wind. There is a problem with the consistency of my blocks. More than half disintegrated as I placed them in position. I should have spent longer on the stomping.

At this rate, I estimate it will take – I calculate the height to go, compared with the height already gained – about twenty more hours to complete the igloo. Given I have four days left until Christmas, I will have to work on it for five hours per day. It's lucky the days are so long but, even so, it's going to cut into my sleeping time. Still, it can't be helped and I'm sure I'm getting some great footage.

I have made an igloo-cam by placing my phone upright on a purpose-built snow mound. Pressing a button, I review my footage. It's certainly indie. In fact it's so avant-garde there's nothing happening at all. The screen shows only white. I fast forward and – *aha* – see myself stagger past with a snow block in my hands. Not totally a wasted effort then.

Stashing my tools inside my fledgling igloo, I make a furtive dash back to the base. I'm knackered, like I've run a marathon. I don't know how I'm going to keep this up.

I glance at my watch. It's only five-thirty am. I have time for a quick lie down before breakfast.

Chapter Fifteen
I discover my inner artiste

Project:	Shoot an episode of *Cougar on Ice*
Objectives:	Be a cool, calm and charismatic media personality
	Impress Adrian

My alarm goes off at seven o'clock. I have the grumpy, scratchy feeling I have not slept at all. Although, I must have slept, because I dreamt I was on television, naked with a big, green nose. I don't need Jung to tell me what that means. Stretching my arms above my head, I moan. My whole body aches. Igloo-building is a cruel and unusual punishment. I'm never going to get that thing built. Knowing the way television works, no-one will remember there was to be an igloo episode. If I keep quiet about it, the whole thing might go away.

Looking out the window at the snow blowing across the rocks I try to visualise the dust and heat back home – the burning trees, the choking smoke. Again, I think how much Marley would have loved it here. He liked nothing more than to be in the wilderness and it doesn't get much wilder than this. His book's on my table. When I pick it up it falls open at Chapter XII – *Between the Polar Circle and the Ice Wall*.

> … it seems as though she had entered a new region, 'that region of Desolation and Silence,' as Edgar Poe says …

The last time I read that line was next to Marley's bed in hospital. I should get ready for breakfast, but instead I pick up my laptop.

To: Marley Lennon Wright
From: Summer Dawn Rain Wright
Subject: I miss you so much

Sitting beside your bed while you were in a coma was the hardest thing I've ever done, Marley. Three days is an awful long time to be next to someone you love, wondering if they're there. I read to you from *An Antarctic Mystery*. I thought you'd like it.

Inside the hospital it was cool, but outside the sun beat down in a way it never did overseas. I'd only been away two years, but it was enough to feel disoriented. The sky was so blue, and so high, the birds so noisy. I'd come home looking for normality, routine – but instead, this. Every way I turned I was met by confusion. There was nowhere safe.

And I'd missed you so much, Marley.

I touched your hand and though it was warm, it was still. No answering curl of fingers met mine.

You always think there'll be another day, endless days … The whole two years I was away, it never occurred to me you might vanish.

Two years is a long time to try and stay in touch. We emailed constantly at first but as time went on you seemed less interested in my stories of London nightclubs and crazy Israeli backpackers. And maybe I was less interested in your stories of the fires you'd put out and the gossip from Nimbin.

But you weren't just my brother; you were part of me – my creek wars opponent, my late-night reading companion, my fantasy games cast. It was different when we were at school. You hung out with your friends, me with mine, but at home we were like Siamese twins.

I save the email and press 'send'.

It's funny how Antarctica makes me think of Marley. You'd think a change of scene would have the opposite effect. But the looming wilderness outside my door makes me cling to him more tightly.

Here in the station it's easy to forget I'm in the most inhospitable part of the Earth. It's warm inside – too warm. The heating dries me out, makes me languid. But outside it's a land people have never made their own. A flurry of snow beats against the window, as if reinforcing my point. *Antarctica*. It's hard to believe I'm here.

But I shouldn't be lying here thinking about Marley. I have a big day ahead of me. I click on my project planning file and inspect my objectives for today. They are not sufficient. Today I need to shoot a whole episode of *Cougar on Ice* and it has to be great. Today I will show the world what I am capable of. Today I will show Adrian.

I think of Maxine's goodbye pep talk – *there's a lot riding on this, Summer*. If I can pull this off my future at Channel Five will be assured. I'll walk into a scriptwriter's job. I'll be able to do what I've always wanted to do.

Chorus: Oo, oo, she's going to be a soap-opera scriptwriter.

If I can pull it off.

And once I'm the star of Channel Five Adrian will come back to me. He won't be able to resist my amazing project management, my celebrity star power. I need to get through this, to come out on top.

There's a knock on the door.

Sliding my feet to the ground, I stand up. I'm wearing only a long T-shirt and suspect my hair is like a bird's nest, but who cares? I stumble to the door and open it.

It's Lucas. He's in no position to judge my hair – his still looks like it's been dried in a wind tunnel. At any rate, it matches his beard. 'Phone call for you,' he says. 'Maxine. From Sydney. I told her you would call back, but she wanted to hang on. She is … forceful.'

I grimace. 'She is more forceful in person.'

'It is expensive on the phone, so maybe you should hurry.' Lucas takes in my appearance. 'Are you okay?'

I grunt. 'Didn't sleep well.'

Lucas gestures towards the window. 'The light throws you off. You'll get used to it.'

'Does it ever get dark?'

'Not at this time of year. Land of the midnight sun,' he says in that faintly lilting accent.

I wonder what part of Scandinavia he's from. Putting on a jacket and track pants over my bed shirt I follow him along the corridor to the phone. I'm in no mood to talk to Maxine, but I suppose I don't have a choice. 'Hello?' I put the phone to my ear.

'What's happening there, Summer? Why haven't you checked your emails? We've decided to go to air early. We need your piece right now. Dianne has sent you the script but you'll need to adapt it for local conditions.' Maxine has mastered the art of talking without pausing for breath. Perhaps she's doing that circular breathing thing, like playing the didgeridoo. 'Channel Four has premiered their new show

Outside with Mack Decker in the Arctic. Can you believe it?' Her voice rises to a shriek. 'I think we've got a mole, so I'm increasing security. Talk to no-one.' She stops.

'I understand, Maxine,' I say in a no-nonsense James Bond way.

'And from now on, when we talk about the show we call it Charlie Oscar India.'

'Pardon?'

'C O I,' Maxine snaps.

'Oh, I get it, *Cougar on*—'

'No!' Maxine yells. 'Use the code.'

'Sorry. Got it. Charlie Oscar India.'

'I know I said we'd air next week, but we've rearranged our schedule and we're going now. We're going to knock those copycat bastards for six. Check your emails and get Rory to send me the teaser as soon as possible. You'll have to start without Mary and Alicia but they'll be there this afternoon. Don't mess this up, Summer. Is anyone suspicious?'

'Um, no. I don't think so.'

'I hope you've made a start on the igloo – that's essential. Bye.'

'Yes, but—'

She hangs up.

My ear is ringing as I put the phone down – Maxine sounded so close. It was disconcerting, like she'd teleported in to check up on me. In my fragile sleep-deprived state, her tirade has left me a little shaky. I lean against the wall and close my eyes, delaying the moment of facing the day as Cougar – putting on that upbeat, bitchy mask. And the igloo … Damn, double damn and blast. I'd been hoping she'd forget about the igloo.

'Everything okay?'

I open my eyes and see Lucas. His hair is still sticking up from his head and his eyes are kind. For a Viking, he looks like he might be good with tea and sympathy. I have a sudden urge to swoon at his feet. That beard – it's so fluffy, like a teddy bear … I suppress an urge to stroke it.

'Hey, Cougar, I've got a coffee for you.' It's Rory. He's carrying his camera and a laptop over his shoulder. His eyes flicker between Lucas and me and one eyebrow lifts.

Instantly I straighten my back, try to channel Cougar – solid ice all the way down. 'I'm fine,' I say to Lucas.

His mouth twitches. 'Leave you to it then.'

'Heard from Maxine?' Rory passes me the coffee as Lucas strides off down the corridor. 'I was just checking my emails.'

I roll my eyes and point at the phone. 'She sounds even scarier via satellite. You'd think she'd get diluted en route.'

'Take more than that. A stake to the heart.' Rory heads towards a table, beckoning me after him. 'Let's check out the script.'

'Maxine said something about sending her the teaser, they're going early?'

Rory nods. 'Yeah. I'll send them the footage from yesterday. They'll edit it up into a teaser and we'll be shooting and rolling from then on. That's what I like – a quick production. Hate it when stuff sits in the can for months.' Rory opens his laptop and clicks. A Word document appears. I lean closer to read:

CHARLIE OSCAR INDIA: EPISODE ONE

COUGAR: IT IS WILD AND LONELY HERE IN ANTARCTICA. SNOW AND WINDS OF UP TO 150 KILOMETRES PER HOUR BUFFET OUR SHELTER. OUR HARDY GROUP OF ANTARCTIC SCIENTISTS KEEP BUSY XXX (NB: FILL IN THE GAP WITH DESCRIPTIONS OF WHAT THE SCIENTISTS ARE DOING EG. COUNTING SEALS). I AM REMINDED OF THE HEROIC EXPLOITS OF THE EARLY ADVENTURERS TO ANTARCTICA, ROBERT SCOTT

I yawn loudly. The coffee is kicking in and I'm less lightheaded, but still sleepy. 'Do we have to keep banging on about Scott? Haven't I done him to death already?'

Rory blinks. 'What's wrong with Scott?'

'Where's the drama?'

'The wind, the snow, the heroic exploits …'

I yawn again. 'Where's the sex, the family feuds, the illegitimate children? Who'd want to watch this? It's boring.'

'This is the script, Summer. That's their job. Ours is to deliver on the script.' He sounds like he's talking to one of his kids. 'We get it in the can, we send it home, we have a good night's sleep and later today Mary's here and we do as we're told. That's the way it works.'

My eyes flick over the script. This script is not going to showcase my talents to the world. Outside I see that shimmer again – like diamond dust raining from the sky. A gust of wind hits the window, making a howling noise. *Oo, oo, scriptwriter*, it seems to say. 'No.' I bang my fist on the table. 'This is not a good script. It's making me sleepy.'

Rory leans back in his chair. He hasn't seen this side of me before. 'Should I get you some toast?'

That's probably what he says to his kids when they throw a tantrum. I hardly know what's got into me. 'I don't feel it.' I bang my fist to my chest. 'There's no heart. That script makes me want to go and watch *Outside with Mack Decker*. I bet his scriptwriters aren't feeding him lines about hardy scientists and heroic exploits that have already been done to death, over and over again. I bet his scriptwriters understand the meaning of narrative tension and suspense.' With a click of the mouse, I delete the script. 'There.'

Rory gasps, his eyes darting around the room as if Maxine might be watching.

'Ha,' I say.

'I had no idea you were so … passionate about this.'

'Well, I am.' I put my fist to my chest again. 'I take pride in my work.' I put on a French accent. 'Zat script, eet was rubbeesh.' I think of something I saw in Adrian's book – *The Extreme Project Manager gets it right the last time, not the first* … This hadn't made sense when I read it, but now I get it. You don't hang around waiting for the perfect plan; you dive in and work it out as you go along. 'We're going to do this commando style. No script.'

Rory's ruddy cheeks go two shades lighter. 'That's not how it's done in television, Summer. Maybe in a war zone, but even then—'

'I'll take full responsibility.' I stand up. 'Imagine you're in the trenches, Rory. Snipers are firing at you. You get to your feet, camera at the ready and you shoot.' I clench my hand as if snatching a prize from the air. 'You capture the moment.' Outside, the sun pokes through the clouds, lighting a shimmering column of diamonds all the way to the ground. I lower my voice. 'You go for glory, Rory. You tackle the krill issue and you go for glory.'

Chapter Sixteen

Going for glory

Half an hour later, Rory and I are in the dining room. I am wearing my snowsuit and balaclava, but I've pulled the goggles up on my forehead as they're too dark for indoor use. I rub my hip where I banged into a table before discovering this.

About ten people are busy eating their breakfast. As anyone who watches soap opera knows, any time more than three people appear on screen, something interesting is about to happen … Taking my microphone, I advance upon Maria the krill woman. After a quick consultation with *Polar Fun for Kids*, I am right on top of the krill issue. I take a couple of deep breaths and try to channel Cougar – *think star power, think bitch queen.* I can do this.

Maria looks up at my approach, a slice of toast held to her lips. Her eyes scan my snowsuit then flicker to Rory and his camera. Her lips purse.

I don't give her time to think. 'Tell me, Maria, is it true the term "krill" is a cover-up for what is in reality a whole lot of different prawns?'

Maria frowns. 'Here, we have seven types of krill only. But yes, there are many.'

'Many types?' I raise my eyebrows as if this is a startling piece of information which she has unwittingly disclosed. 'So tell me … what, exactly, do you do when you are studying krill? Catch them with your hands? Scoop them up with a net?'

'No.' Her mouth curls. 'I am using a CPR of course.'

I raise my eyebrows again but this is a pointless exercise when wearing a balaclava. It's annoying to have to wear so many clothes – sweat is trickling down my sides already. There are bound to be close-ups though so it's best to be safe. 'CPR?' The only CPR I know involves the kiss of life and chest compressions. 'Can you explain to the viewers what that is please?'

'Continuous plankton recorder.' Maria articulates each word. 'We drag it behind the boat.'

'Aha, yes. Notwithstanding, can you explain to the viewers what plankton is? Not everyone is a scientist like you and me.'

'Small plants and animals,' Maria says slowly. 'Krill are small animals. They eat small plants.'

I am in danger of getting mired in scientific irrelevance. This is not going for glory; it's sinking in quicksand. I need drama! Excitement! I lean closer. 'So, what makes a girl say to herself, when I grow up I'm going to be a krill scientist?'

Maria puts down her toast. She looks astonished, as if the attraction of krill is self-evident. As if all little girls aspire to a krill-filled future. 'Krill are …' She gazes up at the ceiling as if awaiting a pronouncement from the heavens. When she speaks she has an almost religious fervour. 'Krill are the source of food for almost all the wildlife of Antarctica. Even though they are so small, there are many of them. If you put all the krill in the world together they would weigh more than all the humans.'

I'm about to ask my next question, but it turns out she is just drawing breath.

'Without krill, there is no ecosystem. Once, when I was in a boat, we travelled over a swarm of krill. It was ten kilometres long. And in each metre was up to sixty thousand krill.' She sounds like she is reporting a religious vision – a heavenly choir, no less.

I nod politely, but I'm not going to blow Channel Four out of the water with the weight of krill. And I'd rather not hear what Maxine has to say about how many advertising dollars a krill feature is likely to bring in. My ears burn at the thought. *Human interest, that's what we need.* 'But was there a moment in your past – did something happen, a trauma maybe – that made you turn to krill for salvation?'

Maria shakes her head.

'Did your Sea Monkeys die?' I'm clutching at straws.

'I don't understand.' Maria takes a sip of tea.

When in doubt, it's time for sex … I dredge a memory out of *Polar Fun for Kids*. 'Is it true krill mate for life and raise only one baby?'

A laugh explodes out of Maria's nose. 'No. Where did you hear that?'

Oh yes, that was the emperor penguins – they were on the same page as the krill. I smile. 'Ha, ha.'

'Krill lay thousands of eggs. And they mate with anyone. They are krill.' She says *krill* as someone else might say *French*. As if the word is synonymous with free love and a sophisticated swinging lifestyle. Cocktail parties, wife-swapping and some light bondage between consenting krill doesn't seem out of the question.

'So it's a crustacean orgy down there?'

'No—'

But I have my story. I put up my hand and turn to the camera, gesturing to Rory to come in for a close-up. 'Few people would be aware the icy surface of the Southern Ocean hides a raging orgy to rival the final days of the Roman empire. The culprit? A little-known but common animal known as the Antarctic krill. Krill scientist Maria Becker says the krill will mate with anyone.' I pause for effect. 'Anyone,' I repeat.

'This puts me in mind of that episode in *Days of Our Lives* where the cross-dressing accountant had a forbidden love affair with an ice-skater who was possessed by the devil. Does that sort of thing happen much with krill?' I ask Maria.

'Certainly n—'

'As I thought. So the question in my mind is – does this casual approach to sex start at the bottom of the Antarctic food chain and work its way upwards? Can we expect the same from penguins and seals? Is Antarctica full of swingers?' I pick up a packet of coffee that I placed on the table before I began. 'After all that excitement, I need to relax with a nice cup of Moccona. Join me after the break for more *Cougar on Ice*.'

Maria is chewing on her toast again. She puts it down. 'That is a very sensationalist view of krill.'

'Thank you.' I might be getting the hang of this TV celebrity thing.

'Nice work,' murmurs Rory as we head for the door. 'Commando style, huh? Haven't seen it done before but you could be right.' He pauses. 'Notwithstanding,' he adds.

'Did I …?'

'Yep.'

An Antarctic Mystery has clearly got beneath my skin.

I hadn't noticed my heart was beating triple time but now it settles. Being Cougar is hard work, I need a little time out. 'I'm suffocating in this suit. Let's go outside.'

'Are we allowed?'

I stare at Rory. 'I thought you were an intrepid war correspondent. Don't you just do what you want?'

'Yeah, that's right. I do what I want,' says Rory with mock bravado.

'We won't go far. Just outside the door. For some fresh air.'

'We'd better switch our tags over.' Rory carefully moves our tags from 'in' to 'out.'

We push our way out through the double doors. It's windier than yesterday and overcast and I sigh with relief as the cool air hits my face. Despite the breeze, it isn't exceptionally cold. I'm glad I've got my snowsuit on, but I was expecting something more severe from Antarctica – frostbitten extremities or numb fingers at least. But inside my mittens my hands are warm as toast. Rory wanders a short distance away to get some shots of the station.

I'm happy to be breathing cold air into my lungs. I look out at the rocks and beyond that, the snow, the endless snow. Like the early explorers, I have an urge to discover far horizons, to press on beyond my normal limits, to—

'Hey.'

Rory and I jump like school kids sprung smoking. Lucas has found us.

I open my mouth. 'Sorry, we needed some fresh—'

'Want to go skiing?' Lucas has his goggles pushed up on his forehead and a pair of skis in his hand.

They are nothing like the skis I'm used to. I've skied before, but only on big, heavy skis built for turning; these are about the width of a box of matches.

'You can cross-country ski, can't you?'

I raise my chin. 'Of course, I cross-country skied all the time when I was living with the Inuits. Across the ice-floes, chasing polar bears … You know.'

Lucas flashes his white teeth. 'Good. Here are your boots.' He holds out a pair of shoes that look like runners. 'I checked your size against your shoes.'

I sit on a rock, pull off my snow boots and slide on the shoes. They are light and comfortable, nothing like the ski boots I've worn before. I take the skis from Lucas and place them on the ground. It's not at all obvious how I should put them on.

'You haven't used this system before?' says Lucas.

'Um, no, I'm more used to …'

'New Nordic Norm?'

'Yes, that's it.'

Lucas bends and, taking my boot between his mittens, helps me into my binding.

I stand up; this should be fun. At last, something I can do. 'Okay. Where to?'

'Down to the beach.'

'The beach?' The word seems bizarre in this location.

'It's not far.'

'Okay, great. The beach.'

Lucas turns to Rory. 'And you? Will you ski?'

Rory shakes his head. 'I cross-country skied once in Afghanistan, but it's hard with the camera. Don't want to drop it. I'll catch up.'

I bet Rory has never cross-country skied in his life.

Lucas pushes off and lopes towards the sea, his skis lifting up behind him as he strides away.

I wave to Rory to follow, push off and immediately fall over. Looking around to see if anyone's noticed, I pick myself up and struggle after Lucas. I'm sure I'll get the hang of these skis soon.

After a few minutes I'm at the sea. Lucas is already there, waiting.

'Okay?' Vapour comes out of his mouth as he speaks.

I'm puffing from the exertion of trying to stay upright.

'Are these skis thinner than the ones the Inuits use?' he asks.

I waggle my head vaguely and survey my surroundings. Ice extends out from the shore, at first in a solid mass, but becoming more fractured the further out it goes. Beyond that looms a tall white outline. At first I think it's a boat. As I stare at it, the form takes shape.

'Your first Antarctic iceberg?'

I turn to Lucas, excited, but trying to keep a lid on it. What I want to do is yell and shout – *look, look, an iceberg*. But Cougar probably saw lots of icebergs when she was living with the Inuits. While the iceberg is a fair distance off shore, I can see it clearly. It must be about the size of a two-storey building. 'It's very blue,' I say, as if comparing it to other icebergs I have known. The iceberg is white on top, but its deep cracks glow an iridescent peacock blue.

'Sometimes they're green,' says Lucas. 'When they have organic material inside them. They're beautiful. Like jade.'

I sniff in a *ho hum* way. 'Yes, I've seen green icebergs before.'

Lucas blinks and turns back to the iceberg.

I try to make amends. 'You must like it, coming here. You've been a few times before, haven't you?'

He nods. 'Once you have been, you are addicted. There is nowhere else like it on Earth.' He pauses. 'Although Greenland is good too.'

I'd like to talk to him more about this addiction, but I'm unsure how to do it in a Cougarish way. It's frustrating having to double-think everything I say.

Lucas and I regard the iceberg in silence. He takes off one mitten and, pulling a plastic bag from his pocket, offers it to me. It's the dried fruit I saw him eat on the plane.

I take a piece, bite into it then almost spit it out again. It is beyond disgusting. It's indescribable. My mouth puckers. I'm not sure what to do.

'You've had dried fish before, haven't you?'

Dried fish. I nod and chew enthusiastically. No doubt Cougar ate a lot of dried fish with the Inuits. Somehow I swallow it down.

Rory catches up to us, which gives me a chance to stuff the rest of the dried fish in my pocket without Lucas noticing. He focuses the camera on Lucas, reminding me I am a commando-style interviewer. I lean on my ski poles. 'So tell me about your work. You're a climate scientist. What does that involve?'

Lucas straightens his shoulders. 'I use available data to try and predict future climate trends.' He was more interesting when he was talking about the iceberg.

'What sort of data?' I suppress a yawn. In retrospect, krill are very exciting. At least they have sex. It's going to be hard to find an interesting angle to Lucas's work.

'Air temperatures, sea level rises, ocean temperatures, ice melt, carbon-dioxide levels. I am investigating ... *blah* ... Southern Ocean ... *blah, blah* ... climate of southern Australia.' A veritable torrent of mind-numbing facts gushes from his mouth. He goes on and on. His face is animated, his mittened hands wave to emphasise his points. There's no doubting his own enthusiasm for his studies.

I lean on my poles and gaze at the iceberg. Its azure caves invite exploration. 'Eeargh.' My skis seem to have sensed my distraction: they slide out from under me. I fall on my face with my skis in a tangle behind my head.

Lucas steps over and untangles my skis.

I roll onto my back and climb to my feet. Note to self – stay alert when on cross-country skis.

'Are these skis more slippery than the ones the Inuits use?' asks Lucas.

I brush the snow from my goggles so I can see him. Is he taking the piss?

Lucas chews his lip but his face is solemn.

I mustn't be paranoid.

He slips back into boring scientist mode. '*Blah, blah* ... sea temperatures, *blah, blah* ... carbon dioxide.'

I want to scream with frustration. It's like he's giving a lecture to a captive audience of scientists. He clearly has no idea of the attention span of your average Channel Five viewer. Commando style isn't working – this is like jumping out of the trenches and being felled by an encyclopaedia. At least Hornby knows how to appeal to a broad audience. *Climate science is crap* – there's a sound bite you can work with. I know what Cougar would do next – build on the Hornby angle, get some controversy going. I steel myself.

'But isn't the science all fairly dodgy?'

Chapter Seventeen

I take the penguin option

My words echo off the ice. *Dodgy, dodgy, dodgy …*

Lucas stops abruptly in mid-stream. 'Dodgy?' He sounds astonished.

I would apologise, but I'm Cougar and I'm not here to make friends. 'Well, inconclusive. Like the Minister says. Scientists say one thing and then it's another. It changes every year. No-one seems to know what's going on. Some people say nothing's happening at all. Or it's a natural cycle. Or even that it's getting colder. What do you say to that?'

Lucas pulls at his beard like a Viking debating whether to attack.

I take an involuntary step backwards, almost tangling my skis, but manage to stay upright.

Lucas takes a deep breath. 'There will never be complete certainty. Climate science isn't like that. The vast majority of scientists agree … *blah* … carbon dioxide levels … *blah, blah* … rising for the last two hundred years, dramatically so for the last—'

I want to yell, *Give it to me in thirty seconds and try to mention sex.* I don't doubt his sincerity, but where's the story? I enliven things the only way I can. 'Would you like a Tim Tam?' I unzip my little backpack and offer him the packet.

'Thank you.' He takes one, but doesn't eat it, instead waving it around to emphasise his points. 'The last sixty years in Australia have been the hottest in a thousand years. Bushfires are getting worse.'

I'm so tired, and Lucas's voice is so soothing, my eyes droop …

'Droughts, floods and storms … *blah, blah, blah* …'

'Don't forget the frogs, pestilence, hail and locusts,' says a familiar voice behind me.

I jump. I've never slept standing up before. Let alone on skis. It's a wonder I'm still upright. Adrian is standing next to me with a large camera around his neck.

He smiles at Lucas. 'Just joking.'

Lucas doesn't smile back.

Adrian glances at me, then out to sea.

My inner sloths pout sadly. I'm glad Adrian will be gone soon. It's hard to know how to behave around him. I'm aiming for a cool, dignified and in control media star aura but it's taking it out of me.

Lucas's mouth tightens. 'Where is the Minister?' Clearly the Minister and, by extension, his minder are his least favourite people.

'He's coming,' says Adrian. 'Sorry. Don't let me interrupt. I just wanted to get a few photos.' He looks out to sea, raising the camera to his eye.

I follow his gaze. The iceberg moves to the left. A current must have sprung up. But Adrian, Rory and Lucas are drifting to the left as well. How do they do that? *Aargh.* It's not them, it's me. My skis are sliding backwards.

Rory follows me with the camera as I drift backwards towards the sea.

Adrian turns and points his camera towards me too.

Aargh. Aargh. How do you stop these things? Are they going to film me while I slide backwards into the ocean?

'Dig your poles in!' Only Lucas pushes off and skis towards me.

I manage to plant my poles behind me and arrest my slide in a cool, dignified and in control manner. Digging them in, I plant my bottom on top. Now I won't go anywhere surely.

As my heart settles, I watch Lucas glide towards me. How can I find a sexy angle on climate change? Every time he talks about it, I drift off. *Literally.* Surely there's a kernel of excitement beneath all the waffle. I need to find it.

He schusses to a stop beside me.

'Just came here for a better view,' I murmur.

Lucas seems to buy it.

Rory stomps towards us with his camera and aims it at Lucas again.

'So, what's happening here in Antarctica? Climate-change wise.' I say.

'The polar regions are changing faster than any other area on earth,' says Lucas.

I nod. 'Of course.'

'In the Arctic, where I do a lot of my research, the glaciers are melting rapidly. It's the same on the Antarctic Peninsula.'

Melting. That's the angle I'm after. In *An Antarctic Mystery* the crew sail their boat right past the South Pole. 'Do you think we'll be able to sail to the South Pole one day?'

Lucas bites his lip. 'Antarctica is made of land, so, no.'

I flush inside my balaclava. How was I supposed to know that?

'But maybe, if the sea rises enough ...' He sounds like a kindly primary school teacher trying to help out a slow student.

I'm glad Adrian didn't catch this exchange. 'So, the ice is melting?'

'Yes. In fact, it is estimated the Antarctic ice sheet is contributing two tenths of a millimetre per year to sea level rise.' Lucas says this with a breathless air.

'Two tenths? Of a millimetre?' I repeat.

'Hard to believe, isn't it?'

'That doesn't sound like a lot.'

'Two tenths of a millimetre is a lot.'

'Lucas, I'm sorry, but two tenths of a millimetre is not a lot. Not to your average Channel Five viewer. Even a millimetre would not be a lot. Even a centimetre. Metres, that would be a lot.' This is the worst interview ever. Mack Decker is probably getting shots of glaciers falling into the sea and polar bears clinging to melting icebergs up there in the Arctic. My stomach jolts at the thought of Maxine waiting for my program to blow his out of the water. Two tenths of a millimetre isn't going to do it.

Lucas is talking again. ' ... seventy per cent of the world's water. If the Antarctic ice melted it would raise the global sea level by sixty metres.' He seems unsure if these facts will meet with my approval.

'Sixty metres.' I perk up. 'Did you get that, Rory?'

He gives me a thumbs up.

Encouraged, Lucas regains his mojo. 'Current climate models estimate ... twenty-four per cent decrease in Antarctic sea ice ... loss of sea ice reduces reflection ... ability of the ocean to absorb carbon dioxide and heat ... globally significant ... uptake of carbon dioxide ... circulation of the deep ocean ... and *blah, blah, blah, blah* ...' He goes on for a while. 'Did you get all that?'

I'm tempted to say he lost me at *current*, but it seems cruel. 'Excellent. Fascinating.' Adrian glances in my direction at this point and I'm sure I'm making an outstanding impression.

None of this will make the cut unfortunately. While undoubtedly important, it's not all that interesting. It's such a pity there are no polar bears here. I bet Maxine didn't know that when she gave the show the green light. Maybe we can do an infographic showing how polar bears would be affected if they did live here …

Voices drift across the ice. Hornby and the station leader are walking towards us. Hornby is probably completing his fact-finding mission with an iceberg viewing before flying back to Australia to announce that all is well. Antarctica is still covered in ice and there is no cause for concern.

Adrian walks back to join them. The Minister points at the iceberg and he and the station leader pose for a photograph in front of it. Adrian snaps away – he's in his element.

Lucas glares at them, apparently wishing he could smite them with his Viking axe.

I look from Lucas to the Minister. *Here* is a great story – drama, conflict, tension. Sadly there's no sex, but you can't have it all. 'Why don't you go on camera debating the Minister about climate change? We can do it now. It will air in Australia tomorrow.'

Lucas grimaces. 'I would love to. But, no.'

'You heard what he said in the airport. Don't you want to set the record straight?'

'I can't take on the Minister. I'd be hung, drawn and quartered.'

'Well … maybe I could.'

'You would do that?'

I shrug. 'It would be great television. I don't know what to say though.'

'I told you all about it.' Lucas sounds baffled. 'Say that.'

'Oh. Yes.' I try to remember what he said. 'Actually, it might be too complex for my viewers. They're not scientists like you.' I pause. 'And me,' I add.

Lucas rubs his head through his hood. 'It is not complex.'

'Not to you and me. But my audience …'

'But that's the trouble. No-one takes the time to understand. And it is not that hard. It means Hornby just needs to plant one small seed of doubt and people leap on it. Because they don't want to think and they don't want to change their lifestyle. They would rather not know.'

I feel guilty, as if I'm one of those people. Come to think of it, I am. Whenever I see the words 'climate change' I turn the page. I decide to change the topic. 'Why don't we talk about penguins? You can't go wrong with penguins.'

Lucas's look places me firmly in the ranks of the people who don't want to think. But it's hardly my fault climate change is so boring and penguins so cute.

Behind us, a red-suited figure runs up to the Minister's party. Raised voices drift towards us.

'Sounds like trouble,' I say.

Lucas seems cheered by the prospect. 'Okay, let's find the penguins.'

Penguins – yay. I practically skip with excitement, before I remember I am Cougar Gale. No doubt I have encountered more penguins than I've had lentil patties. And skipping on skis is a bad idea. 'Yes,' I say. 'I suppose so. We'd better do the penguins.'

Lucas shoots me a strange look.

He probably thinks I have multiple personality disorder. I must try harder to stay in character.

'We can ski there.' He points to a rocky peak a couple of hundred metres away, joined to the mainland by ice. 'There is a penguin colony on the island.'

We ski across the snow to the island. Lucas is soon far ahead of me. I follow in his tracks trying not to think about the deep and freezing water beneath. While the surface seems solid there are cracks here and there, with aqua ice gleaming through. I ski over them quickly. The snow squeaks beneath me as I accelerate. It's much finer than the snow in Chamonix; like talcum powder. As we approach the island I hear a raucous squawking, like kids in a schoolyard.

Rory trudges up behind me. 'Phe-ew.'

My nose crinkles as the acrid, fishy smell reaches it. Penguin colonies seem so clean and serene in the wildlife movies. Who'd have guessed they'd smell and sound like a fish market on a hard day's trading?

The clouds are clearing and as the sun hits the water beyond the ice banks, it shines a translucent blue. It looks good enough to jump into – if it wasn't for the temperature. And the leopard seals. I wouldn't want to encounter one of those. *Polar Fun for Kids* told me leopard seals have large sharp teeth and weigh up to 600 kilograms. Further Googling revealed that a member of Shackleton's party was attacked by one when camping on the ice and an Antarctic researcher was killed by a leopard seal a few years ago. I resolve to stay alert for large, spotty seals.

'That's close enough,' says Lucas.

We stop, some distance from the colony.

The penguins have been busy – squawking, carrying rocks around and flapping their wings – but now they pause and stare at us curiously. I feel like a concert goer arriving late to a performance. 'Sorry, don't mind us. Carry on.'

Despite being incredibly noisy and smelly, they are as devastatingly cute as I'd expected. Some are sitting on eggs, while others guard fluffy grey chicks. *Aww. This* is what our target audience tunes in for. I signal to Rory to film.

'These lovely ...' I hold up my hand for Rory to stop as I inspect the penguins, which are small with black heads and back and a white stomach. I run through the list of penguins I memorised from *Polar Fun*. I know they're not emperor penguins. That leaves gentoo penguins, chinstrap penguins, macaroni penguins, king penguins, rockhopper penguins and—

'Adelie penguins,' says Lucas.

'I knew that. Just clearing my throat.' I cough. 'These lovely Adelie penguins are building their nests out of rocks.' Two penguins peck at each other. 'Competition for mates is fierce.' That's what David Attenborough always says.

Through Lucas's goggles, I discern a quizzical look.

I must have said something wrong. I replay what I said – *competition for mates* ... But if the penguins have chicks and eggs, I suppose they have already mated. 'Just warming up.' I pitch my voice to a deep, mellifluous level. 'These lovely Adelie penguins are raising their chicks here in the harshest place on earth, Antarctica. The cast of *Neighbours* could take a few lessons from these guys. If you thought life was tough on Ramsey Street, you should see the bickering going on here.' I gesture for Rory to zoom in on three penguins that are flapping their wings and biting at each other. 'Love triangle,' I whisper dramatically. 'I suspect one of them is an ex-wife trying to reinstate her place in the family mansion.'

Lucas folds his arms. Clearly, he's underwhelmed, but there's not much I can do about that. I'm in the entertainment biz, after all.

An invisible signal seems to spread through the colony. Several penguins run to the edge of the ice shelf and line up, like kids at a swimming pool. It's a drop of a couple of metres into the water and, considering the penguins are only about half a metre high, it must seem like a long way down.

'The penguins are contemplating a swim.' I use my best David Attenborough voice. 'They are a little tentative, I expect it's cold in there. And let's not forget the leopard seals. The sea is swarming with savage killers.' I decide to get some informal chat happening. 'What do you think, Lucas? Can we expect to see a penguin smeared in fish and tied to an iceberg by its love rival as a leopard seal approaches?'

Rory swings the camera to Lucas.

Lucas stares at me wordlessly.

Rory swings the camera back to me.

'Guess you missed that episode of *Days of Our Lives*.'

The penguins procrastinate madly, jostle each other and eventually succeed in pushing one of their number over the edge into the water.

I laugh loudly, then catch myself. 'Cracks me up every time, the way they do that.'

'Where have you seen Adelie penguins before?' asks Lucas.

'Oh, when I was in, um ...' I have no idea where they live apart from Antarctica – possibly nowhere. 'Oh look,' I cry.

Twenty black heads peer over the edge after their comrade and, apparently deciding it's safe, they take the plunge. It reminds me of how Marley and I used to muck around at the water hole, pushing and shoving until one of us lost balance and leapt into the muddy water below. The penguins hurl themselves out of the water like flying fish as they swim around. They're exuberant, turbo-charged.

Lucas seems to have forgotten his question, which is good.

'Looks like the water's mighty fine,' I say to camera. I haven't watched many nature documentaries, but I know the script.

As I gaze out at the floating iceberg, it reminds me of a drawing in *An Antarctic Mystery* of a ship stranded on top of the iceberg. I'm yet to discover how the ship made it up there. 'Aaeeargh.' I'm sliding again. I'm sliding towards the water. This is bad. The water is cold. And full of leopard seals. I try to push my skis out into a snow plough but they won't go. The snow is shiny and firm here. I attempt to stick my poles in, but they slide away. I'm going faster. The water's getting closer. *Bang.* Something hits me and I fall face-first into the snow. When I lift my head I see Lucas lying on the snow next to me.

Clearing the snow from my goggles, I summon indignation. 'I was trying to get a closer look at the penguins. There was no need to knock me over.'

Lucas stands and brushes the snow off his suit. The light is behind him and I can't see his face. 'You were about to go in the water.'

'I was going to stop.' I struggle to my feet, making sure to cross my skis to prevent further slippage.

'That's not what it looked like.'

'Well I was.'

'If I hadn't stopped you, you'd be in the water now.'

'Rubbish.'

Lucas snorts.

Rory has run after us. He focuses the camera on me and points at my snowsuit, reminding me it's time for more product placement. I unzip the top of my suit, pull out a tablet computer, which is luckily undamaged, and hold it up. 'This tablet is great for taking penguin photos.' I click and hold the image towards the camera. 'Aw, look at that and you can update straight to Facebook.' I click to send but nothing happens.

'No reception here,' says Lucas.

'I knew that, I was just demonstrating. Edit that part out,' I say to Rory.

He nods.

It's time for my signoff. I assume a serious expression and signal to Rory for a close-up. 'You can join me after the break for lots more cute penguins. This is Cougar on Ice. Notwithstanding.'

'Nice one,' says Rory.

'Interesting approach,' says Lucas.

Do I detect a whiff of sarcasm? If so, I don't care, because contrary to what he says, you can't go wrong with cute penguins.

Chapter Eighteen

I find out some surprising penguin facts

A small group is huddled outside the station when we get back. The Minister is pacing up and down in front of them. In his red snowsuit, he looks like a Santa Claus whose sleigh-ride's running late.

As it turns out, this is not far off the mark.

'Ridiculous. Bloody ridiculous. What sort of show are you running here?' he says to Mike, the station leader. Hornby has a deranged, exhausted look I fear I may share. His goggles are pulled up and his eyes are redder and wrinklier than they were yesterday. Perhaps he didn't sleep much either.

'I have a meeting with the PM tomorrow,' he says. 'We're discussing the new emissions trading scheme. I haven't got time for this. I've got a conference call with the US Minister for Science in five minutes. Adrian, sort it out and let me know when we're flying.' He stalks off into the Red Shed.

Unlike his boss, Adrian is unperturbed. 'Let me know if anything changes.' He wanders off without further comment.

'What's up?' Lucas says to Mike as we approach.

Mike, who has the *de rigueur* flowing beard, nods at Rory and me. 'It's too warm to fly. The runway's soft. He's doing his nut, but it's out of my hands. We can't take off while it's like this. CASA would have me for breakfast if anything happened.'

'So, this is unusually warm?' I ask.

'Yeah. We didn't get a good freeze last night because of the cloud cover and now it's up to two degrees. It's not safe to use the runway if the temperature's above minus five. It's designed for ice. The plane took off from Hobart but we've had to turn it around.'

It had never occurred to me that warm weather would stop the plane flying.

'Worst part is, I'm not sure when it's going to get any colder,' says Mike. 'Last thing I want is a pissed-off Minister hanging around the station, but the forecast is for more of the same. Might need to think about getting him on a flight through McMurdo, I don't reckon he'll be up for the two-week boat trip.'

I glance towards Adrian's back, which is disappearing into the station. I'm not sure if I'm pleased or not at the thought of him staying. I turn back to Mike. 'So, my producer and stylist are still in Hobart?' I say in my Cougar voice.

Mike sighs, clearly over his VIP visitors. 'We'll get them out here when we can.'

Rory and I exchange a glance. I'm sure we're both thinking the same thing – *no rush*.

Mike goes inside.

'So do you have enough penguin material?' says Lucas.

'Oh yes. How cute were they?' I catch Rory's look and tone it down. 'I never get tired of penguins, no matter how many I see.'

'I'm going to get a few filler shots.' Rory wanders off towards a snow drift.

'You'd never imagine they're the Jekyll and Hyde of the animal kingdom, would you?' says Lucas.

Jekyll? Hyde? This doesn't make any sort of sense. I hope this isn't the polar bear conversation all over again. 'No, you wouldn't.'

Lucas shakes his head. 'So cute, yet so depraved.'

I stare at him. Are we still talking about those sweet little penguins? What do they do – turn into axe murderers after dark? He must be pulling my leg but his face seems serious.

'You know the story, don't you?'

'Mm. Shocking. Just shocking.' Vague agreement worked for polar bears; I'm hoping it will do the same for depraved penguins. I need to line up Rory to interrupt me when I get into these situations. I glance in his direction, but he's absorbed in capturing some sky shots.

'I'm not surprised people only spoke of it in whispers for a hundred years,' says Lucas.

I give him a sharp look, but his face is grave. I have a brainwave. 'Wait.' I put up my hand. 'We need to get this on camera. Rory,' I call. 'Come over here.'

Rory ambles over. 'Ready to roll.'

'I'm going to play dumb, okay?' I say to Lucas, 'So you can fill the audience in.' I turn to the camera. 'It's rumoured the Adelie penguins have a dark secret. A secret hidden for over a hundred years. It is only in these more permissive times it has finally come to light. Tell us about the dark side of penguins, Lucas.'

'Are you sure you want to know?'

'If there's depravity going on here in Antarctica, my viewers need to know about it.'

Lucas ignores the camera, his eyes on me. 'Well … Way back in 1910, Scott's team came to Antarctica.'

I nod. 'So tragic. All dead.'

'No, not all of them,' says Lucas.

'I meant they're all dead now.'

'Oh. But it was only the team who made the final expedition to the South Pole that died in Antarctica. Others stayed behind doing scientific work ….'

I sniff, as though this isn't all news to me.

'Some of them ended up spending an entire winter in a snow cave when their ship was blocked by sea ice and unable to pick them up.'

An entire winter? In a snow cave? This strikes me as almost too dreadful to be true. I turn to the camera. 'Imagine spending months and months in complete darkness, living in a snow cave. How awful.'

Lucas nods. 'It's hard to believe, isn't it? They had nothing to eat except seals. By the time they came out they were covered in seal blubber from head to toe. In the before and after photographs they are like different men. Before, they were very Victorian. Well-groomed and well-dressed. After … you can imagine.'

I screw up my nose. 'I bet they never wanted to see another seal again after that.'

Lucas nods. 'No. But that wasn't the worst part.'

It's hard to imagine what could beat spending an entire winter in a snow cave. By now, I'm envisaging cannibalism and satanic rituals. We might need a special late night feature – *Cougar on Ice Uncut. Charlie Oscar India … Unicorn.*

'The worst part was they had to watch the depravity of the Adelie penguins.' Lucas shakes his head. 'The winter was harsh, but the penguins were harsher. George Levick, a member of the team, was so shocked by what he saw he wrote his report in Greek, so only scholars could read it. He didn't want to horrify anyone who came across his notes inadvertently.'

He must have been the easily shocked type. Those Victorians … 'Are we talking about sexual depravity?'

'I'm afraid so. When Levick got back to England he wrote a book about the penguins, but his observations on their sexual behaviour were left out. They were too shocking. Women might have swooned. It would have destroyed the penguins' image.'

'Okay, I think my viewers are intrigued. What were those naughty penguins doing that was so shocking?' I laugh in a Cougarish way.

'Are you sure you want to hear?' His face is straight.

'You have to tell us. What were they up to?'

Lucas lowers his voice. 'Homosexuality, sexual abuse of chicks, rape, even … necrophilia.'

'Necrophilia? Those sweet little penguins?' I shake my head, over-acting for the camera. 'I refuse to believe that. It must have been a mistake. I mean, I've had times myself when—' I pull myself up. 'Cut that part, Rory.'

Lucas grimaces. 'They look cute, but …'

'I am never going to see a penguin in the same way again.'

'It is horrifying what they do when we're not watching. We have cameras filming the colony on the island …'

'And they're still at it?'

He nods solemnly.

I turn to the camera. 'There you have it folks, from an expert – the penguin colony is a swingers party from hell. That's a wrap.'

Lucas's face cracks into a cheeky smile.

It makes me uneasy, as if I've had something pulled over me.

'I have some work to do,' he murmurs.

'Yes, yes, off you go. By all means.' I give him a queenly wave as he goes inside. 'Don't you ever leave me alone with him again,' I say to Rory. 'I feel like he's trying to catch me out.'

'Hot stuff though,' says Rory. 'The secret life of penguins. I never would have guessed.'

'Yeah, it is, isn't it? Depraved krill and more depraved penguins … I think we've got our first episode. Let's call it "Sex on Ice".' *Sierra Oscar India*. 'Maxine's going to love it.'

Chapter Nineteen

I am an elegant rock-climber

After lunch – pumpkin soup, salmon quiche and apple crumble – I lie on my bed digesting my meal like a carpet snake with a possum in its stomach. I'd end up the shape of a bowling ball if I spent all winter here; Cherie's cooking is way too good to resist.

I'm drowsy after my restless night, but the dazzling light outside doesn't allow for the possibility of an afternoon nap. I suppose I could draw the blind, but it seems like sacrilege to cut myself off from the snow and the sky.

An Antarctic Mystery is in easy reach, so I pick it up and flick through it …

> No more appropriate scene for the wonderful and terrible adventures which I am about to relate could be imagined …

My eyes are drawn to the window again. It's strange being so warm and well-fed when Antarctica is just out there. It doesn't seem right. I should be experiencing it. Like Scott. Like Amundsen. Like all those other people who have been drawn to this vast southern wild.

Yes, Antarctica summons me and I must obey. My igloo beckons.

Heaving myself off the bed, I open the door to my room and peer out – the coast is clear. Walking quickly I head for the entrance.

'Hey, Summer.'

I jump.

Rory bounds down the hallway. 'Have you seen the rock-climbing wall? We should get some shots of you climbing. You can introduce the next segment of the show from the top of the wall. It is totally a Cougar thing to do – getting in some training, yeah?'

I sigh, drawing my eyes away from the sparkling white outside the window. 'But I haven't rock-climbed before.'

'Haven't you? I figured you would have. Being an igloo-builder.'

'Is there anyone else around?'

Rory shakes his head. 'No, it's empty. Come on.'

'I don't need to wear my puffy suit, do I? It's so hot in here.' Who would have thought heat exhaustion would turn out to be one of my biggest problems in Antarctica?

Rory looks me up and down.

I'm wearing my zip off pants and the dugong T-shirt again. My large collection of thermal layers are hanging up near the entrance with my snow suit.

'Why don't you put a balaclava on?'

'Won't that be weird?'

'Nah, you'll look like that Russian rebel girl band.'

'If you say so. We'd better get some product placement in. What haven't we done yet?'

'How about the Jimmy Choos?'

'The Jimmy Choos? Rock-climbing?' The Jimmy Choo shoes were always going to be a tough call in Antarctica, but they've paid their money and I need to get them in somewhere.

'This is as good as it's going to get. You're not going to wear them in the snow, are you? It'll look good. Sexy.'

'You think? Okay. Hang on a sec, I'll grab them.' Ducking into my room, I slide the shoes onto my feet and pick up the rope I purchased at Outdoor World. With the rope over one shoulder and the silver jangly things the guy sold me over my other shoulder I feel impressive – woman versus wild. And Rory was right about the stilettos – they add a risqué dominatrix touch. Looking in the mirror, I strike a pose, one hand on my hip. I look ruggedly sexy. Cougar had better watch out. I pull the balaclava on and, Rory is right, I'm just like a singer in a Russian rebel girl band.

Rory inspects me as I come out into the corridor, taking in my accessories and my spiky footwear. 'Wow. Serious bondage. You know what to do with all that stuff?'

'Yes.' I twirl, making all my equipment jangle. 'See?'

Rory whistles. 'Good jingling. Hang on a sec, walk down the corridor and I'll film you.'

Once Rory is set up, I mince down the hall, concentrating hard to avoid falling off my heels. I've never been a high-heels girl – I graduated from hippie sandals to sensible corporate footwear – so it's a challenge. The rope makes me feel sporty though, very competent and gung ho. I should incorporate it into my outfit more often. Equipment jangling, I strut past Rory into the rock-climbing room, coming to a halt some distance from the wall. My heels are already sore and my calves aching from the effort of staying upright. I don't know how some women do this high-heels thing.

The rock-climbing wall, however, appears fairly easy – a number of chunky handholds bolted to a blue surface. I swivel to face Rory. 'I always wear my Jimmy Choos when I rock-climb. A girl needs to feel stylish to perform at her best.'

Rory gives me a thumbs up.

'So ...' I look up to the top. Surely my rope is supposed to be attached to something? I survey the wall for a while, but no solution presents itself.

'Climb whenever you're ready,' says Rory.

I tie the rope around my waist, as if I know what I'm doing.

'Take one of those things off your strap and hold it like you're about to do something with it.' Rory gestures at a wire contraption with a semi-circular head that retracts when I pull it. 'How do you use that?'

'Hm?' I retract and release the head a few times. 'Oh, you mmm ...'

'Pardon? Didn't catch that.'

I say the first thing that comes into my head. 'You stick it in a hole.'

'Oh, yeah, I see how it works.'

I'm glad one of us does. I stride towards the wall, wire thingy in my hand, the rope trailing behind me.

Rory follows me with the camera. 'Looking hot, Cougar. Climb when ready.'

Although the rock-climbing wall looked easy from a distance, once I'm close it seems alarmingly vertical. I pause at the base, my eyes travelling up. It is also disturbingly high.

'Good,' says Rory. 'Nice dramatic pause. Go.'

I find the first handhold and pull myself up. This isn't hard at all; in fact I think I have a natural aptitude for it. I find another handhold and haul on it, the rope dangling from my waist like an ineffectual tail. This can't be the way it's supposed to be done. Hanging on requires upper body strength. I puff and pant as I manoeuvre myself towards the next one. As I do so, I catch a glimpse of my foot. It's very elegant. Perhaps I will become a high-heeled rock-climbing girl. Adrian would be impressed. It's a pity he's not here. I drag myself up a bit more. 'Is this far enough?' The ground is a long way down already.

Rory tilts his head on one side. 'I suppose if I get low and shoot upwards …' He kneels. 'Okay, rolling.'

I swivel my head around to the camera. 'Cooped up indoors, it's important to stay fit. That's why, when I'm in Antarctica, I climb at every opportunity.' I pause to catch my breath. 'Once I'm out in the snow, amongst the crevasses, I want to know my skills are honed, ready for a rescue or to save myself if necessary. In my next segment of *Cougar on Ice* I'll be venturing further afield, to a remote weather station. The scientists are trying to find out if Antarctica is getting hotter …' A drop of sweat trickles out from beneath my balaclava. I hang on with one hand and wipe it off. 'It certainly seems that way. If the ice melts—' A voice from the corridor outside interrupts me. I cling on; hoping no-one will come in. I'm pretty sure I'm not doing this rock-climbing thing right.

'What you are doing is unethical.' It is Lucas. 'I don't know how you can—'

Another voice speaks. 'It's not me who's unethical, it's you lot – spreading fear amongst the kiddies, beating the story up so there's money for more unnecessary research. We pour funds into it and what do we get – the temperature is going up in some areas and down in others? So what? I've said it before and I'll say it again, climate science is crap.'

It's Hornby.

'Do you pat a growling dog?' Lucas doesn't wait for a reply. 'No, you don't because it is likely to bite. *Likely*, not certain. You analyse the risk and you act accordingly. When over ninety per cent of scientists believe the evidence shows the earth is warming, isn't that enough reason to act?'

'If ninety per cent of lemmings jump over a cliff, do you follow them? The climate has always been changing. Humans aren't driving this change,' Hornby sneers.

'You have your head in the sand.'

There is some muffled speech before the corridor goes quiet.

'Did you get that?' As I look at Rory my hands slip. 'Argh.' *I am falling, falling, falling* … I land on the mat with a thump. Lucky I was only one metre up.

'I think so. Are you okay?' He fiddles with the buttons on his camera. 'Yes, got it. Great fall. Still rolling.'

I scramble to my feet. Miraculously, my shoes are intact. I point my toe towards the camera, put my hand on my hip and adjust my balaclava, which has ridden up over my mouth. 'When rock-climbing in Antarctica it's important to put your best foot forward.' I catch a movement out of the corner of my eye.

Lucas is leaning against the door frame.

The camera is on, so I try to ignore him. 'In my Jimmy Choos, I'm ready to go from rock-climbing wall to nightclub. Come back for more *Cougar on Ice* after the break. Notwithstanding.'

I hear a muffled snort from the doorway.

'That's a wrap.' Rory coughs.

When I glance back at the door, Lucas has gone. I stare at the space where he used to be. Was he laughing at me?

'I think I might be getting a cold,' says Rory. 'My throat's all scratchy.'

'It's just the central heating,' I say.

Once I've ditched Rory, I double back around and head for the door again. It's a few hours until dinner and my igloo demands attention. Maybe I can finish it off before Adrian leaves tomorrow. A shipshape igloo will prove to him I am an excellent project manager.

As I pass the common room I see Maria inside. She is dressed in shorts and a singlet and doing some kind of workout. Dancing from side to side, she kicks one of her legs in the air in an action that could take your head off if you were in the wrong spot. As I gawk, she puts her hands to the ground and throws her legs over her head. *Wow.* Before I get over this she is spinning on the floor in a squat, pushing with one hand and cartwheeling over like Bruce Lee on steroids.

I'm about to tell myself not to get on the wrong side of her, when I recall that I already have. I sneak off towards the entrance door before she spies me and attacks.

It's a little risky going out on my own at this time of day, but what are they going to do if they find me out of bounds anyway – lock me in my room? Maybe I could be deported; that wouldn't be good …

I avert my eyes from the tag board, push open the doors and run towards my rocky outcrop, expecting a whistle or a yell at any moment, but none comes. As I come over the rise, my fledgling igloo looks less impressive than it did this morning. In my absence several blocks have crumbled or blown away. The snow clearly needs heavy stomping to compact it before I cut any more blocks. Placing my phone back on its snow perch, I press 'record' and march around in circles in the area I have designated as my quarry. *Hut, two, three, four. Hut, two, three, four* … I raise my knees high for extra stomp power and swing my arms like a soldier on parade. After twenty minutes of this, I'm panting hard and the snow is firmer underfoot. Time to chop out more blocks.

Three hours later, my igloo has risen to waist height. The blocks are holding together, but despite my best efforts to make the walls slope inwards – as instructed by the website – they are almost vertical. I follow a mental line upwards … If I continue on my current trajectory, my igloo will be over ten metres tall – a skyscraper – and getting the roof on will be tricky. I'm glad Adrian's not watching as this is clearly a project which is suffering from lack of a plan.

'Where's your Gantt chart, Summer?' I imagine him saying.

Obviously, I should have done one, but I thought I could wing it.

Sinking to the snow, I examine my construction. Despite its shortcomings, I am fond of it. It might not be the finest igloo in the world but it's *my* igloo and how many people can say that? Considering the last thing I built was a Lego castle at the age of twelve, I'm doing alright. Once the Christmas decorations are up, it will be a haven of beauty. I'll put tinsel around the doorway, light some tea candles inside, put up the little plastic tree … Mary has the Christmas decorations, but she'll be here before then. I make a peace sign at my phone, then remember I'm wearing mittens.

Turning my phone camera off, I stand up. I can do no more. And it's almost time for dinner.

I sneak back inside the station and stamp the snow from my boots. As I head for the drying room, I freeze. Someone's there.

Lucas is crouched on the floor beneath the snowsuits, peering into a cardboard box. As I watch, he opens a tin of fish, scoops out a teaspoonful and lowers it into the box. I hear a rustling sound.

Lucas sees me. He stops still, teaspoon in hand, looking sheepish.

I expect I'm looking sheepish too. I still have my outdoor gear on. It's obvious I've been outside without permission. *Sprung.* Well, it's too late now.

I walk over to the box. Inside is a dark-grey bundle of fluff with a pointy black beak and black button eyes. An Adelie penguin chick. It's so cute. 'Can I touch it?'

Lucas shakes his head. 'No. I don't want it to get too used to people. I shouldn't have it here but I found it abandoned on the ice. I just want to feed it up for a little while before I release it.'

'Why was it abandoned?'

'One of its parents must have died. Maybe a leopard seal. It's a team effort looking after a chick. Sometimes this happens if one of them doesn't make it back.'

The penguin opens its beak as Lucas offers it more fish.

'I'd appreciate it if you didn't mention this to anyone,' says Lucas.

'But it would make great television. You with the penguin.'

Lucas shakes his head. 'We're not supposed to interfere. I should have let nature take its course, but …'

'It was too cute?'

'It's almost ready to fledge. It seemed a shame.'

It seems that even Lucas is not immune to cute, waddling penguins. 'I won't tell anyone.'

He offers the penguin more fish. 'Thank you.' He finally registers that I've been outside. 'Where have you been?' he says sternly.

'I have to build this igloo. It's very important.'

'Well' – he takes another teaspoonful of fish, then shrugs – 'I won't tell if you won't.'

Chapter Twenty
I impress Adrian

Dinner – nut steak for me, beef casserole for the others – is slightly strained. Maria ignores me, Lucas seems preoccupied – perhaps he's worried about his illicit penguin-feeding – and even Rory isn't his usual cheery self. He looks a little pale.

Lucas's book, *The Worst Journey in the World*, rests beside him on the table.

'What's that about?' I ask, in an effort to make conversation.

'It's a memoir of Scott's expedition. Written by the assistant zoologist, Apsley Cherry-Garrard.' Lucas toys with his casserole and seems disinclined to go on.

Silence falls again apart from the clatter of cutlery.

'Is it good?' This conversation is flowing like a billabong in drought.

'Yes, it is.' Lucas takes a potato and chews it slowly and just when I think our discussion has come to an end, he speaks again. 'The most interesting part is not Scott's journey to the pole, it is the expedition to gather the emperor penguin eggs.'

I chew my nut steak, mentally cursing Cougar's vegetarianism, and nod encouragingly.

'The emperor penguin nests in winter, so they skied from their base in complete darkness. For five weeks the temperatures were so cold Cherry-Garrard's teeth froze and shattered and their sweat turned to ice. Their sleeping bags were frozen when they crawled into them and they were frostbitten all over.'

Shattered teeth. Frozen sweat. Eating nut steak in a warm dining room now seems the height of luxury. I swallow. 'Why did they want the emperor penguin eggs?'

'They were thought to be important to the study of the evolutionary link between reptiles and birds.'

'And were they?'

Lucas shakes his head. 'By the time they got the egg specimens back to London, the science had moved on and no-one wanted them.'

'Wow.'

The sheer futility of the exercise defies further comment and we finish our meal in silence.

Just when I'm thinking of escaping to my room, Mike gets to his feet. 'You know what tonight is, don't you?'

A barracuda-like smile spreads across Maria's face. 'Trivia night.'

Surely not. I hate trivia nights. I can never remember which footballer scored a life-changing goal in 1978 or what singer was top of the pops in 1987. Some people are not good at storing random facts.

Up at the top table, Adrian smiles too. Adrian is good with trivia.

'The teams are ...' Mike rattles off a list of names and chairs scrape as everyone rearranges themselves.

I end up at a table with Cherie, Hornby and Adrian.

'The topic for tonight is ...' – Mike pauses – 'glaciology!'

'Yay. Lucky us having you on our team,' says Cherie.

Hornby grins. 'Excellent. I like to be on the winning team.'

Adrian stares at me with a neutral expression. 'Me too.'

A swarm of krill occupy my stomach.

'We need a name,' says Cherie.

'Krill orgy.' The words fall from my mouth.

At the table next to us Lucas, Maria, Rory and a bearded scientist whose name I haven't caught are in a huddle. Clearly they are the A team.

Rory widens his eyes at me and twitches his head.

I'm not sure what he's suggesting. Faint? Vomit? Flee?

He twitches his head again.

Claim possession by a demon?

'Question one,' says Mike. 'What is the name given to the loss of ice and snow from a glacier system?'

Cherie and Hornby stare at me expectantly. 'I'll write down your answer,' whispers Cherie.

'Um.'

A whispered conference takes place at the table next to me. Out of the corner of my eye, I see Lucas write something.

Cherie has her pencil poised. 'Quick, he's about to go onto the next question.'

I feel a light brush on my leg. I look down.

Lucas's hand is draped casually over the back of his chair. Beneath the table a piece of paper rests against my leg. A word is written on it.

I look back up quickly. 'Mm, sorry. It's ablation of course,' I say in a bored tone.

Adrian's eyebrows twitch in a suspicious way.

I ignore him.

'Next question,' says Mike. 'What is the name for a jagged, narrow ridge that separates two adjacent glacier valleys?'

Cherie looks at me.

I gaze out the window. Again, the paper brushes my leg. Lucas is helping me. But why? How does he know I need help? Is he onto me? He studiously gazes in the opposite direction.

'Arête,' I mutter. I hope I've pronounced it right.

Cherie scribbles it down. There's something different in Adrian's eyes this time – respect?

Seven more questions follow. Each time Lucas's answers surreptitiously brush my leg.

Adrian is openly goggling at me.

I maintain an aura of cool competence.

'Last question. What is the name for an elongated ridge of glacial sediment?'

Lucas's paper brushes my leg.

This one calls for a German accent. 'Bergschrund,' I spit.

Adrian wipes a small spray off his arm.

'Sorry,' I say.

'No problem.' He smiles at me.

It's a nice smile. My three sloths do a happy dance.

Cherie's pencil stays poised over her paper. 'Are you sure? I thought—'

I frown at her and she writes it down.

Mike gathers up the papers from the five tables. After a couple of minutes he looks up. 'It's a close one. First place and winner of the prize pack of chocolates' – he holds it up – 'are ... the Leopard Seals.'

Maria jumps up and punches the air. 'Yes.'

'In second place with only one question wrong are the Krill Orgy. Sorry, Krill Orgy, drumlin was the answer to the last question.' He laughs. 'I bet you're kicking yourself.'

Cherie and Hornby stare at me accusingly.

'Drumlin.' I slap my hand to my head. 'Brain snap,' I murmur.

'You did well, S—' – Adrian stops himself – 'Cougar.'

As I stand up to leave, I meet Lucas's eyes. He looks at me coolly and I doubt myself – perhaps he didn't mean to show me the answers? But what about bergschrund? He deliberately gave me the wrong answer and kept the right one for his team. What a low act. I'll need to keep my eye on him.

'So, who was the glaciology whiz in your team?' asks Rory as we head down the corridor.

'Me. I've been studying, you know.'

'Wow' – he pats my back – 'Good going.' He sneezes. 'I'm definitely coming down with something.'

'It's the light. It makes you feel weird.'

'Maybe.' He sneezes again as he opens his door.

'Did you sleep last night?' I ask.

'Yeah, of course. Why? Didn't you?'

'I don't think so. Antarctica's giving me insomnia.' I yawn. All the igloo-building, rock-climbing, interviewing and lack of sleep is catching up with me – horizontal is the only way to be.

In bed, I close my eyes, but they open again. I'm not ready for sleep. It's only eight-thirty and outside it looks like mid-afternoon. I gaze at the clouds outside my window for a while then fumble around on my bedside table for my phone. Holding it above my head, I press *record* and talk into the camera. You never know when some extra footage will come in handy.

'I might be warm and cosy in here, but outside all those vast and lonely spaces beckon. It seems possible I could round up a husky team and head off for the South Pole. Become the first Australian female television presenter under the age of thirty to make it unassisted …'

A knock on the door startles me. 'Come in.' I hope it's not Rory with another strenuous filming suggestion.

Cherie pokes her head around the corner. 'Phone for you.'

With an effort I sit up, swing my feet to the floor, pad down the hallway to the phone and murmur, 'Hello.'

'Summer?' The voice is loud, instantly recognisable and entirely unwelcome.

I stand up straighter. 'Hi, Maxine.' I expect she's rung to congratulate me on my 'Sex on Ice' episode.

'What on earth do you think you're doing?' she yells.

Chapter Twenty-one

Seven thousand kilometres is not enough

Maxine's voice is shrill. It has an echo that suggests she's on speaker-phone, although it could be the distance on the line. I picture her at her desk, her scarlet nails darting over the keyboard while she talks.

'This latest show Rory's sent me,' she snarls. 'What happened to the script?'

My stomach flops. Maxine is not happy. She has not yet become a flesh-eating alien, but her claws are emerging. I cast about for a plausible excuse and decide I may as well get it over with. 'The script wasn't very good.'

'Not very good?' Maxine's voice rises. 'Do you think you know more about scriptwriting than Dianne?'

I do, but it seems unwise to say so. I quake, then calm myself. After all, what can she do? She's half a world away and I'm the woman on the spot. She needs me. 'My script was more dramatic. More original.'

'That scientist droning on about climate change was dramatic?' She snorts. I hear the *ting* of an incoming message and the rattle of a keyboard. I was right, she's multi-tasking.

'Um, no, that part wasn't dramatic but it was important. People need to—'

'I'm running a commercial television station, not an educational service. You are aware the major advertisers for Charlie Oscar Indigo are—'

'India.'

'What?'

'You said Indigo. It's Charlie Oscar India.'

There's silence on the line for some time. I shouldn't have said that.

'You are aware the major advertisers for Charlie Oscar Indigo' – Maxine pauses; I keep my mouth shut – 'are a large car manufacturer and a fuel company, aren't you, Summer?' Her voice is unnaturally kind. It gives me the creeps – she's playing both good cop and bad cop.

'Yes, but—'

'Do you think they want to advertise on a show about climate change?'

'No, Maxine.'

'I cut that part out. There will be no mention of climate change on Channel Five. It's boring and it's bad for business. It makes people feel bad. Our job is to make people feel good. Is that understood?'

'Yes, Maxine.'

'And what's this about sex on ice?' I hear teeth grinding. 'The penguins,' she snaps, 'was that true?'

'Absolutely. Adelie penguins are very kinky. I couldn't make up stuff like that.'

There's silence on the end of the phone for some time. 'I'll run the sex part, because I've got nothing else, and sex is sex, but Summer …' Her tone is colder than an Antarctic winter.

'Yes?'

'Do this one more time and you're toast.'

'Yes, Maxine.'

'Dianne's approved script for tomorrow will be there soon.' She hangs up.

It's possible Maxine may need me more than I need her, but even from seven thousand kilometres away, she gives the impression she could kill through the phone.

Back in my room, I lie on my bed for a while contemplating sleep, but my eyes seem glued open. I decide to finish my self-interview. My mobile isn't on the table. I must have left it down the corridor. Groaning, I stand up again, retrace my steps and find my phone lying right where I left it. Its battery is flat. This seems like a metaphor – there is not one skerrick of charge left in me either. Regardless of the daylight outside, I must try to sleep.

Lying on the bed, I'm closing my eyes again when I hear someone playing guitar. I suspect a man. He'd better keep his distance. I want nothing to do with any guitar-playing men.

With the exception of Adrian, every single one of my ex-boyfriends has been musically-minded. Their faces swim before me – Max, who took off with my savings; Dave, who ended up fleeing the country with the drug squad in pursuit; Gary, who eventually admitted he had a wife and kids in Sydney … All of them played a mean guitar. Apart from their fecklessness, it's the one thing they had in common. I'm a slow learner, but I do learn.

I am wide awake again now; this damn midnight sun. Maybe some bedtime reading will do the trick. I open *An Antarctic Mystery* at random and read:

> The desolate aspect of the land remained the same, while the strait was already visited by floating drifts, pack of one to two hundred feet in length …

I must have slept because some time later I wake. The building creaks in a sudden gust of wind; perhaps that was what woke me. I was dreaming my usual dream. It's time I told Marley about it. I pull my laptop towards me.

To: Marley Lennon Wright
From: Summer Dawn Rain Wright
Subject: The usual dream

This is my dream, Marley. I have it all the time.

It is hot.

The sheet is a tangled mess around my feet. My skin is damp. My window is open but no breeze stirs. A brass band of cicadas has set up camp on the gum tree outside. At first it was one – a lone violinist, then it was joined by a cellist, now they have brought in the bagpipe section. You know it's a hot night when the cicadas are singing at midnight. Usually they stop as soon as the air cools.

'Shut up.' I sit up and lean out the window.

They pause for a moment. *How rude*, I imagine them murmuring, before they re-commence what is clearly a symphony in ten parts.

Water. Must have water. I slide my feet onto the bare boards. Something scuttles away. The possum. I don't have a problem with the possum. Unlike the cicadas, it understands the limits of polite behaviour. Every night it helps itself to one banana from our fruit bowl. The skin is left neatly on the kitchen bench. If it knew how to operate the garbage bin I'm sure it would place it in there.

I wipe the sweat from my face with my singlet as I shuffle towards the kitchen. There's no moon tonight, so the house is dark. Inside the kitchen there are more scuttles. Small ones. Cockroaches.

I'm used to cockroaches. Sometimes they crawl across my hair in the night and I hardly scream at all. There's no point in carrying on. The only result would be that the cicadas might shut up for a minute.

I run my hand along the kitchen bench and encounter an object. It is smooth and rounded. My mind flicks through an inventory – zucchini? Too big. Melon? Too small, and, I run my hand along it, too long. The object moves and my body explodes. I leap backwards with a shriek of alarm. It's a snake, snake, SNAKE.

I run out of the kitchen. A figure looms near my front door – a shadowy outline. It's you, Marley. It's time I gave you a piece of my mind.

'Why did you leave me here with all these snakes?' I say.

You are silent.

'I miss you.'

But you don't reply. You are only a shadow, cast by a tree.

As I press 'send' something rattles outside in the wind – the Antarctic wind. I visualise it whipping up the snow, blowing across the South Pole, howling around my half-formed igloo. I'm glad I'm not out there. The building creaks again and I imagine I'm Scott of the Antarctic, lying in my tent in a blizzard. I stretch my toes, grateful for clean sheets, rather than ice-coated seal skin. Around me, the heating hums and the air is dry. I try to go back to sleep.

Five minutes later, I throw off my covers and slide my feet to the floor. My mouth is parched; I'll get a glass of water. I know I'll never settle otherwise.

As a child, I'd often ramble around the house in the middle of the night. This was how I discovered that my family and the resident wildlife were like co-inhabitants of a timeshare apartment. A carpet snake devouring a rat, a bat swooping across the lounge room, a possum caught eating a banana – these were some of the highlights of my night-time explorations. After checking out who was making use of the facilities, I could usually settle to sleep.

Pulling on a polar fleece jacket over my long T-shirt, I open my door. Outside, a low glow lights the corridor. I pad along, heading for the lounge room – I'm not expecting to see anyone, or any animals for that matter; it's after midnight and I don't imagine seals and penguins roam the corridors after lights out.

As I pass the door to the rock-climbing room I see a flash of movement. I pause. A man is climbing. He's high up, but has no rope attached. He's wearing track pants, his T-shirt lies in a crumpled heap beneath him. Climbing fluidly, he reaches the top of the wall, muscles rippling under his skin as he extends for the next handhold.

He turns his head to search for a grip and I see his face. *Lucas.* He looks different like this. His feet bare, his legs stretching from foothold to foothold. He leans back, lets go and dangles from one arm. I notice the determined set of his mouth. The veins stand out on his forearm.

I'm mesmerised. It's better than watching the carpet snake eat the rat. Lucas makes his way along the top of the wall, then climbs downwards. I hesitate. Should I have it out with him? Ask him why he helped me in the trivia quiz? But that conversation could take me in awkward directions. Reluctantly, I move on.

In the lounge, I take a drink from the water dispenser and gaze out the window at the stark beauty of rocks and snow. I lean my head against the cool window, my breath misting the glass. My fingers touch my chest, soothing a dull ache which has emerged from nowhere.

Back in bed, I catch one last glimpse of the glowing night before I curl up in a ball and close my eyes. As the wind howls outside, my mind returns to Adrian and all the things I love about him. And while there are many, many, many things, it occurs to me that maybe, just maybe, one thing is missing – a longing to touch his skin.

But perhaps that is not important.

Chapter Twenty-two
Boring ice-core samples

Project:	Sunday schedule
Objectives:	Complete igloo
	Impress Adrian again before he leaves
	Follow script for Charlie Oscar India
5.00–7.00:	Work on igloo
7.00–8.00:	Breakfast
8.00–9.00:	Show Adrian my igloo
9.00–17.00:	Filming and field trip with Lucas

The night passes in fitful sleep that comes to a decisive end at five am. Plenty of time to finish my igloo before breakfast. As I roll over, my aching arms and back scream. I close my eyes again. Just for a minute.

Many wriggles later I wake to find it's seven am. I'm late. And I haven't finished my igloo. I won't be able to show it to Adrian before he leaves. *Damn.* But at least he'll see it on TV.

I jump out of bed, dress quickly and trot down the corridor, stopping outside Rory's door. We're going with Lucas to film a segment at a remote ice-drilling station today so we need to get a move on. There's no reply to my knock; he must be already at breakfast. I'm turning away when I hear a croaky *come in.*

Rory is lying in bed with the covers pulled up to his nose like the Big Bad Wolf. He sneezes when he sees me. 'I'b sick.' He pulls a tissue from a packet next to him and blows loudly into it. 'I can't go out in the colb today.'

'Oh buck up, it's just a cold. You'll feel better once you've had breakfast.'

'No.' He shakes his head. 'I'b sensitive. If I go out when I'b feeling like this, it will go to my chest.'

'I thought you were a he-man.'

'I ab a he-ban,' Rory sniffles. 'It's a bab colb. You shoulb be bore sybpathetic.'

They do say the big ones fall hardest. I put my hands on my hips. 'Well, who's going to do the filming?'

'You and Lucas can filb each other.'

'Do union rules permit that?'

'No, but—' Rory bursts into a fit of sneezing. 'See. I'b sick.' His ruddy cheeks are ruddier than usual. He shuffles up in bed. Picking up a scarf from his bedside table he winds it around his neck. 'Ibportant to keep by neck warb. Pass be the cab'ra.' He gestures at the floor. 'I'll show you.'

I try to pick up the camera Rory's been using, but I can hardly lift it.

'No, not that one.' Rory points. 'The sballer one.'

I pick up the other camera. It's heavy and bulky, but manageable.

Rory pats the bed. 'I'll show you how to do it. It's easy.' He gives me a quick run-through on the controls, interspersed with sniffles and coughs. It does seem fairly easy.

I edge away as he bursts into a fit of sneezing. 'But what about the script?'

'I printed it out.' Rory picks up some papers from the bedside table and thrusts them towards me. He groans and lies down again, pulling up the covers. 'Better stick to the script, Subber.'

I glance at the date on the top of the script. *December 21.* I knew it was coming up, but I'd tried to ignore it … Today is the summer solstice, my birthday. I'm not feeling festive, so I don't mention it.

Flicking through the script, I yawn. Today, according to Dianne, I'm going to talk about a scientist's life and how they keep themselves amused in Antarctica. Dianne wants me to ask Lucas about his favourite Norwegian recipes and what he is looking forward to when he gets back to Australia.

This script sounds like the sort of conversation you'd have if you wanted your dinner party guests to leave. The mention of a scientist's hobbies would be enough to have them searching for their car keys and murmuring something about babysitters. I'm sure I can do better than this.

One more time and you're toast.

melt   **147**

The hairs rise on my arms – it's like Maxine is here in the room. *She's seven thousand kilometres away*, I tell myself. *There's nothing she can do.*

'Oh hey, Subber,' says Rory as I turn to leave.

'What?'

'Get your footage to be as soon as possible so I can send it to Baxine.'

'Baxine?'

'No, Baxine.'

'Oh, Maxine.'

'That's what I said, Baxine. They have internet out there at the cabp. I checked. You can send a file to be when it's done.'

'Okay.' I turn to go again.

'And Subber.'

'What?'

'You should check out the show website, see what the cobbents are like on last night's intro.'

'Cobbents? Oh, comments. Right.' Last night, they would have aired the teaser from the airport and ice runway. I hope they were able to do something about my green nose first.

'I would have looked, but I'b too sick. Baxine places a lot of weight on the cobbents. They're ibportant.'

'Okay, I'll have a look.' I leave Rory sniffling in bed and head towards the dining room, lugging the camera over my shoulder. I know why I forgot my birthday – because it's Marley's birthday too and I don't want to think about that.

On my way to the dining room, I pass the communal phone and before I know what I'm doing, I'm dialling the country code and his number. The phone rings and rings. There is a click. *Hi, this is Marley, leave a message.* I close my eyes, holding back tears. I'd like to play the message over and over, but that isn't possible. Instead, I stand there silently for a few moments. At last, remembering how much this call is costing, I take a deep breath. 'Hi, happy birth—' But I've reached the end of his message bank.

I place the phone down gently. There's so much distance between me and Marley's phone – the snow, the ice, the cold seas, then the land, the Great Southern Land. How did those early navigators feel, being so far away from home, out of touch with their loved ones? At sea for so many years … How did their families stand it?

There's a computer nearby and I open up the internet, type in *bush-fires New South Wales*.

> Fires still raging out of control … highway blocked … fire-fighters called from Queensland … extreme weather conditions …

Outside the window the sky is grey, but the Australian flag hangs limply; last night's wind has dropped. It seems surreal to be reading about bushfires, standing here in a T-shirt looking out at Antarctica. I feel further from home than I've ever been.

I should call Mum, she'll be trying to get onto me to say happy birthday. I eye the phone, but it's too hard to deal with right now. I would have to pretend to be in Sydney. I'll call this afternoon when I get back.

I'm shutting the computer down when I hear voices in the corridor outside.

'He is saying I manipulated the climate data.' Lucas sounds angry. 'There is going to be an investigation.'

'Who is saying? Hornby?' The second voice is Maria's. 'He's an idiot. It's not in the media yet?'

'No, not yet. It will be bad timing for the climate talks if it goes public. People will lose confidence. But perhaps that is the idea. He says it's a scientific conspiracy.'

Maria snorts. 'Why would you do that?'

'I don't know – to secure government funding? That's what they usually say.'

She laughs. 'So you can afford to buy paperclips.'

Their voices fade as they move towards the dining room. I stare at the doorway as it sinks in. Hornby's saying Lucas manipulated his research to make the climate situation seem worse?

That must be what they were arguing about last night. Lucas doesn't seem like the kind of guy who'd do that, but what would I know? Could the means justify the end? Especially with the climate talks coming up. Well … This is going to stir things up. And it does explain the atmosphere at dinner last night.

Obviously no-one is in a hurry to fill me in so perhaps it's best to pretend I don't know.

I open the door to the dining room, trying to gauge the mood. At the top table Adrian and Hornby are deep in conversation. Adrian is wearing moleskins, a polo shirt and loafers: casualwear. The Minister is dressed for some light alpine hiking – smart-casual pants, collared shirt and walking boots. His eyes are puffy and lined by dark shadows. Clearly he is not sleeping well. I hope I don't look as bad as him.

I head towards my usual table. Lucas and Maria have their heads bowed over their breakfast. Lucas glances at me as I approach.

My heart beats faster at the sight of him. What's that about? Is this because of the rock-climbing? No, it can't be that.

I wouldn't have developed a crush on him because I saw him climbing with his shirt off. I'm not that shallow. I've always sneered at those scenes in the soaps where the hunky guy spills something on himself and has to take his shirt off. So predictable. So stupid. As if women would fall for guys who do that. And besides, he has a beard. I hate beards, so my rapid pulse must be about the climate data thing. Whatever that is … I'm anxious about having overheard his conversation, that's all.

I sit, feeling tongue-tied.

Maria exchanges a meaningful look with Lucas. 'You are best to tell her. So she doesn't hear it from someone else.' She glances at the top table.

Lucas sighs. He has dark circles under his eyes too. Is anyone here sleeping properly? 'There are allegations …'

I decide it's best to clear the air. 'I heard you. In the corridor. I was using the computer, and …'

'It's rubbish of course,' he says.

'Of course,' I say.

'They have hacked my emails from the last ten years and pulled out words here and there, rearranging them to make it look like I was fiddling data.'

'Who is they?' I ask.

Maria frowns. 'Who *are* they?'

She's confusing me. I never thought I'd need English lessons from a Dutch woman, but it appears I do.

Lucas shrugs. 'I cannot say. Not definitely.'

I get the message. Not to a TV celebrity is what he means – more than his job is worth. 'The emails are fakes?' I ask.

'They are a mixture of things I said and things I didn't say. I have no doubt the investigation will clear me but if it gets into the media the damage will be done. In the public mind they won't be able to trust the science anymore.'

'I won't say anything.'

He nods. 'Thank you. It makes me so angry. Years and years of meticulous work … And it could be all for nothing. The timing is perfect of course, before the climate talks.' He sighs. 'I never thought climate science would be a dangerous profession.'

'Dangerous?'

Lucas looks surprised. 'You don't know?'

'Know what?'

'You don't read the papers?'

'I do, but …' In actual fact, I mainly read the entertainment section. 'I must have missed it.'

Maria's head comes up and her lip curls.

I flush.

Lucas gives me a strange look. 'I just assume everyone knows … It was reported widely. You didn't see the story?'

Clearly this is a major failing. I feel bad about it. No doubt Cougar reads the news thoroughly. I try to recover lost ground. 'I've been away. Living with the Inuits.' I address this last remark to Maria.

She snorts and turns back to her breakfast.

I suppose she keeps on top of current affairs even when trawling for krill in the Antarctic oceans.

'Oh, well, it wouldn't have made it over there. I was getting death threats recently. They were anonymous, but when the police investigated they linked them to a group called Real Climate Facts. Their leader is a good friend of …' Lucas's eyes flick to the top table. 'He is big business, mining industry. They couldn't charge anyone, not enough evidence.'

I remember the policeman driving by the airport, his wave to Lucas. Were they keeping an eye on him?

'A fake bomb was planted in my office,' says Lucas. 'They had to increase security at the whole laboratory.'

'But why? What did you say to make them do that?'

'Not much. Not enough, I thought. I published a paper that showed the last sixty years in Australia have been the hottest over 1000 years. I made some predictions that bushfires will occur more often ...'

My mind wanders at the mention of bushfires ... *Happy birthday, Marley.*

' ...extinction of half our plant and animal species by 2100,' Lucas concludes.

'So, why are they attacking you? Do they think you made it up?'

'They pretend to think so. I was the principal author. I compiled data from a number of other scientists. They've made it look like we are in a conspiracy.' Lucas laughs. 'We've been cooking the books together, so they say.'

Maria looks up. 'You could never get two scientists to agree to a conspiracy, all we ever do is poke holes in each other's data. That's the way science works.'

Maria and Lucas turn back to their breakfasts – cold grease is congealing on the side of their unfinished sausages.

'Looks good,' I say. 'I'd better get some. Rory has a cold. He won't be coming with us.' With effort I lift the camera that's dangling by my side and place it on the table. 'I'm the camerawoman today, I'm afraid.' I pour some cereal into my bowl and gobble it down as I'm behind schedule.

Lucas stands as I finish. 'Okay, let's go. I've got a hag to take us out there.'

This seems rather rude.

Lucas notices my face. 'Hagg, short for Hagglund.' He pauses. 'Snowmobile.'

'Ah.'

Lucas catches Adrian's eye and nods stiffly. 'The Minister is coming too,' he says. 'The plane is still not flying today. Tomorrow, I hope, it will be cold enough.'

I glance towards Adrian. There might still be time to show him my igloo.

Lucas and I head for the door. As we don our snowsuits and boots, the Minister catches up.

'Adrian is staying behind. Urgent briefing notes to prepare …'

The likely subject of those briefing notes hangs around us like rotting fish as we turn our tags and step outside.

Chapter Twenty-three

Ice cores are sensational

Our transport, the Hagg, is parked a few metres away. It's the same red vehicle which transported us from the airport, but the back carriage has been taken off, leaving behind what looks like a square tractor. Lucas takes the driver's side and the Minister climbs in the front next to him, which shows either bravado or pig-headedness on his part. I jump in the back, nursing the camera on my lap. A gust of wind whips up the snow outside as I pull the door shut.

Lucas glances back to check I'm settled. 'Should warm up once we get going.' He smiles briefly, before turning to the front.

My heart goes pitter-patter at his smile. This has nothing to do with the data allegations. No, this is pure chemistry. *Brain to heart: settle down. He has a beard, a really hairy one.* And this afternoon when I show Adrian my igloo he will fall back in love with me at once.

As we start off with a jolt, I remember I was supposed to check the comments from the show last night. Too late. If people are making fun of my green nose I don't want to know.

The atmosphere in the front seat is dire. I hum nervously in an attempt to break the ice, but it only emphasises the tension so I stop. It's surprisingly quiet inside the cabin. Only a dull roar from the engine penetrates.

Lucas grips the steering wheel so tightly his knuckles are white. The Minister gazes out the window. Perhaps he too is feeling the tension, as he whistles softly.

'How far is it?' I say.

'We are going to an ice cap about two hours' drive away. It's where a lot of the work on ice-core records is done. An ice-drilling team is camped out there. You can interview them.' *Woodwork and recipes, here we come …*

It occurs to me I should shoot some footage on the way. Taking Dianne's script out of my bag, I look at it again. It's still boring. Scientists' hobbies may be the only topic more boring than climate change.

Although, with the Minister and Lucas here … climate change could make great television. I stifle a pang of doubt. It's exactly what Cougar would do – bulldoze her way through, get the story no matter who she tramples underfoot. Foisting the camera onto my shoulder I direct it at Lucas and press 'go'. 'Do you think climate change is the most boring subject the world has ever known?'

Lucas glances at me as he accelerates over a snow bank. 'No. I find it fascinating.'

The Minister's shoulders tense and he stops whistling. Outside, a flurry of wind whips up the snow into a mini-tornado. The rocks that surround Casey Station have vanished and there is nothing but ridge after ridge of snow.

A blast of static comes over the radio mounted on the dashboard. Lucas twiddles the knobs, but it doesn't become any clearer.

'So fascinate me,' I say.

The Minister taps his fingers on the dashboard. He clears his throat as if he's about to speak.

Lucas beats him to it. 'Today we are going to an ice cap where much of the climate work has been done over the past thirty years.' It starts snowing lightly, fine flakes the size of sugar crystals land on the windscreen. Lucas turns on the wipers.

There's nothing more beautiful than falling snow.

'Our records show that over the past thirty years there has been more and more snow falling here. Now we know that drought in Australia is part of the same weather pattern. And it is most likely caused by climate change.'

'Most likely.' The Minister snorts. 'Is that a scientific term?'

'I can give you the scientific term, but I don't expect you'd like it any better,' says Lucas.

'More snow, less snow, you'd still say it was climate change.' Hornby glances at my camera. 'You can quote me on that.'

I'd already intended to.

Lucas's clenched knuckles on the wheel betray his state of mind.

'It does seem bizarre,' I say. 'How can you link more snow to less rain?'

'Exactly,' says Hornby.

'It is part of the same system,' says Lucas, 'produced by warmer air.'

'Pixies in the garden,' mutters the Minister. 'You can quote me on that.'

Lucas takes one hand off the wheel. For a moment I think he's going to punch Hornby, but he changes gears. He seems to have decided to ignore the Minister. 'Ice cores paint a picture of changing climate.' Lucas shoots a wry glance over the back of the seat. 'Is it boring?'

I'm gazing at the snowflakes on the windscreen. 'No. Um, maybe a little. Why don't we talk about polar bears? People like them.'

Lucas laughs. 'Polar bears, penguins, baby seals … What about fluffy kittens?'

'Yes, if you can work them in, that would be—'

Lucas interrupts. 'I don't understand. What is not interesting about air flow and ice-core samples?'

I open and shut my mouth but no reply is necessary.

'It is our planet, our weather, what could be more important? Wait until you see the ice cores. Then you will understand.'

I like the way his eyes light up when he talks about ice cores, but in a world of fluffy kittens and celebrity fashion disasters I fear they will have little traction.

The Minister taps his fingers on the dashboard again. 'Are we nearly there?' He yawns and checks his watch. 'This is taking a long time.'

Lucas looks at him as if he's just noticed he's there. 'This is Antarctica.' His remark is underlined by another blast of static from the radio.

'Bird egg collecting would solve a lot of problems,' says Hornby.

Lucas and I stare at him. This is a remark of such incredible randomness it's hard to know what to do with it.

'I collected bird eggs as a boy. We need more children out there collecting bird eggs instead of sitting in front of computers. You can quote me on that,' he says to me.

'What about threatened birds?' says Lucas.

'Oh you would say that, wouldn't you? That's what they always say. You don't collect the threatened birds of course, just the common ones – magpies, swallows, that sort of thing. It's character-building, climbing trees to get eggs.'

'You don't think it sends the wrong message?' I say.

Hornby snorts. 'That's typical namby pamby greenie crap. Get kids out there in the wild collecting things. Do them the world of good. Put that in your story.'

'Mm. Yes, I will.' Maxine might like that. I turn the camera off and place it on the seat next to me. Outside the window the snow and rocks are curiously mesmerising. I nod off for a moment and wake to find myself dribbling. No-one seems to have noticed.

Lucas catches my eye in the rear-view mirror and inclines his head to a plastic bag in the central console. 'Help yourself to dried fish.'

I take a couple out of the bag. 'Thanks.' When he's not looking, I stuff them in my pocket.

Eventually some green pyramid shapes appear in the distance – the ice-core camp. I film the tents as we get closer. Three bearded men emerge from under the tent flap at our approach. It appears the Antarctic Division has hired a team of identical triplets.

I climb stiffly from the Hagglund, pulling my hood up over my head and slipping on my large puffy mittens. A brisk wind chills my cheeks and my nose goes instantly numb.

'We are higher here than at the station,' says Lucas. 'Probably at least five degrees colder.' He introduces the Minister and me to the beards – Simon, Scott and Tim. I instantly forget which is which.

'Casey's on the radio for you,' says one of the beards to Lucas. 'They've been trying to call for a while. Isn't the radio in the Hagg working?'

Lucas raises his shoulders. 'Maybe we were in a black spot.'

The beard holds up the tent flap.

Inside, Lucas talks on the radio briefly. 'Affirmative. Copy.' I'm waiting for him to say Seahorse Ice-cream Tango, or some such thing, but he just says, '2351 clear,' before turning to us. 'The Minister and I are needed back at the base this afternoon.' His tone betrays his irritation. 'A conference call, Minister. Regarding the implications of the email leaks on the science program.' He replaces the handset with a bang.

'But we just got here,' I say. 'I need to get some footage.'

Lucas glances at his watch. 'We can stay for an hour.'

The Minister looks around the tent. 'Shouldn't need that long.'

Inside the tent is a metal rig with a drill. A tube of ice is laid out nearby on a mat. It's longer than I expected, about three metres. My mind ticks over Dianne's script again. Should I talk to the beards about what they do on those long, cold nights? How much they miss home? What they eat for dinner? I'm going to risk Maxine's wrath if I don't.

I gaze at the ice-core sample. It's shiny and beautiful. Surely this is my story, not woodcarving, knitting and cunning ways with pasta. If ice cores turn out to be boring, I can always move onto recipe ideas. I start the camera and assume my bossy Cougar persona. 'So, who am I talking to here?'

The three beards glance at each other. The one with the longest beard points at Lucas. 'Him.'

I turn to Lucas. 'You know about this stuff?'

The beards laugh.

'I can get by,' says Lucas.

'Okay, so, tell me about the ice core,' I say.

Lucas squats next to the ice and looks up at my camera. 'An ice core is like tree rings …'

So far, so dull, but I give him the benefit of the doubt. 'What can they tell us?'

'We recently found out the end of the last ice age was linked to rising carbon dioxide.'

At the mention of ice age my mind wanders to images of sabre-tooth tigers and woolly mammoths. I pull it back. 'How recently?'

'Last year.'

'Last year? That's quite exciting.'

Lucas's mouth twitches. 'That makes a change.'

I ignore this. 'What happened?'

'The sea level rose by about a hundred metres as the ice melted.'

I can't believe I didn't know this. 'Why wasn't this in the papers?'

'It was. And the scientific journals. You must have missed it.'

Blood rises to my cheeks. 'It's hard to keep up with everything.'

'Perhaps Kim Kardashian got divorced that day.'

'Wasn't that the most ridic—' I stop. 'Cut that part, Rory,' I say to the camera. I turn to one of the nearby beards. 'Can you train the camera on me while I talk?' I hand it to him, step over to the ice core and crouch next to Lucas.

'Don't touch,' he says, 'or you'll contaminate the sample. You can see the different layers.' He points. 'The next stage is to divide the core up and label each sample.'

I study the ice and eventually discern fine gradations. 'How old is the oldest part?'

'It varies with the depth. This sample is not so old – about ten thousand years?' He glances up and one of the beards nods. 'The end of the last ice age,' says Lucas.

I contemplate the ice. I feel dislocated, like a time traveller, as I try to take it in.

'Ten thousand years is not a long time,' says Lucas.

No wonder no-one understands scientists. 'Ten thousand years … That seems old to me.'

'Not in geological time,' says Lucas.

His mention of time reminds me … I extend my wrist exposing the watch and look at the camera. 'When you're dealing with million-year-old ice samples it's important to stay on time. That's why I wear Seiko.'

An awkward silence falls inside the tent after my product placement. As the hand of my watch ticks around I gaze at the gleaming ice and imagine time going forward for thousands of years to this point. It's hard to get my head around.

Standing up, I take the camera from the beard who's been filming our interview. 'I have a couple more questions.'

'Go ahead,' says Lucas.

'You said we've only just discovered the last ice age ended due to rising carbon dioxide?'

'Yes.'

'So how much did the carbon dioxide rise by before it ended?'

'About the same amount it has risen over the last hundred years. Forty per cent, or so.'

'The increase in carbon dioxide was the same as it is now?' I can't believe I didn't know this. 'And the ice age ended?'

Lucas nods. 'Only now, obviously, it's happening more quickly.'

I hear a snort. 'Completely different situation,' mutters Hornby.

I swing the camera towards him, but he holds up his hand. 'Off the record.'

Why so shy? 'Are you sure, Minister? It's a good opportunity to put your point of view.'

He shakes his head. 'Talk to Adrian, we can set something up later.'

When he's got a script is what he means. 'Pity, this is getting interesting.' I pan around the tent. The Minister moves away from the group to avoid being filmed. My camera comes back to Lucas. 'You should tell people this stuff, they need to know.'

'We tell people constantly. No-one's listening.'

'Well, they're going to listen now.' I aim my camera at the beards.

They huddle together like startled sheep.

'Scientists like these are the whistleblowers of Antarctica, exposing the secrets of the Earth's past.'

The Minister snorts.

I pause the camera. 'Did you have a comment, Minister?'

He shakes his head.

I press *record* again. 'These scientists are digging for facts and bringing you answers at great personal cost to their own comfort and psychological wellbeing. They are camped out here in this barren wasteland, driven by their need to understand what is happening to our planet. And they will not rest until they have answers.' Dianne's script rustles in my pocket. 'They have no time for woodwork or special recipes,' I add. 'They are way too busy saving the human race. This is Cougar on Ice, notwithstanding. And that's a wrap.'

The beards look alarmed. 'That's a very sensationalist view of ice-core sampling,' says one.

'I do my best.'

Chapter Twenty-four
I decipher the krill issue

When we come out of the tent the sky is darker and the wind stronger. Tiny snowflakes settle on my snowsuit.

Lucas surveys the sky. 'Is there a blizzard warning?' he says to one of the beards.

'Not that I've heard. Looks like it, doesn't it?'

'Do you want to visit the snow pit?' asks one of the beards.

This question seems addressed to me, but I'm not sure how to reply. Is 'the snow pit' a euphemism for a toilet? In which case ... 'Yes, that could be good.' Toileting in a snowsuit poses all sorts of challenges, so if a snow pit is on offer, I will take advantage even if I don't yet need to.

The Minister checks his watch. 'We need to head back.'

'We should go to the snow pit.' Lucas is firm.

We? One at a time presumably. I use my casting vote. 'I'd like to go to the snow pit.'

'Make it quick,' says Hornby. 'This conference call is extremely important.'

'I'll be as quick as I can.' The man has a nerve.

Behind the tent some coloured flags on sticks flutter in the wind. We crunch across the snow towards them. Cut-out steps lead into a pit covered with wooden boards. It looks shadowy and cold in there.

Lucas steps down and vanishes into the blue-tinted shadows.

Well, I guess I'll wait my turn ...

'Are you going down?' says one of the beards after a moment.

'Oh, I thought it was one person at a time.'

They shake their heads in unison. 'Fits two,' says one of them. 'Three,' says another. 'At a pinch,' says the third. They appear to have been working together so long they're almost one creature. And clearly they have no problem visiting the snow pit together. They look at me expectantly.

Maybe I'm breaching some unspoken Antarctic protocol that requires you to visit the snow pit in pairs. I'm not sure I'm ready for this, but perhaps I need to get over it. I glance down into the pit and back at the beards.

'It's good down there,' says one.

I don't like to snub their offering; they don't have much in the way of comforts here. *When in Rome* ... Tentatively, I follow Lucas.

I don't know what I'm expecting – toilet cubicles I suppose. I prepare to avert my eyes politely as the space opens up. But how wrong I am – the chamber is breathtaking. A blue glow shines through one of the walls, lighting up the pit. It's like being in an underwater viewing area – as if fish could swim by any moment.

'I was about to come up and find you,' says Lucas.

'Sorry, I thought ... never mind.'

Whatever this is, it's not a toilet. Lucas's shoulder brushes mine. The beards were right; there's room for two, but only just.

'It's gorgeous in here.' My voice is hushed. The atmosphere seems to call for it. 'Why is the light like this?'

'I thought you would like it. There is another pit on the other side of this wall that lets the light through.' Lucas points at the turquoise wall. Layers of snow are illuminated in the glow.

'It's spectacular.' I remember my Cougar persona. Cougar has probably been in lots of snow pits. 'Quite nice,' I add. 'But what's it for?'

'Does it have to be for something?'

'No. But it is, isn't it? The beards haven't made it for sheer pleasure, have they?'

'The beards?'

I tilt my chin skywards.

'Of course.'

I raise my camera, poking Lucas in the shoulder as I do so, and pan across the wall. 'So, tell me, what's going on here?'

'The snow pit is a more recent record than the ice core.' Lucas points. 'The bright layers are the summer snow and the darker layers are the winter snow. Summer snow crystals are larger, so they aren't as dense. The snow is analysed to get temperature estimates and other data such as ...'

I lose track of what he's saying as I gaze at the blue light. A strange urge comes over me to talk about the infinite, about time and snow and ice and what it all means. To leave data and estimates behind and get to the bottom of it all. There is something almost spiritual about the atmosphere in here.

But the Minister is probably tapping his feet in the Hagg and besides, I am Cougar. 'Quite nice,' I say again.

Lucas offers me dried fish and I take some, holding them in my mitten for later disposal.

'So, better get going …' he says.

When we climb up into the light Hornby is in the back seat of the Hagg, as if awaiting his Ministerial chauffeur.

Lucas's face tightens, but he doesn't comment.

I pull the SD card out of the camera and hand it to one of the beards. 'Would you be able to send this footage to Rory at Casey Station? He wants to get started on the editing as soon as possible.'

The beard holds the SD card between his thumb and mittened fingers. 'Should be okay. Sometimes the satellite goes down. You got it backed up?'

I lift the camera. 'Yeah, it's on here.'

'Okeydokey,' he says. 'I'll give it a go.'

I climb in the front seat next to Lucas. A gust of wind blows up the snow around us as he starts the engine. Hornby yawns loudly.

The beards wave as we go. My SD card catches the light in one puffy hand and I feel a touch of nausea at the thought of what Maxine will say – *one more time and you're toast*. But surely the ice cores are more exciting than bush-cooking recipes. And Maxine is too far away to worry about. I think of the snow pit – if she was here she'd understand. Or maybe not.

The wind gets stronger as we drive back. Soon it's howling, raking the snow into billowing sheets of white. A particularly strong blast shakes the vehicle. I grip the dashboard in front of me.

'It's okay.' Lucas glances at me. 'It won't go over.'

Behind us, the Minister rustles paper in a pointed way. Most likely he's getting ready for his phone conference – preparing the case against Lucas. The air in the cabin is thick as custard. Lucas changes gears with a jerk and I gaze out the window. It would be so easy to disappear without trace in all that snow.

There's silence for some time as we jolt along. I eye Lucas's hands on the steering wheel, and have a flashback to the rock-climbing wall last night. My heart skips a beat. 'Do you rock-climb much?' *Oh no.* He has never told me he rock-climbs at all.

But Lucas doesn't seem fazed. 'Only when I'm in Antarctica. It's a good indoor exercise.'

'Have you ever fallen into a crevasse? While taking an ice-core sample, I mean.' I can't believe what I'm saying – my brain must have short-circuited.

'No. I try to avoid that.'

Outside the window the landscape is almost featureless in the flat light. Mountains loom in the distance but it's hard to get any perspective on their height. 'How do you know where it's safe to drive?'

'This route is well-tracked. Things can change though, the ice is always moving.' He taps a monitor mounted on the dashboard. 'I'm following the GPS.'

'Did you say you've been to Antarctica three times before?'

'Yes. The first time I spent twelve months here. I was out camping for three months, taking ice-core samples during the winter.'

'Camping?' Surely I can't have heard him correctly.

He nods as he changes gears over a ridge.

'Really?' A flurry of snow beats against the window. I try to imagine pitching a tent for three months, out in the ice and snow. In the winter darkness. I know the beards are camping, but they're not far from base so they must get back there a bit. For three months, though ... 'Did you go crazy?'

'Maybe.' Lucas laughs. 'But you have to expect that in Antarctica. One of the early explorers, Admiral Byrd, brought twelve straitjackets with him when he came here.'

'Did he need them all?'

'I'm not sure. But I expect there are more painful ways to go crazy than spending time in Antarctica.' He darts me a quick look.

My pulse thumps in my throat. I want him to keep talking. 'What's it like here, in winter?'

'The sun' – he indicates with his hand – 'stays low in the sky. And in mid-winter, for a few weeks, there is no light at all. It is cold of course. It's easy to get frostbite.'

'Does the dark get you down?'

'Sometimes. But when it's dark, the sky is bright with stars. And the aurora ...' He trails off.

Aurora. Even the word is like poetry.

'What's it like?'

'A sheet of rippling light. Sometimes white, sometimes green, sometimes red. It swirls and changes.' Lucas's voice is soft. 'It can last a few minutes, or all night. We saw one every second night or so that winter. It was an active period.'

'Wow.' This is inadequate, but it's the best I can do. I try to imagine the constant darkness, the freezing cold, the rippling aurora. 'And you camped?' I still can't get my head around this. 'In a tent?'

'Not a tent, a caravan. It was heated.'

That sounds marginally better. 'Would you do it again?'

'I'd like to, but ...' Lucas hesitates. 'I've heard astronauts have trouble adjusting when they come back to Earth. I think it is like that. You're a different person afterwards. Things that used to seem important ... don't anymore. Things that weren't important, are ... It gives you perspective.'

A stillness comes over me as he says that. For some reason I think of my white apartment – cool whiteness everywhere. Is that what it would be like? No, it would be the opposite, like ripping down the walls and letting in a blizzard. No morning project routine, no Gantt chart, no city train, no production meetings – just the wind and the snow and the ice. The idea is strangely attractive. *Particularly if I was camping with Lucas.*

'Being here is not hard. The hard part is coming back. Getting used to crowds, supermarkets ... It's stressful.' Lucas pauses. 'It can be hard on relationships too.'

This demands a follow-up. 'Did you—' I start.

'Sastrugi,' Lucas says. The snowmobile rocks and tips as we climb over a ridge of ice.

'Pardon?'

He points. 'The wind ridges in the snow. I suppose the Inuits had a different word for them?'

Sastrugi. The word sounds vaguely familiar. Oh yes, *Polar Fun for Kids* said Scott's team pulled heavy sleds over ridge after ridge of sastrugi. Now I know what it is, I can see how hard that would be. Some of the wind ridges have sharp edges about a foot deep – imagine pulling a sled up that when you're on your last legs. I divert Lucas's question with one of my own. 'What happened to Scott? His body I mean.'

'A search party found him and two of his team dead in their tent. They kept the diaries and a few other things and covered the bodies with snow. They'll be under metres and metres of ice now, moving slowly to the sea. Maybe in two hundred years they'll reach the sea and float away in an iceberg.'

'Oh.' I imagine an iceberg floating out to sea, carrying the bodies with it, like pieces of fruit inside an ice-block. 'It all seems kind of futile doesn't it?'

'That's what I mean: perspective. Antarctica is indifferent to us, yet we can destroy it.'

'With climate change you mean?'

Lucas nods. 'Last year, it rained in Antarctica for the first time in living memory. Even in this wilderness' – he gestures out the window – 'we make our presence felt.'

I touch my camera. I should catch this but I don't want to spoil the mood. Lucas is much more interesting when he isn't being filmed.

'It's the same in the Arctic. The Inuits are hearing thunder for the first time … But you would know that.'

I nod vaguely. Imagine hearing thunder for the first time. You'd think the world was ending.

'On the Antarctic peninsula penguin colonies are disappearing because of the krill.'

Aha – the krill issue, we meet again. I speak before thinking. 'What's up with the krill?'

Lucas shoots me a surprised look.

I've dropped my Cougar persona, but it's too late now.

'The krill issue is—'

'Important. Yes, I know, but what exactly is it?'

'Krill need sea ice for shelter and food.' He sounds like he's being asked to explain something self-evident, like why you should brush your teeth.

Perhaps it is self-evident, but not to me and I'm beyond caring if it makes me look foolish. I need to get to the bottom of this. 'And?'

'Less sea ice means less krill,' says Lucas.

'So, there are less krill than there used to be?'

'Yes, maybe up to eighty per cent less since the seventies.'

'Eighty percent? Goodness. So this is the *krill issue*?' I emphasise the last two words.

Lucas's eyes crinkle. 'It is. Most marine species depend on krill – whales, seals, penguins, seabirds ...'

'I see.' I understand Maria's obsession with the creatures now. 'You know a lot about krill, don't you? I thought you were a climate scientist.'

'Climate science is a broad field. Besides, I am Norwegian.' Lucas doesn't seem to feel the need to expand on this last sentence.

'And?'

'Krill is big in Norway.'

Clearly Norway and krill go together like Australia and kangaroos. 'Of course.' I contemplate the vast whiteness outside my window – to think I'd gone my whole life barely realising this was here. I can see now why you might want to head off with your huskies towards an unexplored horizon. How the savagery and wildness might impose a hypnotic lure. 'Poor Scott,' I say.

'Yes, poor Scott. His wife had an affair with the Norwegian explorer Nansen while he was away. So they say in Norway anyway.' Lucas glances at me, then concentrates his attention outside again as we drop into a small gully.

'I suppose that's what happens when you go off exploring for years. A woman has needs.'

Lucas's mouth twitches and he accelerates to climb out of the ditch. The silence extends and I think I've made a faux pas, but soon he speaks again. 'She was quite a woman apparently; a sculptor. Rodin and Picasso were friends of hers. Scott had to fight off a number of suitors to win her hand. The last letter he wrote before dying was to her.'

'What did it say?'

'I can't remember it all.'

If I was back home, this would be the cue to Google *Scott's last letter*. I'm glad I can't do that, I'd prefer to find out from Lucas, even if his memory is incomplete. 'Tell me what you remember.'

'He said … the worst part about his situation was he would never see her again.'

'Oh.' I blink, looking out the window so Lucas can't see the sudden tears that spring to my eyes. I hardly know why the story affects me so much – because I'm here, in the place where he died? 'That's so sad. But how amazing she got his letter in the end. That his words made their way across the sea to her door. While he lay there … covered in ice.'

Lucas gives me a long look. 'Yes. I hadn't thought about that part of it before. It is poignant.'

A flurry of snow beats against the window and it's not hard to see Scott in his tent, writing a love letter to a wife he'd never see again.

Chapter Twenty-five

A snow cave is practical

In the back of the Hagglund, the Minister coughs and shuffles his papers. He yawns.

I'd forgotten he was there. Has he been listening?

'We nearly there?' He yawns again.

He is definitely suffering from insomnia, like me.

'No,' says Lucas.

'The conference call starts soon.'

'I'm doing my best.'

'I can't miss this,' says Hornby. 'The opposition will be asking questions.'

A smack of wind hits the vehicle like a message from the gods. *Your concerns are trivial*, it seems to say.

I glance at Hornby and see him pick up a book from the seat. It's the one Lucas was reading: *The Worst Journey in the World*. He sighs and opens it.

After about half an hour the snow comes more heavily. Lucas eases off the accelerator. 'Damn.'

'What?'

'Here it is.' He gestures out the front window.

An angry grey haze blankets the air in front of us – an approaching storm. It's getting closer. And darker.

'We're not going to make it back before the blizzard hits. We'll have to bunker down until it goes past.'

'But …' I stare at the angry blackness ahead and my heart races. 'How long will that take?' I check my Seiko watch. It's only one o'clock so even if we wait out the storm for a couple of hours there's plenty of time to get back and ring home. Hopefully Rory will be up and around and we can edit the ice-core show into something Maxine will like. I should finish my igloo too.

Lucas swings the wheel. 'One day if we're lucky.'

'One day?' I can't believe he said that. 'But ... I've got things to do. Places to go ... I need to file my show. It's got to be in Sydney by this afternoon.'

'One day?' Hornby comes to life in the back seat. 'Absolutely not. I need to get back to communications. The Prime Minister is calling this afternoon. I need to go through Adrian's briefing notes beforehand. The independents are talking about walking. It's imperative I speak to the PM. I'm flying out tomorrow. Keep going.'

'This is Antarctica,' says Lucas. 'There's no point in making plans, Minister.'

'How far from the station are we, anyway?' says Hornby.

Lucas glances at the GPS. 'Twenty kilometres.'

'That's nothing,' says Hornby. 'I do that on my morning run.'

'Scott died eighteen kilometres from his food depot.' Lucas turns the wheel and pulls up in front of a large snowbank. 'You know how to dig a snow cave, don't you?' he says to me. He seems not at all concerned about our change in plans. If anything, he seems invigorated at the prospect.

'No. I know how to build an igloo.'

Lucas raises an eyebrow. 'A snow cave is more practical. We'll be at it all night if we want to build an igloo. So, unless we're planning on staying here for a week or so ...' He says this as if it's well within the bounds of possibility.

I shake my head and stare out at the snowbank. 'No. Preferably not.' I haven't accepted my change in circumstances. I'd been looking forward to a hot shower, filing my report, calling Mum. I don't want to end up in an ice-block floating out to sea without giving her the chance to say happy birthday. 'Can't we keep going slowly? Follow the GPS?'

As I say this, a violent gust of wind rocks the vehicle. Ice blasts against the windscreen and whiteness descends. As I look out the window I can't distinguish up from down; it's like being suspended in space.

'Too dangerous,' says Lucas. 'You can't drive blind. There are cliffs and ditches. We drove over sea ice on the way here. It could shift in the wind ...'

I imagine vanishing into a hole in the sea ice, the cabin filling with freezing water, like the Titanic going down.

'We're better stopping here while we have a good spot. It's relatively sheltered.' Lucas softens his voice. 'It'll get damn cold if we have to end up spending the night in the Hagg. It's not safe.' He picks up the radio. 'Casey Station from 2351. Casey Station from 2351.' The only reply is white noise. 'The blizzard is messing up the coms.'

'Disgraceful ... ludicrous,' mutters the Minister. 'The Prime Minister will be hearing about this.'

Lucas leans over into the back seat and, ignoring him, grabs two shovels. 'Let's go.' Turning, he sees my face. 'What's wrong? We'll be fine. Come on. We're not going to die like Scott, if that's what you're worried about.' He pulls up his hood, pulls on his goggles and mittens, opens the door and is gone.

I take a deep breath and remind myself: the extreme project manager adapts to any situation. Even unexpected stopovers in snow caves. Taking the shovel, I open the door. Outside, the wind nearly flattens me. After a fierce struggle I manage to shut the door. By the time I make it to the snowbank, Lucas is already shovelling. He turns and yells into the wind. 'You clear away the snow as I dig it out.'

I glance back at the snowmobile. Hornby's face is pressed to the window like a toddler on the verge of a serious tantrum.

'Don't worry about him,' says Lucas. 'He'll come round.'

Bracing myself against the wind, I dig. An otherworldly feeling takes over as I bend to my task. It's like Lucas and I are the only people on earth. *Perspective* ... Yes, Antarctica gives you that. Just surviving seems like enough of an achievement for the day.

As I shovel the snow, I ponder what it would be like if we were the only survivors of an apocalypse and had to live the rest of our lives in a snow cave, subsisting on seals and penguins. We would be like Adam and Eve, only with more clothing. Naturally we would need to propagate for the good of the human race. My mind returns to Lucas on the climbing wall ... there could be worse fates. I'd persuade him to shave with a sharpened seal bone. A shovelful of snow hits me in the face.

Lucas peers back at me. 'Sorry.' He seems like a different person – the serious scientist has vanished, leaving a wild man behind.

melt   **171**

Lucas digs a tunnel about a metre long, then opens it up into a cave. I crawl back and forth in the tunnel removing shovels full of snow. It's hot work, this snow-cave building. Before long I'm sweating. I glance over at the snowmobile every now and then. The windows are encased in ice and snow, but I can see Hornby's outline. It projects a mixture of incredulity and impatience. I suppose he's not used to having his plans thwarted. No doubt he will deign to enter the snow cave when it's ready.

After what seems like a couple of hours Lucas has excavated a small platform with a curved snow roof. I crawl onto the platform and sit with my legs dangling into the tunnel. The roof is close enough to touch with my outstretched hand and the platform is big enough for three bodies to lie side by side.

Lucas puts down his shovel and wipes his forehead. 'Well, this is home. It's not the biggest but it will do for now.'

I don't like the way he says *for now*. How long are we planning to stay here for? Long enough to turn our snow cave into a snow palace? Hopefully not.

'I'll go and get Hornby,' says Lucas. 'And the survival gear.' He vanishes out through the tunnel.

It's quiet and still inside the cave once he's gone. I feel like a possum in a tree hollow. It's hard to imagine the blizzard raging outside. I'm rather proud as I survey our new abode – we've made ourselves a home. And compared to the tempest outside, it is practically cosy. The light coming through the snow has an aqua-blue tinge like the sea on a sunny day. If we end up building a snow palace, maybe we can put in a stained-glass window …

I'm so absorbed in designing my snow mansion it takes me a while to notice Lucas has been gone a long time. I wait a little longer, mentally adding a pool room and a home theatre, before deciding to go out and investigate.

I emerge from the tunnel into a raging, white storm. Ice crystals blast against the only exposed patch of skin, my nose, and turn it instantly numb. Although the snowmobile is only a few metres away, I can barely see it. There is no sign of Lucas or Hornby. The wind roars around me like a plane taking off. Where have they gone?

The snowmobile seems a long way away. I crawl towards it – I don't dare to stand – it feels like the wind would pick me up and take me away. Clinging to the door handle, I pull myself upright and, wiping away the encrusted snow from the window with my mittens, peer inside. The cabin is empty. My heart thumps inside my chest. The wind howls like a savage ghost. I've never felt so alone.

A hand touches me on the shoulder. I scream – a shriek that disappears into the storm.

'Cougar.' Lucas yells into my ear. 'Hornby's gone.'

Chapter Twenty-six

My dark past is exposed

Lucas and I lean against the vehicle, trying to stay out of the furious wind. Snow lashes against the side of my hood and into my goggles. All I can see is white.

'He's taken the GPS and some of the survival gear,' Lucas yells. 'He must be trying to get to the station. God knows why. I've been searching for him.' He gestures out at the storm. 'But it's hopeless.'

'That's crazy,' I yell.

'I'll try the radio again.'

We crawl inside the snowmobile. Inside, it's marginally quieter.

'I can't believe he'd do that,' I say. 'For a stupid conference call.'

I'm reminded of *An Antarctic Mystery*. How the expeditioners disappeared, one by one. *Of the three who had embarked on the schooner, our number was reduced to two …*

Lucas reaches for the radio. 'I'd have a go at driving after him, but without the GPS …' He points at the mount on the dashboard where it used to sit. Holding down the button of the radio, he calls the station again. 'Emergency. Emergency. Emergency. Casey Station from 2351. Casey Station from 2351.' We wait but there is no reply. Lucas speaks into the radio anyway. 'Nathan Hornby is missing. Last seen twenty kilometres south-west … at coordinates …' He continues for a bit then puts the radio down. 'Sometimes they can receive even when we can't hear them, so it's worth a try.'

We stare at each other, then out at the snow.

'He must really want to talk to the Prime Minister,' I say.

Lucas sighs. 'He's fit, he runs marathons. So …' He looks out at the storm. 'We may as well settle in.'

Hornby has taken the little tent, one sleeping bag, an insulating mat and some food. We take what is left – a mat, a sleeping bag, some energy bars and some water – and pull it inside, through our tunnel. Lucas arranges the mat and sleeping bag and sits, patting the seat beside him.

 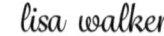

It seems strange that there's nothing to be done about Hornby, but there's no point in us all wandering off into the blizzard. I join him on the mat, my arm brushing against his as I get into position. Our cave may be cosy, but it is far from spacious.

'He'll be alright,' says Lucas.

I nod. 'He's a survivor.'

'He's got the tent. He should have the sense to get into it. He'll be fine in there. It's blizzard-proof it it's erected properly.'

'It's such a strange thing to do.'

Lucas shrugs. 'He's a politician.'

I look at him, unsure what he means.

'They build them tough.'

Silence falls. Here we are in a snow cave, the two of us, for who knows how long. It's intimate, encased in this ice womb together.

Lucas offers me some dried fish and I take some, sliding it into my pocket when he looks away.

'So, it's the summer solstice,' I say when the silence has gone on for too long.

'So it is, I had forgotten. Damn.'

'Why damn?'

'We're missing out on the special dinner. Cherie will have been cooking all day. Solstices are big in Antarctica. On the winter solstice I was here we cut a hole in the ice and went swimming.'

'No way.'

'It was something to remember.' He unwraps an energy bar and surveys it sadly. 'Happy summer solstice.'

'It's my birthday,' I say.

'Really?' He looks up, still chewing. 'I would have brought a cake. How old?'

'Twenty-eight.'

'Happy birthday.'

'I was named after the summer solstice.' I bite my lip. I shouldn't have said that.

'You were called Cougar after the summer solstice?'

I could say Cougar is my middle name, or I'd changed names later, or my parents saw a cougar on the summer solstice, or any number of things, but I'm tired of pretending. 'I'm not Cougar. I'm Summer. Summer Wright. Summer Dawn Rain Wright.'

'Well ...' Lucas laughs. 'Pleased to meet you, Summer Dawn Rain Wright. I believe we have spoken before on the phone.'

'Yes.' He doesn't sound as surprised as he should. I think of the way he helped me with the trivia ... 'Did you already know?'

'I suspected. Strongly suspected.'

'When? When did you first suspect?' I feel foolish. Here I was thinking I'd carried my role off with aplomb.

'In Hobart airport.'

So soon. 'The polar bears?'

He nods.

My cheeks flush as I remember our conversation. I'd been stupid to think I'd got away with it. In retrospect, all my exchanges with Lucas take on a different meaning. 'You've been paying me out the whole time, haven't you?'

'No. I was impressed. I was interested to see where you'd go with it. That's why I helped you out on the Trivia Night. I didn't want you exposed. You should be congratulated on your performance, Summer Dawn Rain Wright.'

'You can call me Summer.'

'Okay, Summer. So, may I ask why you're impersonating Cougar Gale?'

I shake my head. 'It's a long story.'

'And we're so short of time,' he says.

'I'm not supposed to tell anyone. If I told you I'd have to kill you.'

'It may yet come to that. Who knows how long we're going to be here for.' He waits. 'You're really not going to tell me?'

I shake my head. 'Channel Five would put out a fatwah on me.'

'Seriously?'

'Mm hm. There's a plot out in the car park where they bury people with loose lips.'

'I had no idea.'

'People think television is glamorous, but it's not. It's like the mafia.'

'Well, let's speak no more on the topic. As far as I'm concerned, you are Cougar.' He looks around him. 'Good snow-cave building,

Cougar.' He sounds ridiculously satisfied, as if being stuck in a snow cave in a blizzard is the way he'd always hoped to spend the day.

I suppose it beats being grilled by politicians over an alleged scientific fraud, which was the alternative … I find it hard to believe he would do that, but I suppose I don't know him well. 'Have you done this before?' I ask.

'Hung out in a snow cave with an undercover television celebrity?'

'No, just hung out in a snow cave.'

'Yes, lots of times. Here in Antarctica, but before that, in Norway. My father taught me how to dig a snow cave when I was a boy. It's an essential survival skill.'

'Not where I come from.'

'So your father never passed on the art, I take it?'

Usually this would be a cue for one of my signature stories. The Father Story has many variations, depending on my audience. They all got a workout when I was a kid.

My father was a mountain climber who was lost on Everest.

My father worked for the NASA space program and was blown up in a faulty rocket launch.

My father worked as a spy in the Middle East, but he got found out and …

But none of these stories seem right.

'I don't have a father. Not as such.'

'You mean you don't know who your father is?'

'No, I don't have one.' This is not something I talk about much. Being in a snow cave encourages confidences – it's hard to imagine the outside world's still there. 'Mum used a sperm bank. She didn't want a man in her life, just a child. Her boyfriends weren't what you'd call reliable. She wanted to go it alone.' I pause. 'I don't usually tell people that. Usually I make up a story, I don't know why. It's just easier, I guess. I don't feel as much of a freak.'

Lucas gives me a long look. 'It comes naturally to you, doesn't it? Making up stories.'

'Is that bad?'

'Maybe. If you don't know when to stop.'

'Hey, I know when to stop. I came out to you, didn't I?'

Silence falls for a few moments.

'I've never met the child of a sperm donor before,' says Lucas.

'You probably have. We look just like regular people. There are plenty of us out there.'

'I don't doubt it, a little bit of sperm goes a long way.'

'That's what concerns me.'

'What? That you might have siblings you don't know about?'

'Mm, sometimes I worry I'll be about to get married and at the altar the priest will say, "Does anyone know any reason why this man and this woman should not be legally wed?" '

'And a man will burst in through the back door holding medical records in his hands?'

'Yes, and he'll say, "Stop the wedding, these two are brother and sister."'

Lucas smiles. 'Do you watch a lot of soap opera?'

'I do. Do you ever worry about stuff like that?'

'I am not so worried about the wedding disaster myself. I'm more concerned one day a cooking stove will explode in my face and I'll become an amnesiac then I'll be locked in an ice-bound cabin while an arsonist burns it down …' His serious expression falters. 'And if I survive all that, my jealous ex-lover will kidnap me while I'm getting a heart transplant.'

I laugh. 'I don't believe it, you watch soap opera too. You and Rory are the only men I've ever met who watch soaps.'

'I only watch them in a manly way. I am mainly interested in the buildings and the cars.'

'Bullshit.'

He laughs. 'They have a strange DVD collection back at the station. You can't afford to be choosy. The winter I stayed here I saw season one to five of *Dynasty*.'

'But you enjoyed it, didn't you? I can tell.'

'It is strangely addictive. That's not something I would want many people to know about me.'

I put up my hand in the Girl Guide salute. 'Your secret is safe with me, Scout's honour. … As long as my secret about not being Cougar is safe with you.'

'My lips are sealed.'

'I think we understand each other. Damn. If I'd known they had season one to five back there I wouldn't have left the station. I am totally watching it when we get back.'

'So what other unlikely scenarios do you dwell on, Summer?'

'I worry someone will discover my dirty past and turn up at my doorstep to blackmail me.'

'Do you have a dirty past?'

'Kind of.'

'You do? Excellent! We have a long night ahead of us.'

There is something about the way he says this that makes my stomach flip. His arm brushes against mine with a rustling noise and I'm conscious of how close we're sitting. 'I cheated on a history test in primary school once because I hadn't studied. I had the answers written on my thigh.'

'That's it?' He sounds disappointed.

'What do you mean "that's it"? It was terrible. I thought the teacher was onto me. I still have nightmares about it. I could never be a drug smuggler.'

'I was hoping for something more salacious.'

'You're the only person I've ever told.'

'Really?'

'Uh huh. It feels good to come clean at last.'

'What makes you think I'm not going to blackmail you now I know your dark past? You could be stripped of your primary school leaving certificate.'

'You can't because I know you like *Dynasty*. You wouldn't want that to get around. It would be bad for your scientific reputation.'

'Damn.' Lucas smites his forehead. 'You've got me over a barrel. But I can always say it wasn't me, it was my evil twin.' His smile fades when he sees my expression. 'You don't believe me?'

But I'm thinking of Marley. 'I've got a twin.'

'An evil one?'

I shake my head. 'No. I'm the evil twin. You'd like Marley.'

'I expect I would.'

His words hang in the air.

'I'll show you a photo.' I reach into the pocket of my snowsuit. Despite the lack of reception, taking my phone with me is a habit. As I pull out the phone, several dried fish fall onto the snow.

Lucas eyes them. 'You've been hoarding them.'

I blush. 'I don't like dried fish.'

Lucas picks one up and pops it in his mouth. 'We may be here long enough for you to develop a taste for them.'

'I hope not.' I turn on my phone and find the photo. 'This is us on our fourteenth birthday.' I hold my phone out so Lucas can see.

In the photo, Marley and I are holding a carpet python – he has the head and me the body. It isn't a particularly large snake, maybe a metre long; we had much larger ones hanging around our house. Marley always loved catching snakes. He'd dart in and pick them up behind their head. He'd been bitten a couple of times, once badly, but it didn't stop him. At least he was never silly enough to try to pick up the thuggish brown snakes or the timid red-bellied blacks that vanished into the bushes in front of us.

'Where does Marley live?' asks Lucas.

I swallow. 'Marley's not …'

Lucas waits. The silence goes on and on as I remember …

Chapter Twenty-seven

I catch a snowflake

Marley's house was close to the hospital. It was a beaten-up weather-board, one of those old Lismore houses which stand on stilts so flood-waters can wash under them.

When I wasn't at the hospital, I wandered around his lounge room, picking up and putting down books, photos … There was one of me.

Looking at the photo, I felt the snake's warm, muscular body beneath my fingers again. 'You were a mad bastard, Marley,' I said. It was easier to talk to his picture than to the Marley who lay, as if sleeping, on the hospital bed.

'Still am,' he seemed to say.

'Haven't you got yourself a girlfriend yet?' I ran my thumb along the rim of the photograph's frame. I assumed not, or I would have run into her in hospital. The Marley in the photo was the same size as me, but now the hospital bed was barely long enough for him. 'You've got taller,' I said as I put the photo down and turned away.

'Your hair's got so long since I last saw you, Summer.'

I turned back, but of course I had only imagined his voice.

❄

Lucas is still waiting. I swallow again and start to talk …

'He never woke up,' I tell him. 'They pulled the plug eventually. And things went a little strange for me …'

'In what way?'

'It was just, being back in Nimbin. It was like it had always been. Only Marley wasn't there. I don't know, my whole life seemed so pointless, so random, so lacking in direction.'

'That sounds understandable.'

'I felt like I needed to take control, to eliminate risk. It seemed like the only way forward. I thought I could turn my life from this muddle into something manageable if I tried hard enough.' Sitting here in the ice at the southern end of the world, this seems like about the stupidest idea ever.

'Do you still feel like that?'

'I don't know. I thought I had my life worked out, everything programmed in, and here I am. Stuck in a cave in the snow in Antarctica. How random is that? '

He laughs. 'With a mad scientist. Could it get any worse?'

'I'm pretty sure it could.'

'I'm pretty sure it could too.' He holds my gaze. 'So, it must be interesting to be a twin.'

I like the way he puts it in present tense, because that's the way it feels – once a twin, always a twin. 'It's a hard habit to get out of, having someone who knows you so well. Marley's the only person I've ever known apart from me who can do this.' I hold out my hand and, dropping the middle finger, join the fingers on either side at the tips, then draw the middle finger through the hole they make and put it back again, like a rabbit coming in and out of a hole.

'Amazing. I've never seen anyone do that before.' Lucas attempts it.

'No, you're not allowed to hold your fingers in with your other fingers.'

He tries again but can't do it without his fingers separating. 'You are talented.'

I waggle my head modestly. 'It's my only talent and it doesn't translate well to the big screen.'

'It's a good one. So it's the summer solstice, your birthday. We should celebrate.'

'We used to have a ceremony for the summer solstice, back where I grew up. Marley and I always thought it was for our birthday.'

'What sort of ceremony?'

'A pagan ritual.'

'I love pagan rituals. Tell me about it.'

'Euphoria always led the ritual.'

'Euphoria?'

'My mother.'

'Great name.'

'You think? Could be worse, I suppose. The ritual didn't always run the same way. Euphoria used different approaches to keep it fresh. On my tenth birthday everyone carried painted branches – the men's were gold and the women's silver. We danced through the bush and the houses with lines of men and women interweaving.'

'We do something similar in Norway.'

'You do? I thought it was just us.'

'No. Midsummer's Eve we have big bonfires and processions. What happened next?'

'After the dance we all came together in the clearing as the sun was going down. It was always stinking hot. The men and women presented each other with a flower and a blessing.'

'It's good to acknowledge the passing seasons. We're creatures ruled by the sun, after all.'

'Euphoria used to tell me and Marley that the Sun Lord was our father. We believed it.'

'That would make you a sun princess?'

'Something like that.'

He looks thoughtful. 'We should go outside and do it.'

'What? The solstice ritual? But it's a blizzard out there.'

'We'll stay out of the wind.' He pulls up his hood and heads for the tunnel, as if we've already agreed. 'Come on.' He turns back to me. 'If you want to celebrate the glory of light, the land of the midnight sun is the place to do it.'

His enthusiasm is infectious. I pull up my hood and crawl out of the tunnel after him.

The wind and snow buffet me as I come out into the open but, following Lucas's example, I lean up against the snowbank that houses our cave. The blizzard whips around us, but we're in a pocket of stillness.

There's no sign of the sun, though it must be out there somewhere. All I can see is white. I hope Hornby is safely in his sleeping bag inside his tent. I hope we can find him tomorrow. What on earth was he thinking?

Lucas puts out his mittened hand and catches a snowflake, holding it out to me. The flake is a tiny, but perfectly formed, six-pointed star.

I raise my voice above the howl of the wind. 'Is every snowflake really different?'

'Most likely. Their shape depends on the weather conditions as they fall.' Lucas gazes at the snowflake, as if imagining its birth in the clouds, its whirling journey to Earth. 'Each snowflake has a different journey.'

'Like people.'

'But no twins. There was a man in the nineteenth century' – Lucas puts his head near mine so I can hear him – 'Wilson Bentley. Over forty years he took five thousand snowflake portraits. No two were …' A wind gust carries his words away.

I examine the snowflake on his hand. 'Do they always have six points?'

'Sometimes three, sometimes six. Mostly they're just a bunch of crystals lumped together. Not many form a star like this.'

I hold out my hand and catch my own snowflake. It's another six-pointed star, delicate and beautiful. What a shame for all that beauty to vanish when it melts.

With our backs pressed against the snowbank we're out of the worst of the wind. Still, my nose is turning numb; I won't be able to stay outside for long. I imagine Scott's team pulling their sledges into the wind, eventually giving up, battening down in their tent, ready to die. Did he wish he'd never come? I expect so. But Lucas is so at home here, like it's his natural environment. Perhaps it's his Viking blood. I can picture him with long hair and face tattoos, his vessel sailing through icy waters.

Lucas grasps my mitten, shakes his snowflake onto it and yells over a fierce wind blast. 'Happy birthday, Summer Dawn Rain Wright. You are the finest television celebrity I've ever met and I wish you blessings and joy.'

I stare at him for a moment then I get it: he is emulating the pagan flower-swapping ritual. Now it's my turn. Taking hold of his mitten, I shake my snowflake onto it. What to say? 'You are a good scientist and, um' – the wind howls in a tremendous gust – 'strangely sexy for a bearded man.' The words are whipped from my mouth. I hadn't meant to speak aloud. In the bitter cold of the storm, my cheeks heat up. I pull my hood tighter and pray he didn't hear me. The wind roars again and I'm reassured. There's no way he could have heard me.

Nothing in Lucas's face suggests I've said anything inappropriate. Snowflakes have gathered in his beard and on the wisps of sandy hair that protrude from beneath his hood. 'I'm getting cold. Want to go back inside?'

I bob my hooded head.

'When's the next pagan festival?' he yells.

'New Year's Eve.'

'I'll be there.' He bends and disappears into the tunnel.

The noise of the blizzard drops immediately as I follow him in. We climb up onto our sleeping platform. I'm still feeling awkward. I'm sure he didn't hear me, but even so …

Lucas and I sit up on the mat, side by side. He pulls his hood off. His snowflake is still on my mitten; I was careful not to crush it on my crawl back in.

'What's the Norwegian word for snow?'

'*Sno.*'

'The same?'

'Yes, but then there is light, small snowflakes, *fjukr*; larger snow-flakes, *snoflukse*; very large snowflakes, *snofloke*; heavy falling snow, *fana*; snow blowing around, *drivsno*; snowy weather with dry, light snowflakes, *fjautre*; very heavy snow, sudden snow, average snow, wet snow … Is that enough?'

'Enough for now.' I examine the flake on my mitten. 'They're so beautiful, aren't they?'

'In Greenland, the snowflakes have changed; they're not like this anymore, a lot of them. They're duller.'

'Because it's warmed up?'

'Yes, they aren't as fine, they're lumpy, misshapen. You can see it on satellite imagery. It makes the ice cap darker, when viewed from space.'

I stare at the snowflake on my hand. It lies there unmelting, a perfect jewel. 'Is that … a permanent change?'

Lucas looks up at the curving walls of the cave. He picks up his shovel and chips away a sharp edge, smoothing it out. 'Seems so.' He chips away at another protuberance and puts his shovel down. 'Life isn't always good news.'

'I'd never thought about that before. That things have changed permanently.'

'Most people try not to think about it. Sometimes you have to though.'

'Even if it makes you feel bad?'

'Perhaps.' He eyes the roof. 'It needs to be as smooth as possible or you can get drips.'

'It seems too cold for that.'

'Snow is an excellent insulator; it may get above zero in here during the night.'

'It does feel warmish.' With a puff of breath, I blow my snowflake off my hand. It vanishes among its compatriots on the floor of the cave. I pull off my hood and my beanie comes with it.

Lucas takes off his mittens, reaches over and strokes my hair down. 'That's better. You were a little Jimi Hendrix.'

Oh. My stomach flips at his touch. Beneath my puffy snowsuit, my body reacts in a way it never did for Adrian. I'd forgotten how that felt – those leaping crickets, that melting in my legs. I resist the urge to lean closer, to touch his face, to unzip … I stop my thoughts right there.

I'm venturing into scary territory. Touching Lucas would be impulsive. Anything could happen. I'm not a spontaneous person. Not anymore. Bad things happen to people who don't plan properly.

And besides; I'm encased in a metre of down. It is way too cold to take it off even if we were so inclined. And he has a beard, though that doesn't seem so much of an impediment anymore. I imagine it scratching against my cheeks, against my stomach …

Did he hear me, or didn't he?

Chapter Twenty-eight

The snow cave gets crowded

Morning finds me curled up with an arm flung across Lucas's chest. I'm not sure how this happened as I hardly slept at all. I lie there, not moving. Could I remove it quietly without him noticing? We're huddled together under our one sleeping bag. A weak light comes through the snow. It's impossible to know what it's like out there.

I shift my arm a fraction and his eyes open, meeting mine at close range.

His beard tickles my face as he moves. 'Sorry.' I move my arm. 'I didn't mean to accost you in the night.'

'No.' His hand moves, holds my arm. 'Leave it there.'

So I do. It's strange waking up so close to a man who's not my lover, but he seems fine with it and I don't want to abandon my position. It's cosy, comforting. And we are clearly over the danger period.

After our brief frisson – which may have only been my frisson – we'd spent a comradely night discussing *Dynasty* and playing word games, before retiring.

'How did you enjoy your first night in a snow cave?' Condensation rises from his mouth.

'It was warmer than expected.'

His chest rises and falls beneath my arm.

'And more friendly,' I add.

He laughs. 'But not as friendly as it might have been.'

My breath catches. The crickets jump around in my stomach and a warm glow spreads out from there. *We are not past the danger period.*

He sits up and, picking up a pole he brought into the cave, pokes it at the small ventilation hole he made yesterday. A shower of snow falls onto our ice platform. 'It's snowed a lot out there.' His voice is matter of fact.

The crickets stop jumping, my body cools. *Nothing to see, move along.* 'Do you think it's still blizzarding?'

'I'll take a look.' Lucas pulls up his hood and crawls out the tunnel.

While he's away, I pick up the camera and train it on the entrance. When I see him returning, I turn it on. 'So, Lucas Nilsson, climate scientist, how is the climate outside?'

'The weather, you mean.'

'Yes.' I'm not sure what he's getting at.

'Weather is a snapshot; climate is the collection of those snapshots. Sorry, I am being pedantic, but the distinction is important … Important to me, anyway. We have a Norwegian saying: "one swallow does not make a summer".'

'We have that saying too.'

'You do? You must have got it from the Norwegian.'

'It could have been the other way around.'

'Perhaps.' Lucas sounds unconvinced.

'Okay, let me rewind.' I press the rewind button and put the camera to my shoulder again. 'So, Lucas Nilsson, climate scientist, how is the weather outside?'

'Abominable I'm afraid. Going to have to wait it out a bit longer.'

His words remind me of *An Antarctic Mystery*. '"The weather was abominable. Rain, mixed with snow, a storm coming over the mountains",' I say.

Lucas stares at me, as if he is trying to remember something.

An Antarctic Mystery by Jules Verne. It was Marley's favourite book. I've been getting stuck into it while I'm here.'

He smiles broadly. '"So this was the sum of all our efforts, trials and disappointments …"'

'You've read it!'

'Of course I've read it. It's about the Antarctic. It's Jules Verne. What boy with an interest in science would not have read it? "Science, my lad, is made up of mistakes, but they are mistakes which it is useful to make, because they lead little by little to the truth." What's that from?'

'I don't know.'

Journey to the Centre of the Earth. How about this? "I saw the world. I learnt of new cultures. I flew across an ocean. Made a friend."' – his eyes linger on me – '"Fell in love."'

I swallow. *'Around the World in Eighty Days?'*

'Ah, so you do know Jules Verne.' Lucas takes the camera from me. Putting it on his shoulder, he trains it at me.

'So, Summer Dawn Rain Wright, this is the first day of your twenty-ninth year. You have spent the night in a snow cave getting friendly – but not too friendly – with a climatologist.' He pauses here. Perhaps he is imagining how friendly things might have been. I know I am. 'If this was *Dynasty*, what would happen next?' He peers around the camera and studies me closely.

I'm aware I have spent the night wearing a beanie which has now come off. I put my hand to my head and find my worst fears confirmed. My hair is flat on one side and sticking up like a rooster's comb on the other. 'Turn the camera off.'

'No.' Lucas's hand goes to the lens and he twists it. 'Going in for a close-up. I'll be posting this on YouTube by the way.'

'If this was *Dynasty*, I would now find out you have a dark secret which means that while we have had a pleasant night in a snow cave together, we are doomed to never repeat it. A blackmailer will soon appear, forcing you to flee the scene. I will not see you again for at least five years, by which time I will be married to your scientific rival. One night you will knock on my window and—'

'No. You've got that wrong, Summer. And you call yourself a soap opera expert. I'm surprised at you.' Lucas places the camera on the mat and switches it off. His face is serious. 'If this was *Dynasty* you would be about to discover' – he leans towards me and touches my hair – 'that climatologists find nothing more attractive than hair that goes up on one side and down on the other.'

We both laugh. But he wasn't joking because he leans closer and his beard tickles my face as he presses his lips against mine. The beard is unexpectedly pleasant, like cat's fur. I find myself becoming hot, despite the cold air.

He runs his hands down my puffy-jacketed arms. 'Sorry. I shouldn't have done that. This isn't the place ...' He glances at the walls of the snow cave.

My heart is beating fast and I have no idea why I've been so set against beards my whole life. I want to feel his beard against my face again.

He kisses me again. Just once and lightly, but it feels like a pact. *Later*, it seems to say. 'May as well go back to sleep, don't you think?'

'Excellent idea.'

So we lie down again and pull the sleeping bag over us and his arm goes around me. Our chests are together and I wish I could feel his heartbeat, but there is too much down between us.

'Are you worried about your penguin chick?' I ask.

'No. Cherie has been helping me feed it. It will be fine.'

'Oh good.'

I yawn and he yawns too, at exactly the same time.

'"Those who yawn at the same time are not on bad terms",' says Lucas. 'It's a Norwegian saying.'

'It's a good one.' I lie there for a while, my face tingling where his beard brushed against me, feeling his chest move up and down beneath my arm. I can't imagine I will sleep – my heart is beating too fast – but there is something soporific about the stillness of the snow cave and the rhythm of Lucas's breathing. I yawn again …

I must have slept a little because when I open my eyes, the light in the cave is brighter. I turn my head and study Lucas. He's still sleeping, his thick hair tousled and his face serene. I touch his beard with the tip of my finger and he twitches. I take my finger away at once. And then I hear voices.

At first I think I must be imagining it. But the voices get louder and become more distinguishable. I hear Rory, Mike the station leader and, finally – I sit bolt upright – Adrian. I stare at the tunnel entrance. Adrian? Surely not. There's a grunt and a shuffling noise and the round lens of a camera emerges from the tunnel.

'Sorry, Sum, ah Cougar.' Rory is on the other end of the camera, crouching in the tunnel. 'Maxine made me.' He wriggles forward, crawling up onto our platform to make room for the person behind him. Maybe if I close my eyes, it will all go away. It's hardly credible

Rory and Adrian are in our snow cave.

Lucas sits up and I open my eyes again. He stares at Rory then at the tunnel.

'Move forward and let me in.' It's Adrian.

Rory's knee jostles against mine as he wriggles forward.

More voices echo from the tunnel.

'What's happening up ahead? Keep going.' This sounds like Maria.

'Can you get out of the tunnel?' says Mike.

I feel like I'm being smothered. Adrian and Rory perch on our tiny platform while more people try to force their way in.

'What?' Lucas yawns.

I sit up and shuffle backwards to create more space. Lucas does the same. This is a bad move as Adrian and Rory shuffle forward to let Mike and Maria in. Mike scrambles up onto the platform while Maria crouches in the tunnel. My eyes dart around the cave. Damn, it wasn't a dream.

Rory has the camera trained on me from about one foot away. 'What are you doing here?' My voice is croaky.

'Maxine told me I'd better get out here and get some footage. Now the Minister's gone missing. And the email leaks. Things are hotting up.' Rory seems uncomfortable.

The email leaks … Does that mean it's in the media?

Lucas shoots me a glance. There's something assessing about it. He doesn't think it was me, does he? That I leaked the data fraud story to Channel Five? I'd like to clear this up, but it's hard in the present company.

Adrian glares at Lucas from an awkward squatting position. 'Handy for you, isn't it? That Nathan's gone missing.' As he tries to straighten his legs he bangs his head on the ceiling. 'Ow.'

'Speculation doesn't help anyone.' Mike peers around Adrian's back.

And at once I see how the story could play out. Lucas and Hornby were at each other's throats yesterday – it isn't much of a stretch to imagine things turned nasty out there in the blizzard. With Hornby gone, Lucas's main accuser is out of the picture.

Adrian looks between Lucas and me. 'I wasn't interrupting anything, was I?' There's a tense set to his jaw.

I flush.

'No.' Lucas speaks first.

It's the right thing to say, but I feel wounded. There might not have been much happening, but … The snow cave seems claustrophobic and stuffy, as if oxygen supplies are being depleted. 'Do you need me here, Rory?'

He blushes for no obvious reason. 'No. I can do it. You're right.'

'I … I might go outside.'

Lucas's face is impossible to read. 'You got my radio message last night, did you?' he says to Mike.

'Yes, we got going as soon as we could,' says Mike. 'It's all hands on deck. There's two more search teams setting out from the station.'

'I'll get you wired up, shall I?' Rory produces a small microphone and clips it to Lucas's snowsuit.

What has induced him to venture so far beyond his usual job description? He doesn't meet my eyes.

'So Doctor Nilsson, what can you tell us about Minister Hornby's disappearance?' Rory says as I squeeze past Adrian and Mike in the direction of the tunnel.

But the tunnel is blocked by Maria. Behind her, Cherie peers over her back.

'Hi, Cougar,' says Cherie.

I try to ignore the feeling that the walls are closing in on me. 'Could you back up?'

Maria and Cherie crawl backwards out the tunnel as I advance. I push past them and at last I'm free. As I taste the fresh air, they crawl back in.

Outside, the wind has dropped a little and the cloud has lifted. I stand up with difficulty; my body has frozen into crawling position. Another Hagg is parked next to ours and a Ski-Doo sits next to that. I lower my goggles as a blast of wind blows a spray of snow at me. I feel exposed, like a rabbit pulled out of its burrow. My Seiko watch tells me it is one pm. Lucas and I have been in the snow cave all morning. I wave my arms and stamp my feet, keeping my back to the bitter wind.

Some time later, Lucas emerges from the tunnel. He looks my way but the snow whips up around us and he seems far away. I wish we could crawl back inside our cave and stay there. We would eject the intruders and start a dynasty of hardy children who thrive on a diet of seals, penguins and bits of moss.

The remainder of the party crawl from the tunnel one by one, like ants emerging from a nest. Rory first, still looking sheepish, then Cherie, Maria, Mike, and finally Adrian.

'Right,' says Mike, 'we're all going to take different routes back so we cover more ground to search for Hornby.' He hands out maps to Lucas and Maria and points at a dotted line on each. 'These are your routes. They're gearing up some more search parties back at the base.'

Our vehicle is covered in snow. Lucas and I scrape the ice off the windscreen and climb inside.

Lucas turns the key in the ignition and the snowmobile shudders. 'It was nice to spend your birthday with you, Summer.' His manner is reserved.

I don't know what to think, what to feel. For all I know, it's a Norwegian custom to kiss after spending the night in a snow cave. He seems so distant. It's all too hard. But we have the drive back to talk to each other. That's plenty of time to work out where we stand.

Mike and Rory climb back inside the other Hagg and Maria and Cherie climb on the Ski-Doo, Maria in front.

Before we can start, the back door opens and Adrian climbs in. 'Thought I might join you two,' he says.

Chapter Twenty-nine
Good news, bad news

We take off with a jolt and in no time at all, the entrance to our snow cave has vanished. I suppose the cave will gradually sink and there'll be just a small bubble of air, heading slowly for the sea. Perhaps in a thousand years scientists will drill an ice-core sample through it and speculate on what that bubble means. There will be nothing to show that Lucas and I talked about soap opera and Jules Verne and snow-flakes in there. I sink into a reverie as we make our way across the snow.

Lucas drives fast, bouncing over the sastrugi. 'You look out on your side, I'll look on mine.'

'I'll look both ways,' says Adrian.

Lucas seems tense. I suppose he has the media to worry about now. And the speculation about what happened to Hornby. He doesn't think I leaked the email story, does he? I glance at his profile before returning my gaze to the snow. Is he the kind of person who would fake data or resort to violence? I don't think so. But maybe if enough is at stake …

I feel like I should be trying to figure out what, if anything, we mean to each other. But I am tired, and he is preoccupied and our relationship is much, much too vague to pin down. And besides, Adrian is in the back seat.

If Lucas is thinking along the same lines, he shows no sign of it.

The clouds have cleared and the sun is bright by the time we get back to the station. A helicopter rests on the helipad, its blades turning slowly.

Lucas gives me a brief smile as he pulls up, but his face is impassive as he climbs out.

Mike waves him over to the group that has gathered next to the other Hagg.

No-one seems to care what I do, so I head for the station door. I feel at a loss as I wander down the corridor towards my room.

Inside, I open my laptop to check my emails. There are two messages dated yesterday, from Jacinta and Maxine. Maxine's is titled *Urgent* and Jacinta's says *Mega-exciting news*. I feel a pang that no-one has sent me a birthday email, but then I remember only work people have access to my special Antarctic email address. For some obscure IT-related reason, my personal emails don't get through here.

Urgent – I open Maxine's email first. It's best to get it out of the way. Her missive is terse.

> I have received your last segment. Words fail me. This was supposed to be about scientists' hobbies not ancient history.

I imagine her typing – her baby-blue eyes like gimlets, her fingers pounding the keyboard. My stomach takes a dive.

> You were warned. Cougar is on her way, but until then I've told Rory that he's in charge.

That explains the sheepishness.

> Stop broadcasting and return immediately on the next flight. As of this minute, you are no longer an employee of Channel Five. Hand in your keys on return to Sydney.

I take a deep breath as I close the email. So much for instant promotion to scriptwriter. I guess Maxine wasn't too keen on the ice-core episode.

I lie down on the bed. Though I should have expected this, I didn't. Being sacked is a new experience. I don't like it much. What am I going to do with myself? Tendrils of anxiety creep through my body. My life is going off course. I remember Jacinta's email – *mega-exciting news*. I sit up again.

The tendrils go into writhing overdrive as I read Jacinta's message.

> You are going viral! Your shows are an underground sensation. Maxine's freaked out because she can't control it and the advertisers are worried about their brand image. I know Cougar's on her way, but don't stop. You're better than her!

Jacinta has posted three YouTube links. The first is my teaser from the airport and on arrival in Antarctica. I check how many views it has.

Ten thousand! *Oh my goodness.* No, I've missed a zero. One hundred thousand views. This does my head in. Why are one hundred thousand people watching me pretend to be Cougar Gale while encased in down, balaclava and goggles? Is it because I'm a freak? My cheeks flush. I feel like I've been stripped naked in public.

There are about a hundred comments. I scan through them with a sense of dread.

> I've never liked Cougar before, but this is funny!
>
> Love the line that there are lots of scientists and only one Minister. He'd better watch out!
>
> Is this really Cougar? She seems much funnier.
>
> A chocolate treat is what you need when you're stuck in a blizzard – LOL.

My heart is thudding as I click on the second link. My 'Sex on Ice' broadcast has about half a million views and hundreds of comments.

> The sex life of krill – rofl.
>
> … crustacean orgy
>
> … krill mate with anyone
>
> … penguin colony is like neighbours
>
> … penguin swingers from hell

Did I say all that stuff? How was I so stupid?

Below the comments are several links to other videos. My program has spawned off-shoots. I click on a couple. There are kids rapping about penguin love and commentators pondering the significance of Victorian attitudes to penguin sex. Jacinta's boyfriend's indie band has whipped out a song called 'The Krill Issue' featuring a dance move where they all wave their legs and arms wildly. I wonder if it will catch on.

Jacinta's third link – my rock-climbing wall teaser – has over a million views. Who are these people? Why don't they have anything better to do? The comments are taking a more pointed turn.

> Who is this?
>
> Why is she wearing a balaclava?

Is it one of those Russian girls?

I think it's Kitty McIntyre.

Who cares? She's funny. No way is she Cougar Gale though.

It's got to be a teaser for a new comedy show.

I reckon the Hornby disappearance is part of it.

Yeah, clever marketing.

It's because there's an election coming up.

There is a lone dissenting voice:

This isn't Cougar. Cougar is much sexier.

I am a little deflated as I scan to the signature line – Doreen. *Doreen?* I'm not sure what the name tells me about Cougar's fan base, except that it is broad.

I click the links shut. My head is spinning like I'm having an out-of-body experience. I'm an internet sensation. This is not the kind of thing I ever imagined would happen to me and I'm not sure if I like it. It's uncomfortable, like walking down the street and having strangers pass comment on your outfit.

There's a knock on the door. 'Summer.' It's Adrian.

What does he want? 'What?'

Adrian pokes his head through the doorway. 'I wanted to say … happy birthday for yesterday, Summer.'

'Thanks.' Adrian looks like he has more to say, so I wait. I yawn. I'm so tired. I've hardly slept since I've been in Antarctica and I have a weird, floaty feeling in my head. It makes it hard to concentrate.

'I was worried about you. When you went missing.'

I nod and yawn again. 'I was fine.'

'I wanted to tell you … the Cougar thing. It was a big mistake. It's over.'

I nod again. 'Right.' Adrian's words wash over me. They have an echoey quality. Maybe I'm getting sick.

'I've been watching your broadcasts. They're good. They're not right for Channel Five's target audience but they could work well for another market. With more focus and planning, you …' Adrian continues in this vein for a while. I'm not sure if he's offering professional advice or something more personal. It's hard to make sense of it. I yawn again. Can you die from lack of sleep?

'So I was thinking you have potential there for …'

A movement outside the window catches my attention. Mike and Lucas are still talking beside the Hagg. Lucas has taken his hood off and my stomach knots as I examine his profile. I don't get it. One minute he was so warm and the next … Ridiculously, I feel like I've had a one-night stand in a snow cave. I blink. I'm not about to cry, am I?

'Productive partnership … assist with developing your capability …'

Is Adrian offering consultancy services? I'm sure I can't afford them. I can't believe Maxine sacked me.

Outside the window Mike and Lucas make their way towards the building. Lucas's face is turned away from me.

Adrian has stopped. He seems to be waiting for a response.

'Pardon?' I turn back towards him.

'I said I miss you.'

'Oh.' Something loosens inside my chest. I gnaw the inside of my cheek.

Adrian is waiting. He looks solid and comforting there, like a safe port in a storm. I blink again.

Should I say I miss him too? It would be true. I miss the way he made me feel like my life was on track. Life without Adrian is full of uncertainty. It's unpredictable. Just look what happened in the cave with Lucas. Adrian's gaze is strangely hypnotic. His face is earnest.

'We should talk over dinner. Those broadcasts you did. You could go far with that. We need to get a strategy and a marketing plan worked out for you …'

I glance at my laptop – at the thousands of views, the hundreds of comments – and I have no idea how to respond to this, what it means. My heart beats faster at the thought of trying to deal with it. Adrian wants to help. I could do with some help.

'I can make a spreadsheet and get some introductory figures.' His voice is like a warm bath.

I nod gratefully. 'Okay. Let's talk over dinner. That would be good.'

'Great. The dining room, seven-thirty?' Adrian smiles his old charming smile.

'Okay. I'll see you then.' I yawn as he closes the door. It's nice Adrian's taking an interest in my career. It's nice that he cares.

I lean against the pillows, at a loose end after he leaves. *An Antarctic Mystery* is on my bedside table. I flick through it, coming to a picture of one man chasing another. *I was afraid, I ran away from him*, reads the caption.

Outside the window Lucas and Mike have disappeared. Snow blows up around the empty Hagglund. I wonder where Hornby is. I look at the picture again. The men look like Lucas and Hornby. Would Lucas do that – chase Hornby out into the snow? Maybe; how would I know?

I put my hands behind my head. What should I do with myself? It's all been so hectic and although I'm so tired, I can't sit here doing nothing. I'm in Antarctica – I need to make the most of it. Only two days until Christmas. I suppose Cougar will be doing the special in the igloo instead of me … My igloo! If I can do nothing else right, at least I can do that. I am the igloo-building expert. It's my one claim to fame. I can't leave without finishing it. My stomach growls so I open a new packet of Tim Tams and take one out.

Opening my door I glance up and down the corridor. All clear.

The TV news is on in the lounge room as I go past. I pause as I hear the words *climate change*, and lean in the doorway to catch the story. *Accused climate scientist's wife and lawyer Melanie Nilsson says that …* My biscuit turns to sludge in my mouth as I stare at the image of an earnest and attractive woman with a blonde bob speaking. '*… this is completely cooked up. It shows how low …*'

Climate scientist's wife. The words repeat in my head. Why didn't Lucas mention he was married? I swallow with difficulty and put the rest of the biscuit in the bin. Why should I care? Nothing happened. Nothing much. Lucas Nilsson's marital status is none of my business. But it feels like it is.

Outside, the two snowmobiles and helicopter have gone, searching for Hornby no doubt. I shiver inside my snowsuit as I think of him out there in the snow. The blizzard is spent, but the wind lingers.

Although I'm wearing all the usual clobber and have my hood tied up tightly, the air bites at my face. I set off at a brisk pace towards the rocky outcrop and by the time my igloo comes into view, my nose is an ice-block. Hopefully a bit of igloo-building will warm me up and get rid of the lump that has settled in my chest.

A small glow of satisfaction fills me as I approach the igloo. I've got further than I thought; it is quite igloo-like. I stop and take a photo. *My igloo.* No matter what else happens, no-one can take this away from me. I am an igloo-builder.

I'll need to work from the inside now to finish it off. Kneeling, I crawl into the tunnel.

'Ah, you're back, Oates,' says a familiar voice as I emerge into the interior.

Chapter Thirty

I meet Scott of the Antarctic

Nathan Hornby is patting at the snow walls, putting the finishing touches on my igloo. What used to be an opening to the sky is now a rooftop dome. I gape at it. It's hard to know what's more shocking – Hornby, or the fact he's finished my igloo.

The Minister is a little worse for wear. The circles under his eyes are darker, there's stubble on a chin I've only ever seen clean-shaven, and patches of red across his cheeks – which could be frostbite – give him a haggard appearance.

'There, all done.' Hornby inspects the roof, sits and pats the snow beside him. 'I'm afraid I had to eat the huskies,' he says.

He sounds so convincing I almost check for gnawed bones or bits of fur. 'How did you get here?'

'I was looking for the eggs.'

I'm a little worried. He sounds sane, but huskies? Eggs?

He pats the snow again and I join him on the ground in order to inspect him more closely. Perching on the edge of the platform, I dangle my feet into the tunnel entrance. *I can't believe he finished my igloo.*

'It was a terrible journey,' he says. 'The worst in the world.' The book he was reading in the Hagg yesterday lies open on top of a thermal mat – *The Worst Journey in the World.* 'Have you got them?'

'What?'

'The eggs.'

'No. There are powdered eggs back at the station if you want some I think.'

'No, no. The emperor penguin eggs.'

I decide it's best to humour him. 'No. I haven't got the emperor penguin eggs. Sorry.'

Hornby sighs. 'All that effort for nothing. The blizzard' – he shudders – 'I thought I was a goner.'

This, at least, makes sense. 'Did you sleep in the tent?'

'No. I kept on and kept on.'

It's hard to imagine, trekking for hours in those conditions. No wonder he's deranged; I expect I'd be the same. I feel a reluctant respect for his resilience.

It's cosy inside the igloo now the roof is on. I was planning on shooting some more igloo-building footage but it's too late now, thanks to Hornby. I glare at him. He seems oblivious. Making the best of a bad situation, I pull out my phone. 'Do you mind if I ask you a few questions?'

'No.' Hornby straightens his shoulders. 'That's why I'm here.'

I feel like we're having two different conversations. 'You're in the igloo for an interview?'

He snorts. 'No. In Antarctica. My man Alan said you'd be here.'

'Alan?'

'Yes, Alan. You know him. Good man with a spreadsheet.'

'Oh, Adrian.'

'That's what I said. So, let's get going.' He assumes the far-off gaze of a grizzled explorer. 'A last message. For when I'm gone. Let these words and my remains tell the tale.'

His words echo around the snow cave. 'It's not going to come to that, Minister.' I unzip my little backpack. 'Would you like a Tim Tam?'

Hornby takes a Tim Tam and gazes out towards the tunnel. 'Great God, this is an awful place.'

A blue glow comes through the ice; it's beautiful in here, but I can see what he means. This is not a place for people – Antarctica can kill you without trying.

I press the button on my phone camera and aim it at him. 'How did you end up here?'

Hornby looks shifty. 'I wasn't doing anything wrong.'

'No, Minister. I'm sure you weren't. But how did you get to this igloo?'

'I was on the way to the penguins.'

'You were going to the penguins?'

'Yes. The emperor penguins. I wanted an egg. For my collection.'

I glance at the book, remembering the story Lucas told me. 'An egg? But they lay their eggs in mid-winter.'

'I know that,' he says impatiently. 'Emperor penguins have the worst life in the world.'

'But did you set off alone from the snowmobile on purpose, or' – I have to ask – 'did someone chase you away?'

He touches the book on the table in front of him. 'It's all in here. The full story. I've written it down. Egg collecting. It's the only way.'

I sigh. 'Did Lucas threaten you?'

'Nilsson?' Hornby turns a deeper shade of red. He looks into the phone camera and speaks with the conviction of politicians everywhere. 'If that climate change story he peddles is true, my name's not Scott of the Antarctic.' He gets up. 'Better get going. Can't let the Norwegian beat us.'

I give up on getting the truth out of him. Better get him back to the station for medical treatment. 'Okay, let's go.'

'You're a good man, Oates.' Hornby picks up *The Worst Journey in the World* and slips it inside his snowsuit.

I inspect the ceiling before we crawl out the tunnel. 'You did a good job finishing off the igloo.' I suppose I have to give him that.

'Built it from scratch. Man has to know how to build an igloo out here. That's what it's all about. Getting out in the wild.'

'No you didn't,' I squeal. 'I built most of it. You just closed up the gap in the roof.'

'But you just got here.' He sounds like he's talking to a child with a vivid imagination.

'I built it before. I've been working on it for ages.'

Hornby looks wary. 'Settle down, Oates. The mind plays funny tricks on you in these conditions.'

Pot kettle black. 'But I did build it. I've been slaving away on it for days. I've practically killed myself stomping snow and cutting blocks.'

Hornby snorts and heads for the tunnel. 'I think I'd know. I spent the night in it.'

I narrow my eyes at his backside as he crawls ahead of me and it takes every ounce of restraint left in me not to kick it.

Hornby stretches as he gets outside. 'Worst place in the world,' he mutters.

The sun is low in the sky and a pinkish light touches the snow. Beyond the ice is the sea. A tall iceberg catches the sun, burning gold. I can't imagine anything more beautiful, but I don't bother to contradict him.

'Are we far from the pole?' Hornby pulls a GPS from his pocket and eyes the screen. 'This thing says we're there.'

I lean over his shoulder. The *You are Here* arrow is pointing right at Casey Station. He must have followed the GPS all the way to my igloo, not realising the station was just over the rise.

Hornby's stride is sure as he makes his way towards the base. If it wasn't for his Scott of the Antarctic complex he'd seem practically untouched. 'As if it isn't enough to beat me to the pole, he tries to steal my wife,' he mutters. 'I'll show that Scandinavian scoundrel.'

I think he's referring to the explorer Amundsen, rather than Lucas, but it's hard to be sure.

No-one is outside when we get back to the station, but the aroma of baked potatoes drifts towards us as Hornby and I walk down the corridor to the dining room.

'Food lies in front of us, death stalks us from behind,' Hornby intones. 'Where is the food depot?'

'Here, Minister.' I open the door to the dining room. 'Look who I found.' I stand aside to let Hornby in.

Lucas is sitting at a table with Maria. He and Hornby lock eyes.

'Damn,' Hornby mutters, 'the Norwegian got here first.' He backs out, shuts the door and leans against the wall. 'Things have come out against us, Oates, but we have no cause for complaint.'

Behind the door, multiple chairs scrape at once. I lean against the wall next to Hornby and take a deep breath. I know it's trivial, but I can't let this go. 'That was my igloo, Minister. I put a lot of work into it. I want that acknowledged in press statements.'

He snorts. 'You're well paid for what you do, Oates. Everyone knows the expedition leader takes the credit but not the blame.'

He obviously thinks I'm one of his staff. 'It's only fair—'

The door flies open and, led by Rory, the occupants of the dining room swarm out. 'Where have you been, Minister?' Rory raises the camera to his shoulder.

The Minister straightens his back and assumes a statesmanlike air. 'I do not regret this journey, which has shown that Englishmen can endure hardships, help one another, and meet death with fortitude.' He turns to me, as if for support.

Not knowing what else to do, I bob my head like a ministerial sycophant. Someone has to do it and Adrian, who gets paid for this, seems too dumbstruck to fulfil his job description.

Hornby sighs deeply. 'Had we lived, I should have had a tale to tell of the hardihood, endurance and courage of my companions which would have stirred the heart of every Englishman.'

Adrian's eyes go from me back to his boss. 'What happened to you, Minister? We've all been worried.'

'I built an igloo.' He doesn't look at me.

I bite my lip, but it's no good, I have to set the record straight. '*I* built an igloo. The Minister stayed in it.'

All eyes shift from the Minister to me.

'Are you saying you built an igloo for the Minister?' Rory turns the camera towards me.

'No, I—'

'Are you saying you've been outside without an escort?' says Mike.

'No, I—'

'In Antarctica' – Hornby looks from me to Lucas and back again – 'you get to know people so well that in comparison you do not know the people in civilisation at all.'

Is he implying I'm a liar? 'I did build it.' I don't care if I get into trouble for going out of bounds. The igloo is one of the best things I've ever done and I want the credit for it. I don't know why it's so important to me, but it is. 'It's my igloo.'

'Did anyone see you build it?' says Hornby.

'No, I—'

'I rest my case,' he says.

Rory has been swinging the camera between Hornby and me but Adrian puts up his hand. 'No more filming, the Minister needs to eat.'

I am fuming. As I turn away, I catch Lucas's eye by mistake. This gives me a strange feeling in my stomach. I have a strong urge to kick him as well. I don't know what's coming over me. Maybe it's the lack of sleep. I'm not hungry and the thought of being in the dining room with Lucas has no appeal. I decide to retreat to my room before I do something undignified.

Inside my room, I take off my outdoor gear, thinking of Lucas. *The kiss … His wife … Bastard.* I wish I *had* kicked him. There's a knock at the door.

Adrian pokes his head in. He looks handsome, clean shaven and wide awake. The corridor light surrounds him with a golden glow.

I yawn.

'Well done for finding Nathan,' he says. 'God knows how long he would have stayed out there for.'

'Does he still think he's Scott of the Antarctic?'

Adrian nods. 'Hopefully it will wear off. The doctor's checking him out. Sleep deprivation and exposure, she says. Stress-induced psychosis. Happens to some people in Antarctica apparently. She's given him a shot to help him sleep.'

'Sleep deprivation, huh?' I yawn more loudly.

Adrian seems to be waiting for something. 'Do we have a dinner date?' he says at last.

Our meeting had slipped my mind. 'I'm not hungry.'

Adrian pulls a bottle of red wine and two glasses from behind his back. 'Have a drink with me?

I look at the bottle. A drink would be relaxing. And perhaps it will help me sleep. I yawn again and nod. 'Okay.'

Adrian pulls a package from his pocket. 'I've got some cheese. King Island Blue.'

We sit side by side on the bed and Adrian pours the wine. I feel embraced by his capability. Almost hypnotised.

I take a sip.

'Do you like it? It's the Chateau Lafite Rothschild. I brought it with me from Sydney. Can you notice the vanilla and chocolate flavour?'

I take another sip. It tastes like wine. I drain the glass and hold it out for a refill.

'This is special wine, Summer.' Adrian sounds reproving, but he fills my glass.

I take another gulp and the ache that settled in my chest at the sight of Lucas dissipates. 'Yeah, I agree, itsh good.' I gulp again. Something occurs to me. 'In the igloo, Hornby said something about you – that you'd told him I'd be there.'

'I told him you'd be in the igloo?'

I'm not sure if that's exactly what Hornby said; it's hard to remember. Adrian shrugs. 'Not making a lot of sense at the moment, is he?'

'No.'

'I know I said this before, but I've missed you, Summer.'

'I've missed you too.' It's a relief to say this, like giving in to an irresistible force. A gust of wind hits the window as if reminding me of something I've forgotten. 'What happened with you and Cougar?'

'It was nothing.' Adrian's voice is soothing. 'I told you that. It was a mistake. It's over. I'm sorry.'

I nod. 'Anyway, we're here for a planning meeting, right? So ...' I lose track of where I'm going with this.

'The internet thing,' says Adrian.

'Oh yeah. That.' I try to pull myself together. I don't know why it's so hard. I expect I could do with a lie-down. 'What should I do about the internet thing?'

'There are a few different options. You can capitalise on your celebrity to leverage ...' Adrian goes on for a while.

I yawn, and possibly drop into a micro-sleep. When I realise he's stopped talking, I ask, 'But what about Cougar? Aren't you in love with her?'

Adrian puts his glass on the bedside table with a bang. 'Alright.'

I jump.

'I've done the figures. I'm going to show you.' He pulls a USB stick out of his pocket and, plugging it into my laptop, opens a PowerPoint slide titled *Summer v Cougar*. It's a bar graph. He clicks the mouse and the first bar thrusts vigorously up into the slide.

It's mesmerising.

He clicks again and again. Adrian pauses once all the bars are erected.

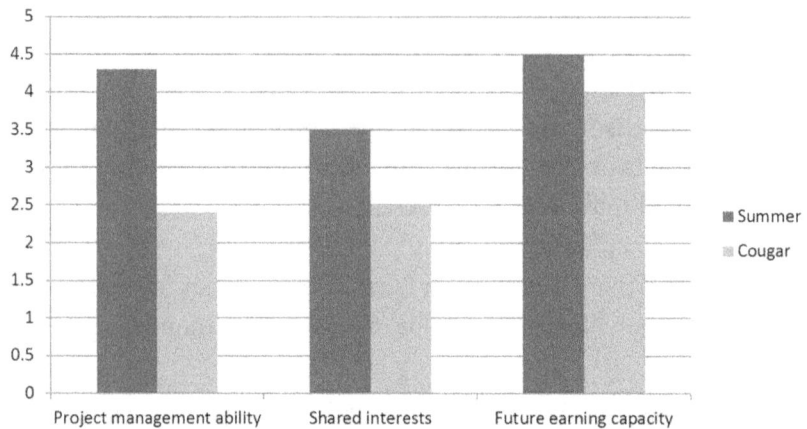

I scan the chart, lingering on the column marked 'Shared interests'. 'I thought you were enjoying the rock-climbing.'

'It wore thin. There's another chart.' He clicks the mouse.

This time there are only two protrusions, which is lucky. I'm not sure I could take much more excitement.

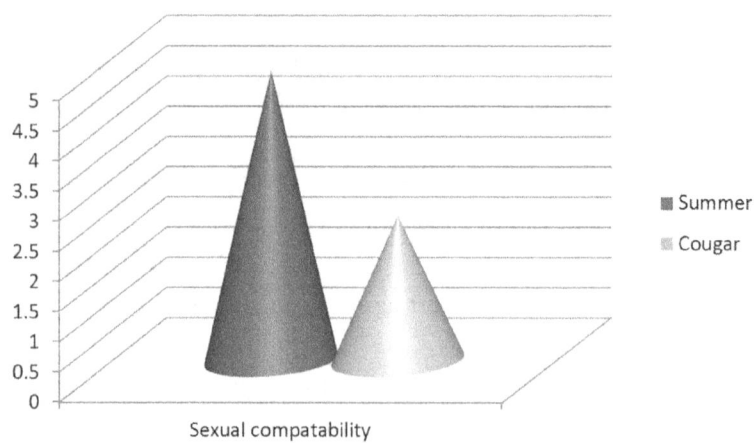

I narrow my eyes as I examine the first cone. 'So, what's that? Four out of five?'

'Four point one.'

I purse my mouth. 'That's not bad. And Cougar was?'

'One point six.'

I stare at the two cones. 'How'd you work that out?'

'It's a complex formula. I can show you my workings if you like. I based it on time and motion studies for construction in the—'

I flap my hand. 'Maybe another time.'

'So, as you can see, Summer, Cougar and I didn't add up.' Adrian shuffles onto the floor and gets to one knee.

'What are you doing, Adrian?' I peer over at him. 'Did you drop something?'

He clicks the mouse again and the next slide appears. This time there are no suggestive eruptions from the bottom of the chart.

Summer, will you marry me?

I read the words, but I'm not sure how to take them.

Perhaps Adrian is conducting a psychological analysis as part of another graph in progress. I must be careful how I answer.

He clicks the mouse again and Burt Bacharach starts singing 'You're Just Too Good To Be True'.

I turn my gaze to Adrian. 'I thought we were having a business meeting.'

'It is, of sorts. It's about combining our enterprises. You and me, Summer, together we'll be more than the sum of our parts.'

Burt Bacharach is still crooning from the computer. Adrian clicks the mouse again and brightly coloured butterflies fly across the screen.

The way their wings flutter makes me dizzy. 'There wasn't something … in the wine, was—'

'I'm sorry I don't have a ring, but as soon as we get back to Australia …' Adrian takes my hand and presses it to his lips. 'I'll take care of you, Summer. You won't have to worry about anything when you're with me.'

Adrian clicks the mouse again and the butterflies arrange themselves on top of the words *Summer, will you marry me?*

I'm swept along, as if I'm in a movie of my life. The room spins. I open and shut my mouth. The wind lashes against the window, but I ignore it: what would the wind know? Unlike last time at Le Max, my hair is unfluffed and I'm wearing neither lipstick, slinky top nor perfume. Despite that, my role is clear. I accept graciously.

My three sloths wake up and applaud. For a moment I think they will morph into Joy, Delight and Gratitude and do a happy dance. They must be exhausted though, as they go straight back to sleep.

Adrian gets off the floor and kisses me. And if I have a slight longing for whiskers on my face, I soon stifle it. I put my wine glass on the table as we sink to the bed.

As usual, Adrian is a skilled and focused lover. We both get off quickly, which helps to dispel any lingering doubts. The room spins and the wind lashes against the window as we lie side by side afterwards, our hands intertwined.

'Only four point one?' I say.

Adrian turns his head to me. 'Four point four.'

'Yay.' I am elated by my upgrade.

But the wind weighs in. *In Antarctica, you get to know people so well that in comparison you do not know the people in civilisation at all*, it whispers. I ignore it. I expect I have a touch of the same psychosis as Hornby, but I'm sure if I can get some sleep, I will be fine.

After a little while Adrian lets himself out quietly as my bed is much too narrow for two. I hear a voice in the corridor as he shuts my door – *Lucas*. Lucas saw Adrian come out of my room … *Well, good.* He knows I'm not sitting around pining for him.

As I close my eyes I am happy. I am very, very happy. The only cloud on my horizon is that the phantom guitar player is at it again.

Chapter Thirty-one
My last product placement

'The plane's leaving at twelve o'clock,' says Mike to me at breakfast. 'So you'll have to get the snowmobile over to the runway at nine. Nice work on your show, by the way. We all had a look on YouTube last night.'

'Thanks. Glad you liked it.' I'm surprised it was his kind of thing. I would have imagined he'd prefer a more cerebral approach. I yawn. Despite the wine and the sex, I slept badly again last night.

My memory of Adrian's proposal is a little jumbled. Did he really play me Burt Bacharach? He must have, as I was humming it when I woke up. *I'm engaged!* I nudge my inner sloths to show some emotion but they are indifferent. Still tired, I expect.

'Are you posting any more shows?' asks Mike.

I touch my pocket where the SD card from the snow cave nestles in a small plastic box. I don't know what to do with it. It's a shame to waste it though. There's also my iPhone footage … 'Maybe.' I glance around the dining room but Lucas isn't there. *Good.*

Apart from the fact that he's tucking into his bacon and eggs with unusual alacrity, the Minister appears almost unscathed by his polar adventure. His cheeks are just a little ruddier than usual. I guess the sleeping injection did the trick. *The Worst Journey in the World* is open on the table beside him. He's near the end.

Adrian winks when Hornby isn't looking. We've agreed to keep our relationship secret until we get back to Australia. With Cougar turning up today, I have enough revelations to deal with. I smile back, stifling another yawn. I'm so tired, I wish Adrian could pick me up and carry me home, but I need to get through one more day in Antarctica.

Maria rises as I head for the door. 'Cougar.'

My stomach clenches. She's probably seen 'Sex on Ice' and wants to punch me out for defaming krill. If so, I may as well surrender at once. I've seen her in action and I have no chance. 'I'm sorry about the krill. I know you—'

Maria takes my arm and steers me towards a corner.

My heart is beating in double-quick time. I glance around, hoping for support, but no-one is looking our way. Will she run up the wall and spring off it, hurling me to the ground with a couple of well-placed feet to the chest? 'I didn't put it up on YouTube. That was my friend, Jacinta.'

Maria looks puzzled. 'Yes, but you made the show.'

'I didn't realise … how important—'

'I want to thank you, Cougar.'

'You do?'

'For what you have done for krill.'

I blink. I'm not sure I'm out of danger. She could be luring me into lowering my guard.

'I was not sure at first, but now I see … you have made krill sexy.' She rolls the word in her mouth. 'You have given them the recognition they deserve. I saw the TV show, and the comments, and now, the song. *Oo, oo, we are small but we are sexy. We are krill and there's no holding us down.* I love that song. Today I am getting ten times more hits on my krill blog and I have been invited to appear on a television panel show when I get back to Sydney. I was wrong. We needed a different approach to the krill issue. Mine was too serious. The krill are grateful.'

'How do you know?'

'I just know.' As Maria walks off she is humming the tune to 'The Krill Issue'.

Well, how about that. My conversation with Maria has convinced me – I have work to do. I glance at my watch. One and half hours until I have to catch the snowmobile – time to film one last episode.

I know I'm not supposed to venture out on my own, but outside the sun is sparkling on the snow and I'm not going to spend my last morning in Antarctica sitting indoors. Grabbing Rory's spare camera from my room, I stride down the corridor. On the way I pass the phone and remember I never rang Euphoria.

Mum picks up the phone on the third ring. 'Summer? I don't know why you didn't tell me you were going to Antarctica. Patsy saw you on the TV. I went and watched it at her place. You were terrific.'

'Thanks, Euphoria.'

'So are they giving you your own show?'

'Um, no. I've been sacked.'

'But that's crazy. We all loved it here.'

'The advertisers weren't happy. They thought it didn't reflect well on their products.'

'Advertisers.' Euphoria sniffs. 'More fool them. I'm sure you'll find something else soon.'

'I have some other news. I'm engaged. To Adrian.'

Euphoria greets this with silence. She has never met Adrian, so it isn't personal; Euphoria thinks marriage is an outdated institution – except for gay marriage, because they still need to have their turn. I hear bird calls in the background while I wait for her to talk. A currawong, a whip bird, a kookaburra … 'You and Adrian will have to come up for New Year's Eve,' she says eventually.

While many pagans don't celebrate New Year's Eve, Euphoria likes to hold a renewal ritual which involves a 'letting go' ceremony. Euphoria always insisted on Marley's and my partners coming along to her rituals. She thinks it's a good opportunity to take the measure of someone. 'No good,' has been her pronouncement on all of the boyfriends I've produced so far and she's been right, but she hasn't met Adrian.

The birds call again in the background and I visualise myself in my cottage on the commune. I haven't been back there for a year. Not since Marley … 'I'll talk to Adrian about it.'

'You're going to have to come home some time.' Euphoria clears her throat. 'I planted a tree. On your birthday.'

I know she means for Marley. 'I'd like to see that.' I pause. 'I'll try.'

After I hang up, I head for the entrance. A pair of skis is propped in the annex, some boots beneath them. They look like the ones I used before. Why not? I'll get there quicker on skis and I pretty much got the hang of it last time.

Boots on and skis in hand, I duck outside, strap on the skis and, slinging the camera and tripod bag over my shoulder, push off towards the bay. Ten minutes, and only a couple of falls later, I'm in front of the deep blue sea.

I set up the camera on the tripod and ski into view with the sea behind me. I've left my hood and balaclava off – there's no need for disguise any more. 'Hello, my name is Summer and this is my last episode from Antarctica. I thought I'd sign off with a weather report. Today the temperature in Antarctica is a balmy minus five degrees. That might sound cold, and it is colder than it has been, but not as cold as it should be. Considering Antarctica holds seventy per cent of the world's water, we don't want it to get much warmer or seaside houses will need to be redesigned as underwater—'

'Summer, Summer …'

Lucas's voice drifts across the snow. What does he want? Perhaps it's time to catch my flight. I talk more quickly. 'Bottom line is, we need to stop pumping all that carbon into the air. If this was *Dynasty*, the evil oil baron would be defeated by the—'

'Summer.' His voice is louder.

I look up. Lucas is running down the hill towards me and for a moment it's like something from an old-time romance. A slow-motion sequence, the lovers running into each other's arms … Except that I'm engaged and he's married, and last night he ran into Adrian coming out of my room, so I suppose that rules that out.

'Run,' Lucas yells. He points behind me.

I hear a grunting noise and spin around towards the sea. My skis tangle and I fall over. A spotted seal the size of a small hippopotamus is racing towards me. Its blubbery rocking gait propels it rapidly across the ice.

'Leopard seal!' Lucas yells.

I untangle my skis and scramble to my feet. Lucas is running to-ward me from one direction. The leopard seal is galumphing toward me from the other. I try to ski up the hill towards Lucas, but slide backwards. The grunting gets louder. I think of the researcher who was dragged to her death. I lunge towards Lucas but my skis cross and I fall over again. A hot, fishy breath hits me as I struggle to undo my skis.

Lucas grabs my arm, hauls me upright and half-carries me up the hill. We only stop when we're up the top and turn, gasping. The leopard seal lumbers up to my camera and nudges it with its nose. The camera topples. It picks it up in its mouth and attempts to toss it in the air, but it is awkward, attached as it is to the tripod. A packet of Tim Tams – my last product placement – lies in the snow. The seal bites it and flings it in the air. The Tim Tams scatter – a hail of chocolate. After poking a lone Tim Tam with its nose, the seal turns away, lips curling. *Not a good product endorsement.* It scans the rest of the detritus. Apparently satisfied its foe is vanquished, it turns and lumbers back to the water.

I stand there, panting, my heart thumping. I feel both foolish and frightened. I hope Lucas didn't notice I was preparing for a romantic moment as he ran towards me. I hope my lips weren't puckering up in expectation.

'You should see what they do with penguins,' Lucas says. 'They throw them in the air so hard, their skin comes off before they eat them.'

The leopard seal slides over the ice bank. There's barely a ripple as it enters the water. I feel sorry for any hapless penguins who are taking a dip but I'm glad it's not me being tossed in the air until my skin comes off.

The water explodes as four Adelie penguins launch themselves onto the ice. *Smart move, guys.* They slide across the ice and come to a standstill.

I steal a glance at Lucas and feel an urgent hum in my chest – *do something, do something.* But there's nothing to be done. Not one single thing.

'Did you know the male Adelie penguin selects his mate from a colony of more than a million?' says Lucas.

'Yeah?' He's acting the tour guide again. Clearly our kiss is the furthest thing from his mind. 'That's interesting.' I gnaw my lip and gaze out at the sea, wishing it was the furthest thing from mine.

'Think of it – to us, they all look the same, but to a penguin …'

'Some are cute and some aren't.'

'Right. A million penguins and he chooses the one for him. Then they mate for life.'

So this is how it ends – with a fascinating discussion on the mating habits of penguins. I am about to burst with unexpressed feelings, but they're going to have to remain that way.

Lucas leans down and picks up a rock. With a flick of his hand he throws it into the air and catches it again.

I suppose he's going to skip some stones now. And follow it up with a lecture on climate change. Just the thing for our last few minutes together.

Lucas slides the stone into his pocket. 'Your plane's landed. The Hagg's on its way from the airport.'

We walk back to the station, not talking, Lucas carrying my skis. I try to think of something to say but nothing can slide past that blockage of unsaid words. I feel like something has passed me by, though I'm not sure what. This feeling persists while I'm packing my bag and walking outside.

Cherie is there, along with Maria, Mike and Rory. It must be traditional to see off departing guests. Adrian and Hornby have their suitcases next to them. Lucas emerges from one of the sheds and comes towards us.

Hornby coughs at his approach and fumbles in the briefcase he holds in one mittened hand. 'Your book.' He holds it out towards Lucas.

Lucas takes it.

'Interesting story,' says Hornby. 'The egg collecting.'

Lucas nods.

Hornby beckons Lucas closer. He murmurs, 'Emperor penguins ... climate change ...' The rest is indistinguishable.

'Not good ... sea ice ...' Lucas replies.

I'm astonished to see them talking to each other so civilly. Cherie and Maria look astonished too. Adrian looks cross.

There's a rumble and a Hagglund approaches. It comes to a standstill, the door opens and out climbs Mary the producer, Alicia the stylist and finally ... Cougar.

Cougar is not wearing the regulation over-sized red snowsuit. Hers is black and form-fitted. Her thick, black hair hangs over her shoulders from beneath her beanie. Only Cougar could be glamorous clad in down.

Rory picks up his camera and Alicia darts forward to rearrange Cougar's hair before nodding to him to continue.

Maria, Mike and Cherie look from me to Cougar and back again.

'Long story,' I say. 'I'm Summer. That's the real Cougar. As you can tell.'

Cherie can't take her eyes off Cougar. 'She's exactly the way she is on television.' She turns back to me. 'You're similar, just not so …'

'Yeah. I know.'

Cougar spots me. She raises her hand. 'Hello, Autumn, we meet again.' One of her feet is encased in a large down bootie that must fit over the top of her bandages and she's carrying a ski pole for support. Her injury doesn't inhibit her much. She takes a few steps and stops in front of me.

'What happened to your broken ankle?' I say.

'Turned out to be a hairline fracture, it's healing quickly. Well, things have been exciting here, haven't they?' She looks at Lucas. 'A climate scientist with a grudge.' Her gaze turns to Hornby. 'A Minister lost in the snow. Anyway. Channel Five thought they'd better send in the A-team so you can scoot on back. Time to check the Positions Vacant, I gather.' She seems surprisingly friendly. Her eyes linger on my head. 'I'd do something about your hair first if I were you.'

Adrian heads towards the Hagglund. His eyes meet Cougar's for a moment, but he continues on without a word.

Well, it looks like that's over.

There's a general movement towards the Hagg and Cougar and I are left alone. Rory's camera is elsewhere. She steps closer. 'You should know … Nothing happened with me and Adrian. Nothing physical.'

'What? But you said how great he was. In bed.'

Cougar's mouth twitches. 'I don't do guys.' And she looks like she's about to say more, but Rory swings the camera back towards her and zooms in. She steps away from me, smiling in a practised way. 'I've arrived at Casey Station in Antarctica, and …'

Cougar doesn't do guys? But what about all those guys she's been with in the social pages? Were they just for show? And in that case … was Adrian for show too?

I make my way towards the Hagg with my backpack, but Maria intercepts me. 'I should have known you were an imposter.' Her eyes flicker to the real Cougar. 'You had no idea about krill.'

This is a little unfair. I thought I'd carried off the krill segment with some aplomb.

'It's funny, how having no idea about a topic can sometimes be the best way to approach it,' Maria says. 'It's been nice having you here … Summer.'

I can see Hornby's face through the window of the Hagg, and in the seat behind him, Adrian. They seem impatient to depart. I'm not in as much of a rush, myself.

Lucas is talking to the driver. He gives me a lopsided smile, picks up my backpack and swings it inside the snowmobile then turns back to me. 'Bye, Summer.'

'Bye.' I look over his shoulder as if I'm in a hurry to get inside. I don't want him to see the tears that are prickling in my eyes. I've got no idea what that's about.

'Better be off,' says the driver.

I climb in and gaze out the window; Lucas is walking towards the station. The snowmobile chugs and he turns and waves. I raise my hand in reply, but he's already opening the door. *That's that then.*

The plane is waiting when we get to the runway three hours later. By the time I find my seat, Hornby is already bent over some briefing papers with a self-important air. I liked him better when he was Scott of the Antarctic. Beside him, Adrian stares out the window looking pensive. The seat next to me is empty. Rory has stayed behind to film with Cougar of course.

'I'm going to miss going for glory with you, Summer,' he'd said as I headed for the Hagglund.

'Rory,' Cougar trilled.

Rory rolled his eyes. 'You did good, Lexie. Don't let the bastards get you down back in Sydney.'

'Thanks, Roars.'

'Rory.' Cougar was louder.

'Gotta go.' Rory high-fived me and was gone.

The plane taxis down the ice runway and my seat shudders beneath me as it lifts into the air. I stare out the window, feeling like a different person to the one who touched down a few days ago. *Antarctica – it gives you perspective.* The plane banks and my igloo is below me. A small figure stands next to the station. It looks like Lucas, but it's impossible to be sure. I wave, though of course he can't see me. The figure raises his hand as if in reply. A little further and I see the ice-core camp. Three figures emerge from the tent and wave at the plane.

We rise higher and the continent stretches out into the distance – all that ice and all that snow and all those human dreams and aspirations made small by its indifference. I crane my neck until the snow becomes a haze of white then the plane climbs into the clouds and it is gone.

Chapter Thirty-two
A high-achieving Christmas

Four hours later we descend into Hobart. A heat haze shimmers across the runway as we land. I've already shed my snowsuit, but now I take off my polar fleece jacket and pants as well. Amazingly, I've had the foresight to wear shorts and a T-shirt beneath.

Across the aisle, Adrian has stripped off his snowsuit too – he's back to the polo shirt and moleskins. Hornby is still wearing his snowsuit – no doubt expecting a media opportunity. Adrian goes ahead, but Hornby lingers.

He glances up and down the aisle as I approach, as if checking we're alone. 'I'm sorry I took the credit for your igloo. I wasn't myself.'

I hadn't been expecting that. 'That's alright, no big deal. But thanks.'

He strides off down the aisle, smoothing his hair into position as he goes.

The heat hits me as I climb down the steps onto the tarmac. While the sun in Antarctica was dazzling, this sun is harsher. It feels like it could burn in an instant. It's a relief to get into the air-conditioned terminal. My phone beeps as I turn it on. I have over three hundred new messages. That must be a mistake but I don't have time to deal with it. I turn it off again.

In front of me, Hornby pats his hair again as he spots the media contingent. No doubt he's sweating inside his snowsuit, but it will be worth it for the photo op.

There are more media reps here than on the outward journey – at least six cameras. They rush towards us and Hornby straightens his shoulders.

'Minister, Minister' – a microphone is thrust in his face, then another and another – 'How did you know how to build an igloo? Have you done it before?'

I can see him struggling with his conscience.

'The Minister has always been interested in outdoor survival,' says Adrian. 'He showed great enterprise by building a wonderful igloo.'

Hornby and I look at Adrian.

'How long did it take you to build the igloo, Minister?' says a blonde woman.

Hornby hesitates, glances at me, but the temptation is clearly too much for him. 'About three hours. First I cut the blocks …'

I slink towards the door, but as I do so, another TV crew rushes in. I stand back to let them at the Minister, but they pull up in front of me. The reporter is a trendy young woman who looks like she takes style tips from Jacinta. She holds out her microphone.

'So, Summer, how does it feel to be the latest YouTube sensation? Do you realise you've been trending on Twitter for three days? Is it true Steven Spielberg's called you about movie rights? Have you signed with …'

A ripple passes through the crews grouped around the Minister and one by one, as if by a herd instinct, they swing towards me.

Hornby heads for the door, trying not to look like he's been snubbed. Adrian hangs back and comes to my side.

'I, I don't know anything about any of that,' I stammer.

'No interviews.' Adrian holds up his hand. He passes around his business card. 'You can talk to Summer through me.'

The news crews run alongside us as Adrian and I head for the exit. We're booked into the same hotel again for one night. A gust of wind blows my hair across my face as I step outside. I pull it back, clumsily.

Hornby is standing next to his limousine. He raises one hand. And standing there in his snowsuit with his wind-battered face he does have the grandeur of a failed polar explorer. He mouths the word *sorry*.

I feel a strange affection for him – like we've been through something together. I shrug and raise my hand in reply. My hair immediately lashes across my eyes and by the time I've restrained it, he is gone.

Sydney is ringed by smoke as Adrian and I fly in the next day. An orangey-brown haze stretches to the horizon and a hot wind dries my skin as we walk the few steps from the plane to the airport entrance. Already Antarctica seems a fantasy.

I thought I'd sleep for about ten hours straight last night but even when it got dark I was still restless. Every time I closed my eyes I saw Lucas running down the hill towards me and heard the leopard seal's wheezing bark.

As we make our way to the train station, I'm jaded and disorientated like a soldier returned from combat. On the train I turn on my phone again to sort through my messages.

I only got to message number one hundred and sixty last night – about one hundred and forty to go. Bizarrely, most of the messages are fan mail. There are also offers. Would I like to be the face of a new chocolate biscuit, do an ad for a mixer drink or participate in a reality TV show? A few agents are keen to take care of my public image. It hasn't occurred to me until now that I have a public image, let alone one that needs taking care of. It's lucky Adrian is here to help. 'Take a look at these.' I pass him my phone.

He scans through my messages. 'You do need someone to take care of your image, Summer.'

The train rushes into a tunnel and my reflection appears in the window. I look like I've been held hostage for months. My hair is sticking up from my head and my eyes have a long-distance stare. Adrian is right, my image is problematic.

Adrian's stop is before mine. 'I'll see you in a few hours.' He kisses me before he gets off.

It is like we've never been apart.

My apartment smells musty when I open the door. Should I bring out the cleaning products? The thought doesn't hold its usual attraction. Instead of turning on the air-conditioning, I open the windows – let the hot air blow through the room, ruffling papers and lifting the sheets on my bed. It's nothing like the wind in Antarctica.

It is part of the same system. Lucas's words linger in my mind. The thought is comforting. I open the windows wider, imagining the fishy smell of penguins wafting in. I gaze at my white walls; comparing this shade of paint to Antarctica is like calling a sandpit the Sahara.

Now what? I turn on the TV and head into the kitchen for a drink.

My fridge is purring. Opening the door I lean forward, letting the chill hit my cheeks. I'm pouring myself a cold drink when I hear familiar music – *Cougar on Ice*. I rush back into the lounge room and there she is. The sun is shining and the sky is that clear violet unique to Antarctica. Behind her, a green-tinged iceberg juts from a turquoise sea. I scan the screen expecting to see Lucas. Is he behind that seal? Behind that chunk of ice? Maybe he's out of camera and will appear at any minute.

Holding my cold drink to my face, I step closer to the TV.

'Antarctica is home to seven species of penguin and four species of seal. Look at these cute penguins,' she says. The traditional cute penguin music starts, making the Adelie penguins look like little Charlie Chaplins as they waddle towards the sea.

Cougar's delivery is a little flat. I stare at her, remembering her whispered message – *I don't do guys …* So why does she work so hard to give the impression she does? Commercial reasons to do with prime time television, I suppose. Family viewing. I feel a tug of sympathy. I know what it's like trying to pretend to be someone you're not.

A quick-paced montage of Cougar building an igloo comes on. She's making light work of it; the blocks appear in position as if by magic. I suspect she's getting a lot of off-screen help. 'This igloo is a big secret,' Cougar whispers to the camera. *Not anymore, it isn't.* 'I'm going to be building all night.' *Ha – fat chance of that.*

Cougar pitches her next show. 'Tune in tomorrow for my last episode from Antarctica. It's the Christmas Day igloo special and it's going to be fabulous …'

I punch the off button. That was supposed to be *my* Christmas Day igloo special.

As I stare at the screen, it hits me – tomorrow is Christmas and I don't have a present for Adrian.

Adrian sleeps over at my place. His breathing reminds me of the leopard seal and I have trouble sleeping again. Perhaps I need a shot, like Hornby. But there's no chance of seeing a doctor on Christmas Day.

On Christmas morning Adrian and I have a cup of tea while we plan the day ahead. Adrian has a scheduling app on his iPhone which he likes to fill out every morning. He bought me a scheduling app for my iPhone too, but I haven't worked out how to use it yet.

'This is the first day of the rest of our lives; we need to set the bar high.' Adrian taps something into his iPhone and holds it out.

6.30: Ten kilometre jog

Jogging. Jogging is good. Maybe if I get some exercise, I'll sleep. I nod with what I hope passes for enthusiasm.

'I've set the running app so we can build up for the New York marathon. Won't that be fun?'

'Terrific.' Could be worse. We could be training for the Bikram yoga convention.

Adrian taps his iPhone again. 'There's a special deal for Bikram yoga in the New Year. You can go to as many classes as you want for a set fee, so it's good value if you go every day.'

'Great.' That's a week away, so I don't need to worry about it yet. Maybe I can develop a condition that requires me to stay cool. I make a mental note to research this.

9.00:   Breakfast

I nod with genuine enthusiasm.

9.30:   Go home to commence turkey cooking

'You have a turkey at home?'

'Yes. Of course.' Adrian flicks over to his Christmas Day project plan. 'See?'

I peer over his shoulder. Adrian's Christmas Day planning is comprehensive.

'You've already got a plum pudding, crackers and a Christmas present for me? But, how did you know we'd be having Christmas Day together?'

'I planned it three months ago, Summer.'

It's silly to be uncomfortable about this. It's nice he planned to spend Christmas Day with me. *Prior planning and preparation prevents piss-poor performance.*

Adrian types in the next item.

13.00: Christmas lunch

I nod.

14.00 – 21.00: Give Christmas presents, chat about future plans, watch television etc.

'Et cetera? That's not like you.'

'I thought we could leave it a little loose, seeing as it's Christmas.'

'I suppose that's alright. Just this once.' What will he put in next? If he's in an et cetera kind of mood, there's no telling how far it will go.

21.00: Bedroom activities

Adrian puts his hand on my knee.

My seductive smile is interrupted by a loud yawn. 'Sorry.' There's nothing unromantic about programming in sex. That's what all the women's mags say you need to do – schedule in your 'us' time. I wonder how long Adrian will allow for this agenda item.

21.30: Sleep

'Is half an hour long enough?' he asks.

'That should be fine, darling.' I think fifteen minutes would do it.

'Perhaps we should allow more time. After all that turkey and pudding, we might need more, um … And I've got a few new ideas.'

New ideas? I raise my eyebrows.

'You know that chart I showed you?'

'The sexual compatibility one?'

'Mm. I think we can do better than four point four, don't you?'

'Oh. Yes. Absolutely.'

'I might make it twenty-one forty-five. If we finish early, it's a bonus. It's always nice to exceed expectations.' Adrian saves his schedule with a satisfied air.

Adrian and I set out on our run. Unfortunately ten kilometres proves to be a bar too high. 'Might need to' – huff, puff – 'work up to' – puff, huff – 'that one, darling,' I say after ten minutes or so. I feel a little dizzy. I yawn.

'You're not trying, Summer.'

'Sorry. It's … it makes my legs hurt.'

'That's no reason to give up.'

I give him a pathetic puppy-dog look. 'I know I need to work on my running and I'm looking forward to it, but I'm tired. And I don't want to burn myself out. We've got a full program …' I run my tongue across my lips enticingly.

Adrian smiles. 'I suppose it is Christmas Day … I'll re-set your training schedule to start tomorrow.'

'Okay. Great.'

Adrian kisses me goodbye and pounds away, his muscular legs pumping in his high-cut shorts.

He is so incredibly focused; as long as I stay in his orbit some of it is bound to rub off on me.

By seven o'clock I'm home again and the excellent part about this is, it gives me time to make my home-made muesli before Adrian notices I haven't done so already. Muesli-making is surprisingly easy once I get around to it. I glance at my watch once it's done. Yay – time to catch some soap opera highlights.

Christmas Day is a special time in soap land. You can be sure if anyone has a dark secret, it will be exposed. As soon as you hear, 'This is going to be the best Christmas ever,' you know things are about to go downhill quickly. I click from show to show, sampling the following storylines:

Christmas gifts from beyond the grave – *aw*.

A Christmas gift of a land title to a woman who is dying of cancer and won't live to see the house built – *aw*.

Warring sisters ruin Christmas dinner with a catfight – *awesome*. *Lucas would love that one*. The thought appears from nowhere. I squash it and flick the remote to the next show.

A lonely divorcee cries in the street while her ex lives it up with his new wife – *aw*.

An overweight father gets rushed to hospital after—

I click off the screen as Adrian opens the door.

He glances at the TV. 'What have you been watching?'

'Oh, that old movie by Lars Von Trier. You know the one where the two guys are walking through the desert. And they get lost ...'

'That's Gus Van Sant.'

'Oh, yes. I love that movie,' I gush.

Adrian nods. 'It's his seminal work.'

'Mm, amazing. So metaphorical.'

'Wouldn't mind seeing it again.' Adrian picks up the remote and presses the power button.

'I'll make this your worst Christmas ever,' screams Olga as she slashes the tyres of her lover Brandon's car, now cosily ensconced inside with his pretty wife who makes the best roast turkey this side of Dallas.

'Must have finished,' I murmur, my eyes glued to the screen.

'Incredible, the rubbish they run.' Adrian turns it off. 'Who watches this stuff?'

Apart from the running, the day progresses according to plan. After breakfast, Adrian goes back to his apartment to commence Operation Turkey. At twelve o'clock I join him. Wine is poured – another Chateau Lafite Rothschild (different vintage), smoky with a hint of almond, or something to that effect. It tastes like wine.

By two o'clock I'm so full of turkey and plum pudding I can hardly move. Adrian is a good cook. He made the plum pudding himself to a special recipe handed down through his family for generations. 'My grandmother won the Adelaide show with this recipe,' he says. He explains to me how he made the pudding way back in October. 'Next year you can make it.'

Considering the last thing I baked was cornflake biscuits in year seven, this makes me anxious. But October is a long way off.

'I'll give you my project plan.'

'Oh good.' Once I have my life properly planned, plum-pudding making and marathons will all fall into place.

Adrian goes over to his side table and picks up a small, beautifully wrapped package. 'Happy Christmas, Summer.'

How exciting. Small packages are always the best. I undo the bow and peel away the paper. What can it be?

Inside is a techie-looking watch. It has little windows displaying figures, a dial that swivels around and a band made of silver links.

'Here. I'll put it on for you.' He fastens the watch around my wrist.

It's heavy and cool against my skin.

'It's a GPS watch which collects data on how much you exercise each day. It also has a heartrate monitor. The best part is, I've set it up to automatically download its data onto my iPhone whenever you go near a wi-fi zone so I'll be able to keep track of your progress and help you.'

I inspect the watch. 'So, you'll know exactly where I am and what I'm doing at any time?'

'Yes, isn't that great?'

It's clever; and obviously I do need help with my exercise program, so if the watch makes me feel like a prisoner on day release, I need to get over it. It's nice that Adrian wants to help me get fit. 'It's lovely. Thank you. Very thoughtful.' I twiddle the dial on the outside of the watch.

'That's so you can time your run,' says Adrian.

I give Adrian the *Business Essentials* magazine I picked up at the train station last night. 'Sorry, it's … hm.' There's not much to say.

Adrian looks a little disappointed, but he rallies. 'Thank you, darling, I've been wanting to read this one. I've got another little present for you, but I'm saving it for later.' He smiles suggestively.

I gather this is to do with his *new ideas* for the bedroom. My stomach flutters nervously. 'Can't wait.'

According to Adrian's schedule, it is time for life planning. And now I really am nervous, because how can I plan my life without filling Adrian in on my secret, secret goal?

Chapter Thirty-three
Adrian and I exceed expectations

Adrian sits on the couch in lotus pose. He says it's important to stretch the hips at every opportunity. 'So, where do you see yourself in ten years' time, Summer?'

I flop on the couch next to him. My face flushes and I swallow hard – I've got to get it over with. 'Adrian. I … I … I …'

Adrian raises one eyebrow and adjusts his position.

My heart races. *Say it, Summer.* My tongue is thick in my mouth, so I have trouble forming the words. 'I want to be a scriptwriter.'

Adrian laughs. 'That's funny. It sounded like you just said you want to be a scriptwriter.'

'I did. I do.' This must be what it's like to come out.

'Oh. Huh.' Adrian cocks his head, pulling his feet further up his thighs. 'That's an interesting idea, Summer, but you need to focus your energy on leveraging off your celebrity, not retiring into a cave to write a script. Strike while the iron's hot.'

I take a sip of wine – woody with a hint of soap – trying to push aside a lump in my throat. 'I've been working on a script. Do you want to see it?'

'Okay, sure.' Adrian glances at his watch. He picks up the remote and turns on the TV. 'Not right now, let's watch this. Then we'll get back to the planning. I've got a special announcement for you. You're going to love it.' He smiles in a mysterious way as he massages his instep.

Familiar music comes from the TV: Cougar's Christmas Day special is starting. *Maybe Lucas will be* – I stop that thought in its tracks. As the credits fade, Cougar is sitting inside an igloo with the three beards.

I inspect the igloo. Yes, I recognise that wonky part on the side where it collapsed and I had to push it back up again. 'That's *my* igloo.'

Adrian's eyes flick to me. 'I thought Hornby built it.'

'No, he just put—'

'Sh.' Adrian gestures at the screen.

It no longer seems so important to be acknowledged as the igloo-builder anyway. I let it go.

'What do you do for recreation here in Antarctica?' Cougar is using the script I rejected for my ice-core camp episode.

The beards are wearing paper crowns – possibly a Three Wise Men reference – while Cougar has a red Santa hat. Candles are dotted around the igloo, their glow dancing on the ice walls, and a small Christmas tree in the corner has a pile of presents beneath it. I gnaw my cheek. Though I've let go of my igloo, it's hard to see Cougar take all the credit.

'I like woodcarving,' says one of the beards.

'Photography,' says another.

'I write poetry,' says the third.

'Poetry?' Cougar mugs surprise. 'Would you like to read us some?'

The beard coughs and pulls a piece of paper from the pocket of his snowsuit. 'It's a haiku.'

Cougar nods encouragingly.

He reads:

> 'Antarctic ice cores
> Secrets of the Earth's past
> Exposing the truth.'

That's almost exactly what I said in my ice-core report. And at the time he said it was sensationalist. Clearly it's grown on him. Seeing the beards reminds me I have unused Antarctic footage at home. I should have a look at it.

Cougar is outside the igloo, pointing at an iceberg. Some cutesy Christmas carols start up.

'You know that funny thing you do with your fingers?' says Adrian.

As the program fades we see Cougar in her paper hat opening a present. 'You mean my greatest talent?' I hold up my hand and do the rabbit through a hole trick with my middle finger.

'Mm. Cougar can do it too.'

'No way.'

'Mm, hm.'

'Oh, what fun, it's a snowball!' Cougar throws the snowball at one of the beards in a forced display of gaiety. She seems a little off her game.

'Wow. I've never met anyone else who can do that before.' I stare at Cougar. 'I suppose she's coming back to Australia now that's over.'

'I suppose so.' Adrian picks up the remote and turns off the television.

I suppose Lucas is coming back too. He was only there as liaison for the TV show and he needs to be here for the inquiry into his alleged data fraud. But of course Lucas's movements are neither here nor there.

'So ...' says Adrian, 'do you want to hear my special announcement?'

I nod. It's obvious I'm going to. Adrian's pent-up expression suggests he might explode otherwise.

'It's all hush, hush, but ... you're looking at the new Director of Communications for Channel Four.'

I try to match his smile. 'Congratulations.' I raise my glass. It sounds impressive, but I'm bewildered. 'Here's to you. I didn't know that was your line, having a job I mean. I thought you were more of a consultant.'

'I have many lines.'

'What happened to your job with Hornby?'

Adrian glances out the window before replying. 'That was a specific project. It's finished. Besides, I'm not sure he's the right sort of client for me. He's a bit conventional – doesn't like to get out of the box.'

I think of Hornby in the igloo. He seemed pretty out of the box to me.

'Channel Four is more cutting edge, more open to suggestion,' Adrian continues. 'Leapfrogging, that's what it's all about – hopping from one opportunity to the next. Onwards and upwards, Summer. Staying still is going backwards. That's not all though ...' Adrian raises his eyebrows at me.

'Go on, tell me.'

'A little birdie tells me they're after a new outdoor presenter.'

'What happened to Mack Decker?'

'Losing ratings. His Arctic series didn't cut it. Couldn't find enough polar bears, I hear. They want someone new. They want you, Summer.'

'Me?' My mouth drops open. 'But … how do you know?' It seems bizarre I have come to the attention of Channel Four.

Adrian smirks. 'I'm the new Director of Communications.'

A number of cogs fall into place. 'Adrian, you weren't the Antarctic mole who tipped off Channel Four about my show, were you?'

'Yep.' Adrian appears unrepentant.

I have no reason to be loyal to Channel Five, but this doesn't feel right. 'But, you undermined my show.'

'You were their stooge, Summer. Maxine dropped you like a hot potato, why should you care?'

He's right. 'I don't.' Obscurely, though, I do. Wasn't that a little mean of Adrian to undercut my show's exclusivity?

He takes my hand and squeezes it. 'Hey, you're not worried about that, are you? All's fair in love and war. They would have found out anyway. The whole operation was leaking like a sieve.'

It seems silly to be upset on behalf of Channel Five. What did they ever do for me? 'So they offered you a job?'

'Uh huh and now they're offering you a job. Channel Four is sharpening up their image. You've got street cred.'

'Street cred?' A nervous giggle explodes out my nose. This is about as likely as discovering I'm heir to a European kingdom. Street cred is for hipsters with fashion sense. 'I haven't got street cred.'

'Of course you have. They want you to help draw the YouTube audience back to television.' Adrian frowns. 'What's wrong?'

I don't know how he can ask me that. 'It's not wrong, it's just … weird. I expect they've made a mistake.'

'There's no mistake, Summer. You're the new Mack Decker. Congratulations.'

An overwhelming tiredness grips me. It would be easy to say yes, to go with the flow, but yet … 'I appreciate it Adrian, I do but … I'm not sure if it's what I want to do.'

'There are a lot of people who would jump at that offer.' He glances at the silent TV and his meaning is clear. Cougar would jump at that offer.

I take a deep breath. 'Adrian, I want to write scripts. It's all I've ever wanted to do.'

Adrian sighs. 'I suppose I can ask if there's a part-time spot for a scriptwriter on the current affairs team. You might be able to fit that in around your presenting commitments.'

'No. Soap opera. I want to write soap opera scripts.' *There, I've said it.*

Adrian laughs loudly, shifting the cross of his legs. 'You crack me up, Summer.' His laugh dies as he sees my face. 'You can't be serious?'

I open and shut my mouth but no words come out.

'Don't be silly, Summer. Those things are written by morons.'

My cheeks flush.

'Soap opera scriptwriter.' Adrian chortles again. 'You can do so much better than that. You'll have your own show. You'll be a star.'

I toy with my GPS watch. 'How long have I got to decide?'

'What's wrong with right now?'

'I don't know. It's … I need to think about it.'

'Well, I guess not much happens between Christmas and New Year, so you can have until then. You'd be mad not to take it, Summer. It's a once in a lifetime opportunity.'

'Give me a few days. Okay?'

Adrian doesn't look happy, but he shrugs. 'Okay.'

It's only eight-thirty, so I have time to ring Euphoria before the next item on our agenda. She doesn't celebrate Christmas, but I feel I should wish her season's greetings.

'Summer?' she says as she picks up the phone. 'I knew it would be you. I watched your show again last night, but they had that other woman on. She's not as good as you, there's something about her though …'

'She's very popular.'

'Something familiar, I meant. Cougar's a funny name, isn't it?'

'Yes. It suits her though.'

'So are you coming up for New Year?'

I'd forgotten about New Year. But maybe it's a good idea. I do need some time out – time to think. About this Channel Four thing, about other things … I can't get everything straight in my head. Maybe I'll be able to sleep there. And I can't stay away forever. 'Okay. I'll come tomorrow if I can get a flight. Adrian's got stuff to do here, but I'll tell him about New Year's.'

'Good. It will be good to see you. I'm opening a bed and breakfast. You can help me with that. Make sure Alan knows what to bring,' she says.

'Adrian.'

'That's what I said.'

I transmit Euphoria's invitation to Adrian when I put the phone down.

'There won't be nudity, will there?' I've told Adrian I grew up on a commune.

'Would it matter if there was?'

'I'm not keen on nudity. Except with you, darling.'

'I'll make sure there's no nudity. I'll tell Euphoria.'

'So, what's this … ritual thing?' Adrian looks like he's sucked on a lemon.

'You have to bring along a symbol of something you want to let go. More than one thing if you want. It's not weird or anything. It's just a turning over a new leaf ceremony.'

Adrian appears unconvinced. 'What are you going to bring?'

'Let's keep it a secret from each other. It will be more fun.'

Adrian agrees to join me in Nimbin on New Year's Eve. 'I should meet your mother … Hysteria?'

'Euphoria.'

'That's right.' He glances at his watch. 'Nine o'clock. Time for your next present.'

To: Marley Lennon Wright
From: Summer Dawn Rain Wright
Subject: My unexpected Christmas present

I will draw a veil over the surprising activities that followed, Marley. Suffice to say, Adrian appeared to have drawn inspiration from a best-selling book, but introduced his own special slant. Making love with Adrian used to be like building a bridge. Now there were so many stages it was more like a trans-national highway upgrade.

'Did you like that, Summer?' he said afterwards as we lay panting side by side.

To be honest, I felt like I'd been done over by a Gantt chart. 'It was, um … ambitious.'

Luckily, he took that as a compliment. 'There's lots more where that came from, I've got a new app.' He picked up his phone from the bedside table and scrolled through it. 'Have you ever tried backwards-facing cowboy?'

I glance at the picture. It looks challenging. 'I don't think so.'

'I'll save it to favourites.'

Even with all the extra props and positions, Adrian and I exceeded expectations, so I had time to book a flight to Ballina before we went to sleep. And to write this email.

There's no need to be concerned, Marley, everyone is into this sort of thing. Or so I hear.

Chapter Thirty-four
I worry about fire-walking

The airport is chock-a-block on Boxing Day morning and my flight is delayed due to strong winds on the north coast.

Finding a free table in a cafe, I open my laptop, order coffee and a muffin and, putting in headphones, review my footage of the leopard seal attack. From the safety of Sydney Airport, it's pretty funny. There I am, looking seriously at the camera, and there's the leopard seal sliding out of the water behind me.

The next part is like the climactic scene of a horror movie. Lucas yells … I glance behind me and run … my skis tangle and I fall … Lucas pulls me up … the footage goes all over the place as the seal knocks over the tripod. There's a flash of me and Lucas, both aghast, a flash of teeth, a flash of sky and a flash of sea, then the screen goes white as the camera lands face-down in the snow. All it needs is a scream and a splash of red on the snow to complete the picture.

I'm no film editor, but after half an hour's work I have an episode that more or less hangs together. I add some gothic horror music, give it a name, *Fear on Ice*, and load it onto YouTube. At the bottom, I post a note – *behind the scenes footage coming soon*.

My flight is still not boarding so I order another muffin and browse the news sites. Climate change is much in the headlines at the moment. Or maybe it always was and I'm only noticing it now.

Today a Swiss village is complaining of a glacier problem. In 1678 inhabitants of this village inaugurated an annual pilgrimage to banish their local glacier with prayers and holy water because they were sick of it taking up good pasture land. Their prayers were so successful that the glacier shrunk at a rate of ten metres a year and has now developed cracks which threaten to unleash dammed floodwaters onto the village. The villagers have petitioned the Vatican to modify their pilgrimage. They'd like to ask God to stop the ice shrinking now. This story reminds me of the magician's apprentice – be careful what you wish for.

While I'm reading this, little messages keep popping up on my screen. *Fantastic! Can't wait for your next one. I've subscribed to your channel, waiting eagerly. I hope it's not too long…* These messages make me anxious. My fans are waiting. I'm not used to people having expectations of me. With each message that pops up, my stress levels increase. What am I going to do next?

The Swiss story is paired with one on melting icecaps in Greenland. A satellite image depicts how the snowflakes are changing. This reminds me of Lucas. I scroll down and there's more …

Upcoming climate summit wracked with controversy

> With only one day to go … crucial evidence is suspect … climate scientist Lucas Nilsson … alleged data fraud.

Closing the news site quickly, I push my muffin away and glance at the Departures screen. Time to board.

Euphoria meets me at Ballina airport. She has dressed up for the occasion in a brightly-coloured skirt and top but her waist-length grey hair and deep suntan mark her out as 'one of those Nimbin folk'.

I give her a hug and smell patchouli oil.

She stands back and inspects me, shaking her head.

'What?'

'Your aura's cloudy.'

'When hasn't it been?'

Euphoria sighs. 'Yes, but something's going on.' She hugs me again. 'You can talk to me about it when you're ready.'

This is one of the reasons I avoid coming home – Euphoria has a gift for weaselling out things I would rather keep hidden.

'Jeez, the driveway's gone downhill,' I say as we bounce up the track to the commune one hour later.

Euphoria glances at me and I bite my tongue. Maintaining the driveway was Marley's job. I look out the window. The rainforest is dry. The vines are dusty and the dark green leaves of the figs and palms are not as shiny as usual.

Euphoria changes down a gear as we climb out of a pothole that threatens to engulf us. 'Desperately need some rain.'

We pull up outside the main house. It looks as it always does – like the kind of dwelling a koala or a possum might build if it had a mind to, all cosy hollows and tree-top bedrooms. My own cottage is a few hundred metres away, on a narrow path into the rainforest.

'Got something to show you.' Euphoria leads the way towards the creek.

I know where we're going, but there's no avoiding it.

Unlike the other trees, Marley's fig tree is well watered. Just under a metre high, it is healthy and full of promise. Scooping some water from the creek in my hands, I dribble it slowly over its leaves. A matching trickle makes its way down my cheek.

Euphoria put her arms around me. 'Don't keep it all inside, Summer.'

But a sprinkle of rain doesn't break the drought.

Later, when I unpack my bag, a dried fish falls onto my bed. I place it in my mouth without thinking. Although it is disgusting, I chew slowly, making it last.

※

I settle into a strange routine over the next couple of days.

In the morning I help Euphoria with the bed and breakfast. This is more of a concept than a reality, but soon we have a sign out the front and three tidy cottages. All we need are some guests. I introduce Euphoria to the idea of project management.

'You see' – I show her a Gantt chart I've whipped up on my laptop – 'You decide what your aim is – in this case a money-making bed and breakfast – and you put in the steps you need to get there.'

She is taken with it. 'Might have to get myself a computer. I expect someone around here's got an old one they don't need.'

In the afternoon, I fiddle around with the rest of my Antarctic footage, trying to edit it into a show. I also work on my secret project – a new soap opera. And of course I am planning my wedding. My wedding project plan has over five hundred tasks – guest list, flowers, catering, outfit, cars, speeches … Building a trans-national highway would be easier.

Adrian and I will leave for a two-week honeymoon in Fiji straight after the wedding. Adrian has organised it all. He rang me yesterday to tell me about it.

I had to go to the main house to take his call as there's no mobile reception here on the commune.

Adrian spoke fast. I expect he was in the middle of some important work project. 'It's one of those package deals where you stay in a five-star hotel and every day something is scheduled in – cultural tours and snorkelling trips. We should try fire-walking too.'

'That sounds terrific, darling,' I squeezed in when he paused for breath. Our honeymoon will be stimulating. Not as exciting as sleeping in a snow cave in Antarctica maybe, but much warmer obviously.

'The breakfasts are good at the Isa Lei Resort,' Adrian said. 'They have a special option for fitness …'

I lost track at that point as I was thinking about how to get out of the fire-walking.

'Have you been exercising? I haven't been able to download your progress report for some reason,' he said.

'Oh. Yes.' I twirled the dial on my new watch. 'I've been running every day, but there's no wi-fi here.'

'Not even when you go into town?' Adrian sounded shocked.

'No.' There *was* wi-fi in town, but I made sure I left my watch behind when I went in there because, of course, I hadn't been running at all.

What I had been doing a lot of – oh joy, oh bliss – was sleeping. Back in my old bedroom I sank into the sounds of the forest, waking in the morning like ascending from the bottom of the ocean. Each time I woke, I felt like I'd put back a piece of myself I hadn't known was missing.

Yesterday, I carried my laptop to the creek and sat next to Marley's fig tree to work. It was shady there and would have been pleasant if I'd thought to bring some insect repellent. While I used to be immune to the predators my years away had apparently removed this protection.

'I know; hilarious, right?' I said to Marley's tree as I stood up, pulling a leech from my ankle. But Marley's tree was just a tree.

It didn't answer back.

Chapter Thirty-five

I struggle with my love interest

Today I set up office on the verandah of my cabin. My 'behind the scenes' feature is coming along slowly. Sorting through the footage is quite a job.

I open one of my movie files and leave it playing while I make a cup of tea. Sipping my tea in the kitchen, I scan my wedding spreadsheet. Are gardenias in season? Adrian has placed a lot of trust in me, leaving me the wedding project plan. I would hate for anything to go wrong.

A voice comes from my laptop. *'So Lucas Nilsson, climate scientist, how is the climate outside?' 'The weather, you mean.'* There is a discussion about swallows and summer, then we move on to Jules Verne – *'Science, my lad …'*

As I go back out to the verandah, Lucas is talking again. *'So, Summer Dawn Rain Wright, this is the first day of your twenty-ninth year … If this was* Dynasty, *what would happen next?'*

I see myself on the screen. My hair looks like I've been dragged through a hedge backwards, but my face …

'If this was Dynasty, *I would now find out you have a dark secret …'*
I look so happy.

'I will not see you again for at least five years—'
And the way I'm looking at him … I click the program shut and sink into my desk chair. His words replay in my head. *Science, my lad, is made up of mistakes, but they are mistakes which it is useful to make, because they lead little by little to the truth …*

It's not only science that is made up of mistakes. It also applies to life. And to love. *Don't be silly, Summer, you hardly knew him. Love is based on shared goals and* – I glance at my wedding plan – *spreadsheets. Besides, he's married. And I'm engaged. And once I'm married to Adrian, the Cone of Certainty will be mine forever.*

I take a deep breath and banish Lucas Nilsson from my mind.

There's a lot to be done and it's only three days before Adrian comes and whisks me away to my new job at Channel Four, a wedding and a honeymoon in Fiji. But for now ... I open my secret file, as guilty as a woman having an affair. Adrian will be so cross if he finds out I'm frittering away my time like this.

My soap opera, *Love on Ice*, is set in Antarctica and already I have the first ten episodes plotted out. It features a lively cast of characters who are sure to keep the action rolling.

Love on Ice — cast list episode one

Autumn: a naive TV presenter

Nigel: a manipulative politician

Carla: a sultry krill researcher

Alan: the politician's minder

Bjorn: a grumpy Norwegian climate scientist

I get stuck whenever I come to write this character. I need a love interest, but a scientist with a beard doesn't fit the bill. I've tried to write him as a more typical hero, but it falls flat.

I flick through my notes, but they raise more questions than they answer.

Will there be a hot and steamy sex scene in an igloo? Or will he become an amnesiac following a cooking-stove explosion? Or be locked in an ice-bound cabin while an arsonist burns it down? Will he ever shave off his beard? In an effort to make sense of this character, I fill out a checklist – something I only ever do as a last resort.

Name: Bjorn Larsson.

Age: 34

Height: 6 foot

Weight/Build: Strong - looks like he knows how to find his way out of a crevasse

Birthplace: Norway

Colour hair/eyes: thick sandy hair that sticks up from his head, eyes that see right into you, as if he understands

I stop and delete everything after *eyes*. I don't know what got into me.

> Educational background: PhD in climate science
>
> Hobbies: rock-climbs, studies snowflakes, interested in pagan attitudes to climate
>
> Physical peculiarities: scar on face from ice core drilling, big fluffy beard that scratches your face when he kisses you, making you feel like you want to

I stop and backspace. As I reach *beard* my stomach leaps like I'm on a downward swing. *What's with that?*

'Beard,' I say. My stomach leaps again and this time my legs tingle too. *Weird.* 'Beard, beard, beard, beard, beard.' By the last *beard* my stomach has settled. Glad that's out of my system.

I think about the character some more. *Strangely sexy*, I add. *Particularly for a bearded man.*

Despite my efforts to get inside Bjorn's head, I'm having problems. I should make Alan, the politician's minder, the love interest and Bjorn the villain. That's the best solution to my scriptwriting dilemma. Bearded men make good villains.

I decide to rest my script before making any major decisions. In the meantime I can sort through the footage for my behind-the-scenes episode.

This episode will feature the phone camera footage of my igloo-building which I've saved onto the computer. I open it up, fast forwarding through the first igloo-building episode. Mainly it's just a snowscape with occasional glimpses of me staggering past, a snow block in my hands. Those bits are funny. I make a note of their location.

Soon I come to the part where I'm lying on the bed talking into the camera – *I could round up a husky team and head off for the South Pole ...* This makes my chest ache in a way I can't explain.

I take a sip of tea and when I look back all I see is a shot of a ceiling with the corner of a chair in the foreground. The shot goes on and on. Realisation dawns – I must have left my iPhone on *record* when I abandoned it next to the phone at the station. As I press *fast forward* to get through this boring bit, I hear a chipmunk squeaking – someone is talking.

Curiosity gets the better of me and I press *play*. The recording is faint and crackly but I can make out a few phrases – ... *email in the system? ... cover your tracks ... Nilsson*. It is a man's voice, but not clear enough to recognise. This is intriguing. Stopping the recording, I replay it. This time I get a few more phrases. *Emissions bill ... fake data ... leak it through ...* I replay it again, but get only a muffled *Roger that*. My eyes drop to the date on the bottom of the recording – the twentieth of December. Clicking on Google, I type in *Nilsson, climate data, leak*. As I thought, the story broke on the twenty-first of December. I tap my fingers on the table, pieces falling into place. Someone in Antarctica set up the bodgy climate data scandal. Someone set Lucas up.

What am I going to do with this?

❄

Euphoria knocks at the door of my cottage the next afternoon.

I'm struggling with a dramatic scene from *Love on Ice*. Nigel the politician has been pushed down a crevasse by Carla the krill researcher and Autumn the TV presenter is trying to get him out. Meanwhile Bjorn the climate scientist is analysing ice-cores when he inadvertently spills a whole mug of coffee down the front of his polar fleece jacket necessitating a quick change of ...

Euphoria leans against the door. 'There's a man here. Says he knows you. Lucas Nilsson.'

My stomach leaps as if I've bungy-jumped. *Beard, beard, beard, beard, beard.* The repetition calms me. 'Is he by himself?'

'Yes.'

'What's he doing here?'

'He's taken one of the cottages. He said he's interested in pagan climate rituals. I invited him to stay for New Year's Eve.'

'But that's three days away.'

'He's paid four nights in advance for the Bangalow Cottage.'

The Bangalow Cottage is our most expensive. I can imagine how excited Euphoria is to have her first guest.

'I told him I'd tell you he's here.' She cocks her head. 'Your aura's a little … confused. Anything you want to tell me?'

'No.' I pull my aura into line. *Beard, beard, beard, beard, beard.*

She hovers for a few moments, shrugs and disappears.

After Euphoria leaves, I tap my fingers on the keyboard for a while, attempting to return to writing. It's no good. I can't sit here, waiting to run into Lucas around the place, I'm going to go over there and talk to him. I'll enquire about his wife and fill him in on my wedding plans. That would be the correct etiquette when meeting anyone with whom you'd once shared a snow cave.

I survey my reflection in the tiny mildewed mirror which hangs in my bathroom. My hair is at an awkward stage – neither short nor long. I'll need to get it cut before the wedding. Finding a comb, I drag it through, then splash some water on my face. The summer sun has coloured my shoulders and my nose. In the dull mirror, I'm not all that dissimilar to the Summer who grew up here. I square my shoulders. May as well get it over with.

My heart thumps as I approach Bangalow Cottage. Which is ridiculous. This is a courtesy call. That's all.

Then I see him.

The reality of his presence blows me off course. Lucas is sitting on a couch on the verandah, plucking at a guitar, his back towards me. I recognise the tune from Antarctica. And now it's obvious – Lucas is the guitar-playing guy. Of course. He would be, wouldn't he?

Given my bad history with guitar-playing men, avoidance is clearly the only strategy. As I turn to go, I step on a stick. It cracks loudly and he turns.

He's shaved off his beard. I can't believe it; he's a guitar-playing man and he's shaved off his beard. Without the beard he looks like the kind of man a woman might …

I stop that thought before it forms. This isn't going to happen. I'm getting married. And he's already married. This is a polite and friendly meeting. I raise my hand in a casual wave. 'Hi.'

A broad smile stretches across his face.

He seems so happy to see me I find myself feeling happy too.

We smile at each other for some time.

I mentally edit the description of my climate scientist, Bjorn. There is no 'strangely' to the 'sexy' anymore. I also note his eyes are exactly the same shade of blue as the Antarctic sea. 'Are you really here to research pagan climate rituals?'

'Partly.'

'And the other part?'

'Sit for a moment? I've got something to show you.' He stands and walks inside. He's wearing loose khaki shorts. I've never seen his legs before. *Damn*, things were so much easier in Antarctica.

I perch on the edge of the couch. It's nice here at the Bangalow Cottage. Even though it's so dry, the stream in front of the cottage is flowing. The sound of water is always soothing.

'I think I might owe you some thanks.' Lucas sits on the couch, but not too close, and hands me a folded copy of a newspaper. It's dated the twenty-eighth of December – today.

Scandal rocks first day of climate summit.

My head spins as I read the headline. I scan the rest of the article.

Nilsson cleared – emails are frauds. Government inquiry closed …
Hornby not available for comment …

'That's great.' I look up. I can hardly put two thoughts together. The combination of Lucas – *no beard!* – and the newspaper article is frying my brain. 'But why thank me?'

Lucas tilts his head to one side and observes me closely. 'There's back room gossip, something about an anonymous recording from Antarctica. Someone in the Minister's office must have spoken out of school. Lips are sealed, but … birds don't fly into our mouths fully roasted.'

'Pardon?'

'It's a Norwegian saying. It means … well, someone roasted this bird. For some reason I thought of you.'

My stomach clenches. He's here to thank me. That's all. Yesterday morning's rushed trip to the internet cafe in Nimbin has brought results. It has also brought Lucas to my door, which was not what I'd intended. Not at all.

'I've got a recording,' I say. 'It sounds like someone setting you up. I sent it to Hornby. I wanted to give him a chance. I would have given it to the newspapers next. If he hadn't done something. He's not a bad egg Hornby, just a little misguided.'

'Egg is apt.'

I laugh, remembering Hornby's egg-collecting obsession.

'You didn't send it to me,' says Lucas.

I raise my shoulders. 'It seemed cleaner to keep you out of it.' But this is only part of the reason. The other part I can't articulate – not since he's only here to thank me. 'How did you know where to find me?'

'I knew you lived in Nimbin. I asked at the bakery and they gave me directions. And you did invite me for the New Year's Eve ritual you know.'

'Did I?'

'Perhaps I invited myself.' He pauses. 'Your mother tells me you're getting married soon. Congratulations.'

'Yes.' I get to my feet. 'I'm very busy organising it. I should get back. I've got lots of spreadsheets …'

'I hope you don't mind me staying for a few days. I really am interested in the pagan rituals. And I need a short break. I've got a project starting in Greenland soon.'

Greenland. Could he go any further away? Not that it's anything to do with me. 'No. Euphoria's pleased. You're our first guest.'

'Have a fish?' Lucas holds out a packet.

'No thanks.'

'I thought you might have developed a taste.'

I shake my head. 'What happened to your penguin chick?'

'I set it free before I left. It was fat and strong. I think it will be fine.'

'Oh good.' I twist my hands together. I wish he hadn't shaved his beard off. Things were hard enough already. 'I really have to go.'

Lucas picks up his guitar again as I leave.

Guitar music drifts down from Bangalow Cottage that night but I put earplugs in and keep typing. My life is on track, I have a lot of spreadsheets to do and I can't afford to get distracted.

Chapter Thirty-six

I attend a powerful pagan ritual

The next morning I wake with the realisation that my usual snake dream has been replaced. I get out of bed and sit at the kitchen table, pulling my laptop towards me.

To: Marley Lennon Wright
From: Summer Dawn Rain Wright
Subject: My new dream

This is how it goes, Marley.

I'm at a church and the organ is playing, 'Here comes the bride'. I walk down the aisle and join Adrian in front of the pulpit. After the 'we are gathered here today part', the priest says, 'If anyone can show just cause why they may not be lawfully joined together, let them speak now or forever hold their peace.'

There is silence in the church. The priest takes a breath, about to continue.

'I do.' A man interrupts.

Adrian and I turn. The whole congregation gapes at a man in the back row. He stands. His cheeks are freshly shaved and yet his eyes are the same blue and his teeth are the same sparkling white.

'She is the child of a sperm donor.' Lucas brandishes some medical records. 'I would have got here sooner, but I had amnesia from a cooking-stove explosion.'

Guess you don't need to be Freud to figure that one out, huh?

When I go outside, I find a bowl with a small collection of objects from the rainforest sitting on my writing desk. There's a blue feather, an empty snail shell, a black bean pod and a sprinkling of red berries carefully arranged on a flat rock from the creek and placed inside a bowl. Like an altar.

There's a rustle in the trees. I raise my head. A man's back disappears through the forest. *Lucas.*

Why would he do that? My first impulse is to throw the collection into the bushes, but I hesitate as I pick it up. It's so beautiful, it seems a shame. All day as I work it sits there, like a message I don't know how to read. By midday my neck is aching with the effort of not looking at it and my wedding plans have stalled. I pick the bowl up and throw its contents into the undergrowth, rubbing my chest to banish the lump that's settled there.

That night a guitar and a mandolin are playing in Bangalow Cottage. I grind my teeth. *Euphoria.* How could she? But I haven't told her about Lucas yet – about how he kissed me even though he's married. About how he went all strange and distant afterwards. When I do, she will know to avoid him. Although … I suppose there isn't much to tell.

In the morning I find a collection of pebbles sitting on my table in a water-filled jar. They are like jewels – all colours and sizes, and too pretty to throw out even if they make my heart hurt. And when Euphoria calls by for a cup of tea the story stays untold.

'We're going to have a jam session at Bangalow Cottage tonight,' says Euphoria. 'Why don't you come up and play your tambourine?' The tambourine was the only instrument I ever mastered.

I shake my head. 'I'm busy.'

That night, the guitar and the mandolin are joined by bongo drums. *Aunt Patsy.* My family has taken to Lucas in a big way. I stuff the earplugs in my ears and pull out *An Antarctic Mystery.* I'm getting near the end of Marley's book. The good ship Halbrane has slid from the top of the iceberg to the bottom, shattering and vanishing into the abyss of the sea …

> Three of our men had perished and in what frightful fashion! I had seen Rogers and Gratian, two of our most faithful sailors, stretch out their hands in despair …

I put down the book and stare out at the night. *Rogers* ... Why does that give me a feeling of déjà vu? I pull out my earplugs – the party is still going on at Bangalow Cottage. 'Are you trying to tell me something, Marley?'

I listen, but there's no reply.

On New Year's Eve when I step outside, my writing table is awash – flowers float in bowls, leaves are arranged in the cracks of the table. Why is he doing this? He's already said thank you. I should go over there and tell him to stop, but I don't trust my stomach in his presence. I wish he'd go away.

I go back inside and get dressed. Adrian is flying into Ballina today. Things will be clearer once he's here. Adrian will take control.

The ute doesn't have any air-conditioning so on the way to the airport I wind the windows right down and let the hot air whip my hair across my face. I turn the radio up loud and sing along to the greatest hits of the year, yelling over the noise of the wind.

Outside the window the country is parched and brown. I remember what Lucas said about the link between more snow in Antarctica and drought in Australia. It doesn't seem far-fetched anymore. The planet is not so big – what goes around comes around.

Half an hour out of Ballina I see smoke in the air. A stiff breeze is tossing the branches of the gum trees that line the road. White flakes drift from the sky. *Like snowflakes.* I turn on the wipers and they smear a grey sheen across the windscreen.

Ahead of me on the road, a figure in an orange suit holds up his hand. I lean out the window as I pull up, smelling ash, my skin drying on impact with the air. The firie is familiar – it's Jack the dope dealer, my high-school sweetheart.

'Hi, Summer. We're about to do a backburn here, you'll be right to go in a sec as soon as that truck turns around.' He points at the big fire-truck with 'Lismore' on the side which is blocking the road in front of us. Jack has the awkward air Nimbin people always have around me. It's because of Marley. They don't know what to say. Jack is covered in black soot from his head to his toes. His hair is wet with sweat and as he runs his hand through it, he leaves a trail of black lines on his forehead.

'You should be wearing a helmet,' I say.

'Yeah.' He gives me an ironic salute, picks it up off the bonnet of his truck and puts it on. 'Gets hot. We've all been watching you on TV.' He glances at his three crew members, who are raking leaves back from the road. 'Haven't we?'

The men murmur their assent. They seem a little shy.

'It was awesome,' says Jack.

I should murmur 'it was nothing' or some such thing, but I'm new to this celebrity game. 'Do you want my autograph?'

That is not the sort of question you can politely say no to, so a dirty scrap of paper is found which I sign with a flourish four times, tear into four and present to them.

'You're right to go, Sum.' Jack pockets his autograph.

Only people I went to school with call me *Sum*. 'Wear your helmet, huh?'

'Yes, ma'am.' I'm about to drive off when he puts his hand on the window ledge. 'We miss Marley here.'

'Thanks.' I blink to stop the tears. 'Thanks for telling me. I miss him too.'

They raise their rakes to me as I drive off.

Standing inside the cool of the airport, I watch Adrian walk across the tarmac to the glass door. He's wearing a polo shirt and smart-casual long pants and has a satchel slung over his shoulder. He looks handsome, fit, clean and well-organised. His new job is obviously agreeing with him.

He gives me a hug and an aftershave-smelling kiss then throws his bag in the back of the ute and we squeeze in the front.

I wind past the flying-fox colony towards the highway. 'All set for the ritual?'

Adrian shifts uncomfortably.

'It will be all right.' I pat his knee. 'You don't need to get naked.' A naughty impulse seizes me. 'Everyone else will be, but it's not compulsory. I like to wear a flower behind my ear myself.'

Adrian opens his mouth. 'I'm not—'

I hit him on the shoulder. 'I'm joking. There's no nudity.'

He relaxes.

I've had a word to Euphoria about this. I told her Adrian and I would not be attending if she planned to strip off her sarong in the heat of the moment as she was wont to do.

'Oh, but that's silly, Summer,' she'd said. 'There's nothing wrong with a healthy attitude towards your body.'

'That's not the way we do things in Sydney,' I replied.

She'd reluctantly agreed to refrain from going the Full Monty.

Adrian holds onto the rim of the window to brace himself as I turn the wheel sharply towards our driveway. 'Nice flags.' He sounds like an intrepid explorer in a strange land.

Euphoria runs out of the house at the sound of the car, her hair flowing behind her, suntanned feet bare. She is dressed up for the ritual in a colourful sarong. A multitude of beads rattle around her neck.

I jump out of the ute and Adrian climbs out behind me. He is smiling, but I can tell it's an effort. Euphoria puts out her arms and he leans down to give her a stiff hug – an explorer doing his best to observe the native rituals.

'Prepare to be embraced,' I murmur as he gets his bag out of the ute.

'I've got another guest,' says Euphoria. 'Just arrived. The bed and breakfast is taking off. You'll meet her later. She's joining us for the ritual.'

I hadn't realised the rituals would be such a drawcard. 'We should add it to the sign – "Bed, Breakfast and Rituals".'

'Maybe "Bed and Breakfast. Rituals for any occasion".' I can see Euphoria's mind ticking over. 'It could be our unique point of difference.'

I'm startled to hear this expression come from her mouth.

'I went to a tourism workshop in Lismore yesterday. They say that's what every business needs. What do you think, Adrian?'

Adrian nods. 'Separate yourself from the herd. Excellent advice.'

Over the next few minutes I suspect Adrian doubles his lifetime hug tally. The entire commune is keen to meet Summer's man. And when you get a Nimbin hug, you know you've been hugged, there's no half measures or delicate cheek-kissing here. First comes the deep eye contact and an opportunity for breath to mingle as you absorb each other's essence. Then you move into the clasp with full chest to chest contact. This lasts a while, as no hippie worth their salt will be the first to break away. After the clasp, there's an option for deep eye gazing again. Most people take this up. Adrian is dishevelled and wild-eyed by the time we escape to my cottage for a short break before the festivities.

Adrian puts his suitcase in the lounge room and checks his watch. 'How long is it until the … ritual?' The word sits uncomfortably on his tongue.

'Half an hour.'

'Let's have sex.' He taps at his iPhone. 'Yes, here it is. Backwards cowboy.' He puts down the phone and unbuttons his shirt.

'Um …' The creek pebbles on my table catch my eye. 'Let's save it up for when we've got more time. Then we can get right into it.'

'Roger that, you saucy minx. You want to do forwards cowboy too? I've got that here.' He scrolls through his phone.

Roger … Déjà vu strikes again. And it is gone. What is it with Roger? 'Yes, absolutely.'

Adrian looks down at his shirt, which would be just right for drinks at Potts Point. 'Am I suitably dressed?'

I maintain a straight face. 'You're fine.'

Soon it's time to gather for the ritual. A large group is already up at the main house by the time Adrian and I get there. More hugs ensue – because even if you hugged someone half an hour ago it doesn't mean you can skip them this time. A protocol must be observed. Adrian is a high performer. He's worked out it's a three-phase project – the eye contact, the clasp, the eye contact again – and he dispatches each hug with his usual efficiency. I hope he manages to stop when he gets back to Sydney – it can be hard to know where to draw the line. Before you know it, you're greeting your bank manager with an affectionate embrace.

Lucas is there. I manage to avoid hugging him. It seems he's not keen to hug me either as our orbits don't collide. He gives me a half-smile when he catches my eye.

My stomach does its usual thing. *Beard, beard, beard, beard, beard.* I'll be glad when he's gone.

'The circle is about to be cast,' Euphoria cries. She enters from the east and, placing a sunflower on the ground, walks slowly to the south, placing another flower. She continues around, placing flowers at points west and north. 'You may enter the circle in love and trust.' She directs the men to one side of the circle and the women to the other.

Adrian and I aim for the divide between the genders where I can be next to him to help with any ritual problems.

'We are a field of sunflowers,' Euphoria calls.

Everyone knows the drill. They rustle and sway.

'One half is the wind' – she points – 'and one half is the sun.'

The group members offer a range of artistic interpretations of wind and sun. I am enjoying being a little sunbeam, when I catch a glimpse of Adrian. The man next to him flings his head and his long, dark hair flies into Adrian's face. Adrian lifts his arms and waves them in a motion that reminds me of a wind-up toy.

I don't look at Lucas – it would make my brain hurt.

'Oh, hello dear.' Euphoria waves her arm. 'Come and join us. We've only just started.'

A woman approaches from the direction of Blue Fig Cottage. She wears a singlet and quick-dry shorts. One of her long brown legs terminates in a bandage around her ankle and she limps as she makes her way towards us.

'Cougar?' Adrian and I mutter her name at the same time. What on earth is she doing here?

Cougar insinuates herself into the circle between Adrian and me.

Euphoria steps into the middle. 'The wheel is turning,' she cries. 'It is time for new insights.'

'You shouldn't have come here,' mutters Adrian.

'Don't worry, I didn't come for you,' Cougar mutters back out the side of her mouth.

'New Year's Eve is a tipping point – a time to look back at what we've accomplished. What do we want to take with us and what to give away?'

Cougar turns to me. 'I've been watching your YouTube videos.'

My heart beats faster. Is she angry I've smirched her image?

'Are there achievements that are hollow as we gaze to the future? Remember, this is where the story starts,' calls Euphoria.

'They're interesting.' Cougar makes no attempt to become a ray of sunshine.

Euphoria seems to sense a small cloud passing across the sun. 'We will split up into a men's group and a women's group, in preparation for the offerings.'

The women's group turns on itself to huddle together and I find myself face to face with Cougar again.

'Embrace the god and goddess in each other,' calls Euphoria.

Cougar steps forward and puts her arms around me. They are strong and wiry and even if I wanted to escape it would be difficult. 'I didn't come here for Adrian, I came to see you,' she mutters in my ear.

I don't struggle, but neither do I put my arms around her. I've never seen her this closely before. Her eyes are light hazel with flecks of green. *Exactly like my own.*

I turn my head for a moment. In the men's group, Lucas embraces Adrian. Neither of them seems happy about it. They look like two seals about to butt chests.

I turn back to Cougar. What does she want?

'Adrian says you can do the finger thing.'

I hold up my hand and her arms drop to her side. I draw my middle finger up through its neighbours, put it slowly back down and raise my eyebrows at her.

She puts her hand up, does the same and smiles.

And I'd like to hug her properly then, but Euphoria calls us to order.

Cougar glances at Adrian as we wander over to join the circle. 'He wasn't interested in me either, you know. Not in a physical way. It was more of a fact-finding excursion for him.'

'How do you mean?'

'Well … he lost interest once I was taken off the Antarctic trip.'

Euphoria glares at us. She raises her voice. 'Two offerings must be made. One is a symbol of something we have been working on this year, but we haven't yet finished. This symbolises the harvest not yet in. The other is a symbol of something we are letting go. Something weighing us down, that we don't need as the season changes and we head into winter. Something to keep and something to give away. This is where the story starts.'

Euphoria has built an altar out of rocks and other objects from the rainforest. She puts a bowl containing a few pieces of fruit and vegetables beside the altar. 'To symbolise my garden, which is growing.' Next, she puts down a jar of honey. 'To symbolise my addiction to sugar, which I am leaving behind.'

Euphoria does this every year. She has a sweet tooth.

A few more people go – sheets of music, wood carvings, drawings, scribbled pages of writing, bottles of beer, mobile phones and chocolate gather before the altar. I have my two symbols ready in my little shoulder bag. I pull them out – something to keep in my left hand, something to give away in my right.

'Roger?' Euphoria calls on a tousled redhead.

Roger. I have that feeling again. What is it with Roger?

Roger comes forward, his offerings in his hands.

And at last it comes to me. *Roger that.* That's what the mystery caller in Antarctica said. *That's what Adrian said.* The phrase replays in my mind, over and over. And the jigsaw pieces fall into place.

Chapter Thirty-seven

Antarctica gives you perspective

Antarctica gives you perspective, Lucas said. And it seems that it's true.

Adrian's watch ticks in my hand, reminding me that ten thousand years is not a long time. Geologically speaking. And that being the case, my twenty-eight years are the blink of an eye. This thought could be depressing, but instead it's empowering.

An image of life with Adrian stretches before me – a house on the North Shore, accounting for my time to the minute, ascending the corporate ladder. And still my watch ticks. Do I want to spend the rest of my all-too-short life ascending the Cone of Certainty with Adrian?

And, geologically speaking, isn't all certainty an illusion? I imagine the woolly mammoths and sabre-toothed tigers heading for the hills as the floodwaters rose at the end of the last ice age ten thousand years ago. Project management wouldn't have saved them.

With each tick of my watch, another piece falls into place. *Adrian lost interest in Cougar when she wasn't going to Antarctica. Adrian told Hornby I was going to be filming in Antarctica. Adrian was the mystery caller. Adrian framed Lucas.*

'Summer?' I realise Euphoria has called my name several times.

I am frozen. Everyone's eyes are on me. Adrian, Cougar, Euphoria, Lucas … But there's someone missing. The wind rustles in the tree tops. It dances along the creek stirring the leaves of Marley's little fig tree.

This is where the story starts, Summer Dawn. His voice is in my head.

And as I walk out to the middle of the circle, I swap the items in my hands. 'Something to give away.' As I place my GPS tracking watch in front of the altar, I feel like a prisoner being set free. 'And something to keep.' The first page of my new script, *Love on Ice*, joins it. The first line catches my eye – *Ten thousand years is not a long time.*

Adrian is the only person here who would understand what these objects mean. An angry red colour passes across his face. Holding his gaze, I lift my shoulders and mouth the word *sorry*. But I'm not.

As I go back to the circle, I feel so light I could almost float away. And while I have no idea where the breeze might take me, right now that seems okay.

After all, when you're dealing in geological time, there's not much point in counting minutes.

On New Year's Day I wake to the sound of a kookaburra laughing. 'Shut up,' I mutter as I pull on a sarong.

Adrian departed in a taxi straight after the ritual.

I saw him off. I didn't need to explain the situation to him – seemed like he'd been expecting it ever since the true data-fraud story surfaced.

He leaned out of the taxi window. 'That recording – did you …?'

'Yes. I'm not planning to do anything else with it.'

He knew he'd got off lightly.

I thought Cougar would join him on the last flight to Sydney – that Channel Four job's going begging after all – but she's still here.

The ritual became a blur for me after my turn. I vaguely recall Cougar tossing a *Who Weekly* cover of her with one of her many escorts onto the altar. Was that something to keep, or something to give away?

Last night I finished *An Antarctic Mystery*. It is lying beside my bed and I pick it up and reread the last page.

> Thus terminated this adventurous and extraordinary expedition, which cost, alas, too many victims … discoveries of great value still remain to be made in those waters!

End of the voyage extraordinaire, reads the final line.

I think of sending Marley an email. Or leaving a message on his phone. But now, that doesn't seem necessary. If he is anywhere, he is here. 'I like your book, Marley,' I say to the air.

Outside, on my doormat, I find a piece of dry wood carved into the shape of a snowflake. I snatch it up. I have got to put an end to this.

Lucas is on his couch again, a guitar on his lap. He looks up as I approach.

The snowflake dangles from my fingertips, forgotten. Neither of us talks for some time. I can feel the energy between us but my bruised heart keeps a tight lock on my mouth.

He puts down his guitar. 'Can we talk?'

I sink onto the edge of the verandah, my back to him. My legs can hardly hold me anyway.

He gets off the couch and comes to sit beside me.

I appreciate it that he doesn't come too close.

'Did you hear about the Carbon Bill?' he says.

I can't believe it. That's the last thing I expected him to say. He wants to talk about the Carbon Bill? I shake my head.

He reaches behind him and picks up his phone. 'You're cut off here, aren't you? I had to climb that mountain over there to get reception.' He points at a distant hill.

'You climbed all the way up there?'

'I had to know what happened.'

'Euphoria's got a radio at the house.'

'I didn't think of that. Too late now.' He holds out his phone towards me, showing me the screen with today's newspaper headline.

> Shock as Hornby Votes Yes. Government pledges to reduce carbon emissions.

The story continues with commentators from both sides saying their bit.

> Return to the dark ages …

> Bring us into line with other countries …

> Job losses in the mining sector …

> Job gains in the renewable energy sector …

> Emperor penguins at risk, says Hornby …

And, near the bottom:

Nilsson data provided key evidence of need for change. 'I expected nothing less,' says Nilsson's lawyer and former wife.

Former wife? 'Former wife?' I say.

He looks at me quizzically. 'We've been separated for a year. Now divorced. Just last week. Amicably. She's a good lawyer.'

'What happened with you two?'

He blows a tiny spider off his arm. 'Same thing that happened to Scott of the Antarctic.'

'But you're alive.'

He laughs. 'I spent too much time in Antarctica. She found someone else.'

'I'm sorry.'

'It was for the best. Though it was painful at the time.'

I wait.

'It would have been better if she'd told me straight away. But she kept pretending nothing was wrong. She was quite a storyteller too.' He gazes at me.

'My stories are harmless. I wouldn't lie about something like that.'

'It's not that I blame her. I wasn't the person she'd married; Antarctica changed me. Like I said, it gives you perspective. We both knew it wasn't right, but we kept trying to make it work.'

'So …' I look at the screen again. 'This is good news, right?'

He nods. 'Best for a while.'

'Will it make a difference?'

'You have to start somewhere.'

'Take care of the little things and the big things will take care of themselves?'

'I'm not sure if that's true, but … you do what you can.'

The sky has darkened while we are talking. There's a rumble in the distance. 'Summer?'

As I turn to face him a single raindrop lands with a splash on my nose. Like a blessing.

'You and Adrian?' he says.

'Finished.'

'Are you okay?'

'Relieved. It never seemed right, but I kept thinking I had to try harder.'

'My whole marriage was like that. Melanie is great, but she is so …'

'Organised?'

He laughs. 'And I am not.'

'I should have known. If a wedding is extensively planned it is obvious it will never take place.'

'In soap opera?' says Lucas.

'Yes, it's rule number seven.'

'And if a man and a woman spend a night in a snow cave?'

'They will never see each other again until their political rivals and love interests have been dispatched.'

'And then?'

'Everyone will clear the floor and they will dance the tango.'

Lucas nods solemnly. 'Of course.' He pauses. 'I'm sorry about the way I acted. After the snow cave. I know I was a bit distant. It was just … hearing that Channel Five was covering that data-fraud story …'

'You thought I'd told them?'

'I shouldn't have thought that. I would have talked to you about it on the way back to the station, but then Adrian got in the Hagg. I came to see you, back at the station. To apologise. But when I bumped into Adrian coming out of your room I figured I'd blown my chance.'

I chew my lip. 'What did you put on the altar yesterday?'

'A rock.' Lucas reaches into his pocket. 'Like this one.' He pulls out a rock and places it on my lap.

It is about the size of an apricot stone – grey and weathered. Up close it looks familiar. 'This is a symbol of something I want to keep,' he says.

'What was the other thing?'

He touches his chin.

'Your beard? You want to leave your beard behind?'

'I'm not usually a bearded person.'

'You're not? I assumed you were.'

'No, only when I go to cold places. It keeps me warm. I heard what you said outside the snow cave, by the way.'

'What?' I blush fiercely. I know exactly what he means.

'Strangely sexy for a bearded man. I wasn't sure if it was a compliment.'

'I didn't say that.'

His eyes crinkle. 'What did you say?'

'I was speaking … Chinese. *Strai ji sen shui fo abead deman*. It means "Blessings on us both for the Summer Solstice".'

A snort bursts out of Lucas's nose. 'That sounds more like Hungarian.'

'Yes. Hungarian. That's what I meant.'

'You are multi-talented, aren't you?'

'Yes. Yes, I am. I don't like to brag about it.'

'Chinese, Hungarian … Do you have any other languages?'

'Only Inuit.'

He laughs.

'Anyway, I may have changed my mind about beards.'

'You may?'

'Possibly.' The rock rests on my lap. 'Did you bring that with you from Antarctica?'

'Maybe, but don't tell anyone. Remember how I told you about the Adelie penguin? How he chooses his mate from millions of penguins?'

I nod, wondering where this is leading.

'After he's waddled around checking out a million penguins, he finds a perfect stone and rolls it to the feet of his loved one.' He holds my gaze. 'If she accepts his gift, they stand belly to belly and sing a mating song.'

'That's so romantic.' A hot blush spreads from my toes to my head. I put my hand to my cheek in an attempt to cool it.

'It is, isn't it?' He almost whispers.

'So …' I roll the rock on my lap with the palm of my hand. 'What does she do if she accepts his gift?'

'She sits on it.'

I gaze at the rock. 'Penguins must have softer bottoms than me.'

'I'm pretty sure she'd pick it up if she had hands.'

I pick up the stone. 'Like this?'

'Yes, like that.'

A second raindrop lands on my face and another. The rain gets heavier. I hold my free hand up to the sky, catching the drops before they touch the ground.

Cougar and Euphoria run out of the main building. They seem to be getting on like a house on fire. Euphoria cracks a broad grin when she sees Lucas and me sitting together. Cougar stamps in a puddle and splashes Euphoria. Euphoria squeals and splashes her back.

I stare at Cougar and I don't know why I've never seen it before. Has everyone else noticed before me? I look at Lucas.

He nods. 'She is.'

'She is what?' Although I think I already know what he means.

'The child of a sperm donor.'

'How do you know?'

'Euphoria told me.'

'Euphoria told you? Why didn't she tell me?'

'Maybe she wanted you to find out for yourself.'

Cougar jumps up and down in a puddle and for a moment I see a fourteen-year-old boy playing in the rain. I blink and the illusion vanishes. But the resemblance is breathtaking.

Then, as if this downpour was a warm-up, the rain increases tenfold. The wind blows in under the verandah roof and immediately we are sodden, our clothes clinging to our bodies. The main house vanishes, as if under a waterfall.

And now I'm grateful for the rain as something breaks inside me. The tears surge up from a deep well inside.

Lucas sits quietly beside me, the rain running down his face, his leg pressing against mine.

The tears keep coming – they've been banked up for over a year and they're not stopping now. It's like a dam bursting. At last my crying falters and slowly peters out, leaving me drained but calm. The rain eases a little too and the air smells ripe and fresh. Frogs croak. Where have they been all this time?

Lucas turns to me and wipes some water from my cheek, puts his finger to his mouth. 'Slightly salty.'

I smile weakly.

But the storm is not over. A clap of thunder shakes the house. Tiny balls of ice clatter on the tin roof and bounce over the edge. I stick out my hand and catch some. They are pure and cold and soon they litter the ground in front of us like snow.

'I have some snowsuits with me,' Lucas yells in my ear. 'We can put them on if you like?'

'That's presumptuous of you,' I yell back.

He laughs, his hair wet with rain, his shirt sticking to his chest, rivulets of rain running down his cheeks. 'I'm a born optimist, Summer. Always prepared.' He stands and puts out his hand, pulling me up. We run inside. The noise of the hail lessens, but only slightly. It sounds like a giant wombat tap-dancing on the roof.

'So where are these snowsuits?' I look around.

Lucas grimaces. 'I'm sorry. That was a total lie. I've brought you here under false pretences.'

'You cad. I should slap your face and leave.'

'Perhaps we don't need the snowsuits?'

'Do you think that's wise?'

'No, I think it's risky.'

Suddenly I can't put two thoughts together.

Lucas runs his hand down my arm, wiping away raindrops. 'So, the dance floor is clear. Shall we tango?'

I shiver. 'I might have got that wrong.' I put out my hand, lift his T-shirt, and place my palm against his chest. His heart is beating – fast. 'This falls into the category of men with wet T-shirts will always take them off.'

He steps closer, wraps his arms around me and presses his nose against my neck.

And if I was a penguin I'd throw my head back and sing a mating song right now.

Epilogue

Dear Cougar,

Thanks for all those media clippings. That was a great story in *Who Weekly* about you coming out. I wouldn't worry about Maxine, she'll come round when she sees your audience is on side. I loved the photo of Nathan Hornby riding his bike to parliament. He's quite the greenie now, isn't he? I also enjoyed the link to *Woman's Weekly*. *Krill and Me, the Untold Story* is a catchy headline. I don't like Maria's chances of getting krill incorporated into the Australian Coat of Arms, but it's worth a shot. I was interested to hear you two met up for a drink … Anything you're not telling me?

Lucas and I arrived in Greenland five days ago. Already we have photographed two hundred and fifty snowflakes. They really are all different. As well as photographing them, Lucas makes models by catching the snowflakes on a glass slide which he's painted with liquid plastic. When the snowflake melts he's left with a plastic case that shows its structure.

The first day we were here it was cold and the snowflakes were as you would imagine – like delicate stars. Lately it's warmed up and they are star-shaped but blobby – like wax models left in the sun. Lucas posts his pictures to his blog every day and I write a story to go with them. We have a lot of followers already. Our plan is to produce a book about snowflakes.

Lucas knows the most amazing facts about snow and ice. Did you know a Swedish army marched across the frozen sea to Denmark and invaded Copenhagen in 1658? Or that the River Thames in London used to freeze so hard in winter that for over two hundred years they held a frost fair on it? He has grown his beard again now we're in the Arctic. I rather like it.

My script for 'Love on Ice' seems to be turning into a musical. There will be singing penguins, a ferocious seal and an intensely romantic scene in an igloo. It will be performed on an ice-rink by skating actors. I have a production company interested already. It's amazing how popular those 'Summer on Ice' clips still are on YouTube by the way. Tomorrow Lucas and I are heading out in the field to get more snow samples. We will build an igloo and sleep in it for four nights.

I hope all is well in Nimbin and you're getting enough rain. Put a corn dolly on the altar for me when you do the Lammas festival and give my love to Euphoria.

Love and kisses from your sister,

Summer

Acknowledgements

I wrote *Melt* as part of a Master in Philosophy in Creative Writing. My advisor, Venero Armanno, provided feedback and whole-hearted encouragement on several drafts. Thank you also to Melissa Harper and other staff within the School of Communication and Arts at The University of Queensland. I am very grateful to the university for supporting my writing with a scholarship.

My publisher, Linda Nix at Lacuna, provided thoughtful edits which made this a much better book.

My writing group – Helen Burns, Jane Camens, Jessie Cole, Siboney Duff, Michelle Taylor and Jane Meredith – laughed in appropriate places and gave wise advice.

My agent, Jane Novak, gave me warm encouragement and helpful feedback.

The Byron Writers Festival staff past and present have been a source of support over many years.

A big thanks to my family: John, Simon, Tim, Sue and all my extended family too. It's been quite a journey.

The following books provided inspiration: *1912: The Year the World Discovered Antarctica* by Chris Turney, *An Antarctic Mystery* by Jules Verne and *The Worst Journey in the World*, by Apsley Cherry-Garrard.

Any errors in fact or theory are, of course, my own.

About the author

Lisa Walker is a full-time writer living in northern New South Wales. She has previously worked in environmental communication and as a wilderness guide. She has Masters degrees in creative writing and natural resource management and is currently a PhD candidate in creative writing at the University of Queensland.

Lisa's writing has appeared in the *Review of Australian Fiction*, *Griffith Review* and *The Age*. She was winner of the Byron Writers Festival Short Story Award in 2008 and finalist in the ABC Short Story Award in 2007. Her radio play, *Baddest Backpackers*, was produced by Radio National in 2008. She was awarded the Varuna HarperCollins Award in 2011 and the Varuna Litlink Award in 2009 and 2015.

Lisa's other novels include:
- *Liar Bird* (HarperCollins Australia, 2012)
- *Sex, Lies and Bonsai* (HarperCollins Australia, 2013; Harper-Collins US, forthcoming 2018)
- *Arkie's Pilgrimage to the Next Big Thing* (Random House Australia, 2015)
- *Paris Syndrome* (HarperCollins Australia, 2018)

You can follow Lisa at:
- website: www.lisawalker.com.au
- blog: lisawalkerwriter.wordpress.com
- Facebook: lisawalkerhome
- Instagram: lisawalkerwriter
- Twitter: @lisawalkertweet

www.ingramcontent.com/pod-product-compliance
Lightning Source LLC
Chambersburg PA
CBHW050338030726
47503CB00008B/2500